Built for Pleasure

Kerrie Maxon

ISBN-13: 978-0-6459584-2-3
eISBN-13: 978-0-6459584-3-0

Edited by Word Emporium – www.wordemporium.co.uk

First Edition 2024

BUILT FOR PLEASURE

To Karma for giving me the push, literally, and lots of free time to get started on this journey.

Acknowledgements

I would like to thank the following people for their support, advice and patience and everything else.

My husband for his patience and putting up with an 'absent' wife while I am busy writing and for taking care of the housework and other chores so I don't have to. His love and support mean the world to me.

My daughters for listening to me prattle on for months, for your advice regarding aspects of the story, and for your faith in me. I am forever thankful that I have been blessed with you both as my gorgeous girls.

To my family, dear friends and work colleagues who I have confided in along this journey, thank you for your support and for enriching my life.

To my beta readers for your constructive criticism in the early stages of writing.

To Sarah from Word Emporium for being my savior, turning an awkward draft into a meaningful cohesive story. Thank you for your patience, wisdom and editing mastery. Without you, I wouldn't have gotten this far. https://www.wordemporium.co.uk/

To my dearest friend Rae, my soul sister, for pointing me in the direction of TL Swan's books and Facebook group, and for being an unwavering loving amazing friend.

And to TL Swan, for your inspiration, generosity, guidance and mentorship via your Cygnets groups and video tutorials. And for keeping it real. Words can't describe my gratitude to you for providing the tools and encouragement and Cygnet Inkers and Swan Squad networks that have allowed me to embark on this journey.

To my fellow Cygnet Inkers and Swan Squad colleagues for your never ending support, advice and patience.

Without you all, this book wouldn't exist.

CONTENT WARNING

"This book contains references to emotional abuse from a survivor's point of view."

Contents

Chapter One

ETHAN

The nightclub pumps out a heavy pulsing beat that the crowd on the dance floor is throbbing to in synchronized waves. The electric atmosphere enlivens our senses as we stride toward an empty table on one side of the room.

It's a warm night and, knowing it would be even hotter in the nightclub, my brother Xander, Mario, and I left our suit jackets and ties in the car with our driver after a late dinner meeting. My shoulders move in time with the intoxicating music, excitement zinging in me as it seeps like a drug throughout my body.

Flashing Mario a wide grin, I chuckle as his voracious gaze scans the crowd. As usual, Mario, who is visiting for a week from our Los Angeles office, insisted on letting his hair down before going back to his hotel, most likely not alone. Xander though, always Mr. Cool, gives nothing away as he perches on a stool and casts a broody glance around the throng while he takes a swig of his beer.

Standing next to him, I hold a beer in one hand, my arm resting on the edge of the high table and the fingers of my other hand sit in my trouser pocket. While my body can't stop moving to the music, my eyes avidly check out the number of potential bed partners I can see, my face creasing with a grin. Looks like I might get lucky tonight too, I think excitedly. Mario, Xander, and I have been friends for years and although we live on separate continents, we are all very similar—our wealth allows us to enjoy a playboy lifestyle; we are happily single and our love lives are rich with variety.

"Okay. This is more like it. Let's have some fun, Ethan," Mario announces as he slaps me on the back, laughing. His excitement is palpable as he rubs his hands together, surveying the bevy of beauties gyrating in front of us. If his previous track record is anything to go by, tonight he will score bed partners for the remainder of the week. He knows that Xander is unlikely to go near the dance floor and is far more selective about who he beds, whereas Mario and I tend to be opportunists, availing ourselves of those deliciously wanton women who are hot to trot. Mostly one-night stands, but occasionally a couple of repeat performances when the sex is outstanding. So, we take our time perusing the crowd, sussing out the women that appeal the most.

"Hey Zee, that looks like Georgina over on the far table." I point my beer bottle in that direction before bringing it to my mouth while I watch my brother's head spin to where I pointed. His eyes narrow as he focuses on the attractive dark-haired woman sitting alone at the table, bouncing along to the music. Even though he won't admit it, Xander is seriously attracted to Georgie.

Mario, whose focus also shifts in that direction, gives a low whistle. "Wow. She's hot. Who's she?" I chuckle to myself as Xander glares daggers at our unsuspecting friend.

"Georgie is a colleague on one of our projects," I elaborate. "We met her when Xander was in hospital, and she came in to visit her grandfather, whose bed was across the room. Xander being Xander pissed her off from the outset, but soon realized she is a brilliant landscape architect, so she has been working with us for a short while now."

Mario looks at Xander questioningly, and Xander gruffly retorts, "Her tongue is as sharp as her brain, and she is an innovative designer. You saw some of her work today."

"Yeah, she doesn't take any of Xander's crap either," I add, giving Mario a wink as I tease my brother. "She is quite a woman." Glancing her way again with admiration, I take another swig of beer.

Mario, whose devil-may-care attitude masks his perceptiveness, glances between Xander and me, shrewdly watching as he asks, "So, which one of you is screwing her?" I nearly spurt my beer out at Mario's frankness and quickly gulp it down, then laugh as Xander's baleful expression impales Mario, who is impervious to it. He loves jibing Xander as much as I do and seems thrilled that his comment has hit its mark.

"I can't speak for Xander, but Georgie is a good friend, and she's like a sister to me." Despite my smiling, playful grin, my words are sincere. She and I initially felt an attraction when we first met, but soon realized that there was no spark between us, although we still have a soft spot for each other. She also confessed to me that Xander is the one that lights that spark for her. Xander remains non-committal though, but his intense attraction to her is evident. His eyes always follow her, as they are now.

While we watch the crowd, a tall, striking woman dances over to Georgie and drags her onto the dance floor, toward a small group of other women who all appear to be friends. They are all attractive, but my interest is piqued by the smaller one of the group. Her shiny red hair is tied up in a ponytail, which swings savagely to and fro as she bobs around. Her skin is pale under the bright flashing lights and her huge, infectious grin lights up her whole face, making me smile. She intrigues me, and no matter how many times I look away to check out the other women in the room, my gaze keeps returning to her.

Although she is small, her body is perfectly proportioned. Unlike most of the women here in skimpy clothing, her sleeveless, dark colored, knee-length dress accents her body, providing enough mystery to make me inquisitive about what lies beneath and the thought of exploring her petite body causes a stirring in my balls.

"I'm going in Mario. What about you?" I challenge as I stride toward the dance floor.

"I'm right behind you, bro. Let's party." Rolling my eyes, I shake my head when Mario struts past me like a hungry man at an all-you-can-eat buffet, raising his forearm and clicking his fingers to the beat, apparently thinking he is *John Travolta*.

"Geez. There is something wrong with you, man," I groan mockingly.

"Yep. I don't have a woman on my dick. That's what's wrong with me," he parries, and I roar with laughter.

"Good luck, man." I slap him on the shoulder as we edge into the crowd, each heading in a different direction. Looks like Mario has his eyes on someone and seems keen to zero in on her. As I work my way deliberately through the crowd in the direction of Georgie's group, heads turn in my direction. Still, I make eye contact with a couple of women that I pass, who are giving me sultry looks. A busty blond even winks at me. I grin and wink back, keeping her in the back of my mind as a fall-back option in case I strike out with Georgie's friend.

Catching Georgie's eye, I smile warmly and wave as I slowly maneuver closer, while I watch curiously as her red-haired friend leans in to ask something of Georgie, who responds with a shake of her head. I suspect the question is about me when the redhead ogles me as I move toward them.

Encouraged that she seems interested, I hold her gaze as she continues to stare at me dreamily. *Mmm, much cuter up close than I first thought. Almost pixie-like. Luscious full lips, high cheekbones, and natural-looking eyebrows. Not like most nowadays that are drawn on.* But I'm taken aback by her stunning eyes, sparkling light green like sunlit shallow water on a sandy beach. The sort you just want to immerse yourself in. I like the way she moves her body too. A vision of her gyrating hips grinding on my cock flashes through my head, stirring the said member like a sleeping serpent.

Mouthing *hello* to Georgie as I approach, I lean in closer still and shout above the music to introduce myself to this little angel. Her cheeks flush as we continue to watch each other, and her eyes gleam as she gives me a flirtatious smile. She yells her name back at me, but I can't hear it above the music. It dawns on me that she is about a foot shorter than my six-foot-three stature, only just coming up to my shoulder. For some reason, my instinct to protect her kicks in, which is weird, but is quickly replaced by inventive ways I can maneouver her petiteness for sex.

We try to chat above the noise, but it's difficult, so we dance; close, but not touching. After a while, I nod toward the bar, and when she nods in agreement, I lightly touch her elbow and lead her off the dance floor, surprised by the tingling in my fingers from our physical connection.

I stop at the bar, dropping my hand, and leaning casually against it as I wait to be served, while she stands next to me, fanning herself with a cardboard coaster.

"I'm sorry. I didn't quite catch your name out there. Is it Emmy?" I ask politely.

Smiling, the corners of her eyes crinkle as she shakes her head. "No, it's Emily," she clarifies. "And you're Ethan?" she queries as the barman approaches.

Nodding, my smile is genuinely warm when I peer into her eyes. "Would you like a drink, Emily?" I feel drawn to her for some reason. Maybe because she is Georgie's friend, or maybe because the name Emily suits her somehow.

She seems nervous under my gaze and turns to the waiting barman. "Yes. A bottled water, please." She rummages in her small over the shoulder purse.

"And a beer for me please," I add, tapping the card machine the barman holds out for me to pay before she has a chance to reach for her money.

"Thank you," she tells me as she picks up her drink.

I point to a quieter corner nearby and Emily plops into a chair when we get over there, as if relieved to get off her feet. She fans herself some more with her coaster and blows air over her flushed face, then uncaps her bottle and gulps down her water. I watch as her throat bobs when she swallows, and that feeling stirs my balls again, as a mental image of her swallowing my cum flits through my brain.

"How do you know Georgie, Emily?" I enquire, curious about her, and although I enjoy the buzz in my crotch, I need to distract myself for now, so I watch her delicate hands as she recaps her water bottle.

"Georgie and I shared a flat in university with Simone and Allie—the other girls I was dancing with. We became best friends, so we have known each other for a long time and try to catch up regularly." Her smile crinkles the corners of her eyes before she continues, "Georgie said you met in the hospital while you were visiting your brother."

"Yes. My brother can be quite grumpy and really was out of sorts that day, so I enjoy ribbing him about how much he annoyed Georgie." I take a swig of my beer, as there is a lull in the conversation. Emily seems unlike most of the women I usually meet in these sorts of places. They would normally have their hands roaming up my leg or arm, being overtly obvious about their intention to have sex with me. Emily seems quite reserved, almost proper, and not forward, or throwing herself at me. However, her eyes rove over me as if she enjoys what she sees. Changing tack, I decide to make her feel a bit more comfortable, so ramp up the charm.

"I really love the color of your hair. It's very striking." She lowers her eyes and the blush on her pale freckled skin is delightful, then she raises her head with a smile.

"Thank you." Her tone is bashful at first, but then she continues with self-mockery. "The downside of red hair, though, is that I fry up in the sun and look like a lobster. I was told once that I live on the wrong continent for my skin." Chuckling wryly, she uncaps her bottle and sips at her water again. "You're English aren't you, Ethan?"

"Yes, but Sydney feels like home now because I've been out here for so long," I acknowledge, sipping at my beer. With a lopsided grin, I impart, "I know exactly what you mean about the sun here. It's brutal. I ended up with sunstroke not long after I arrived."

"Oh, that's no good. I'm always the one on a beach covered from head to toe and wearing a wide-brimmed hat. I also think I should buy shares in a sunscreen company." Again, she chuckles.

"Where do you work, Emily?"

"I'm a schoolteacher, working casually at a primary school in the CBD for now." Her eyes light up with what looks like pride.

"Oh, that must be interesting. And challenging. Do you enjoy it?"

"Yes, I do, particularly seeing the kids develop and learn new skills. But there's a lot of unpaid hours outside of the classroom that need to be put in to stay on top of the curriculum." She bounces her leg as if she's nervous.

Despite the friendly conversation, I'm finding Emily hard to read. Her eyes are telling me one thing, and her body language is saying something different. She seems interested enough to chat but doesn't seem a forward person. In similar circumstances, other women would be giving me a come on, playing flirty games, or throwing sexual innuendos into the conversation. However, she seems like a baffling mix of shyness, flirtiness, and wholesomeness. Unlike most of the women I pick up, I get the impression from her nervousness that she won't be an easy lay and I will have to work to get her into bed, which probably won't be tonight. Even more intriguing is that I am keen to look past this fact and get to know her better.

"Are you in a relationship, Emily?" The thought crosses my mind as a possible explanation for her reserved nature. There are few things that are off limits to me in my sexual relationships, and the woman I'm bedding being involved with someone else is one of my big hard nos.

"No." The word shoots out of her mouth, surprising me with its vehemence, as if the thought is unpalatable, and she shakes her head decisively. Looking me in the eye, her expression is serious, but her tone softens as she explains, "No. My ex and I broke up five months ago. Tonight is the first time I've been out since."

I nod my head and take a swig of my beer, considering that her situation would certainly account for her apparent nervousness and unease. Before I can say anything more, I notice Emily looking past me and nodding her head. I spin in my seat and see one of her friends.

Almost in relief, Emily stands, explaining, "My friends are heading home, so I will have to go too." Then she adds in what appears to be embarrassed justification. "It's cheaper if we all share a taxi."

"Okay. Can I grab your number before you go, though?" She nods hesitantly and keeps an eye on where her friends are while giving me her number, which I punch into my phone. I quickly type a message to her, and press send.

"Now you have my number too." My eyes give her a once over and my mouth curves into a smile. "It was a pleasure meeting you tonight, Emily. I hope we can catch up again."

She scrutinizes my face as if trying to gauge my sincerity, then answers. "Yes, me too." Then she scurries off to catch up with her friends, who look like they are trying to maneuver a very tipsy Georgie out of the club.

I watch the group to ensure they aren't harassed on their way out and briefly wonder what her story is as I return to my brother and Mario, who I notice is still woman-free and back at our table.

Clapping both Mario and me on the shoulders, Xander leans in close. "I'm out of here. What are you guys doing? Staying or going?"

"I'm staying for a bit longer. You up for a bit more partying, Ethan?" Mario answers in his suave American accent.

"Yeah, I'll stay too. Just to keep your party-hardened Los Angeles ass out of trouble while you're visiting," I mock him with much less interest than he seems to have. Now that Emily has left, and with a persistent, subtle ache in my balls, I contemplate whether any of the other ladies excite me enough to pursue them. Casting my eyes around the dance floor for the buxom blond, I see her rubbing herself against Mario, who's already back on the dancefloor. Chuckling and shaking my head at Mario's form, I plop on the stool and entertain myself with the antics of the crowd.

Chapter Two

ETHAN

Sitting at the large boardroom table in Xander's office we discuss the outcome of last night's meeting while waiting for Mario and a few other key staff to arrive.

Mario's boisterous laugh sounds out in the outer office where he's probably stopped to charm Xander's Executive Assistant, Paula. Rolling our eyes at each other, we turn to watch Mario breeze into the office as if he doesn't have a care in the world. His brash, often loud, flippant personality belies the sharp intelligence and eagle-eyed attention to detail that earned him top spot in our American division.

"Hey, bros." He nods to each of us and sits opposite me, asking, "What's up?" as he registers our scowling faces.

"You're cutting it a bit fine, mate. I was expecting you fifteen minutes ago," Xander grumbles.

"Didn't get much sleep, huh?" I tease when I notice the puffy shadows under his eyes.

"No, and she was fantastica," he chuckles, slipping into his Italian accent.

"Bastard," I utter.

"Fuck off," Xander adds.

"You snooze, you lose." Mario raises his eyebrows smugly, but his retort is left unanswered, as other attendees begin to enter the room.

***

The meeting drags on for what feels like hours, so it is a relief to get out of there. Needing some fresh air, I decide to grab a coffee from the café across the road and Mario joins me.

As we stride into the elevator, I text my PA where I am going and check if she needs a coffee too. Carly does so much for me that I frequently like to get her coffee as a way of saying thanks. While we walk to the nearby café, Mario and I discuss the impacts of the meeting and potential workarounds. After ordering, the topic eventually shifts to the nightclub while we wait.

"So, a long night of loving for you last night? Where did you end up, her place or your hotel?" I quiz him, more to stir him than really being interested in the ins and outs of his sexual liaison.

"Yeah, she was hot to trot. She took me back to her place and her friend came too. Man, it was intense, but so much fun. It's been a long time since I've had to keep two women satisfied simultaneously." He chuckles and looks very pleased with himself, while I stare at him open-mouthed and wide eyed.

"Oh, no way. How does that always happen to you, you horn dog? Fuck off."

"What can I say? I have a gift, my man." Mario cheekily wiggles his eyebrows, and smirks at me before continuing, "Did you get the number for the cute little redhead you were talking with last night?"

"Yeah, I got her number. I'm thinking of texting her tomorrow." When our order is called, we collect our coffee and walk out of the café. Mario's phone rings and as he answers I offer him a wave, letting him know I will catch up with him later.

While I walk back to the office, the thought of Emily has me pondering what I will say in my text. *Would I have scored with her, like Mario did with his women, if Emily didn't have to leave? Hmmm, I doubt it. She didn't seem the sort to jump at a one-night stand. More the type to want marriage,* I deduce begrudgingly. Despite her air of shy confidence, there seemed to be a fragility about her. *Do I want to put in the effort to get to know her? A coffee date or two should give me a better idea if she's worth the effort.* And I'll need to make it clear I am not the marrying kind, I remind myself.

Reflecting on my supposed playboy image and realizing there is an element of truth in it, I justify to myself that I am certainly not with a different woman every night, as people expect. I have a few regular fuck buddies that I alternate depending on my mood, who are fully accepting of the casual nature of our relationship. Typically, I am always interested in a new conquest as well. What man isn't? And, if I am truthful with myself, I really enjoy the variety and ease of attracting bed partners. Much like Xander and Mario, my tailored clothes and designer accessories (signs of my evident wealth) are a major drawcard but when combined with my toned and taut physique and reasonably good looks, they draw a lot of female attention. Still, between my long hours at work, my daily runs and gym workouts, and being a football coaching assistant occasionally, I usually don't have a lot of free time to actively seek out new conquests.

My thoughts are interrupted by a colleague when I re-enter our building, and the rest of my day is filled with a flurry of meetings. After work, Ramon drives Xander, Mario, and me straight from the office to a farewell dinner for Mario, where a few of our top company executives are in attendance.

While Xander, Mario, and I remain after the others have gone home, we discuss our planned skiing trip to Aspen later in the year and Xander's business trip to Europe.

In true Mario fashion, he boasts that he is meeting up again with the blond from the previous night. He scoffs when I remind him of his red-eye flight out the next morning. "Of course I'll make it. Who needs sleep when I can do that on the flight?"

I am feeling on edge after Mario's dinner for some reason, even after a grueling workout at the gym, and I know from past experience that the only thing that will release that edginess is a good lay. I have been jerking off more frequently than I like of late, so I quickly shoot off a text to Tahni, one of my 'situationship' lovers, to see if she is available. My balls stir at the thought of her deliciously seductive curves, double D breasts, and her energetic sex play. As I had showered after my workout session, I quickly change into some smart-casual pants, shirt, and zip up jacket and pour myself a whiskey shot, in anticipation of a return text, which doesn't take long to hit my phone. Grabbing my keys, with a grin on my face and a spring in my step because my night just got a whole lot better, I make my way down to the garage and climb into my red Audi RS5.

Chapter Three

ETHAN

Standing in the café near the office while I wait for my morning coffee, I reflect on how much more relaxed I feel, despite not getting back home till the early hours. Tahni loves sex as much as I do, so I am pleased we were able to hook up.

Recalling our sexual exploits reminds me that Mario messaged to say he also hooked up and I wonder if he made his flight, so I shoot off a quick text to check in on him. By the time I have my coffee and am walking back to the office, his reply comes in advising that he is well on his way home and that I had woken him from a nap. The smug bastard then tells me about a flight attendant named Emilia that he is eyeing up.

I then type out another message before I get distracted with my day.

Ethan

Hi Emily. We didn't get much chance to get to know each other over the noise the other night. Would you like to catch up for a coffee and chat on Saturday?

I press send just as the elevator doors open and, readjusting my laptop bag on my shoulder, I stroll toward my office, greeting my PA as I saunter past her.

Carly looks me up and down as if I have had a personality change before uttering a good morning in return. She allows me a few minutes to settle in before she arrives at my desk to go through our daily schedule.

"You seem in good spirits today. Mario's presence must have been good for you," she speculates as she sits across from me, her dark hair pulled back into a bun that makes her appear older than I know she is.

I know what she is asking and I give her a sly grin. "Yes, the dinner was great, and Mario was his usual boisterous self. Then I caught up with a friend afterward." Carly lifts an eyebrow at my cockiness. She knows far too much about my sex life than she probably should and often has arranged the parting gifts for women I no longer want to be associated with.

"Will there be anything else, Ethan?" Her tone is matter-of-fact, as she stands.

"No, that will be all, thanks Carly." Our conversation is quickly pushed aside as I answer my ringing phone.

The rest of the day is lost in meetings, phone calls and reviewing contracts and reports, like most of my days. Part of my job as Chief Property Manager for Drake Enterprises is to review potential acquisitions of hotels and large stately homes to add to the company portfolio. The company, which Xander established and has built into a multi-billion dollar conglomerate, has several main facets, but the predominant one is property acquisitions, including buying, managing, and operating luxury hotels and apartment blocks. So, there are always obstacles to negotiate, whether it be from a redevelopment, contractual or legislative angle. I love the variety of my job and the travel and wealth it provides. I have been in the Australian office now for about twelve months, working alongside Xander on a problematic hotel redevelopment, which is how we both met Georgie.

As I pick up my phone and my laptop bag before heading to the gym, I notice a message from Emily, forgetting I put it on silent earlier.

Emily

Yes, that would be lovely.

Perplexed by its brevity, my forehead scrunches as I re-read the message. *Yep, still says the same thing.* I guess it's a confirmation, but I am surprised by the message's lackluster tone. Is she being polite or maybe she's shy? Or, is she feeling half-hearted about a coffee date now that the alcohol has worn off? Is she regretting giving me her number? Then I inwardly mock myself for questioning her response. *A 'yes' is a yes, man. Take it.*

I shove my phone into my laptop bag and zip it up before heading to the elevator. Punching the ground floor button, I acknowledge that Emily's seemingly indifferent manner annoys me, and as I drive to the gym, I weigh up whether to persevere. Pushing thoughts of Emily aside, I throw myself into an intense work out, hoping to exorcise my frustration over her.

***

After showering at home, I'm sitting at my marble kitchen bench eating a healthy dinner of chicken with roasted vegetables and brown rice when I decide that I will need to talk to Emily some more to better gauge her level of interest, so I shoot her a quick text.

Ethan

How does The Coffee Club at The Quay at 10am sound for Saturday? I'll send you the address in case you don't know it.

Emily

Sounds wonderful. See you then, Ethan.

Encouraged by the speed of her response, and feeling less uncertain about her enthusiasm, I check my emails, then check in with Mario.

Ethan

Hey bro. How was the flight? You home yet? Any tapping ass with the flight attendant?

He doesn't respond, so I figure he is making out somewhere. He is such a man whore. I don't know how he keeps it up, I ponder in awe. Then the odd question pops into my head about why he is so driven to lose himself in an endless stream of women. He rarely talks about his past, and I wonder if his behavior stems from a long forgotten emotional issue. *Wow, that's deep,* I scoff at myself and shake my head, tidying the kitchen before filling my night in watching some baseball on the television.

Chapter Four

ETHAN

Saturday morning comes around quickly, and I arrive at the rendezvous point about fifteen minutes early. Standing outside the café's boardwalk barrier, I scour the area, trying to find an empty table. An approaching waiter asks me to wait till a table becomes available, which shouldn't be long, so I take the opportunity to look around.

The Quay is bustling on this beautiful warm sunny day, the ripples on the surface of the water sparkling like diamonds in the bright sunshine. Inhaling deeply, the air is tangy with the scent of the sea and, unfortunately, the occasional waft of diesel fumes from the ferries.

Pleased that I opted for lightweight chinos and a short-sleeved shirt, I smile at how much I absolutely love the weather here. No matter what time of day or night, there are always people by the harbor in all modes of dress scurrying from one place to another, and today is no different. A large white cruise ship that looks like a floating apartment block sits imposingly at berth on the other side of the Quay, its majestic size dwarfing the passenger ferries. Seagulls squawk, ferry horns blast, buses lurch past, and music blares from a nearby busker. This part of the city is vibrant, and I lift my grinning face to the sun, soaking in its warmth and vitality, feeling happy, satisfied, and at ease with the world.

A couple exit the outside dining area and the waiter signals me to the table under a large white umbrella. As he wipes it down, I sit and check my phone for any messages from Emily. None yet. I hope that means she is still coming. I sip at the glass of water the waiter has just filled and casually watch the passersby, hoping to spot Emily.

"Ethan," a woman's voice that I recognize calls out.

"Oh, shit. Not now," I groan to myself before I turn toward my sister Louisa, standing outside the barrier with some friends. Plastering a grin on my face, I stand and hug her when she approaches my table. As I look past her to her two friends standing nearby, they giggle and finger wave at me. *Great. Her friends are fangirling me,* I bemoan. So, tilting my lips up, I give them a fake smile then straighten and address my sister.

"Louisa. What are you doing here?" She looks amazing, dressed in a light pant suit with matching shoes and handbag, and her long dark hair tied loosely in a scarf as it hangs down her back. She appears every bit the wealthy, confident woman she is.

"Oh, we are heading to brunch and a show." She points further down the promenade to the magnificent white sails of the Opera House. "What are you doing here all by yourself, Ethan?" I love her dearly, but she is such a sticky beak and I know she will enjoy interrogating me when next we catch up.

"I'm waiting for a friend," I answer, my eyes catching sight of Emily standing outside the barrier, her stance stiff and chin tilted up, her facial expression taut and seemingly annoyed. Her eyes are hidden behind sunglasses, but I imagine them glaring at me, because hugging another woman is not a good way to start a date. I bury my frustration with Louisa, commenting, "And here she is now."

"Emily, come meet my sister," I encourage charmingly in a louder voice so she can hear me over the chatter and background noise, extending my arm and waving her in. I suspect she was debating whether to stay or go, but now that I have spotted her, social niceties dictate that she should join us.

Moving her sunglasses to sit on top of her head as she steps into the shade of the umbrella, Emily's features change slightly and I guess this is her schoolteacher face.

I let out a small sigh, pleased and relieved that she is here, because her earlier reticence had me wondering if she would even show up. Covertly, I appraise her curvaceous figure in a yellow patterned summery dress, short sleeved white cardigan, and white sandals. Her hair is loosely pulled back, shining like a halo around her head, and neatly tied at the nape of her neck, draping between her shoulder blades. Out of the corner of my eye, I see Louisa scrutinizing Emily as well. Emily stops next to me, giving me a small nod and polite smile. I gently touch her elbow and extend my other palm upward toward Louisa, as I introduce them.

"Emily, this is my sister Louisa. Louisa, this is Emily." My eyes glance from Emily's to Louisa's then quickly return to hold Emily's gaze as I smile at her appreciatively. She extends her hand to shake Louisa's, giving her a congenial smile.

"Lovely to meet you, Louisa." Her voice, although quiet, is self-assured and genuine.

"Lovely to meet you too, Emily," Louisa responds warmly, as if liking Emily, which I find strange after such a short acquaintance. Louisa hasn't met many of my dates, but she never seemed to like those she did meet, so I wonder what it is about Emily that impresses her so much.

As if it suddenly dawns on Louisa that she is interrupting, she announces that they will be late for their brunch, quickly pecks me on the cheek, and says goodbye, smiling and nodding farewell to Emily before she turns to join up with her friends. As they walk past, I notice the two of them huddling in closer to Louisa, obviously trying to get all the gossip.

I turn my attention back to Emily. "I'm sorry about that. I had no idea she would be coming here today, or I would have suggested somewhere else," I apologize, holding out a chair for Emily to sit, then I return to my seat across from her.

I notice a flicker of irritation sparking her pale green eyes before she drops them to the table and places her bag on the ground next to her. Lifting her eyes again, she replies, "It's not a problem, although I thought it was strange when I saw you hugging each other. I can see the resemblance between the two of you though." Emily holds my gaze as she enquires politely, "Is Louisa younger or older?"

"Younger by a couple of years and still a pain in the ass," I joke, grinning wryly, distracted as my eyes focus on the delicate features of her face, noticing the freckles that peek through her light makeup. But I am mesmerized by her mouth, which looks delightfully kissable with its archer's bow shaped top lip and plump, pouty lower one.

The hovering waiter interrupts our conversation when he appears next to us and asks if we are ready to order.

"I'll have a flat white coffee please," Emily replies, then points to a nearby table where a woman is eating. "Is that a pecan tart?" When he nods, she continues, "I'll have one of those as well, please."

"I'll have a flat white as well please, and a slice of banana bread too." I am not particularly hungry but am considerate enough to not let Emily eat alone.

Sitting back in my chair, I cross one leg over the other knee, smiling at Emily while she fidgets with her sunglasses, removing them from her head and putting them on the table, then she casts her glance around the café and promenade.

"Why is your sister a pain in the ass?" she questions. Her eyes glint with humor and the corners of her mouth turn up slightly, like she is holding back a grin.

"Oh, don't get me started." I roll my eyes and pitch my voice in mock frustration. "Because she is the youngest, and the only girl, she always got everything she wanted and has Xander and I wrapped around her little finger. She is always sticking her nose in our business and bossing us around. And criticizing the way I dress." Emily chuckles at my rant and it is a beautiful melodic sound, and very sexy. "See, I told you not to get me started," I pretend to grouse as I flash a flirtatious smile. She chuckles again and my balls tighten at the delicious sound.

"Do you have any siblings, Emily?"

"No, it's just Mom and me. My father died when I was very young," she divulges matter-of-factly with a tight smile.

I study her face for a moment, trying to imagine what it would be like growing up with a single parent and no siblings. "That must have been hard," I state with genuine empathy.

"It is what it is. I didn't know any different." She shrugs her shoulders with nonchalance. Returning with our coffees and food, Emily gives the waiter a polite smile, thanking him as she draws the tart closer to her.

"True," I ponder aloud, pausing to stir my coffee, then change tack, reverting to some of my usual 'first date' questions. "If you could travel anywhere right now, where would you go?"

"Good question," Emily chuckles, her eyes crinkling. "I haven't been outside of the country, so anywhere would be great. If I had to choose, it would be Europe, specifically Italy, Spain and France. I imagine you've traveled extensively, Ethan."

"Yes, I have, and they're some of my favorite countries , too. But I also love being here. The people are so laid back, and the weather is glorious."

"How long are you here for?" Emily sips her coffee, and seems to be relaxing a bit more, willingly engaging with me, which is a good sign.

"I've been here for about twelve months and will probably stay another two or three months, depending on how some of our projects go." I leave it a moment or two before asking my next question, because I don't want Emily to feel like she is being interrogated. Instead, I take the opportunity to bite into my banana bread, watching as Emily daintily cuts her small tart into bite size pieces. She stabs at one, then opens her mouth, closing her lips over the fork and sliding it out again. I groan inwardly as I imagine her luscious mouth doing the same thing to my cock and I have to lift my cup to my lips as a distraction.

"What exactly is it you do for Drake Enterprises, Ethan?"

"I'm the Chief Property Manager, which involves acquisitions, and often redevelopment of properties to add to our portfolio. So, it means I get to travel a lot."

"Do you have a favorite place to visit or holiday?"

"The usual places. French Riviera, Lake Como in Italy, Aspen and Whistler. But I don't normally get more than a few days away, and even then, there are always work issues that need to be addressed."

Emily smiles and nods and, as the conversation pauses, she pulls her phone from her bag, which surprises me. Then she explains, "Georgie and Allie are waiting nearby. I'll just text them that I'm okay so they can go home." After she sends the text and replaces the phone in her bag, she sits upright and says, "Sorry about that." As if recognizing my puzzlement, a flush creeps across her face and she clarifies in a soft voice, "I was nervous about coming today and they provided some moral support."

"How do you feel now?"

"Very much at ease with you. So there is no point in them hanging around for my sake."

"Okay. That's great and I'm pleased." She seems more relaxed, and I wonder to myself if that sort of moral support is common practice. *I might ask Louisa about it next time I see her.* "Why were you so nervous?"

"Isn't everyone nervous before a date?" she quips, then fidgets with her fork, adding quietly, "It's been a while for me so I'm out of touch with the dating game."

"Fair enough."

After another lull in the conversation, while we eat and drink some more, I ask, "What's something you want to learn or get better at?"

"Hmm, that's a difficult question." Emily tilts her head to the side and her eyes shoot heavenward contemplating her answer before they return to mine. "I'd like to learn at least one other language. And I'd like to get better at reading people."

"Languages I can understand if you are intending traveling, although most countries nowadays speak English well enough for you to be understood. And you'd only have to smile to have men flocking to help you." Cheekily, I add this last bit tongue in cheek, knowing many men, including myself, would find Emily very attractive. "Why do you want to read people better?"

"I figure it will help with the kids and parents at school, and also with dating and life in general," she answers.

Grinning, I suggest, "Okay, let's see how good you are. How do you read me?"

"Oh, that's a bit unfair, Ethan. You're putting me on a spot here." She blushes, and sips her coffee, glancing up to see me patiently waiting for her answer. The corners of her mouth quirk as she gently mocks, "You already know what women think of you."

"I promise I won't hold it against you. Go on, tell me," I challenge. Not because I need an ego boost, but more to gauge her thoughts about me, suspecting she will sugarcoat her response.

Holding my gaze, she draws in a breath. "Okay then." She sits up straighter, her chin lifts, jutting with determination and she responds in a clear confident voice, "Well, I would say you're an astute business-man, proud of your achievements. Playful and cheeky, a man's man, you genuinely care about those close to you, despite downplaying that fact. I feel that you are loyal, trustworthy, honorable. But you don't suffer fools lightly, and I suspect you like to get your own way in most things." Emily stops suddenly, as if she thinks she's said too much, then rests her elbow on the table while her thumb and forefinger grasp her chin. "Or you could just be a very good actor." She tilts an eyebrow and gives me an impish grin, as if to cover for her frankness.

"Very close to the mark, Emily. I feel you're better at reading peo-ple than you realize," I admit in awe, because very few people have achieved such a keen assessment of me, or haven't been brave enough to speak so frankly.

We chat for a while longer, and I am captivated as her voice and face glow, lighting with animation as we exchange views and I acknowledge to myself we have a lot in common.

After some time, my coffee is finished and I decide to dig a bit deep-er. "You mentioned the other night that you broke up with your ex a while ago. What are you looking for now?" Emily's happy expression fades and a mask of reserve seems to cover her face. Sitting back in her chair and drawing in a deep breath, she answers with reluctance while she toys with her empty coffee cup.

"Good question. I am still finding my feet again, so certainly not something serious right now." She pauses, angling her chin up as if she finds the courage to answer honestly. "Something fun and genuine, respectful and trusting, where a relationship can develop, whether that is just a friendship or something more."

I get the impression that there is more to Emily's story, but she doesn't want to bombard me with her woes on our first 'date'.

"What about you? What are you looking for?"

Sex. That is my first thought to that question. But instead, I answer in a polite manner because I feel Emily isn't ready for my honest candor.

"I'd like to get to know you some more, Emily. You intrigue me. You are beautiful and intelligent and interesting. I sense there's more to you and I'm curious to see where that leads if it's okay with you."

"Thanks. I'd like that very much." She grins at me, her eyes glinting and crinkling in the corners as she quips, "You intrigue me too."

The waiter arrives to clear our table and Emily looks disappointed that it signals the end of our date.

"It's such a beautiful day. Would you like to go for a walk around the harbor?" I suggest, keen to spend more time with her. She grins, nodding as she puts her sunglasses on again. Standing, I wait while she picks up her handbag and am surprised when she pulls out her purse.

At my questioning look she speaks. "I'd like to pay my share, Ethan."

"No need. I've got this." I brush her off with a smile and go to move past her toward the cashier, but she grabs my arm, halting me. When

I turn and throw her a quizzical look, her face is set in a determined expression, and she drops her hand.

"Ethan, it's important to me that I pay my way, particularly after you brought my drink the other night. Please let me pay for my coffee and tart."

Bemused, I shrug at her request. "Okay, if it's that important to you, Emily. It doesn't worry me either way." Her insistence strikes me as odd, though, because most of my dates make the initial offer out of courtesy, with no real intent on paying their way. For Emily, however, it seems important. I'm not sure how I feel about not paying. I certainly respect her independence and forthrightness, but rarely am I the one awkwardly waiting while someone else pays the bill. Maybe with family, but not with a date.

We settle the bill, and I push my sunglasses onto my face, to guard against the glare of the water and stark pavement, and Emily dives into her bag and produces a cotton floppy brimmed hat. She chuckles at my surprised, quizzical look as I watch her put it on, pulling it tight so the light breeze doesn't blow it off.

"Sorry, but with this color hair, I burn easily, and my face will be glowing red in minutes, even with sunscreen." Laughing at herself, she is unapologetic about the hat. Not that it worries me, because my balls are tingling at her sexy laugh. I wish I had thought of a baseball cap too because I can feel the heat of the sun beating down on my head and the back of my neck.

Wandering along the Quay, we chat idly some more about our favorite things, dream jobs and more travel destinations as we pass the ferry terminals, and the cruise ship, marveling at its size up close.

While we sightsee, I slow my normal fast stride to cater for Emily's shorter gait, ironically realizing that I'm noticing my surroundings more at this slower pace. *Maybe it's the company*, I muse, because I certainly find Emily interesting and inquisitive. Meandering into the colonial historic area, we admire the beautifully maintained old sandstone warehouses and former two-story homes which have been converted into shops and offices, then roam around the shaded grounds of a historic observatory, appreciating the picturesque views from a different part of the harbor.

Resting in the shade admiring the view quite a while later, I arrange an Uber to take me home while Emily advises she will catch a bus home from a nearby stop, refusing my offer of a lift.

"I've had a great time today, Emily. I'll call you," I tell her honestly before giving her a quick hug when my Uber arrives. Clambering into the back of the small car without looking back at her, it whisks me away into the traffic.

Chapter Five

ETHAN

What is it about Emily that intrigues me so much? I reflect on our day during the ride home. If I use all my other dates as a comparison, then today would be considered mundane, maybe even dull. But it didn't feel that way. It felt nice, comfortable. That surprises me because 'nice' is not usually in my vocabulary. Nice is not something I seek when I date a woman. Normally they are over the top flirtatious, even provocative, and ready to be fucked, (the naughtier the better) and I am more than happy to oblige. Emily is different, though. Her innate attractiveness and sexiness are alluring but she seems oblivious to the fact. She lacks artifice and seems to have no expectation of anything more than a platonic relationship from me. I have never felt so at ease with someone before and yet so unsure of where I stand with her. It is unnerving.

When I think about it, the only women 'friends' I have I am bedding on a regular basis, but we don't normally idly chat when we catch up. In fact, the only conversation is usually a sex directive, like "open your legs," or "take it deeper." Any other female 'friends' are business colleagues, like Georgie and our Marketing Manager, Cynthia, as well as Carly.

Do I want to be Emily's friend? I ask myself as I take the elevator to my apartment. *Yes, as long as I can have her underneath me, moaning my name.* I suspect it will take a bit of wooing before she allows me that privilege though.

Is she worth the effort? I ask myself next. *For now, yes,* but I won't be waiting long, particularly when there are so many other willing bed partners around. Still, I feel that there is much more to Emily than meets the eye. Setting myself the challenge of having my dick inside Emily by the third date, I decide to shower off the day's heat. As I undress though, my conscience prods me about the callousness of 'thinking with my dick'. Briefly I question why I think of the women in my social life differently from the women in my working life. *If I give the social women the same respect that I afford my female colleagues, would I have different experience with women socially?* Quickly I push the thought aside.

While I wash, I chuckle when I remember Emily and her hat. She looked very cute, decidedly unphased and understated. And very genuine. Not like the glamorous women I normally hang out with, who are fully made up and swathed in designer labels, no matter the time of day. Emily's sultry laugh resonates in my balls for some reason, and I fondle them now as I remember the sound. My cock awakens with the thought of it plunging into her luscious petite body, and I wonder if her mound is covered in glorious red pubic curls or if she is neatly trimmed. Stroking a few more times, I envisage Emily's long red hair swathed around my hand while I set the tempo as her sweet lips go down on me.

Astonished that I am jerking off over Emily when I have arranged to have hot sex tonight with Tahni and her flatmate Brianna, who she's invited to spice things up, I go back to washing myself. Needing to save all my juices for later, I relish the lingering horniness that thoughts of Emily create.

As I step out of the shower and dry off, my thoughts turn to Tahni and Brianna, anticipating what they might have in store for me. All I need to know about them is how they want it. The only deep and meaningful where they are concerned relates to my cock in one of their orifices. It's as simple as that. And that's the way I like it. Like a business transaction, I give them what they want, they give me what I want, and I can walk away without any emotional entanglements. *Geez, that makes me sound like a cold hearted bastard. That's what you are, you prick, so stop getting soft and sentimental.* Giving myself a stern lecture as I dress in sweat pants and t-shirt, I decide to watch the replay of last night's game to fill in time.

Switching on the television, I sit at the nearby desk and open my laptop, checking my emails while I eat a chicken and salad sandwich. Settling into viewing the game, I occasionally yell with frustration at stupid referee decisions, or at the players for their mishandling of the ball. When half-time comes around, I am so annoyed with the game that I fast forward it to only watch when the goals set up and scored.

However, the game reminds me of my best mate Jason and the many soccer seasons we played in university, so I quickly text him to see how he is going. We met at Cambridge University and bonded through our love of sport, particularly soccer. After graduating, he was snapped up by a big name tech firm but after a few years, set up on his own back in his home country of Australia.

Ethan
Hey mate. What are you up to? Feel like catching up tonight?

It's not long before his reply pings my phone.

Jason

Hey man. How's it hanging? Yeah. Love to. Usual place?

Ethan

Yep. Sounds good. Meet you there at 7.00.

***

A few hours later, I lean one arm against the chunky timber bar, while the other hand holds a glass of beer, keeping an eye out for Jason. O'Malley's Bar is an Irish pub with dark timber wall paneling, dark red booth style seating against a brick wall, and lots of walnut colored timber tables and chairs. Like the décor, the food is good and hearty, the ambiance is jovial and friendly, and they serve great beer.

The dinner crowd is building, the tables are filling up and I am just considering ordering their magnificent Guinness Pie when Jason ambles in, casually dressed in jeans and t-shirt emblazoned with a large bright logo. His brown curly hair is tousled, and his cheeks and jaw are covered in whiskers like he is trying to grow a beard. As he casts his gaze around the milling crowd, I straighten and wave to him and, as he approaches, we simultaneously raise our forearms and clutch hands, then pull each other in close and slap the other on the back in a bro hug.

"E, it's been too long, man," Jason cries, pulling back to give me the once over, as I do with him.

"Jace, when did you start growing pubic hair on your face?" I snicker.

"Oh, fuck off. It's not that bad," Jace counters, rubbing his palm over his fluffy cheeks. "Another couple of days and it should look more like a beard."

"Yeah, you go on believing that," I mock as he orders himself a beer and a burger. Taking the opportunity of having the barman nearby, I order the Guinness Pie and another beer. When our drinks are promptly handed over, we move to a table at the back of the room.

"What's been happening, bro? It's been, what? Two months since we last caught up?" I question Jason, noticing even in the dimly lit room that his features look drawn and tired.

Jason is an IT genius who developed a very popular video game years ago. He has since gone on to establish his own software development business, which has gone from strength to strength. Xander and I believed in his product and business acumen so much that we each invested some startup funds, which were paid back in the first year, and we remain minor shareholders in the business.

"It's been hectic, mate. We have a new gaming product being developed and the release date is looming, but we keep hitting hurdles so the capacity for meeting deadline is slipping." Pausing to run his fingers down his chin, and breathing in a heavy frustrated breath, he continues, "So I am faced with the corporate embarrassment of pushing back the deadline or releasing a sub-par product. Bad press either way." The disappointment apparent in his tone obviously weighing him down.

"What hurdles? Have you looked at the programming yourself?" I quiz him, knowing full well the anxiety he is going through, as I have been there many times myself with property developments not running to plan.

"Software glitches that shouldn't be happening. No sooner do we fix one then another crops up, but it is taking hours and hours of staff time to find the embedded problem, then developing a workaround." I can hear the exasperation in his voice.

"What's at stake if you don't meet the deadline? Other than the corporate embarrassment."

"Financially, it will be a disaster, which we can't afford right now. We have had a larger competitor sniffing around, but I have been sweating on this product to give the business more market share and less vulnerability."

My cynicism kicks in as I ask, "You recruited any new employees since the takeover bid? Do you think it could be sabotage to make you more susceptible to accepting their offer?" Staring at me, his mouth drops open as he contemplates my question. I can almost see the thoughts spinning around in his head, dropping into place just as the buzzer for our food goes off.

"No, it can't be," he utters, with a confounded look on his face, like he has been punched in the stomach, while I stand and collect our plates from the bar, then return to the table.

"You look like the wind has been knocked out of your sails, mate. Tell me what you are thinking." I set his food down in front of him.

"We recruited a new software engineer a few months ago, just before we became aware of the competitor's interest. She came with excellent credentials and her work is amazing. Now I think about it though, that was also about the same time that the problems started."

"That's a pretty huge coincidence," I state. "Why was a new employee working on such a major project?"

He looks offended by my question, and clips out the words, "She has specific experience in the coding language that was necessary for this product." However, I can see that he is also asking himself the same question.

"Sounds like you need to do some investigating, mate."

"Yeah, I think so. Problem is though, we've been dating for a month or two. I just can't see her doing something like that." His brooding expression shows he is perplexed and irritated, wanting to believe good about this woman, but questioning her possible duplicity.

Raising my eyebrows and pressing my lips together into a straight line, I express my concern. "Sorry to hear that, Jace, but people will do all sorts of horrible things for money. Potentially, you have a mole. You should probably do a deep dive into the coding because I know you will find the issues and fix them before the release date. However, you should also probably hire a specialist security investigator to do a thorough background check of all your employees before you go accusing the wrong person."

"You're right. I'll get onto it. Know any good investigators?"

Nodding because I have a mouthful of food, I pick up my phone and shoot him off Ramon's number, a man I trust completely. As well as being a driver for Xander and me, and a very good friend, Ramon has his own private security firm that Xander and I utilize daily. As a result of a few instances a while back with disgruntled community members near some of our developments, as well as paparazzi issues, we decided a security detail would be necessary, not only for us, but our staff. So Xander called on Ramon, a friend from his boarding school days.

"Thanks, bro," Jason responds with relief. "Now tell me what is happening in your world."

After filling him in on some of the business issues and family up-dates, I tell him about my date with Emily and how much I enjoyed it.

"She is so different from other women I date. She is quiet, reserved, almost shy, genuine, and very much a 'girl next door' type. Small and beautiful, with long orange-red hair and freckles."

"Not your usual type, that's for sure. They are usually super confident, egotistical, man eaters." Jason laughs, mocking me. "How did you meet her? Will you see her again?"

"We met at a nightclub. She's a friend of a friend, and my balls paid attention when I laid eyes on her. Not an easy lay though, and a bit of an enigma." Pausing, I recollect the challenge I set myself earlier, believing it is attainable. "I've set myself a target of three dates to win her over and into my bed," I tell him, recognizing that Emily poses a challenge I haven't felt for a long while.

"Three?" Jace scoffs. "You softening with age, mate?

"Oh, fuck off," I express laughingly.

Dropping the subject, we continue to chat about football, family, and life in general for some time before I look at my watch and realize I need to get moving.

"I've got to go Jace. I've got a couple of hot and horny lovelies to lose myself in tonight," I inform him as I order an Uber.

Jace almost spurts out the last of his beer, then swallows and laughs at me. "You're such a hedonistic bastard. You brunch with a girl-next-door whom you see as a pleasurable diversion, and fuck two nymphomaniacs later that night."

"What can I say? I am an expert in pleasuring women." Throwing him a smug look and a wry grin, mocking myself, I stand and bro-hug Jace.

"See you, dirty dog." Jace quips as I step back and turn to walk away.

Chuckling, I taunt him back, "Let me know how you get on with the investigation. Oh, and the pubic hair beard." I hear his laughter as I stride across the room.

Chapter Six

EMILY

Today feels like I have turned a corner. Finally. After two years of emotional manipulation from my ex, Bradley, and five months of counseling since we broke up, today I felt a vestige of happiness and my self confidence returning, instead of the numbness and anxiety that used to overwhelm me. Of course, my friends rallied around this morning, reassuring me that I would be fine on my date with Ethan. Knowing they were somewhere in the crowd keeping an eye on me helped ease my anxiety immensely.

Before meeting Ethan last weekend, my friends and I had caught up for dinner to celebrate my birthday, my first social outing since the breakup. Their camaraderie, with lots of laughter was just like old times, and buoyed by their friendship and support, we continued to a nightclub, having a ball, laughing and dancing the night away. My self-confidence was boosted by a few admirers keen to dance with me, but I was not fooled into thinking it was anything more than opportunistic fishing for sex.

Then Georgie's friend Ethan turned up with his brother and friend; all stunning, virile men. Ethan's good looks outshone the other men in the room, with his chocolate brown hair, swept back off his high forehead and clipped short around his ears and nape. I'd probably had too many cocktails by that point, but I couldn't take my eyes off him as he danced. His blue shirt fit snugly across his chest and biceps without gaping, accentuating his taut, trim build, and quite surprisingly, my dormant libido kicked into gear when our eyes met.

When he leaned in closer to me to introduce himself, his deep-set hooded green eyes gleamed into mine and I became breathless as heat flushed over my body. Smiling up at him, hoping it was flirty rather than creepy, I felt small and diminutive in comparison to his tall, well-built frame as we danced. His dark pants emphasized his narrow hips and thick muscular thighs, and I admired how well he moved for such a tall man, blushing again when he caught me checking him out. I thought I would melt on the spot when his hand touched my elbow to lead me off the dance floor and had to fan myself with a coaster, pretending I was overheated instead of the effect he was having on my body.

Alone with him, nervousness and self-doubt crept in that he wouldn't be interested in me and that I couldn't think of anything to say, but then I remembered lessons from my counseling sessions and I gripped onto my newly restored sense of self-worth to get me through. His deep, sexy voice rumbled over me as we sat with our drinks in a corner of the bar area, putting me at ease.

Surprising me by complimenting me on my hair color, which made me blush again, I made some inane comment in response about my fair skin and needing to cover up on a beach. Groaning at the recollection, I hope I managed to cover my embarrassment by deflecting a question back to him about his nationality.

When he asked for my phone number, I never believed that he would contact me, and was taken aback when he texted me his number straight away.

Only having a chance to read my text messages when the kids are in the playground at lunch, I was even more surprised when, earlier this week, he invited me out for our coffee date.

He wanted to see me again. I couldn't get my thoughts together and felt nervous and jumpy. *Why did he want to see me?* Obviously, I deduced that sex was his ultimate motivation, but why me? There were so many more beautiful women, ready and willing, that he could have selected instead of me. *Did I want to see him?* It had been fun to flirt, despite my amateurishness, when I hadn't expected it to go any further, but now, what should I do? I knew I didn't feel confident enough yet for anything sexual, but did I want to open myself up to hope that another man would find me attractive, only to be rejected after a second date? I was so confused, with contradictory thoughts swirling through my head, so I messaged Georgie, asking her advice.

My ever practical friend responded.

Georgie
What have you got to lose? Ethan is not like Bradley, thankfully. He is respectful and caring, and he wouldn't have asked you out if he didn't find you interesting and attractive. And he won't pressure you into anything you don't want to do. The choice is yours though, love. If you feel it is too soon, then don't go. If you feel you want to go but are concerned, then we can shadow you for moral support.

That was an option that I wouldn't have even considered and proved to me again how much my dear friends cared about me. They meant the world to me, and their strength and the wise words of my counselor bolstered me to a level where I could reply when the kids had left for the day.

This morning my girls and I rendezvoused not far from where I was meeting Ethan, telling me that I didn't have to do anything I didn't want to, that nervousness was natural, and reminding me how hard I had worked and how far I had come since Bradley left me a timid, frightened shell of a person.

As we clustered in a group hug, I asked, "Where will you girls be?"

"You don't need to know, because you will keep looking over for our reassurance. You need to know that you can do this by yourself. But we won't be far away," Georgie pointed out in her usual pragmatic way.

"Remember, there is no shame in ending it if you feel uncomfortable," Allie added. "You are in control. You are strong and independent."

I hugged them again before taking a deep breath, turning to walk in the direction of the café.

I nearly ran when I spotted Ethan with another woman in his arms, feeling like he was playing me for a gullible fool. It was the sort of stunt Bradley would have pulled to reaffirm my worthlessness. But Ethan spotted me before I could go anywhere. I hesitated, waiting for the callous sneer of ridicule that I had experienced before, but when he invited me to meet his sister, I approached with suspicion, expecting to be the butt of their joke. However, when it didn't happen, and social niceties were upheld, I felt more comfortable with the genuine warmth that Louisa offered me before she departed, as if she were the interloper. Ethan's apology about the situation seemed genuine as well, so I decided to stay. And I'm glad I did, because Ethan proved to be entertaining company, quickly putting me at ease. I had even messaged my friends to say I was fine, and they could go home. His interested questioning, intelligent conversation, and cheeky sense of humor complemented his good looks and devil-may-care attitude. And he smelled so good—fresh like a rainforest.

Our date ended, and Ethan departed in his Uber. While the bus takes me home, I realize that I can't remember the last time I had such a good time or felt so stimulated both physically and mentally. And when Ethan pulled me in for a hug as he was leaving, my brain fizzled, and I forgot my left from my right. I blushed like a schoolgirl and my stomach clenched, dampening my panties.

There is a spring in my step as I walk briskly back to the apartment that I share with Simone and ponder that, even if nothing further comes of the situation with Ethan, he has made me see possibilities for the future, where I can be treated with respect, and have my opinions heard.

The apartment is empty, as I knew it would be, because Simone is away for a week on a stint to Europe as a flight attendant. Shutting the door behind me, I drop my keys in the bowl near the door and shimmy with excitement at how well today went. Simone is gone for two to three weeks every month, so it works out well for me. I am so grateful to her for allowing me to come live in her apartment after I left Bradley with only a small amount of clothes and personal items. The scumbag and I had shared an apartment in the suburbs near the school where we both taught, so Simone's place in the city gave me the opportunity to lay low for a while and find another job. Fortunately for me, a nearby primary school needed a relief teacher, so I was able to slot right in.

I plonk myself on the lounge and conference call Georgie, Allie, and Tash (who couldn't join them this morning) to update them on my day. These girls have been my support network and picked me up when I was down, without judgment, letting me find my way in my own time. They witnessed how I lost myself in my previous relationship and have been with me every step of the way in my recovery.

"Woohoo. You did it, girl," Georgie exclaims.

"We are so proud of you, Em." Allie rejoices. "Congratulations on a huge achievement."

"Look at you. You're glowing. I haven't seen your eyes sparkle or your infectious smile for ages now. The date looked like it was going well," Georgie praises, and then effervescent mother hen Tash butts in.

"Tell me, tell me. What happened?"

"Well, you would have seen that when I got there, Ethan was with another woman. I thought I was being set up, but it turned out that it was his sister. After she left, we chatted for a while." I take a breath, then continue to gush, "He said I intrigue him, and he wants to spend some time getting to know me. He seemed a bit perplexed when I insisted on paying my way, but dropped the matter, and then, when I pulled out my hat, he must have wondered what he had got himself into by asking me to go for a walk around the harbor. But it was glorious. We ended up at Observatory Hill and parted ways there. He hugged me and said he'll call, but whether he does or not, I feel like I will be less anxious with dating now."

"Oh, wow, that's great, Em. Well done you," Allie praised.

"Thank you all for your support and getting me over the line today. It means so much to me that you've helped in so many ways." My voice wobbles as I express my appreciation and love for these women. I know I would do the same for them if ever they needed me, but as my self-reliance restores, I promise myself that I will become as strong and resilient as each of them.

We chat for a bit longer before I end the conversation and hang up.

The night slips away while I go about my chores and analyze my elation. *Is it from pride in myself for overcoming my anxiety today and not running away when everything in me screamed to get the hell out of there? Or is it just that Ethan's charm and easygoing personality put me at ease like he would most people? Is the fondness I am feeling the result of a rebound distraction—finding someone totally opposite to what I have known? After all, Ethan is so far out of my league, but he certainly is an appealing man.*

My head spins, but one thing I know is that Ethan is a player. I can tell from the way he was checking out women on the dance floor the other night, and Georgie confirmed it, warning me to not get too attached. So I continue to question what it is he sees in me. I know nothing serious will come from us getting to know each other and decide to enjoy his company while it lasts, using it as a way to keep rebuilding my self-esteem.

Convinced that he is a rebound distraction (because he is so very different from my ex) I also remind myself to take Georgie's advice, because getting attached is the road to further heartache. *Of course, this is all dependent on him calling me again, which is unlikely,* I admonish myself, trying to be a realist.

Regardless of what happens, I send up thanks for the experience as I climb into bed and write about my day in my journal, knowing in my heart and mind that Ethan has set a benchmark for me today in how I wish to be treated in the future.

***

The rest of the weekend passes in a blur of routine and my mood is still upbeat after yesterday's date. Ethan has been popping into my mind all day, and I've caught myself a few times smiling at nothing. I feel like I should thank him for the date, but don't want to appear too forward. To him, it was probably just an innocuous time filler, but to me, it was a huge step up the ladder of self-esteem and I am filled with gratitude. I ponder for hours over whether to text a thank you or wait till he contacts me. Politeness wins out eventually and I send off a quick text before I change my mind.

Chapter Seven

ETHAN

I slept late this morning because of my sexual exploits last night, grabbing brunch and a coffee when I finished my run earlier. Now, instead of focusing on the work in front of me, thoughts ricochet around my head. My sigh is heavy and audible as I lean back in my chair, crossing my arms over my chest. A dull ache near my ears makes me aware how tightly my jaw is clenched, and my lips are flattened together into a grim slash. My chair bobs in time with the staccato beat of my tapping foot. Why? Because I allowed thoughts of Emily to creep into my night of sex with Tahni and Brianna, that's why.

As much as I enjoyed their attention, there were times when Emily's cute face popped into my head, making me question what fucking her would be like; whether her deliciously ample breasts are soft and heavy, what noises she makes. If anything, imagining Emily fired my drive and amplified the intensity of my emotions, creating explosive orgasms like I have never felt before. Each time I came... and I came a few times with these incredible women, felt like it was coming from my toes, and that my whole body was sucked into the vortex of release. It was incredible, amazing, and I hope my fantasies of her live up to the reality, because I am even more determined to get Emily into my bed. By the time I left in the early hours of the morning, Tahni and Brianna were both sated and didn't know that I'd been fantasizing about Emily.

I am irritated though because I should have been more present in the moment, enjoying them wholeheartedly. They are very good to me, and for me, by allowing me to get my rocks off with them, often at short notice. I don't want to upset that applecart.

My thoughts return to Emily, and I feel a buzz in my balls that I am beginning to associate with her. And I am at a loss to understand why. I have had twangs of arousal before with far more beautiful women, but they have never invaded my thoughts the way Emily has. And that annoys me because I don't want any emotional entanglements. I have freedom and spontaneity, and my life is just the way I like it. I huff out another breath, push myself to my feet, and wander to the large plate-glass window a few feet away to my left. The blustery weather outside seems to represent my thoughts, which are scattered like the wind. *Do I want to see Emily again?* I know myself well enough that if I don't pursue her, I will forever feel like she is unfinished business, and it will keep nagging at me. For me, the thrill is in the chase, and once I have bedded a woman, the flame of attraction is snuffed out. So, I know I need to fuck her to get past whatever this attraction for her is. *But why is it that I worry about hurting her, which will inevitably happen if I see her again?*

"Enough," I bark at myself, harnessing my thoughts back to the work I have bought home. Plopping back into my chair, I swivel my legs back under the desk and tackle the paperwork with fierce determination, eventually getting everything in order.

Just as I am putting the folder of finished documents in my briefcase to take back to the office tomorrow, and thinking about the workout session I have planned, my phone pings. Glancing down at the upturned screen, I am surprised by a message from Emily, and my mouth spreads into a grin.

Emily
Thanks again for a great day yesterday.

That is all it says. No suggestions to catch up again. Emily is all about subtlety, so is this her way of hinting that she would like to see me again? The thought thrills me more than I expected. Or is it simply just a thank you?

Quickly, I check my upcoming schedule for the week on my phone then, I fire off a reply.

Ethan
I had a great time too. I'd like to see you again. How does dinner on Thursday night sound?

Realizing I am running short of time to get to a family get together with Xander and Louisa, I grab my phone and keys and rush to the elevator, which opens directly into my apartment. Its doors shut, and once I exit into the lobby, I walk out onto the busy promenade, figuring that it would be quicker than waiting for an Uber to go the short distance to Xander's place. I love living in this part of the city because everything is so accessible by foot, and there is always something to see or do. When I moved here from London to help Xander with this branch of the business, I had initially stayed in a corporate apartment. However, since then I purchased my own larger, fully serviced penthouse apartment with stunning views of the nearby harbor. When Xander and I travel between London, Sydney and America every couple of months, our apartments in each city provide a stable base for us; somewhere that we can call home for the duration, filled with a smattering of our own possessions.

"Hi Vincent. How are you tonight?" I greet the doorman, pausing to enquire how his sick daughter is. When he assures me that she is much better, I grin and express my best wishes, shaking his hand before sauntering toward the private elevators with their own secure foyer area near the back of the main lobby.

Pressing the video intercom, Xander buzzes me in and I enter the elevator and ride to Xander's full floor penthouse on the fifty-fifth level, also overlooking the harbor.

The doors open to a very plush entry area and Xander greets me at the door as the delicious smell of dinner wafts through to me.

"Hey, bro. How come you're so red in the face?" he asks, raising his eyebrows and casting a cursory glance over my features before stepping aside to let me in.

"I've just walked here at a blistering pace. My best time, too." I grin with satisfaction and slap him on the chest.

"Yeah right." He shuts the security door as I move past into the lounge area where Louisa is sitting.

"Hi, sis." Helping myself to a bottled water from the bar, I notice Xander and Louisa already have wine and I pour myself a glass from the open bottle of red.

We chat idly about Louisa's holiday as she is returning to England tomorrow. Like Xander and I, she does a lot of commuting between our international offices, so has friends all over the world, but her visit to Australia is the first real holiday she has taken and she'e managed to see a large part of the country.

As we eat the delicious roast beef and vegetables that Xander has ordered in, she regales us with humorous stories of vehicle breakdowns, small aircraft flights and swimming mishaps.

"How did your date go on the weekend, Ethan?" Louisa queries with avid interest during a lull in the conversation, her big hazel eyes twinkling with merriment as she delights in taunting me.

"What? What date?" Xander spins his head toward me, his dark eyes questioning. "How come I don't know about this?"

"Why would my love life interest you, Zee? I'm sure you don't want to know what I am doing or who I'm doing it with, just as I don't want to know the ins and outs of your love life."

"Damn right," he mumbles, then he gives me a slightly miffed look, which for the 'Iceman' Xander is unusual, so I mollify him by responding.

"Rest assured, I'll let you know if I get serious with someone."

He nods his head. "So you damn well should."

"Boys, enough of your squabbling. Are you going to answer the question, Ethan?"

"Quit with the attorney interrogation, Lou." I pause and sigh, rolling my eyes at her. "There is not much to tell. Emily is a lovely girl. We had coffee and then wandered around the harbor. Did you know that there is an interesting historic observatory there?" I try distracting her, and fortunately, Xander pipes up.

"Who is Emily? And how come you've met her Lou?" His glance ping-pongs between us. Xander doesn't like being left out of the loop with anything, so his question is not surprising.

Bored with their integration into my personal life, I answer Xander in a flat tone. "Emily is a friend of Georgina's that I met when we went to the nightclub last week. I invited her for coffee and Louisa just happened to be walking past and spotted me." I pause to take a sip of my wine before continuing, "We were hugging when Emily arrived, so I introduced them."

"She appears to be a very genuine person," Louisa adds with affection. "Quite different from the narcissistic, fame-grabbing model-types you normally go for." Of course, she couldn't let the opportunity go to have a dig at me.

"Yes, she is," I reply with a bland expression, then look up at her while cutting my beef. "Tell me about the show you went to see," I say, hoping to take the focus off me. Louisa took the hint and prattled on about the show and for the rest of the night, the conversation remained on neutral ground.

After saying goodnight and wishing Louisa a safe trip home to England, I headed back to my apartment, pondering on Louisa's view of the women I date. *So why do I feel so bothered by Louisa's perception of the apparent shallowness of those flings, when the lack of emotional entanglement is exactly why I bedded those women?*

This internal battle is way too deep for my liking, so I push the irritating thoughts aside while I pause, leaning on a metal fence, to admire the city lights shimmering on the inky water in the still busy harbor and breathe in the cool salt-tinged air.

I had never realized how much inner peace the water views and smells would provide until I lived here. Often taking refuge down by the harbor after particularly grueling days in the office, I find it always lifts my mood, clears my busy mind, and allows me to decompress. Thoughts of returning to my home in London are bleak because I will be so far removed from the cathartic effect of the ocean. Even though I live in a high rise near the river in the city, its muddy color and sometimes foul smell are uninviting.

Taking another deep breath of the invigorating sea air, I turn and walk the short distance to my apartment, greeting the concierge on the way to the elevators. Although it is a little after 10pm, and still relatively early by my usual nightly routine, I debate whether to use the gym or pool facilities or just relax in front of the television for a while. Opting for the latter, I enter my penthouse, drop my keys in a bowl near the front door, and grab a cold drink from the fridge before collapsing onto the lounge. Flicking through the television channels, nothing grabs my interest, so I pick up my phone to trawl through social media when I notice a message from Emily that I have missed.

Emily

Thank you. That sounds amazing. Looking forward to seeing you Thursday.

"Yes." I fist pump the air as I read her message, a grin spreading across my face and a warm feeling filling my chest. Excitement bubbles inside me as I contemplate where to take Emily on our dinner date, and whether I will have the opportunity to kiss her. As I remember her delicate, delicious-looking pouty lips, I fantasize about their taste and texture, and the feel of her tongue as I plunder her mouth.

My imagination runs riot, picturing her luscious red lips circling my cock, gliding up and down the shaft, taking in as much of my engorged flesh as she can.

A delicious ache settles in my balls, and my cock hardens. My hand skims over them and I give my balls a squeeze. Then I unzip my trousers, shimmying them down my hips, and readjust myself into a semi-reclined position, pulling my cock and balls from my jocks.

I am surprised at how hard I am over Emily—someone I know so very little about—but then I remind myself that I know very little about any of my other conquests. If I get horny and laid, that is all I need to know. Losing that train of thought to my current intoxicating horniness, I imagine Emily's tongue flicking and circling the head of my shaft, then lapping up the underside like she is licking drips off an ice cream cone. I stroke my proud cock, feeling it twitch. Gripping it harder, my strokes quicken into a steady, familiar rhythm while I visualize her sweet, shapely body lying spread-eagled in front of me, inviting me to fuck her deep and fast. Her soft sensuousness morphs into a demanding wantonness as I picture her small frame bucking against each of my thrusts, insatiable and wild.

Groaning as the piston-like stroking of my hand brings me to imminent release, I reach for the nearby tissues and, throwing my head back against the lounge, I bellow and catch the explosive rush of cum just in time. Sucked into the storm of the intense orgasm, I breathe deeply until my vision clears and my senses return to normal having just experienced the most extreme fantasy-driven climax I've ever had, and I can't help but hope that Emily in the flesh has the same effect.

Sated and sleepy, I stand, holding my pants at my waist while I amble to the bathroom to clean myself up in the shower, remembering that I haven't replied to Emily's message, but decide I'll do it in the morning after I've booked a table for our date.

Chapter Eight

ETHAN

Thursday finally comes around. I have been antsy all week and keep telling myself it's because I haven't had sex since I jerked off in my lounge room on Sunday, but I now realize it has been because of an eagerness for tonight's date with Emily.

Carly booked a table at my favorite Italian restaurant for 7pm, and I have arranged to meet Emily outside. I offered to send Ramon to pick her up, but she insisted on finding her own way.

We have shared a few texts during the week, mostly about the arrangements, but also chatting about what each of us has been up to, and I have caught myself impatiently awaiting her replies, telling myself to snap out of whatever is going on.

Because I have a late meeting with Xander and some clients, I won't have time to go home to shower and change, so have come prepared with a fresh shirt for this evening, knowing I can shower and shave in my office's private bathroom.

Carly pokes her head around my door and wishes me goodnight as I am unplugging my laptop, grumbling something that I don't quite hear about my date before she disappears again. I stare out the door after her, then shake my head at her odd behavior lately. Standing, I stroll out of my office toward the boardroom for our meeting, reminding myself to check on Carly tomorrow, to see if she is okay. Just over an hour later, I race back into my office, locking the door behind me so I can ensure my privacy while I shower and change, then grab my suit jacket and laptop bag and head out the door to meet Emily.

The swanky bar and grill isn't far from my office, and the balmy night is delightful for walking. I arrive with fifteen minutes to spare, stopping in the small square opposite the restaurant, which is busy with commuters scurrying like ants making their way home. A slight breeze wafts by as I lean against the memorial in the middle that faces the restaurant to look out for Emily.

While I wait, I admire the architecture of the old sandstone building that houses the restaurant. With its tall slabs of polished pink granite surrounding the lower two floors, a grand polished black granite porch with bronze bas-relief sculptures worked into the top face, it creates an impressive art deco statement.

It isn't long before I spot Emily hopping out of a car nearby, so I go over to greet her as she stands looking around for me. A familiar excitement bubbles through me, the usual thrill of anticipation I enjoy while getting to know a woman when I'm on a date.

"Hi, Emily. Thanks for coming," I beam, facing her, my eyes surreptitiously absorbing her natural beauty. Tonight, she is dressed in a classically simple black, knee length dress, cinched at the waist with a narrow red belt. Her bare legs are pale with lightly scattered freckles, and modestly heeled red sandals accentuate the shapeliness of her calves and ankles. Her glossy red hair is hanging loose down her back, and a red and black headband keeps it off her face. A small black handbag hangs near her hip from a long black strap that crosses her body between her breasts, making me salivate with thoughts of exploring them. Overall, beautiful in a lowkey way. Like our last date, it seems Emily's style is to hint at and flatter her shape rather than be overtly clingy and seductive, which I admire because it says a lot about her personality; there is more than meets the eye.

She turns, lifting her face to mine, and flashes a beaming smile, her round, deep-set eyes shining and crinkling at the corners. "Thank you for asking me, Ethan." She inhales deeply, and I assume she has caught a hint of my cologne, then she drops her eyes.

Thankful that I took the time to shower, I turn so I am alongside her and lightly touch the small of her back to direct her forward. "Let's head in then," I suggest, my voice slightly huskier than I intended because her floral scent wafts toward me in the light breeze, stirring my balls.

"Have you been here before?" I inquire with genuine interest as we cross the road.

"No, I haven't, but I have heard great things about it," she discloses. "It's owned by a hatted chef, isn't it?" Her eager tone makes the corner of my mouth lift as we step up the flight of black slate stairs of the entrance porch.

"Yes." Watching closely for her reaction to the interior as I hold open the art deco styled brass framed etched glass doors, I wave her through.

Emily's expression is that of a kid in a candy store, her head swiveling as she takes in the beautifully maintained features of the vestibule that pay homage to its early twentieth-century company headquarters heritage. Marble lines the tall walls, and an expansive curved leadlight window sits above the doors to the restaurant, which are metal framed replicas of the external doors.

"Incredible," Emily utters, her eyes appreciating the old worldliness of the entry foyer.

"Wait till you see inside," I chuckle, knowing the best is yet to come. Again, I hold open the next set of doors and usher Emily through.

"Whoa." She stops, rooted to the spot, mouth agape, her eyes wide and incredulous. The cavernous central grand chamber is an impressive dining hall with five massive marble columns running down each side supporting a towering ceiling. Two wings with lower ceilings adjoin the central hall. One is an open kitchen, the other contains more table seating.

Emily pivots on the spot, her face alight with joy. I feel a wide grin split my face as I peer at her, delighting in her genuine enjoyment of the décor, which has been lost on several other women I've brought here.

"Oh, Ethan. This place is amazing. Thank you so much for bringing me here." Her gushing words are halted as the maître d' approaches. He takes my name, checks his booking list, and then escorts us to a table between two massive green marble columns.

Once we are seated opposite each other and water has been poured Emily hangs the red cardigan she has been carrying on the back of her chair, and gazes around the room again in awe, before returning her attention to me.

"Do you come here often, Ethan?" Blushing when she realizes her use of the hackneyed pickup line, her inquisitiveness turns to a look of insecurity as she bites her lower lip, and her eyes drop to her clenched hands on the table. She quickly regains her composure. "Oops."

Smiling warmly at her, my voice is light-hearted and friendly as I answer, "Yes, I come here occasionally. Mostly for business lunches with clients because it's central to our offices and the food and service are exceptional."

Emily nods, then picks up and peruses the menu. "Do you have any recommendations?"

"The seafood or pasta are incredible. So is the open fire grilled steak." I smirk to myself when Emily's eyebrows shoot up at the price of the premium steak. Even I hesitate to pay a couple of hundred dollars for something that will be consumed quickly, but I have had it before, and it is heavenly.

I am conscious of Emily's insistence on paying her own way and don't want to embarrass her or make her feel inadequate by ordering the most expensive dish on the menu for myself. We discuss the menu options and eventually decide on a starter plate of prosciutto and cheeses, then prawn tortellini for Emily and pork chop for me. When the waiter comes to take our order, I nominate a wine for us as well.

"What are your favorite foods, Emily? Are you an adventurous eater?" I probe.

She chuckles. "I would say I am adventurous because I like most foods and cuisines, but I wouldn't go to the extreme of eating fried crickets or roasted bat." Her face scrunches with a look of revulsion at the thought, then relaxes into a lopsided grin. "My favorites are seafood, particularly prawns, and most Asian and pasta dishes. What about you?"

"I'm a red meat type of guy but adore Italian and French cuisine. I particularly love the seafood out here too." Our conversation continues around food until the delicious looking cold platter arrives and we nibble at the cheese and prosciutto while the waiter fills our wine glasses.

"Why did you choose to become a teacher?" I enquire, probing a bit deeper to get a better understanding of her. My eyes are transfixed by her soft pink wine-wet lips as her delicate slender fingers slide a rolled slice of thinly shaved meat between them. Guilelessly, her tongue peeks out to lick the tips of her fingers, as if she's savoring the salty taste. She doesn't seem to recognize the effect that innocent action has on me or my groin, as I try to recollect my thoughts.

A quizzical look flashes across her pretty face before she answers, her gaze distant, as if she is recalling a memory. Her face is reflective, her lips moving into a small, unfocused smile as she reveals, "When I was young, I was a slow learner and didn't enjoy school very much. Fortunately, I had a teacher who took the time to encourage me, coaxing me to try different techniques, and firing my enthusiasm and learning ability. After that, I got good grades and continued to feel proud of my achievements. I would like to have the same impact on the children I teach, to enrich their lives through learning, help them to feel seen and heard." I am intrigued by how mobile Emily's face is when her guard is down and her work satisfaction is apparent. "What were you like in school, Ethan? Did you have a favorite subject?"

I chuckle as I remember some of my antics. "Yeah, learning came easy for me, so I did pretty well through school, mostly trying to impress my big brother and parents. By the time I got to middle and senior school, I was incorrigible. Thought I knew it all, like most kids at that age, but mostly I was bored because I picked things up so quickly. Fortunately, Xander and my parents kept me in line, encouraging me to pursue my interest in maths and science, which helped later with understanding construction and engineering."

Our meals arrive and conversation halts while we savor the first few mouthfuls, commenting on how amazing the flavors are, and the beautiful presentation of the food. We chat about a variety of topics, including our hobbies, of which I have none other than the gym and running. Oh, and soccer, both helping with coaching and as a spectator. Making love is my most frequent pastime, but not something I can,t openly discuss here. Although Emily cheekily implies she knows of my penchant for sex when she comments drolly, "With your athletic physique, I guessed you love intense indoor physical workouts."

We chuckle about how we seem to have 'grown out of' our childhood sports, and Emily enlightens me on her favorite pastime of bushwalking and day treks around the harbor's headlands. We also laughingly compare our mishaps as novice drivers.

Our meals are finished, and I lean back in my chair, my forearm on the table and the other resting in my lap as I gaze at Emily. She is sitting relaxed and looking happy, her eyes shining and her cheeks plumping with her grin, her hands clasped in front of her on the table.

"Do you have a car, Emily, or do you rely on public transport and Ubers to get around?" I ask with curiosity and note her veiled expression as her gaze drops to her hands.

"No, not anymore. I have a scooter that serves me well for most things and I borrow Mom's car if I need to travel any distance, although I don't like leaving her without a vehicle for long."

"Do you live with your mom? That must take a bit of getting used to." I try to imagine living back at home with my parents, and a shudder runs down my spine. I love them to death, but I have been living alone for so long that I couldn't handle someone, no matter how much I love them, curtailing my movements.

Emily's fingers fiddle with the napkin on the table. "No, I share an apartment with a girlfriend who works away a lot, so it is a great arrangement. I thought about moving back with Mom, but didn't feel it was safe to do so." Her eyes shoot to mine, as she's obviously just said something she didn't want to divulge. Even though I acknowledge her slip of the tongue, my well-practiced poker face remains in place.

"Why is that?" My tone remains friendly and encouraging, hoping she will be honest with me.

Sighing heavily, Emily's eyes, dulled by resignation, return to look at me, her face grim. "I don't want to go into all the details, Ethan, but my ex is not a nice person, and I thought he might do something horrible to my mom out of revenge if I was living there. So far, he's left her alone, thankfully."

I feel a seething rage that a man she cared about could treat her in such a way, but also a conflicting urge to protect her. My hands clench as I try to reign in my haywire emotions, and I express my compassion with a hard-edged tone. "I'm sorry to hear that you had such a rough time, Emily. Is that why it took you a while to get out socializing again?"

She nods and answers in a small quiet voice. "Yes, and also why I had to get a job at a different school."

"Was he physically abusing you?" My words are clipped. I want to find this guy and beat the daylights out of him for hurting Emily. I grab my glass of wine and take a hefty swig to control myself.

"No, his weapon of choice was emotional manipulation." There is an understandable sting of bitterness and loathing in her tone, which she softens when she continues, "But thanks to my counselor, I'm in a far better place and much stronger than I was back then." Inhaling deeply and brightening her features as if in gratitude for escaping the situation, Emily peers at me and diverts by asking, "Have you had any bad life experiences, Ethan?" She sips the last of her wine, waiting for me to answer.

"No. I'm not one for serious relationships and have never lived with anyone other than family." I give her a cheeky grin, hoping to make her laugh. "There was a time when I was sixteen where I had my heart broken by the most popular girl in school."

Emily chuckles. "That's a rite of passage, isn't it?"

"Yes, it is, but please don't think I am denigrating the seriousness of your situation. I am very proud of you for getting out of there and seeking help to get yourself into a better place."

"Thank you, Ethan. That means a lot to me."

"Now, do you feel like dessert?" I ask, changing the subject.

"You've got to be kidding. I am so full I can't fit another thing in," she exclaims, blowing out her cheeks.

Chapter Nine

ETHAN

"Would you like to stay here, or move into the bar area? Or we can go for a walk if you like?"

"I think I'd like to walk if you don't mind?" Emily's eyes light with apparent pleasure, and I wonder if that is because the date is not ending with dinner. I am also surprised that I want to spend more time in Emily's company, and not just to get her into bed, but I find her conversations and personality interesting, making me want more. There is a connection there that I can't explain, but I know I don't have to work to establish it or think about it. I almost feel like I don't have to try being anyone but myself.

"Certainly." I signal the waiter for the bill, and he arrives quickly with it in a small black folder. I sign the docket, dropping my black charge card into the folder, and hand it back to him before he quickly disappears again.

"Ethan, please let me pay for my share," Emily insists, trying to hand me some cash.

"I respect how much you like to pay your way, Emily, but this place frowns on split bills or cash, so it is far easier to pay with one card. You can pay for the next one. Deal?"

Begrudgingly, she accepts, and we chat about some options of where to wander to while we wait. Standing when the waiter returns with my card, I put it away and adjust my laptop bag over my shoulder. Emily gets to her feet, collecting her bag and cardigan, then we walk side by side to the exit, my hand barely touching the small of her back.

The night air is cool now as we step outside, pausing while Emily puts on her cardigan, then we stroll a few blocks away to a bar I know. Again, I adjust my stride to cater for her smaller step, but it feels like a nice, relaxed pace in comparison to my normal long, fast stride.

Entering a hotel lobby, we take the elevator to the fourth floor and come out at an opulent bar with a dimly lit, intimate setting, and comfortable lounge seating. As we enter, I nod to the barman, and wander past the bar toward a two-seater lounge near the back.

We settle side by side into the lounge and order our drinks from the attentive table wait staff. The heat of Emily's body next to mine is delicious.

She gazes around, as if she's absorbing the vibing atmosphere, which is surprisingly hushed for the number of people in the room. The dark furniture and small table lamps exude a warm intimacy and pockets of seclusion while the multi colored wall panels and full length curtains add an uplifting element, drawing the eye to the rafter beams and skylight ceiling. There is low background music playing, varying from dinner music to chart toppers. No room for dancing, but it is not that sort of place, more suited to settling in for the evening after dinner.

"I like the feel of this place, Ethan. It has a calmness about it. Do you come here for business meetings too?" Emily inquires with a wondrous expression lingering on her face as she turns her gaze back to me.

"Occasionally. And sometimes by myself if I get sick of sitting around at home." My blasé answer has Emily smirking and lifting her eyebrows, no doubt assuming that I come here to pick up when I am bored. To be honest, there is an element of truth in her assumption, but sometimes it is just for noise and company, and I like watching people. It is interesting what random strangers will tell you in a bar. *I can understand why a lot of bartenders feel like counselors,* I chuckle to myself.

The waiter arrives with our drinks and places them on the low table in front of us, and Emily leans forward, grabbing her Bacardi and coke, sipping it before placing it back on the table. As she sits back, her body twists so that it is more angled toward me. Her eyes glitter with mischievousness, almost as if the comfortable atmosphere allows her to relax and bring out more of the real Emily.

"Tell me more about your family, Ethan. Do you have any other siblings besides Xander and Louisa?"

"No, it is just the three of us. Technically, Xander is my half-brother, and he only stayed with us when it was school holidays until he was much older, when he moved to England, living with us full time. Up until then, he had been between his father in Greece, boarding school, and Mom in England. Mom struggled financially for a while, then after she married my father and had me and Louisa, she fought for custody of Xander because she knew how lonely his life was at boarding school. Regardless of the distance, we were close, and Mom missed him terribly."

My right arm rests along the top of the lounge, almost touching Emily's shoulder, and my palm is itching to rub against her upper arm or stroke her lustrous hair that cascades over her upper chest. She looks so beautiful as she studies me with bright, curious eyes, listening intently.

Unable to hold back, the back of my fingers brush her shoulder as I continue to peer into her gorgeous green eyes, noting her pupils as they dilate and her tongue as it licks her lower lip. It is an innocently sultry look that shoots straight to my balls, adding to the continual ache she generates, and I am pleased that she seems to feel the same spark that I do.

Blinking as if to regain her self-control, Emily tilts her head slightly, and a slight flush colors her face and neck. She tosses her hair over her shoulder, exposing her creamy, kissable neck. Wanting desperately to taste her, my tongue swipes across my lower lip. There is a husky edge to her voice, tinged with cheekiness, as she questions, "How would you describe yourself in three words?"

I burst out laughing, not expecting that response. "Hmm. Good question. Let's see." I watch as she leans to pick up her drink, taking a sip as she waits for my answer. "Three words," I continue, dragging my mind back to her question. "Cocky. Voracious. Thorough," I respond with a mocking grin, observing her closely and wiggling my eyebrows comedically at my double meaning as she splutters on the mouthful of drink she has just sipped.

"You're naughty." A beaming expression lights her face. I feel the hairs rise on the nape of my neck and a fluttering in my chest.

"You better believe it." I hope she is visualizing just how naughty I can be. "Your turn."

As she ponders the question. I lean over and reach for my drink, my knee accidentally knocking Emily's as I do, liking the warmth that spreads from her. "Okay, here goes," Emily announces. "Adaptable. Creative. Caring. That's harder than you realize, isn't it?"

"Yes, it is, and I can see all of those traits in you, Emily," I confirm fondly. Complimenting her is easy because she seems a beautiful person inside and out. *Too good for you*, a self-deprecating voice whispers in the back of my head, and I quickly push it away. I am enjoying her company too much to allow those thoughts to intrude.

Our banter continues over another drink or two amidst much laughter and a bit of teasing. The occasional brush of my hand against her shoulder, and her hand against my knee builds an excitement in me that I haven't felt for a while, and I notice a similar light in her eyes. Emily squirms in her seat a few times, and after a while, I notice her stifling a yawn and realize that it is close to midnight and we both have work in the morning.

"I can see you're getting tired, Emily. How about we call it a night?" Trailing the back of my fingers down her upper arm, a zinging sensation shoots through them and up my arm. I have tried hard to keep my hands off her because she seems to have the uncanny ability to arouse me with just a simple touch or look, and now is not the time or place to explore that further.

"It's probably a good idea." We both stand and make our way to the bar to pay. When I get my wallet out, Emily places her hand on my forearm to stop me. "My turn to pay," she states firmly, but with a warm smile.

Nodding graciously, I put my wallet away inside my jacket, taking the opportunity to check out her shapely behind, which is defined beautifully by the soft fabric of her dress. My imagination runs riot, picturing my hands firmly gripping her cheeks and pulling her hard against me, and my cock stirs appreciatively, eager to delve into her feminine depths. *Settle down, boy,* I remind myself.

As we head back down in the elevator, I wonder out loud how Emily is getting home.

"I am just going to get an Uber. It won't take long," she answers matter-of-factly as we walk back out onto the street.

"Not by yourself at this time of night, you're not," I retort, my tone sharper than intended.

She flinches momentarily, reminding me of what she must have experienced at the hands of her ex. Then she stiffens her spine and lifts her chin. "I'll be fine, Ethan."

I try to explain my outburst in a far more compassionate way. "Emily, there are too many women being taken advantage of by ride share drivers. I'm concerned for your safety." Pausing to let that sink in, I continue, "As I see it, you have two options. I accompany you home to make sure you get there safely, or you come to my place."

I see her mind ticking over before she sighs resignedly. "Ethan, I like you. A lot. But I don't think I'm ready just yet to come back to yours, regardless of whether anything happens or not. Please don't be offended. But seriously, I will be fine traveling home by myself."

Gazing directly into her eyes so she can see my sincerity, I grip both her shoulders. "I'm not offended, Emily. I totally respect your decision about coming to mine, but going home alone is not happening. Please let me make sure you get home safely. It's the least I can do to repay you for such a pleasurable evening."

"Smooth. Very smooth, Mr. Ethan Wiggins," she quips. "Are you sure? It's totally out of your way?" At my nod, she offers me a grateful smile. "I guess I had better arrange an Uber for both of us then."

I am at a loss to understand why I feel so protective of her, but relief floods through me at her acceptance. Sliding my hands down her petite arms, I notice the faint outline of her perky nipples, my thumbs itching to swipe over them. Instead, I hold her cool hands in mine, watching my thumbs circle over the back of them. Softly, I croon, "Thank you, Em," before raising her hands to my lips and kissing them, lifting my eyes to hers as I do. Her eyes widen in surprise, and an audible gasp escapes her parted lips. I feel her shiver slightly, but am not sure if that is from my touch or the cool night air.

When I release her hands, she steps back, blinking a few times as if collecting herself, then she takes her phone out of her handbag. Her hair falls forward, hiding her face for a moment while she books the ride. I know I need a moment or two to restore my equilibrium, as well. This woman knocks me off kilter with her genuineness and sincerity, her cheeky sense of humor, her fragility contradicted by her stiff determination.

"It should only be five minutes." Fortunately, Emily interrupts my introspection before I discover any more self-revelations, and we move to a nearby seat to wait.

The trip to Emily's apartment doesn't take long due to the light traffic at this late hour and we spend it lost in conversation, our legs occasionally brushing against each other. When the driver pulls up outside the tall, white apartment block opposite a prestigious school, I ask him to wait while I see Emily into the building, rebooking him before we get out of the car.

"Thank you for seeing me home, Ethan. I really appreciate it. I had a great night." She speaks quietly and her warm, genuine smile is reflected in her soft liquid eyes while her hand gently touches and rests on my forearm. Brushing loose hair off her shoulder with my free hand, I slip it underneath the silky swathe and lightly grasp the back of her neck. I feel her shiver at my touch, a small moan escaping her throat, an erotic sound that stirs my blood. Her heat permeates my skin, ramping up my libido to the point that I want to drag her against me, to feel her soft, sensuous body against mine, but I remind myself to take it slow and be gentle.

I slowly bend and lower my head, tilting it slightly, my eyes shifting to focus on her lips. I move the arm where her hand is resting so that it wraps lightly around her, resting my hand on her back, while her hand creates a trail of delicious sensation as it glides along my upper arm, coming to rest on my bicep. My lips feather against hers, and I feel her anticipatory breath brush against my lips. I kiss her again with a soft gentle chaste kiss, and she lifts her mouth to meet mine, an aroused sigh escaping and touching all my senses. I follow with several small delicate kisses, our lips meeting and parting before separating again, sampling, and lingering, like sipping at a fine wine, before I slowly lift my head and kiss her on the forehead. I want so much to continue this intoxicating discovery of all that is Emily, and sense the same yearning in her, but bow to the overarching desire to take it slow with her.

"Thank you for a wonderful evening, Emily." Murmuring, I gaze down at her, then pull her against my body in a brief hug, loving the way her body fits against mine, sure that she can feel the bulge in my pants. I reluctantly release my hold on her and step back, noticing the shape of her nipples outlined against her dress.

"Good night, Emily". My words are husky because I need to get out of here now. I nearly groan from the delightfully warm lustful sensations flooding me, like sinking into a hot bath. It takes all my willpower to refrain from engulfing her in my arms and ravaging her on the spot.

"Good night, Ethan," she responds in a breathy voice.

Turning and walking away, I look back over my shoulder to see her sauntering toward the elevator and admire the shape of her bottom and the swing of her hair, noticing that she also is looking behind her and waving me goodbye.

Exiting the building, I hop back into the waiting car, casting one last glance toward the building as we move away into the night, my body thrumming. I am not used to walking away when I am this aroused and curse my innate sense of chivalry.

By the time I get back into my apartment, I am edgy. My thoughts on the ride home have been cycling between enchantment with everything about Emily and images of slaking my lust in her deliciously sensuous body. Pacing around, trying to decipher my reeling thoughts and feelings, I know I am enjoying getting to know her, seeing pieces of her personality open up like a flower as she becomes more comfortable with me. She has a quick wit and a sharp mind, and I love the banter we have established and our intellectual discussions. Already, I feel a tender protectiveness toward her. She is a really nice genuine person. I get the impression from what I have seen that she is a wonderfully loyal and caring friend because our conversations have been peppered with snippets of how she voluntarily does little things for her friends, like ensuring there are home cooked frozen dinners for Simone when she comes home from a long flight. The part I am struggling with most is that I want to fuck her till neither of us can walk, and I can play hard and sometimes rough in the heat of the moment. Emily seems very strait-laced and vanilla, and I would be mortified if I hurt her, either physically or emotionally. I feel like I am out of my depth with her, because most women that I pursue are blatant about wanting to get down and dirty with me whereas Emily strikes me as being very conservative, although her body cues gave away the lust she was trying to hide. *You never know though*, I muse. *I have been with some blatantly sexual women who are very narrow-minded and conventional in the bedroom.*

Realizing how tired I am, and fed up with my introspection and the continued stirring in my balls from thoughts of Emily under me moaning my name, I undress and step into the shower. *Maybe I need to apply a bit more physical interaction next time we meet to gauge Emily's receptiveness. Yes, that will work.* Gripping my cock, I jerk off to x-rated sexual fantasies with a very hot and horny Emily.

Chapter Ten

EMILY

Wow. Oh Wow. Leaning against the closed door of my apartment, I press my fingers to my lips, which are still tingling from Ethan's sweet, gentle kisses, sensuous yet respectful, and promising intense passion and heat. I know he was gauging our chemistry and my willingness, and quite frankly I am surprised by my body's reaction to him. His fingers on my nape shot sparks down my spine and moisture pooled between my legs just from his lips simply touching mine.

It has been a long while since I felt such arousal from so little physical contact, but then Ethan is intelligent and charming, and his wicked sense of humor had me laughing a lot of the night. I've always found that if my brain is stimulated, my body will follow, so a world-wise, astute businessman like Ethan, with movie star looks, a cheeky personality and a catchy joie-de-vivre is sure to get my motor running. I admire his integrity in safeguarding me by accompanying me home and respect that he didn't push his advantage when we were kissing downstairs, unlike men I have dated before, including my ex, Bradley. *I wonder if he realized how turned on I was,* I ponder. *He is an expert at reading people and their reactions, Emily, so, of course, he knew.*

Pushing myself off the door, I wander to the bathroom to wash off my makeup and change into my pajamas. *Was he turned on though?* I am sure he was because when he hugged me, I could feel a firmness in his groin. I'm sure he wouldn't have continued kissing me if he wasn't feeling something.

Sitting on the edge of my bed, my thoughts turn to having sex with Ethan. Delicious thoughts, which ignite my libido further, causing a fluttering in my lower belly and a tingling awareness between my legs. My mind spins. Ethan licking me there. Ethan driving his cock into me. Him sucking my nipples. *Oh, Stop.* Throbbing hot wetness seeps from the apex of my thighs, dampening my wide-legged pajama shorts. My nipples jut prominently through the soft fabric of my top and my boobs are heavy and aching, so crazily horny with these rampant imaginings. Reclining back against the pillows, I touch myself, slipping my hand under my top, orbiting and tweaking my sensitive nipples. Groaning with pleasure, my index finger slips under the bottom edge of my shorts and between my folds, landing on my clit and circling it. As it slips further down my crevice, it glides into my opening then out, in again and out, back to my clit and I am amazed at how wet I am. My head falls back as my back arches, and my pebble-like nipples scream for more attention as the pleasure builds. *Ohhh. Fuck. So good.*

My phone pings interrupting me with a message. Sighing, I grab my phone with my free hand.

Georgie
Hey, lovely. How have you been? What are you up to?

Emily

Not long home from a night out. How are you?

Georgie
Ooh, do tell.

Emily

I'll tell you all about it next week when we catch up. I'm exhausted and have to be at work early. Night, kiddo. Xxx

With my fantasy-driven ministrations interrupted, I plug my phone into the charging cable dangling over my nightstand, clamber between the sheets and snuggle down, closing my eyes.

I lay there for ages, my body still thrumming from unsated desire, various images of Ethan on our date replay in my head like a movie, trying to understand why my body is reacting this way to his simple touches.

I have never had this sort of intense reaction before, particularly so early in a relationship. Not even with Bradley. Is it because Ethan makes me feel secure and comfortable, and very much at ease, so I'm more able to present my real self? Is it a result of the counseling and personal development that is finally culminating in inner peace and confidence? Or is it simply that Ethan is a charmingly talented womanizer who knows how to play women and the dating game like a musical virtuoso plays their instrument? All I know is that I need to slake this craving Ethan has created in me. I also realize that I need to get laid, for no other reason than enjoying a guilt free sexual experience.

Bradley always blamed me for my inability to orgasm when he had put in no effort, just fucking me when it suited him. It got to the point where I faked it just to shut him up. So, getting laid by Ethan would signify a release of the final remnants of Bradley's emotional hold over me, and hopefully prove to me that I am more than capable of an orgasm in the hands of a considerate lover.

With that in mind, I get out of bed, padding across the room to get my trusty vibrator from my underwear drawer. Stripping naked and sliding back under the covers, I run the buzzing smooth oval-nosed vibrator through my still slick and swollen crease, jumping as it touches my sensitive clit, sighing as the intense shot of pleasure floods my body. With my eyes closed and breathing heavy, I slide it in and out, up and down, my back curving off the bed as I imagine it's Ethan teasing and pleasuring me with his rock hard cock, while my fingers squeeze and scrape my nipples. My heart is pounding, my breath panting and my hips pulsating as the rapturous sensations crescendo in an almighty orgasm. A vision of beautiful wild gold-flecked eyes shining from a captivated face ready to devour me fills my mind as I scream out Ethan's name.

***

The next morning, while I grab a bite to eat before rushing out the door, I check my phone, hoping there is a message from Ethan. There isn't and none appear at any of the multitude of times I check throughout the day.

Disappointment begins to set in, but I remind myself that he could be busy, or have some sort of dating rules about when to call after a date. By the time school finishes, I am annoyed with myself for falling back into letting someone else control my happiness. *You are an independent, liberated woman, Emily. What is stopping you from asking him out on another date? That way, you will know if he is still interested or not.* I decide I like that idea.

I feel that I still owe him for my share of last night's meal and won't feel comfortable till I have repaid him, but I know he won't take money for it. I also don't know very many of the better eateries in the city, so am reluctant to go to another restaurant where a certain formality is necessary. I'd like this date to be more casual, where I can show Ethan more of the things that interest me, and hopefully be a different but enjoyable experience for him too.

Pondering the possibilities while I pack my lunch bag and bottle into a larger tote bag, the idea of a picnic strikes me. Yes. We can incorporate a walk along the headland and picnic in a park overlooking the beach. Excitement builds within me while on the bus home as I search through maps on my phone plotting a possible route, then it dawns on me that I haven't invited Ethan yet. Quickly, I remedy that situation before I lose my nerve.

Emily
Hi Ethan. Just wanted to thank you again for a wonderful evening last night, and to see if you are available on Sunday for a walk along the foreshore.

What if he declines? Well then, I will still go and enjoy the day by myself, I resolve. Working through the logistics in my head of where to start the walk, where to stop for a picnic lunch, and how to get there and back, my trip home flies by, and just as I walk into my building, my phone rings.

"Ethan. Hi. How are you?" My breath catches as I answer, and I chide myself that I sound like a lovesick teenager while I amble to the elevator.

"I'm well thanks, Emily. Thanks for the invite. I have a bit going on this weekend but would love to meet up with you on Sunday if I can. What did you have in mind?" His voice is smoky, sultry, and toe-curlingly delicious with a tinge of business pleasantry mixed in.

For a moment there, I thought he would decline, but am thrilled he seems interested. "Oh, I was thinking of a leisurely trek along the Summerland Bay headland, stopping at a beach or park for some refreshment and then playing it by ear." Pausing, trying to gauge his reaction which isn't forthcoming, I elaborate lightheartedly, as if his answer doesn't matter. "Time wise, probably a couple of hours. So, I can fit in with whatever time suits you."

"Sounds great. Let me see if I can shuffle a few things around and I'll get back to you with a time." His businesslike tone suggests someone is with him and he confirms my assumption by continuing, "Sorry, I have to go to a meeting. I'll be in touch."

"Okay. Bye, Ethan." Hanging up, I try to settle my simmering nerves as I step into the elevator. He didn't blow me out of the water with a flat no, but he didn't sound enthusiastic either. No point in getting my hopes up because his other appointments might not be able to shift. That is, providing they exist at all. Maybe he was just saying that to let me down gently. *Well, if that is the case, Emily, you know where you stand. Don't sweat it.* The words of my counselor run through my head, and I chuckle at how pleased she would be at my renewed pragmatism.

Unlocking my door, I drop my bags, kick off my shoes, and stroll into the kitchen to make myself a cup of tea while I prepare dinner. My night is planned out—marking student's papers, and prepping for some classes next week. Tedious, but necessary to be an effective teacher. Before I know it, I am yawning, and my eyes sting from reading inconsistent, scrawling handwriting.

Packing up the paperwork and stretching out my back that has been slumped over the dining table for hours, I pick up my phone to check it and realize as I walk to the bedroom that I have been so engrossed in my work that I haven't given Ethan a thought. I don't have any messages from him, but there are a few from Allie and Georgie, and one from Simone telling me she will be home on Monday, so I respond to those then, yawning, I have a shower, turn into bed and fall asleep in no time at all.

Chapter Eleven

EMILY

When I wake up the next morning, I feel like I tossed and turned most of the night and am so tired I don't want to get out of bed. Thank goodness it is Saturday, and I don't have to go to school because my brain would be as effective as wet firecrackers. I need a coffee to fire up my system, so get up out of bed, grab my phone, and check it for messages, thrilled to find one from Ethan. 1.15am. Geez, he is a night owl. I can't help but wonder what he was doing till so late.

Ethan
Hi Emily. Sorry for the late response. I'm free from 2pm tomorrow if that suits you. Looking forward to seeing you.

Feeling encouraged and enthusiastic about our date, I pour some granola into a bowl, add a generous dollop of yoghurt, make myself a coffee, and sit at the breakfast bench to revise my plans for tomorrow.

Emily
How about we meet out the front of White Head Bay ferry wharf at

3pm? From there we can walk to South Head, then down to The Bluff, if we have enough time. It should take about 2-3 hours with some beautiful scenery along the way. I would suggest casual clothes, a hat, and good walking shoes. Is that ok with you?

It is not long before Ethan replies.

Ethan
Ok, sounds good. See you there at 3pm.

Emily
Great. I'll bring some snacks along. See you then. *smiley face*

I let out an excited squeal, pleased that Ethan has no qualms with the plan. Regardless of whether he cancels on me at the last minute tomorrow or not, I decide to still do the walk, but will obviously enjoy it so much more with him.

***

Sunday morning arrives bright and sunny, the temperature promising to be in the mid to high twenties so I ensure that my sunscreen is packed as well as a jacket, because South Head opens to the ocean and is likely to be breezy and at least five degrees cooler.

After tidying the house for the rest of the morning, I depart for my bus to the city, then a 30-minute ferry trip to White Head Bay. I am bubbling with excitement, telling myself not to get too carried away because there is a chance that Ethan won't show. Although from what

I know of him, if he says he is going to do something, he commits to it.

Biting my bottom lip, I debate whether a walking trek in nature is the sort of activity a multi-millionaire like Ethan would find interesting or consider even remotely fun. Reminding myself to think of him as a friend, nothing more, and honored that he seems willing enough to let me organize today's adventure and go along with my plans, I bask in the warmth of the sun and the glorious harbor views as the ferry powers across the slightly choppy water.

The wide bottoms of my light cotton trousers ruffle in the light breeze as I disembark the ferry and walk the long jetty to the board-walk, while the white, long-sleeved shirt that is unbuttoned like a jacket wafts behind me. It provides protection from the sun for my fair skin because, as much as I would like to walk around in my dark blue singlet top, I know that I would end up with a severe case of sunburn without it. My hair is tied back into a ponytail, with elastic bands at midpoint and end to prevent it getting knotted from the breeze, and my sunglasses are perched on my nose.

Knowing I am half an hour early, I make a toilet stop and then dig around in my backpack for my soft wide brimmed hat, holding it while I wait in the shade by the road out front of the ferry terminal. Assuming Ethan will come by ferry, I am sitting under a large tree, on a stone wall separating a park from the boardwalk, close to the jetty entrance, and facing it so I can see the passengers as they come off the next ferry.

Checking my phone for a message from Ethan, I jump when his deep, suave voice, as smooth as silk, croons from behind me. "Emily." The way he says my name, a smoky tone with a tinge of huskiness, sends a delicious, warm sensation all over me. I am sure I am blushing as I turn and bestow a warm smile on him, pleased that my sunglasses mask my eyes that are devouring him. *Damn, he is one fine specimen of manhood.*

His neatly cropped, dark hair is brushed off his broad forehead, his sunglasses hiding his beautiful hooded eyes and thick eyebrows. Wearing stylish, ivory colored button up shorts that taper and define his muscled thighs, finishing just above the knee with a rolled cuff, he has teamed them with a gray-green polo shirt. The sleeve cuffs fit snugly above his protruding tattooed biceps (which surprises me). The material drapes over his wide shoulders and prominent pecs but hangs loosely over his flat stomach, pooling fashionably over the top of his shorts at his narrow hips. His bare lower legs are lightly tanned with a fine covering of light brown hair and his feet are clad in black sneakers with white laces and soles. There are straps over his shoulders, indicating he is also carrying a backpack.

My mouth is dry as I utter breathlessly, "Hi," while my eyes rove over him again, paying closer attention to the tattooed tribal banding with a lion's head mid centre. Not normally a lover of tattoos, I find Ethan's a turn on. *But that might have more to do with the thick muscular shape of his upper arm than the tattoo itself.*

He sits next to me on the stone wall, lifting his sunglasses atop his head, and places his hand in the small of my back, leaning in to peck my cheek. "Hi," he purrs in a tone I imagine is his morning-after, sexually sated bedroom voice, because it melts me to the core. "Have you been waiting long?" he enquires in a more congenial, everyday tone.

"No, not long. I'm just admiring the scenery." Despite my cheerful smile, my response is a bit stilted because the sight and smell of him knock me off kilter, reminding me of my fantasies last night. As I pull myself together, I continue in a more natural tone. "I assumed you would come by ferry. Did you drive?"

Ethan nods and casts his gaze around the bustling waterfront. "Yes. I thought it was the most direct way of getting you home later." His sparkling green eyes return to mine, focused intently on my face, and he smiles down at me as if enjoying the thought of taking me home.

"Oh." I am surprised by his goodwill and puzzled by that smile, so stammer, "Thank you." Pulling a map of our proposed walk out of my bag, I point out the route. "We can start in this direction and head up to the lighthouses, but there is a lot of backtracking. Or we can head over to the other side of the peninsula and down past a shipwreck to another lighthouse." I look up at him expectantly as he pores over the routes.

"You okay if we aim for both?" He continues when I nod, "How about we do the northern part first and come back to The Bluff and see how we are feeling?"

"Good idea. Let's make a start then." Standing, I put my hat on, pulling it tightly on my head, then watch as Ethan drops his sunglasses to his nose, removes his backpack, and grabs a baseball cap by the brim from within, flipping it on his head. Standing, he replaces the pack on his back, adjusting the straps on his shoulders, then his hat.

"Okay. Let's go," he announces with enthusiasm as we wander alongside each other onto the concrete promenade slotted between the beach and housing perimeter fences.

"Have you been to this part of the city before?" I ask as he adjusts his gait to mine.

"No. Most of my walking has been around the CBD but I've heard some good things about a seafood restaurant in this area." Chuckling, I point to the building we are passing, with outdoor tables and umbrellas fronting the promenade and overlooking the bay. "Is that it? I'll have to come back here one time and give it a try. Great outlook."

We chat about the stillness of the teal colored bay, the boats moored not far offshore, and the upturned dinghies lying on the sand next to the path. We admire the exclusive houses bordering the pathway and the bustling activity on the beach.

Stairs at the end of the beach pathway lead up to the street, and we follow other walkers as they traverse the residential streets to the entrance of another small beach. More stairs lead us along a timbered path through some shrubbery, then opens up to an exposed gravel path with large rocks on one side and expansive views on the other across the bay to the CBD skyline.

I point out that a military base is nearby as we pass some historical stone bunkers with armament holes that formed part of the city's defense during World War II, and a bit further along, we come across a historic cannon. Stopping for a closer look, we sip at our water and reflect on the views and the history.

While Ethan inspects the cannon from all angles, I clamber along the small wall carved out of the natural stone, finding pathways to different parts of the armament. I also have a better view of the harbor from up here but nearly fall off when Ethan barks from behind me, "What are you doing up there?"

"Getting a better look. I don't have the advantage, height-wise as you do," I chuckle, turning my head to look at him, noticing that for once, I am slightly taller than him. Our camaraderie and openness have increased today, probably because we are both in a different en-vironment and experiencing something new together, so I feel more comfortable teasing him.

Taking my hand, his tone firm and his gaze steely, he urges, "I'd be much happier if you were down on the ground." I raise an eyebrow questioningly, and he replies, a wry little smile quirking his mouth, "I can lift you down if you like?"

"No, I'm fine thanks." I walk along the wall for a few feet, while Ethan still holds my hand, then I jump off, landing off balance at his feet.

He wraps his arms around me to steady me and I hear him utter softly, "Much better," as he gives me a quick hug. When he releases me, his voice is pleasant and distinct as he reveals, "Sorry if I overreacted. When I was young, I was playing with a friend who was walking a wall just like that and slipped off, cracking his skull and breaking an arm. I always felt that I could have done something to avoid it happening and didn't want the same to happen to you." His serious tone lightens as he continues, "Besides, I don't think I could piggyback you to the lifeguards on the beach."

"Huh. I'm not that heavy," I mock with a straight face, flicking him on the upper arm with one hand.

"What?" His face reddens with embarrassment, realizing his gaffe and he clarifies, "Oh no. I meant that I would be running back to the lifeguard, so it wouldn't be practical or comfortable for you if I piggybacked you."

"Gotcha. Good comeback." I throw him a closed-mouth smile, feeling my eyes crinkle cheekily.

I see his expression shift fleetingly from relief to something I can't put my finger on. He frames my face with his hands and looks deeply into my eyes, then growls, "Minx," before lowering his mouth to crush my lips, hard and fast. Then he lifts his head, hovering over my mouth, while his thumbs rub my cheeks. I can feel his desire all the way to my toes, gasping in surprise at the instant heavy ache between my legs and I grasp his forearms as my knees almost buckle.

Chuckling softly to himself, he drops his hands, letting one arm rest across my shoulders, and turning his body away from mine, he presses his fingers softly against my shoulder, propelling me forward, asking in an affable manner, as if that kiss didn't happen, "Where to next, Miss Tour Guide?"

Addled, I manage to murmur, "Um, let's follow the path." Walking together, with Ethan's arm still across my shoulder, feels like a promise that we will spend more time together. I feel very attracted to Ethan, physically and emotionally, and we certainly seem compatible in lots of ways. I am glowing like a bright light in his company, and I hope he has growing feelings for me too. Our conversation along the way is funny, interesting, enlightening, intelligent, and sometimes serious. We discuss anything and everything from favorite ice cream flavors to world politics, laughing and teasing each other in a rapidly developing companionable way.

As we progress along the headland, the concrete path changes to a timber boardwalk shrouded by shrubbery. We occasionally hold hands or walk closely beside each other, often having to maneuver in front or behind as we navigate steps or returning walkers who share the same path heading back to the start of the trail. But the closer to the point we get, the light breeze becomes stronger and cooler, with no land to buffer it. Donning jackets as we inspect the lightkeeper's cottage, we continue around the loop to the lighthouse, holding our hats so they don't blow away. Open ocean is to our left and the wind across the barren, grassy clifftop buffets us, my ponytail swishing like a whip. Peeking over the steep cliff face to the rocky ledge below, we admire the force of nature as waves crash against it, throwing sea spray high into the air. After pausing to drink some water, Ethan holds my hand again, practically dragging me against the wind as we complete the trail loop. Relishing the shelter of trees, Ethan takes advantage of the seclusion to pull me against him for an earth-shattering kiss before we retrace the path to the beginning.

It is almost dusk by the time we get back to the promenade by the beach near the ferry, and much warmer now we are sheltered from the wind, so we decide to get some takeaway fish and chips because we have worked up a hunger. Not only for food either. We have kissed several times along the route, each longer and more probing than the last, so my body is thrumming with lust. I am totally mesmerized by Ethan, who is the best kisser I have encountered, his lips coaxing yet insistent, firm but soft, and very tasty.

Taking a seat on the sand with our delicious looking seafood, we watch the sun set as we eat. Breathtakingly beautiful red and pink clouds streak the sky, their reflection coloring the water pink, while the moored boats in the bay are silhouetted black against the vivid backdrop. We sit in silent awe, breathing in the cooling salty air, enthralled by the beauty of nature.

My thoughts start pondering if this is where the date finishes. I certainly hope not because my desire is clamoring for release, and as Ethan is the one who ignited the fire, he is the only one who can douse it. I recollect him saying he would drive me home, wondering how I can raise the subject of leaving without him thinking I want today to end. As if reading my mind, Ethan bumps his upper arm against my shoulder, then brushes some stray windswept tendrils off my face, peering at me with avid fascination.

"Shall we go?" His sultry voice is bewitching, and his gaze drops to my lips, as if captivated by them. I can only nod as the lust that flares in his eyes takes my breath away, and I am sure it is reflected in my own eyes as I gaze back at him. He stands and brushes off the sand as I pack up our rubbish, then he takes my hand and pulls me to my feet, hugging me and kissing the top of my head. Strolling hand in hand up the street to the car, we squint under the bright building lights until our eyes adjust.

Ethan stops beside a sleek, dark green, late model Mustang and grins at me like a Cheshire cat. My head swivels between him and the car, gawping, and I gibber, "Oh, no way. Is this yours?" One of the conversations we had today was about favorite cars, and I stated that a Mustang was mine. No wonder Ethan had been so evasive about what he drove.

"Of course, it's mine." His grin changes to a smile, pride evident in the way his chin lifts and his chest puffs out slightly. "Did you check out the number plate?"

Giving him a sidelong glance, I walk behind the car and grin when I read 'VROOOM'.

"Cool, huh?"

Returning to face him, I chuckle and, shaking my head. "You are such a motorhead."

Chapter Twelve

EMILY

The car beeps when Ethan presses the key fob and, as it unlocks, he opens the passenger door of his pride and joy. "Hop in." My hand slides over the plush gray leather, inhaling the aromatic smell of newness as I slide down onto the sumptuous seat and buckle the seatbelt. Shutting my door, Ethan paces around to the driver's side and hops in, proud as punch, as he turns his head to me. He is like a little boy with a new toy. "Ready?"

"Yes," I laugh, his enthusiasm catching.

As Ethan presses the start button, a deep throaty growl reverberates through the street, turning into a ferocious roar, sounding just like his numberplate, when his foot presses the throttle and we accelerate up the street.

"I imagined you would drive an Italian sports car, Ethan. Isn't this more of a muscle car?"

"Yes. And it gives me the best of a sports car and a muscle car while still providing enough space and comfort for my height."

"Mmm. Impressive." We continue to chat on the drive home. As Ethan parks near my building, I ask, "Would you like to come up?"

"Mmm. Sure would." His voice is a husky drawl, and his eyes soften, raking over me.

He walks me into the lobby again, my palms tingling where his warm hand holds mine, and then he moves it around my waist when we are in the elevator. A frisson of nervousness hits me because I haven't been intimate with anyone since my breakup. I sense that Ethan has seduction in mind, as do I, because the chemistry between us has been electric all day and I hope I don't disappoint him.

Following me into the apartment, Ethan has a look around when I drop my keys near the front door.

"Would you like a drink or anything?" I squeak out past my dry tongue, not sure what else to do or say as my cheeks heat with a blush. *Geez, get a grip, girl. You are acting like a virgin, for God's sake.* Taking a deep breath, I try to portray the confident person I know I can be; straightening my back, I flick my ponytail over my shoulder.

"Are you on the anything list?" Ethan purrs softly as he steps closer, taking both my hands in his, his darkened eyes drinking me in.

Warmth suffuses my neck and cheeks, and I am certain that I must be beetroot red, but looking up through my lashes, I ask in a quiet, hopefully flirty manner, "Do you want me to be?"

"Bloody hell, Em. Of course, I do. But only if *you* want to. I've been thinking all day of all the things I want to do to you. But I'm not pressuring you if you're not ready yet." Sincerity and respect ooze from his demeanor and some of my nervousness disappears with his enthusiastic response. As if a switch has been flicked inside me, the latent lustful embers spark and combust, fueled by the intensity of Ethan's words.

As I step closer, so our bodies are nearly touching, his heat washes over me. I pull my hands out of his grasp, sliding them up his arms, stretching to clasp them behind his head. "I'm ready."

A flash of fire lights his eyes at my words, and his hands cup my elbows, searing their warmth and strength into my senses as he drags me against him, inflaming my core. Tilting his head to the side, he gives me a fleeting whisper of a kiss. I pull his head closer, opening my mouth and pressing my eager lips firmly onto his in a silent, impassioned plea for more, sighing into his mouth when he applies more pressure. Eventually, he breaks away, pressing his forehead to mine.

"Are you sure, Em?"

Nodding, I feel his banked desire when his palms run up my arms, caressing them. Lifting his head, he closes his eyes, and his fast breath puffs against my hair. Wanting to coax him into losing control, my fingers stroke his nape and I delight in his feverish heat when his fingers dig into my fleshy biceps.

"It's not my first time, Ethan," I murmur, hinting that I can take more.

"It's your first time with me, Em, and I don't want to hurt you," he growls, his fingers moving to rest on my nape while his thumb strokes down my cheek to my chin.

I give him a quick peck on the lips and lift one hand to his cheek, feeling the slightly roughened texture of stubble. "How about we go with the flow but promise to back off if one of us thinks it's too much?"

His eyes shine and darken like jade. He growls again as his mouth smashes against mine with a burning passion, giving me his answer without the need for words.

His hot tongue pushes into my open mouth and I am pulled hard against his firm body, his hands roaming frenziedly up and down my back, gripping and massaging my buttocks. My arms circle his waist, replicating his movements as my tongue explores his mouth, entwining with his hot, probing tongue. We physically can't get any closer, but I feel that we aren't close enough, and I desperately press myself harder against him, my stomach firmly against his bulging cock, making me moan. He feels big. And hard. His heat seeps into my flesh, and I drop my hands to cup his buttocks, desperately wanting more of him.

His smooth, soft fingers slip under my top, and he moans with pleasure. Sliding his hands higher, dragging my singlet top up, they blaze a trail of fire as he strokes my bare skin, then his thumbs glide over the ribcage under my breasts. My hands frantically drag at his shirt, untucking it from his shorts, creeping underneath to feel the velvet soft skin of his lean, toned torso. I am flooded with warmth and my pulsing core yearns for him, dampening my panties with warm wetness.

Ethan breaks the kiss, tilting his head to plant small kisses up my neck while pushing my overshirt off my shoulders. I move my arms from his waist to let the shirt fall to the ground while lifting my chin, exposing more of my neck to his kisses, inhaling his intoxicatingly sexy, musky, sandalwood scent. Sighing against my skin, his deep voice a seductive purr, he murmurs in my ear, "Where's your bedroom, Em?"

A delicious shiver runs through me and, blinking a few times, I gaze tenderly into his smoldering gold lit green eyes. Breathily, I manage to voice, "This way." Taking his hand, and feeling his gaze raking over my body, I lead him to my room, eager to feel more of his touch.

Turning on the light and standing alongside Ethan just inside the doorway –thankful that I tidied this morning– my eyes are fixed on him as he has a cursory glance around the neutrally colored room, his gaze landing on the queen size bed covered in a monochrome, textured velvet duvet. "Nice," he croons. He throws me a lopsided grin and raises an eyebrow, his eyes sparkling as he teases, "Just one thing missing."

I glance around the room to review what he feels is lacking. "Oh?"

Tugging on our still clasped hands, he pulls me back against his firm, tight body, his free hand grasping the back of my head. He stares into my eyes, his hunger piercing them, then utters huskily—"You"—before claiming my mouth with his unleashed passion.

I moan, my tongue matching his in its probing exploration. Our hands skim over the other's body, intensifying our lust, scattering all thought, focusing only on the torrid sensations our touch provokes.

Ethan loosens his hold of my head and moves his hands to lift my singlet, breaking the kiss to pull it over my head. Throwing it to the floor, his fingers brush under the edge of my bra, raising goosebumps of excitement before they trail over my breasts and flat stomach. His eyes follow, his expression mesmerized. My hands glide over his forearms, then drop to catch the hemline of his still buttoned shirt, lifting it to his chest but getting stuck under his armpits. While Ethan grabs his shirt and yanks it over his head, letting it drop to the floor, my hands explore his flat, taut stomach, following the ridges of his six pack abs.

His lips blaze a trail from my mouth to my neck and back, pecking and plundering my mouth as my fingers run through his soft, lush hair. He takes a sharp intake of breath when my fingers circle his nipples, then flick at them. He squeezes my butt cheek, pressing me against his hard, bulging erection that digs into my stomach. My eyes widen and flare at the size of him and he chuckles at my surprise, his face hovering over mine.

"All for you, Baby Girl." My heart palpitates in my chest. I want him naked. Now.

My hand drops to cup his crotch, the thumb running over his contained cock, and I give him a wanton smile. "I need you, Ethan." I sigh at the feel of him in my hand, while the other one tugs at his belt, desperate to feel him flesh to flesh.

Ethan drops his hands to help, kicking off his shoes and lifting his feet to remove his socks, while I slip my shoes off and trousers, dropping them to join his clothes on the floor. His eyes never leave mine and I groan at the sight of him semi-naked, lightly tanned, toned all over, with the material of his navy blue trunk style jocks stretched across his cock. Sighing heavily, I lick my lips, salivating at the thought of his huge member plunging into me.

"Fuck, Em. You are gorgeous." He croaks out the words, and I stretch up to loop my arms around his neck, just wanting to get as close as I can to him, kissing him with feverish, rampant desire.

He undoes my bra and I groan as the weight of my breasts shifts while they are squished against his chest. Ethan hooks his hands behind my thighs, then scoops me up so I am forced to wrap my legs around his waist, my clad hot wet sex against his covered cock and balls. I feel his cock twitch in anticipation as if wanting to be free of the restrictive clothing.

He carries me the few steps to the bed, as if I am light as a feather, then kneels on it and crawls close to the middle, lowering me gently. His arms rest near my head, his body hovering above me, his hair roughened legs between my spread thighs, as his mouth delights in ravaging mine, our groins pressing insistently against each other. I take great delight in languorously stroking the contours of his firm bulging biceps and shoulders, savoring their silky strength before gently scraping my nails down his back.

Straightening and kneeling upright, Ethan mumbles, "Too much clothing," as his smooth, strong hands find my breasts, cupping and gently squeezing them. Then his index finger slides through my cleavage, hooking under the center of my bra, and with a swift tug, he removes it, flinging it behind him. His lust filled eyes focus on my ample breasts, their aroused, jutting pink peaks craving his touch. Moisture floods my panties and, moaning, I arch my back invitingly.

He swoops to engulf my erect nipple in his mouth, his tongue flicking and laving it, cupping the underside of my breast with his hand, molding and shaping it. I writhe against him as his moan vibrates around my nipple. He moves to the other breast, paying it the same lavish attention, and my hips lift off the bed, impatiently wanting his hot, stiff rod inside me. He slides my panties down to the top of my thighs, shifting his body backward to trail kisses down my abdomen, pulling them further down as he moves, exposing my hairless mons.

"Ooh, fuck." I lift my head at his long drawn out sigh, worried that my penchant for a smooth pussy might be distasteful to him, but I catch his rapturous expression before his head drops to lick my slick crevice. My hips buck when his hot, firm tongue laps at my swollen, sensitive clit, and an ecstatic moan escapes my half-open mouth. "Mmm. You are so wet, Baby Girl." He licks me a few more times, grinning in between strokes to look up at my blissful face, then suddenly stops.

Pushing himself off the bed, he quickly pads out of the room, and before my lust-addled brain registers his absence, he returns a moment later with a strip of foil packets in his hand, placing them on the bed. Standing near my feet, he swiftly disposes of my panties from around my ankles, his enthralled eyes raking my body, naked and spread open for him.

I lift my back off the bed, resting on my elbows, and watch him tug his jocks down. His stiff, thick cock stands at attention, ready for service, as it is released from the confines of his underwear. My eyes widen and my jaw drops at his size. I knew he was bigger than I felt earlier, but seeing his ramrod flesh, I don't know whether to panic or salivate.

Ethan stands proudly with his hands on his hips, his rigid staff pointing in the direction of where it intends to be, like a signpost, and he smirks at my stunned expression. "You ready for me, babe?"

"Ethan, you won't fit."

He detects the worry in my voice and his face softens. Kneeling on the bed, he leans over me, claiming my mouth again, French kissing me till I am breathless, and his occasional nipple squeeze has me squirming beneath him. My arms collapse underneath me, my shoulders drop to the bed, and my back arches in sheer joy. I can feel his hot rod resting against my thigh, so close to where I want him that my pussy gushes with anticipation.

"I'll be gentle with you, Em. Just let your mind go and give into the pleasure," he murmurs as he trails small kisses down my neck and across my chest, circling and flicking each nipple with his tongue. My hands grab his head, pushing my nipples further into his mouth, before he continues his seductive exploratory path down my flat stomach. As his tongue dips into my navel, his thumb slides through the slippery channel between my legs, pausing to press and circle my engorged nub. With a slight adjustment of his hand, his thumb returns to my clit, and a finger slips easily inside me. He lets out a sinful groan.

A raspy moan flows like a sigh from my mouth and I feel Ethan's chuckle vibrate on my belly, matching the fluttery sensations inside me. He lifts his mouth, blowing softly on my navel as he pulls his hand back. My bottom twitches on the bed, craving the warmth and pressure of his fingers, then he continues the multi-pronged attack on my senses with his tongue and hand.

This time, two long fingers push into my opening, pausing, then a third finger on the next entry. My breathing is heavy and fast, close to orgasm, my ears are buzzing yet I hear Ethan croon "That's it. So good, Baby Girl." I whimper when he removes his hand, frustrated at the loss of him, wanting to feel the fullness in my pussy.

Reaching for the foil packets, he rips one open with his teeth, his eyes blazing down at me while he sheaths himself. My hungry gaze devours this magnificent male specimen, and I am overwhelmed with affection for him. Rarely have I been so turned on, and most of my previous lovers would have been in, out, and finished by now.

In a flash, it dawns on me that Ethan's genuine, caring, and relaxed nature, his acceptance of who I am, has allowed me to see who I want to be; an equal in a relationship. Not a person who suppresses their emotions for the sake of someone else's feelings. Not a person who shies away from communicating and expressing herself honestly. Feeling liberated, my inner seductress emerges and I grab hold of my fledgling sexual confidence with both hands.

Ethan kneels back between my legs, his body above me, supported by his hands planted next to my shoulders. His dick prods my pubic bone near the top of my slit. He leans in to ravage my mouth, and I wrap my legs around his hips, clasping my feet together in the center of his back, and my hands grip his biceps. Throwing my weight to the side, I manage to topple him, rolling him onto his back, so I am sitting astride him. He lifts an eyebrow and the corner of his mouth tilts in a sly smile, assessing my next move.

I am still gripping his biceps as his arms lay flat on the bed next to his body while I straddle his hips. Lowering my head, my tongue flicks over his nipples and I delight in his sharp gasp. I lift my head and smile with satisfaction, circling them with my fingers, before my tongue finds them again. This time he growls and twitches his hips. I slide my sex up his shaft, lowering my body so my breasts scrape along his abdomen, and with my hands on his shoulders, drag myself up his torso, stopping to rub my pebbled nipples over his tight pink nubs.

The head of his cock edges the opening of my drenched pussy and, desperately needing more of him, I rock my hips so his tip slips inside me. I moan at the amazing tightness, feeling the burning stretch. Each movement of my hips allows him to go deeper until his thick shaft is buried inside me. The sensation is too much, and I cry out in pleasure, his eyes fluttering closed as he whispers my name. Pushing myself upright, my pussy stretches, slowly acclimatizing to his girth. An overwhelming feeling of completeness engulfs me as I savor the delicious sensations.

"Ooh fuuck. That's it, Baby Girl. Take it in," Ethan encourages, groaning as I slowly ride him. His large hands palm my breasts, squeezing and releasing them, with an occasional flick on my oversensitive nipples. His erotic moans and sighs drive me wild and I slide up and down his fleshy pole. "Aah. Fuck yeah. So tight. Take it all, baby. Take it." His strangled, gruff voice is almost an order, and he grips my hips, pulling me up and down his length with more force.

Panting, I throw my head back, letting the sensation of him filling me take over.

As I grind against him, he must sense my impending orgasm and he takes over, flipping us so I am on my back. He pulls out and stands, making me cry out from the loss of him inside me. But I don't have to wait long as he grabs me behind the knees and drags me to the foot of the bed. Nudging his cockhead to my entrance, pushing up inside me excruciatingly slowly, teasing me. "That's it, baby, take it. All of it."

Panting, the intensity inside me at fever pitch, I watch his enthralled face as he pushes as deep as he can go, feeling his pubic bone hitting my lower pelvis like we are glued together. I push my hips against him, teetering on the edge, wanting to lose myself to the euphoria that is hovering close by.

He stills for a moment then withdraws part way before thrusting, disappearing inside me again. Growling, he utters, "Mmm. So good," before pulling all the way out then plunging again, gliding into my slickness with ease. "Fuck, Em. You. Feel. So. Good."

"More." My rapid breathing doesn't allow any niceties. Demandingly, I push against him. "More, Ethan. More."

Again and again, he draws back, then hammers into me, my pussy delighting in slurping and sucking him in as I skyrocket into oblivion. Grabbing the sheets with my fists, my body tensing, a keening cry escapes me as my vaginal muscles clench, contracting around him as my orgasm takes hold. Fireworks explode behind my eyes, blanking my vision, and my breathing is ragged, my heart thumping crazily. Through the roaring in my ears, I hear Ethan howl, "Fuck. Fuck. Fuck" as he rams into me repeatedly, frenziedly, his fingers digging into my hips. He stills inside me, crying out as his dick erupts with his cum. His cock twitches as he spurts the last of his semen, then he pulls out, releasing my hips. My back and hips drop to the bed, my limp legs flopping over the edge. Ethan collapses onto his back on the bed beside me, as if his legs can't hold him up any longer, and drawing in deep breaths, he murmurs, "Sweet Gee-zus." We lie in silence, except for the sound of our breathing, waiting for our senses to return to normal, our sated, softly smiling faces turned toward each other.

My vision clears and I drink in his magnificent masculine body that has given me the best orgasm of my life. Everything about this man is built for pleasure.

I blink a few times as a shocking thought flits through my head. I have a serious case of like for Ethan. *No, it's more than like, but not yet love. Attachment? Fondness? Infatuation? Pre-love??* All I know is that I am totally into him, and it scares the shit out of me. *Surely, it's too soon after Bradley to feel such an intensity of emotion. Maybe it is the effect of post-coital hormones. Yes, that must be it. That is what I am going with for now.*

Chapter Thirteen

"You okay, Em?" Ethan's soft gentle voice breaks me out of my daydream.

"Hmm? Yes, I'm in heaven," Cooing, I give him a beaming smile. "That was incredible. Thank you."

A quizzical look flashes across his face before it shifts to a look of lustful intent, his admiring eyes raking over me. Propping himself on an elbow, he grips my chin between thumb and forefinger, then leans down, turning my head to meet his lips, and kisses me with heated reverence. His flaccid cock lays temptingly against his thigh, so, unable to stop myself, I reach over and stroke his balls then cup them. He gasps and lifts his head, his eyes devilish.

"Yes, it was amazing. But I'm not finished with you yet," he challenges. His hand skims over my breasts, teasing my nipples before trailing his fingers down and circling my navel, then continuing into my still slick crevice, pressing on my sensitive clit and making me jump.

Chuckling, he pushes himself off the bed, standing over me, as if he's admiring the post sex flush covering my body. "Where's the bathroom, Em?" Sitting up, I point in the direction and ogle his firm, rounded butt and beautifully sculpted back as he leaves the room.

Feeling thirsty, I get up, pick up my overshirt, and put it on, leaving it unbuttoned as I sashay to the kitchen. I have poured us both a glass of water and am standing in the lounge room when Ethan comes out of the bathroom.

"Would you like a drink of water?" I ask, salivating as I stare at his magnificent physique. Nodding, he saunters over to take the glass out of my hand, and I watch his Adam's apple bob as he drinks. Noticing that he has removed the condom, I hope it doesn't mean the night is finished, despite what he said earlier.

Ethan puts the glass down on the counter, then clasps my face in his hands. My hands rest on his warm, hairless chest and, as if reading my thoughts, he reveals huskily, "You drained me dry, beautiful. But we can still have lots more fun if you like."

"What do you have in mind?" Raising an eyebrow and with a lopsided smile, my soft voice is playfully sexy in what I hope is a flirtatious manner.

"Let me show you," he murmurs, his twinkling gaze glued to my lips. Lowering his head, his featherlight kiss brushes my lips, lifting then descending again and again.

His tender, adoring manner takes my breath away. All I can do is breathe, "Okay," against his lips. Ethan moves his hands to cup my bottom, then lifts me once again so we are face to face. I wrap my arms around his neck and my legs around his waist while he continues his sensuous onslaught on my mouth as he carries me back to the bedroom.

Stooping, Ethan gently deposits me at the foot of the bed. My shirt falls open, and his hands slide over my breasts, tweaking my overstimulated nipples. Kneeling between my thighs he pushes my boobs together, teasing the tight, rosy buds of my nipples between his lips and tongue. My lower back curves, my hips squirming as I moan, and his chuckle vibrates against my nipple.

I gently drag my fingernails down his contoured back, either side of his spine, producing a deep growl from him. My turn to chuckle, but it quickly shifts to a yelp as he nips my sensitive buds. Lifting his head, he throws me a devilish grin that lights his face, and a fleeting look crosses his eyes as if he enjoyed my reaction. His head lowers again, licking at my nipples, swirling his tongue tip around them while holding my gaze, before removing his touch completely.

"Aah. Don't stop," I plead on a moan.

"You like that, Baby Girl?" he taunts with a wicked twinkle in his eyes, knowing full well that I do, squeezing my nipples, this time with a slight tug.

"Yesss," I hiss, my neck and upper back bowing with pleasure. Again, he squeezes and tugs, chuckling when I moan and twitch beneath him, need thrumming between my legs. Suddenly, he removes his hands again, running them down my flat stomach, onto my thighs, pushing them open wider, draping my calves over his shoulders.

His thumbs explore my outer lips, building the yearning within me. His lust-filled eyes grow wild and are riveted to where he's touching me. Every hair on my scalp stands to attention, every skin cell tingles, every neuron fires at the look of reverence, as if he is praying at the temple of womanhood.

"Mmm. Beautiful," he murmurs, then slides a finger through the cleft. "Ohhh yes." His moan is scorchingly hot and husky and he shifts his hands upward slightly so his fingers surround my pubic bone, resting below my navel, while his thumbs spread my outer labia lips, exposing the heated bright pink swollen inner lips. The fleshy pads at the base of his palm press against the junction of my legs and vulva holding my legs open.

His head dips and his skillfully silky tongue flicks my sensitive clitoral bud, making my hips buck. "Mmm, so fuckable." He licks again, then blows on the hot, wet button. Lifting his head, he taunts "You want me inside you, Baby Girl?"

"Yes. Yesss," I exclaim, feeling moisture gush from my vagina, my hands clutching the bedsheets, lost to the mind-blowing sensations he stirs in me.

His head and mouth descend again, his tongue swiping my clit then gliding down dipping into my molten core. I breathe out an ecstatic sigh. Once, twice more his tongue glides through my slick lips, eliciting the same reaction, the volume increasing with each dip of his tongue.

Ethan lifts his head again and I glimpse a self-satisfied smile and an intense gaze taking in my rapturous expression. Craning my neck, I move my hands to either side of his face, cupping his head, my eyes pleading as I huff, "Uggh. Don't stop." He gives me a roguish look, dropping his gaze as he readjusts his hold on me and glides his index finger over my swollen clit. My hips buck as he circles a few times then inserts his finger into my heated center, which is aching for fulfillment again. My head tips back to the bed, my neck craning and my eyes close as I'm overcome by scintillating pleasure.

"Mmm. So fucking tight," he murmurs then adds a second finger, uttering, "Good girl." He begins pulsing his fingers, slowly at first, but as I react to his touch, he thrusts harder, pushing deeper as I get lost to the feelings building in my core. Groaning, he adds a third finger, making me feel a stretch very much like the thick girth of his cock, then he purrs, "That's it. Take it all, Baby Girl."

His mouth covers my clit and he sucks hard as he curls his fingers stroking my G-spot, driving me wild.

Digging my heels into his shoulder blades, I arch off the bed, riding his face and bucking against his hand, chasing the release I'm desperate for. I lose control and scream out as my muscles clench around his fingers. He doesn't stop touching me, forcing every drop of pleasure from my body, lapping it up until I am a quivering mess.

Eventually, Ethan kisses down my inner thigh, before removing his fingers, and sliding my legs off his shoulders, every movement causing mini explosions of pleasure to erupt in my over-stimulated body.

He stands, our eyes lock and he wiggles his eyebrows and throws me a cheeky grin before sauntering to the bathroom. Hearing water running, I assume he is washing his hands and mouth. When he returns with a washcloth, he cleans me up too, then stands peering down at me, the gold in his eyes fading leaving them a beautiful sage green. Smiling at him and sitting up in an ungainly listless manner, he lingers for a moment before going back to the bathroom. While he is gone, I ponder that the gold must be his aroused state, and hope that I get to see a lot more of that indescribable color combination in his eyes, because I can never get sick of looking at any part of him.

"Give me your hands Emily," he says on his return. I obey his request and, licking my lips, shift my eyes back to his face because his cock is sitting semi-erect in front of my face, and I desperately want it in my mouth. Ethan pulls me to my feet and hugs me. "You okay, Baby Girl?"

Chuckling, I beam up at him, "More than okay. I feel amazing."

"Let's climb under the covers for a bit," he suggests, letting go of my hand and walking around the side of the bed, grabbing and flinging back the duvet and top sheet.

Settling in a half sitting position on the bed, he drags the covers up to his chest. Doing the same on the other side, I clamber in and shuffle over next to him. Stretching his arm out invitingly, he wraps it around my shoulders and tucks me under his arm where I snuggle against his side.

"Every part of today has been fantastic," I gush as I tilt my head back and flash him a smile.

Turning his head toward me, he brushes some loose tendrils of hair from my face, a tight smile and quizzical expression on his face as he says, "Yes it has, hasn't it?" and lightly kisses me on the forehead. Despite his smiling agreement, his tone is lackluster, and he seems to be avoiding direct eye contact, which perplexes me. He seemed to be really into getting me off and now seems flat and indifferent.

"Are you okay, Ethan? That was quite a workout."

"Yes, I'm good, Em." Again, he gives me a tight smile that doesn't reach his eyes, his gaze ping-ponging between my face and some point over my shoulder.

"How did you get that scar under your chin?" I hope my question distracts him from his pensive frame of mind.

"Hmm? Oh. I went over a jump on my bicycle and hit my chin on the handlebars when I was a kid." Nodding my head at his ambivalent distracted tone, I feel hurt that he seems to be biding his time as if he can't wait to get out of here. *Is it a case of now that he has had his way with me the thrill of the chase has vanished?*

His fingers rub circles on my upper arm as we lay silently, each lost in thought. The coziness and sense of security of being wrapped in his arms and the warmth of his body, as well as two shattering orgasms, soon have my head nodding and I drift into sleep. Feeling Ethan move beneath me, he silently disentangles himself from my arms, then lays me gently on the pillows.

Stirring, I mumble in a muffled voice, "Don't go."

Chapter Fourteen

ETHAN

My phone beeps with a message, and when I check it, I groan at seeing that Emily is thanking me again for a fantastic day on Sunday. Deleting it, I toss the phone on my desk, frustrated and disappointed with myself. I feel bad that I have not been in touch with her over the last five days since we slept together, and no doubt her message just now was to gauge the lay of the land between us. However, I will not be contacting her again. Hanging my head and holding it in both hands, I reflect on the decision I made when I left her place on Sunday night.

She is a beautiful person inside and out, and I thoroughly enjoyed my time with her. The sex was phenomenal; the best I've had. Too good. In fact, it scared the bejesus out of me. Seeing her lying in bed, sated and asleep after the double orgasm I gave her made my heart flip. All I wanted to do was stay there next to her, listening to her cute little snuffling noises, and it took everything I had to get out of her bed and leave. I have never slept over at a lover's place and wasn't about to start now, no matter how strong the temptation. All my previous sexual encounters have revolved around hooking up, making sure the woman was well satisfied, then getting out. And if I returned to the same lover, it was the same deal, no matter how many times I came back. Just like with Tahni and Brianna. No emotional entanglements.

Emily was different though. For some reason, I felt a strong emotional pull with her. Last time I felt anything like this 'beyond-physical' attraction I was sixteen and totally smitten with Jocelyn Bennett in my science class. She had seemed shy and reserved but quite giggly and flirtatious once she got to know me. We had been holding hands and kissing for a little while and I was trying to respect her virginity even though I had a hard on every time I looked at her or thought of her. Then she dumped me for one of the football jocks who paid her a lot of attention and took her V-card. I was hurt, badly, and assumed that my gangly, youthful physique and features were the cause. She had wanted to get back with me after the jock dumped her once he'd had his way with her, but I couldn't forgive her and swore from then on to never get emotionally involved again. And I haven't... until Emily.

Funny how that memory has resurfaced now, I muse, questioning whether that is why I have been unable to commit to anything serious.

Poo-hooing the idea, I push it aside, telling myself I am not the 'settling down' kind, and enjoy the variety of my love life. I can't say I am emotionally involved with Emily either, but there is more feeling with her than I have previously encountered, and there has also been a far stronger desire for her—an insatiable hunger, a heavy ache in my balls at just the thought of her. Even now. Not only am I battling my guilt for running away, but I am battling my body's craving for her. The sound of her orgasmic cry echoes in my dreams, waking me during the night. At the time, it filled me with a sense of elation, pride, an animalistic yearning to claim her as mine, to hold her and not let go, and to fuck her till we were both spent. Feelings that speared me in the heart, taking my breath away. That's when I knew I had to get out of there, fast. Before those fledgling feelings turned into something I couldn't escape, trapping me in a situation where I would ultimately hurt her. Better to rip the band-aid off now when we barely know each other.

"Oh, fucking get over yourself." I rant aloud, thumping my fist on the desk, berating myself further. "When did you turn into this touchy feely, mamby pamby soft cock?" Jumping up from my chair, I pace around my desk, desperately needing a distraction.

"Ethan." Carly interrupts as she enters my office.

"What?" I bark, lifting my head to glare at her as she approaches. She raises her eyebrows at me in her best, and very familiar, 'don't you talk to me like that' expression. "Sorry. I've got a few things on my mind."

"Hmm. Obviously." Her tart tone softens into the calm professional assistant voice I know so well. "Anything I can help with?"

"No, I'll work it out. Thanks. Was there something you needed?" Mollified, I run my hand through my hair and perch on the edge of my desk.

"I'm heading home now, but Xander wants to see you before you leave."

"Okay, thanks. Have a good night, Carly." She nods and turns and I watch her shapely figure in a detached manner as she leaves my office. Her looks are the sort I would normally go for, but her irritable, controlling ways and the fact that she works for me, reinforce my resolve not to go there.

My phone pings. *Oh God, I hope it's not Emily again.* Glancing down at the message, I chuckle.

Jason
Wanna catch up and check out the progress of the pubic hair beard?

Ethan

Sure thing, man. Tonight at O'Malleys?

Jason

Great. See you at 6.30.

I send him a thumbs up emoji, and checking my watch, realize I don't have time to get into work now, so pack up my things and walk down the corridor to Xander's office, greeting his PA on the way past to knock on his open door.

"What's up, bro?" I ask as he waves me in and I saunter toward where he sits on the sofa, his laptop in his lap, and his foot up on the coffee table.

"I'm planning on going to the gym tonight. Can you give me a hand and spot me?"

"Are you sure that's wise, Zee?" My brow furrows, as I stare pointedly at his healing foot, not wanting him to injure himself any further. The bones might have healed to the point where he can walk unaided again, but the soft tissue is still very delicate, and his leg is often aching from overuse. He was such a pain in the neck when he was injured in a car accident, I would hate to think what we would have to put up with if he did any more damage.

"I'm working out my arms, not my ankle," he bites testily, glaring at me, then shifts his tone into one of steely practicality. "Doctor's orders were physiotherapy on the leg. Can't see why I can't lift weights lying down."

Nodding my head and giving him a tight-lipped smile, I concede, "You have a point there." Besides, I know that look of determination. He will go with or without me.

"I was going to meet Jason at O'Malleys at 6.30. Do you want to come along, and we can go to the gym afterward?" I propose.

Considering that for a moment, Xander responds with a far more relaxed expression. "Yeah, that'll work. It'll be good to see Jason again too. Thanks, E." Checking his watch, and quickly scanning the laptop bag slung over my shoulder, he continues, "You ready to go now? I'll come with you."

He packs his things and slings the bag over his shoulder, then we head out to the car where Ramon is waiting.

***

I hold the door open while Xander walks with a very slight limp into the noisy bar. Spotting Jason sitting at a high table at the far end of the room we weave through the throng.

We exchange the usual backslapping greetings and while Xander catches Jason up on why he is limping, I move to the bar and order our drinks and some food. Scanning the room, I reflect that this is just the distraction I need so I don't have to think about Emily. Lots of noise, lots of activity, and lots of potentially fuckable women. In fact, there is a very attractive, very shapely blond on the other side of the bar giving me the eye. Smiling I take a swig of the beer that's appeared in front of me and then raise my glass toward her. I'll have to keep my eye on her, I muse, and make my way with the drinks back to our table.

***

"What happened with those software issues you were having, Jace?" I enquire as I cut my medium rare steak.

"Well, I contracted the private security guy you put me onto, and they have a couple of leads and just need some hard evidence now to back up their theory." He pauses to fill Xander in on the situation while I glance across the room to see where the blonde sex bomb is, locking eyes with her and raising my eyebrows suggestively before turning back to our conversation.

"Any more push from the competitor wanting to buy you out?" Xander asks, his shrewd business acumen kicking in. Jason shakes his head, and Xander verbalizes what we are all thinking. "Sounds like they are waiting for you to hurt financially so they can offer you a low price for the business."

"Yeah, exactly," I chime in.

"Yeah, I suspect that is the case, and the investigator believes the same, surmising sabotage to drive the reputational damage and financial hardship," Jace clarifies, looking worried.

"What about the woman you were dating? Is she involved?" Probing further into his dilemma, I notice Xander's head swing toward Jason.

"Fuck, you're not dating an employee, are you?" Xander groans, aghast that Jace seems to have broken the golden rule of not mixing business and pleasure.

"Yes. Initially, I was quite attracted to her, but after this happened, I was going to break it off, but the investigator had some concerns that if she was the saboteur then she could wreak more damage out of spite. He thought it best to keep her close to keep an eye on her. I have moved her to a different project though, so I can determine her coding signature. That way I can work out if she is the one creating the issues, or just an innocent pawn."

"Holy shit. That's a complicated situation to be in, man," I sympathize. "Don't get in too deep in case it is her."

"Yeah, it's hard. I've detached myself emotionally and am seeing less of her, citing work issues, but I know she's noticed a difference in me."

"Let us know if you need any financial assistance to tide you over and keep the competitor wolves away for a while," Xander adds.

Conversation turns to more general topics again, and I continue to glance across the room watching the blonde woman, feeling a stirring in my lower belly as she flings her head back laughing. Her movements all night have been alluring as if she is here looking to pick up.

Catching me watching her, she throws me an inviting smile, deliberately wetting her lips, a promise of sexual attraction and she has me in her sights. I am happy to oblige, so on the excuse of getting us some more drinks, I move to the bar near where she is sitting, to see if she will approach me. Sure enough, she sidles up to me, a bit inebriated and tottering on her eight inch hooker heels. Her short clingy skirt leaves nothing to the imagination and her tight-fitting, button up blouse stretches across her huge melon sized tits.

"Hi," she purrs in a deliberately sexy voice. "I'm Roxy."

"Hi, Roxy. What are you up to?" My eyes roam over her intentionally seductive body, and she seems older than she appeared from across the room. Hmm. One very hot to trot cougar, ready willing, and for the moment, available for a hot fuck.

"Looking for a bit of fun. How about it?" she propositions, vampishly running her fingers up my forearm, sending a cold shiver up my spine, which I find odd.

The barman arrives and I order drinks for me and the boys, and one for Roxy as well, before I turn back to answer her.

"What did you have in mind?" I have no aversion to being hit on by a woman, and Roxy certainly seems the sort of woman whom I would normally accept, but for some reason, something feels off. I believe in following my instincts, so I play along with her game for a bit to avoid creating a scene. My tight smile and suspicious gaze are lost on her.

"Well," she drawls. "You and I could go to the bathroom now, or I could go home with you and your friends." She looks past me and wiggles her fingers in a wave, and when I turn around, I see Xander scowling at me. Inwardly, I chuckle because I know he is warning me off this woman. The barman arrives with our drinks, and I decide to make my escape.

"Well, Roxy, see here's the thing. I would love to take you to the bathroom and delight in your obvious assets, but my friend, the one scowling, needs to get home soon for some medication before he starts ripping this place apart. So, I can't take you up on your offer now." She adopts a pouting downcast pose, then I continue, "How about you call me later and we'll try to arrange something." I scribble down a phone number on a napkin and slide it over to her. I watch a look of triumph flash across her face, before she masks it with a seductive smile. Her fingers circle the back of my hand before taking the napkin, folding it, and slipping it between her boobs.

"Sure thing, Darlin'. See you later." She winks at me and then blows me a kiss. My skin crawls and I hastily grab my drinks and head back to the table.

Xander is ready to blow a fuse by the time I get back. "What the hell was that all about? You seriously didn't just give that mantrap your phone number, did you?" He likes to think that he is protecting me from myself, and I love to taunt him when he comes on heavy like this. I don't need a protector, but I appreciate his looking out for me.

"Relax, Zee. I gave her a number." Pausing, I wait for him to take a mouthful of beer before I continue, mocking, "In fact, I gave her *your* number." He splutters and the corners of my eyes crinkle and my lips twitch in merriment as his nostrils flare. "I reckon you could do with an easy lay, seeing how your sexual activity has been so limited with your recent broken ankle." I glance at Jason, who is struggling not to laugh, nearly choking on his drink.

"You fucking better not have, you moron," Xander roars with indignation. "And I don't need your pity or assistance to get laid." He slowly registers my roguish grin, and his expression shifts to disgruntlement as Jason and I laugh. "You fucking bastard. Just because I've been laid up doesn't mean my cock is also broken. It's been getting plenty of workouts."

"Yeah, the five finger variety, I bet," I murmur drolly.

We chortle and Xander grouses, "Fuck off, both of you."

"Seriously, Zee. I made up a number. I wouldn't do that to you. I'm all for a 'wham, bam, thank you ma'am', but there was nothing subtle about her. She even offered to do all three of us."

This time both men nearly spurt out their drinks and take a long hard look at the sexily audacious woman, maybe contemplating the idea momentarily. I continue in a hushed serious tone, "I suspect she's a high-class hooker." At their nods, I add, "Let's get out of here then. I told her I had to take you home for your medication," I jibe Xander again.

"You're a fucking asshole, E," he mumbles, standing slowly to steady himself. Jason just laughs at both of us as we make our way back through the crowd to the door to our waiting car.

After dropping Jason back to his apartment, we continue to Xander's place. He gets changed into some gym gear, and I borrow some shorts and a t-shirt from him so we can head down to the well-equipped gym in his apartment block. We work out on various machines, and I spot for Xander while he punishes himself with some grueling bench presses. Eventually, we head upstairs to Xander's apartment where I arrange an Uber, collect my things and head home.

Later, as I lie in bed, I think back over the Roxy situation. I was seriously contemplating a quick, dirty fuck in a restroom till I got a sense of foul play afoot. On the rare occasion, I've taken what's on offer into a nearby bathroom, but it's not really my thing. However, I know lots of men who look for that opportunity whenever they go out. Roxy was a very attractive woman, and I would certainly have made the most of her attributes in different circumstances. The question still nags at me why I felt I needed to have sex tonight. It's not as if I am blue-balling it. In fact, now I think about it, I haven't felt sexually driven since Emily, which is unusual. Even after the hottest sex with Tahni and Brianna, I was on edge, looking for more after two days, and here it is five days since Emily and I have only vague stirrings for more. Recalling that my orgasm with Emily was the most powerful I have ever experienced, I put my lack of arousal down to my body restoring its supply of testosterone. But that supposition feels shallow, as if there is something underlying that I can't put my finger on. I don't normally do a lot of introspection, but my keenness to accept what was on offer seemed to be more of a mental urgency, a reassurance that I am fine, almost a case of clutching at straws (in this case Roxy,) and I wonder if my moment of madness was a subconscious attempt to replace the lingering effect of Emily, and the guilt I feel in icing her.

You fucking idiot. Chiding myself, I rationalize that I have frequently hooked up with women in bars and nightclubs, but instead of doing the deed then and there, I have occasionally gone home with them that night or taken their number and followed through, just like I did with Emily. No point in laboring over it. Emily was an anomaly and won't be repeated. I'll arrange a meeting with Tahni and that will erase any lingering Emily effects.

Chapter Fifteen

EMILY

It's been a month and a half since Ethan left my bed, and despite me texting a few days later to thank him for a great night, I haven't heard a damn word from him. Apparently, my supposition was proven correct in that he was only after the thrill of pursuit and the eventual sex. My emotions have been on a roller coaster ride ranging from anxiousness hoping he was okay to indignation that he couldn't bother to let me know he wasn't interested anymore, to the sting of rejection. Shadows of my low self-esteem returned to haunt me for a few days where I wondered if I had been too clingy, or not showed him enough affection, then felt I was unworthy of his attention. Then I realized he is the one with the commitment issues, demonstrated by his inability to commit to sending me a simple damn 'it's over' text.

I am resigned to the fact that I have been ghosted but it still rankles that he could be so rude and disrespectful. I thought he was a better person than that, but apparently his ruthlessness extends beyond the boardroom to the bedroom as well.

Once a player, always a player, I remind myself with disappointment while I sit under the shade of a tree sipping a coffee, swearing off dating and relationships for a while. Friendship is all I will be seeking in future until I know the person well enough to entrust them with my heart. Because my heart has certainly been left bruised and aching. I am alarmed at the strength of emotion I feel for him after such a short acquaintance. Even my couselor thinks I have formed a rebound attachment to him that I will get over in time.

One good thing I can say about Ethan, though, is that he set the intimacy bar pretty damn high. Sex with him was the best I've ever had, setting a benchmark that I hope can be matched in future.

"Emily?" Mom's quavering voice calls from her bedroom. Resignedly, I reflect that Ethan did me a favor in a way by dumping me because Mom was diagnosed with terminal cancer a week later, and I have left my job and moved home to care for her full time. I am only a half hour's drive away from Simone's apartment, but staying there would have been too problematic for Mom's intense daily chemotherapy regime. So having a relationship, even a casual hook-up, would be a hassle that I don't have the mental or physical energy to cope with right now.

I hear Allie's footsteps on the wooden floorboards as she treads down the hallway to Mom's bedroom. "It's alright, Mrs. B. I'm here. What can I help you with?"

They say it takes a village to care for someone, and I have certainly needed that support, even though pride wouldn't let me accept it at first. My girlfriends have been a godsend, helping keep an eye on Mom. My heart bursts and tears prick my eyes in gratitude for their generosity and support, and I don't know how I will ever repay them.

Mom has had good days where she has been up and about, and bad days like today, where she is bedridden from the effects of her last chemo session. Allie came over to give me some respite, and she shooed me out to the garden when I got home from shopping.

The fresh air and some alone time have partially restored my energy reserves and, with a heavy heart, I check my watch, sighing as I notice it is time for Mom's medication so I trudge back indoors to take over from Allie, pushing Ethan to the dark recesses of my mind.

The doctors say Mom doesn't have a lot of time left, six to eight months at best, so I am trying to make her as comfortable as possible for the duration. She nurtured and cared for me even when she was hurting after my father died, giving me a good life despite the difficulties, so now it is my turn to give back to her. My life for the foreseeable future revolves around Mom.

***

A week later, feeling frazzled, I arrive at the restaurant. Mom was particularly upset about me leaving tonight, even though Mrs. Simmons from next door was with her, so I left later than I intended. Sometimes she is harder to manage and more needy than the schoolkids I used to teach, but I understand. Her treatment this week has left her sore, irritable, and depleted. However, despite feeling guilty for leaving her, I also feel like I need some me time, but my warring emotions have elevated my anxiety levels to the point where I nearly canceled. But then the words of the cancer center's counselor ran through my head, reminding me that my health and wellbeing are important too, so I can provide the best care for Mom.

After driving around in circles for ten minutes trying to find a parking spot, I powerwalk the three hundred meters to the restaurant, arriving flushed, windswept, and emotionally on edge. The girls take one look at me as I approach the table and collectively stand, each encasing me in a huge hug. Tears prick my eyes and I swiftly wipe away the pooling moisture and plaster a bright smile on my face.

Their lively conversation bubbles around me, uplifting my spirits, and it is not long before I am laughing with them. Their realism in treating me no differently from before allows me to temporarily forget my problems and bask in their warmth and care.

As usual, each of us has a turn in discussing what has happened in the last month, and in most cases, there is a funny story, sometimes the airing of baggage or difficult situations to get an honest appraisal from our trusted friends. My turn comes around and my stomach churns anxiously because I don't want them to pity me for my contribution.

"Well, you know what I have been doing for the last month." I attempt a bright smile and a lightheartedness in my voice, but both fall flat. Simone pats my arm as I take a deep breath. "What you don't know is how much your love, support, and friendship mean to me. You are the wind beneath my wings, uplifting my morale when things get tough. I couldn't get through this without you, and I am truly grateful for each of you." Tears well again in my eyes and my voice wobbles.

"You would do exactly the same for us, Lovely," Tash declares, the emotion clear in her voice.

In an effort to lighten the mood, I try to change the subject. "Something else you don't know is that one of Mom's doctors is the most gorgeous specimen of manhood I have ever seen. Every time I see him, I am barely able to get my words out and I sound like a blithering idiot. He has dark hair, and a neatly trimmed beard, broad shoulders, and bulging biceps, and his legs are as thick as tree trunks. All I can do is stare open mouthed at him. He is the only doctor I look forward to seeing, and I'm sure I leave puddles on the floor from melting over him."

Chuckling, the girls make lewd comments about other parts of his anatomy, and we all end up in a fit of giggles.

When it is her turn, Georgie mimics me, "Something else you don't know…" Then pauses for effect before announcing, "Xander proposed." We exclaim at the same time, "What." "Where." "Fantastic." The night I met Ethan in the club, Tash had mentioned some chemistry between Xander and Georgie. They had eventually gone away together for a weekend but, like Ethan, Xander had run scared. However, they were able to work things out and have been together for a short while, and make a gorgeous couple, so the proposal is fantastic.

Georgie answers our questions, and soon the conversation lulls when, in a quiet voice, Tash asks a question that I have been expecting for a while, but not wanted to answer.

"Emily, did anything ever happen between you and Ethan? You haven't said much about him since your first date."

Feeling all eyes on me, I give them a tight-lipped smile and a restrained answer. "We went on a couple of dates, but nothing since. You know the type. Once a player, always a player. Sorry, Georgie, I know he's a good friend of yours, and soon to be brother-in-law."

"I'm sorry it turned out that way for you, Em," Georgie adds to their groans and tsks.

"It's probably for the best, because a relationship would have been unsustainable with Mom's situation." Nodding in agreement, we chat for a while longer, until I notice the time. Like Cinderella, my happy time is over, and I must return to the drudgery that is my life at present. So, I say farewell, pay my portion of the bill, and scurry back to my car, and Mom who will be waiting anxiously for me.

Chapter Sixteen

EMILY

Six months later...

Today is Georgie and Xander's wedding day. They are celebrating in the hotel that brought them together; the nuptials in the garden Georgie designed and the reception in the hotel ballroom that Xander and Ethan's company redesigned.

My intention has always been to attend, and Georgie knew it was dependent on Mom's health, so I haven't been able to assist much in the preparations. However, in the last week, Mom has been admitted to palliative care, freeing me up to go. Even though it will be a joyous occasion, I am filled with reluctance; worrying whether I will miss Mom's passing by being at the wedding, and at the thought of seeing Ethan.

Ethan has popped into my head a lot lately, particularly as the wedding drew closer, wondering if he ever thinks of me. I don't really expect him to, as I was just a passing fling for him. Another meaning-less notch on his bedpost. But for me, he touched my heart deeply. He saw me for who I am and treated me with respect while in each other's company. I love the way he called me Baby Girl, not just the words, but the adoration intoned in them, making me feel precious and important. I've come to realize that feeling, that sense of completeness, is what I will strive for in future relationships. Regardless of whether Ethan thinks of me or not, I will always recollect that feeling and settle for nothing less, because Mom's situation has taught me that life is too short.

Mom didn't want me to leave this afternoon, so now I am running very short of time and the traffic to the city is frustratingly slow. I manage to snag a parking spot nearby, and after grabbing my garment bag and accessories from the back seat, I race into the hotel lobby, scanning it for the nearest restroom. The other girls have booked a room for the night, but I haven't got time to wait for the elevator, to track them down, or to see Georgie before the ceremony.

Fortunately, there is a vacant cubicle, so I quickly change into my long, sleeveless dress and stilettos, shoving my jeans and light sun top into my bag. A quick twist and pin of my hair makes it look stylishly messy, then I apply light makeup—mainly mascara and lipstick. My cheeks are rosy from the heat and rushing and there are dark shadows under my eyes, so I add a light dusting of mineral powder to camouflage most of it. Adding earrings and necklace, I cast a cursory glance at myself in the mirror, accepting that my appearance will have to do.

Inhaling deeply to steady my nerves, and grabbing my belongings, I saunter into the lobby in the direction of the garden. Stepping out into the magical, shady pocket where the ceremony is taking place, I pause to look around, admiring the view and setup.

Lit with fairy lights overhead, rows of white fold-up chairs stand on either side of a beautiful red carpet. At the far end stands a white timber arbor draped with white and gold material, a perfect foil for the lush leafy greenery behind it. *This area feels like an oasis*, I ponder, acknowledging once again Georgie's extraordinary talent in landscape architecture.

Standing near the arbor are Xander and Ethan, looking resplendent in their tuxedos and bowties as they chat to who I presume are their parents in the front row. Xander's tux is white, while Ethan's is royal blue to match the bridesmaid Tash's dress. My heart flips in my chest and my mouth goes dry seeing Ethan. I want to turn and run but fight the impulse, reminding myself I have every right to be here, and he means nothing to me.

Most of the guests are already seated and I slip into a row near the back, on the end farthest from the aisle, allowing plenty of space for other guests, and hoping Ethan won't be able to see me behind so many people. Fortunately, Georgie's younger brothers, Ryan and Zack, sit next to me. Before we can do more than greet each other, some guests scurry into seats behind us. I notice Ethan saying something to Xander then they both turn to face the front, standing with hands clasped in front of them.

Music begins to play and everyone stands, turning and gasping at the beautiful sight of Tash first, then a radiant Georgie walking down the aisle, her arm looped in her father's crooked arm. The look Xander gives her as she stops in front of him brings tears to my eyes. It is the look of all-encompassing love, the look of deep passion, wild lust, undying devotion, pride, honor, protectiveness. All those things and more wrapped together in one reverent stare, his eyes sparkling with a warmth that doesn't exist for anyone else.

Oh, steady my beating heart. Where do I find a man that will look at me like that? Certainly not the man standing next to the groom, that's for sure.

The ceremony is beautiful, and not very long. After the official signing of certificates, the new Mr. and Mrs. Drakos greet their guests.

When it's my turn, I give Georgie a hug and she is genuinely pleased I'm here. Xander is talking with another couple until they move away. Then he turns and gives me a fond smile as I congratulate him.

Further away, Ethan stands talking to his parents and sister. Out of the corner of my eye, I see him turn toward me, probably hearing Xander greet me by name. When I turn my head and smile warmly at him, he nods in acknowledgment, wearing an amiable expression but a tight smile, which slips from his lips when his expression becomes deadpan. Holding my expression firm, I watch him blink and turn his attention back to his parents, picking up their conversation again.

"Whoa, that was cold," Georgie utters in a hushed voice, squeezing my hand in comfort. "Are you okay, Em? What was that about?" Hearing her words, Xander, like a typical male unable to read the nuances, bounces his gaze between Ethan and me trying to work out what Georgie meant.

"I'm fine thanks, Georgie. Thought I saw a ghost, but it was nothing." The words drip from my mouth with saccharine sweetness, loud enough for Ethan to hear. Georgie snickers, turning away from us, pretending to greet someone next to her. I notice Ethan's head snap around and catch his glare, and Louisa's tight-lipped smirk, before I walk away, telling Georgie and Xander I will catch up with them later.

Shaking and infuriated with Ethan's snub, I don a cloak of civility and mingle in the crowd, finding Allie and Tash with their partners and Simone not far away. Each of them greets me with a sympathetic hug for Mom's situation and I am warmed by their pleasure at seeing me. Not knowing anyone else here well enough, other than Georgie's family, I seek solace with my friends, allowing their laughter to ease the sting of Ethan's cold shoulder. Despite knowing months ago where I stood with Ethan, I had hoped that civility would prevail today. As we wander into the Grand Ballroom for the reception, I remind myself that I was only ever an easy lay to him. *So, no point in pining for the worthless creep.*

Thankful that I am seated at a table with my friends and Ryan and Zack at the opposite end of the room to Ethan, who is sitting at the bridal table, I am determined to not even recognize his presence, but it is hard. I keep my happy face on because I need this night of revelry and hadn't realized how desperate I've been for social contact over the last few months.

The night is filled with amazing food, some very moving speeches, and all the usual wedding festivities. I am even surprised that Louisa came to say hello to me, but suspect it was more to say hi to Ryan because she kept glancing across the table at him. He, on the other hand, had gone unusually quiet but didn't take his eyes off her.

Not long after the cake is cut, and the photos have been taken I slip out to the garden to ring and check on Mom, as I do every night. The beautiful, lush garden has spot lit elements, shadowed pockets creating solitude and privacy, and darkened areas, with seating scattered throughout. I traipse along the path into one of the shadowed parts and make my call.

Relief fills me when the nurse on duty tells me that Mom is comfortable and sleeping. Noise from the hotel is a faint echo out here, and when I hang up I sit for a while inhaling the cool air and hints of perfume wafting from the nearby shrubs, absorbing the peacefulness into my troubled psyche. The moon is high and bright, illuminating the garden in a silvery glow, but the occasional cloud dims it to a dull grey. I try to envisage what I will do when Mom eventually passes and what my life will look like. Pain pierces my chest, my throat chokes up, and tears well in my eyes. Everything I am, I owe to my mother. Her selfless love and many sacrifices, her wise guidance and strength of spirit, her dependability and always being there for me. I will miss her terribly.

Hushed voices murmur nearby, startling me out of my reverie, and after checking my watch, I decide it's time for me to head home. I have another busy day ahead tomorrow, packing up some of Mom's stuff and visiting her in the hospice, sitting with her for several hours like I do every day.

I follow the dimly lit meandering path, rounding a bend just as a cloud drifts away from the moon, illuminating a couple engaged in a passion-fueled embrace. They are sitting, well practically lying, on a bench in a hedged alcove, her blonde head is thrown back, her shoulder strap slipped off, and he is suckling her naked breast. I gasp silently as he lifts his head to kiss her, and I recognize Ethan. As if he can feel my eyes on him, he turns to look at me. His eyes are in shadow, but I can feel his glare, so I scurry away to say my farewells, burying the stabbing pain I feel in my chest.

Chapter Seventeen

ETHAN

Georgie and I don't discuss Emily. It's like a tacit agreement between us, neither wanting to raise the subject. I don't know how much Emily has told her friends and expect she may be embarrassed about being dumped so unceremoniously. And I haven't wanted to let Georgie know what a fool I've been by running scared. As a result, I had no idea whether Emily would be at Xander and Georgie's wedding today or not but assumed she would be for Georgie's sake.

The festivities are now over, and I am lying on my hotel room bed reflecting on the day. As I still have some post-wedding chores to do from here in the morning, I thought it would be easier to stay overnight, and after all the stress and running around today, I'm thankful I am.

Thinking back to earlier in the day, I was relieved that I hadn't spotted Emily as guests had started to filter into the beautifully decorated garden, because I am quite embarrassed at the way I treated her. I know I should have apologized to her months ago, but as time slipped by, I assumed she had moved on with someone else, writing me off as a bad experience.

Then, after the ceremony, I heard Xander say her name and caught the sound of her musical voice, and I was surprisingly thrilled that she was here. Adopting a congenial expression, my heart was pounding as I turned to see if it was really her.

Stunned by how beautiful she looked and the warmth in her gaze that she quickly shielded when our eyes met, my stomach dropped and I felt sick at how I had hurt her, but the pervading emotion was to flee, just like the last time I saw her. My balls tingled at the sight of her, but I couldn't speak to her because I would have sounded like a babbling idiot. Then her snide veiled remark about me being 'nothing' hit straight at my ego, making me angry.

Telling myself she knew nothing about me, I reminded myself I had left because I wanted to spare her from getting hurt. So, I tried ignoring her, and for the most part, that worked well, particularly when Xander's stepmom's younger sister started openly flirting with me. I was aroused and put it down to the lusty, busty Geneva, then when I was able to glimpse Emily across the room, she was laughing with one of Georgie's brothers, making me wonder if they were an item. That thought was like a sucker punch in the gut and for some reason I was angry again, wanting to march over there and claim her as mine. Instead, I skulled my fourth scotch, played up to Geneva, and took advantage of what she was offering by slipping out to the garden with her. At the time, in the back of my alcohol-addled brain, I thought about trying to make Emily jealous, but now realize that's not possible when a person doesn't have any feelings for you.

I had been trying to distract myself from Emily's presence by making out with Geneva in the garden. Even with her boob in my mouth, I felt detached, like I was just going through the motions. It was intended to be a bit of meaningless fun, a means to a physical release without leaving lingering emotional aftereffects. But then I heard a noise, a hushed gasp that made me look up.

My throat instantly thickened, aching, and my chest tightened with guilt when I saw Emily standing there watching us, her face pained like I had just wounded her. My alcohol buzz was instantly doused as reality hit me. *Fuck, I've hurt her again.* Emily scurried away into the night, and I silently berated myself. *Fuck. Fuck. Fuck. What a mess you've fucking created, you fucking moron.*

The woman I care about was running away, while the partially naked woman beneath me wanted me to finish what I had started. *Where did the idea that I care for Emily come from?* I told myself that pangs of guilt and self-disappointment created the delusion, then, pawing at my hair, I took a deep, pained breath and momentarily closed my eyes. I didn't want to hurt Geneva's feelings too, but needed to extricate myself somehow. So, I gave her several swift lukewarm kisses, replaced her shoulder strap and suggested we cool it for now as it was such a public place, and reconvene later in her room.

"But I'm not staying in this hotel," she pouted, seemingly disappointed.

"Oh, that's a shame," I utter, feigning regret, as I stand and pull her to her feet.

Tidying ourselves, we stroll back to the ballroom, my eyes scanning the room for Emily's beautiful, lustrous, burnt orange hair, but I soon overhear Georgie discussing with her friends that Emily had left. Although feeling deflated by that news, I don't know what I could or would have said to her if she was still here.

After most of the guests have left the ballroom, Georgie's brothers, Ryan and Zack assist me in taking the wedding presents down to the underground car park and loading them into an SUV I hired for the occasion because Ramon attended the wedding as a guest, not an employee.

My instructions from Georgie are that the gifts are to be dropped into Xander's apartment in the morning and that I am not to let her brothers know she and Xander are staying there tonight. Something about her suspecting they will want to play a prank for their wedding night, so she wants to let them think they are still in the hotel.

I quite like the brothers, who are both younger than Georgie, and there are quite a few laughs as we make several trips to the garage. I've also been able to rule out either of them being involved with Emily, which is a relief. Confused, I realize that, despite my rejection of her, I don't want anyone else to have her either.

The ballroom is being packed down by the hotel staff when we return from the last trip, and the few remaining guests still wanting to party relocate to the modern street-fronting bar area, which is still vibing. Ryan and Zack say their goodbyes as they head in that direction, and I notice Louisa and Ramon doing the same.

I head back to my hotel room with the plan of getting some sleep, but I spend hours tossing on the bed and unable to settle, my mind running over again how poorly I have behaved toward Emily. I feel like I should message her to apologize, but we haven't had any contact for over six months—*and whose fault is that,* the nagging voice in the back of my head pipes up—and I owe her nothing. Why then does my chest feel like there is an elephant sitting on it? And why does hurting Emily bother me, when I have behaved like this with so many other women without a qualm?

Flinging the covers back, I turn on the small bedside lamp and clamber out of bed, padding to the bathroom to shower. Despite already showering, I figure the warmth of the water might switch my brain into sleep mode, so as the water washes over me, I turn repeatedly like a chicken on a rotisserie, soaking the warmness into my back, chest, and limbs. Tilting my face under the spray, I tell myself, like a mantra, that the water is washing my concerns down the drain. Eventually, the load feels lighter, and tiredness engulfs me, so I fall back into bed and am soon asleep.

***

Downstairs later that morning, I spot Ryan and Zack in the breakfast restaurant, selecting their items from the buffet. Walking up to them, I notice their unshaven jaws and shadows beneath their eyes.

"You two look a bit rough," I say, chuckling as I reach for some bacon.

"You can't talk, mate." Ryan quips, giving me the once over, "You look like something the cat dragged in."

"Yeah," Zack scoffs." Chewed up and spat out."

Each of us moves around the buffet, grabbing an assortment of food, and piling them on our plates.

"Do you want to sit with us?" Zack offers and I nod, following them to a nearby table. After placing my plate down, I return to the buffet for coffee and juice, followed by the brothers. When we all return to the table, I place my phone on the table and we discuss last night as they regale me with stories of their antics in the bar, and their backfired plan to prank Georgie and Xander, surprising Georgie's parents instead who were staying in the bridal suite.

"Look out. That woman you disappeared with last night has just come in and she is on her way over," Ryan warns me in a sotto voce tone, as I have my back to the door.

"Thanks," I utter just as Geneva approaches with an inviting smile and eyes that eat me up, as she stops far too close to me.

"Hello, Ethan. Gentlemen." Her glance flicks to the brothers, who are ogling her shapely figure and deep cleavage appreciatively, before it returns to me. Her eyes gleam with suggestiveness as she tosses her long hair over her shoulder.

"Geneva. This is Ryan and Zack." Casually, I make the introductions and she nods at the brothers with a flirty smile. "What are you up to today?" Making small talk, I feel the unfulfilled lust from last night rising again in the pit of my stomach, my tongue darting out to lick my lips as I watch her hand skim down her body to smooth out non-existent wrinkles in her form-fitting dress.

"Nothing much. Just some shopping this morning with my sister, then some free time before I fly out tomorrow." Tilting her head slightly, she raises an eyebrow and smirks, her voice lowering slightly as she queries, "Any suggestions?"

I hear Ryan splutter on his coffee and Zack snort, knowing they have taken her words exactly as she intended and are eagerly waiting for my response. Ignoring them and raising an eyebrow, my focus on Geneva, a devilish grin plays at the corner of my mouth as I drawl, "Mmm. I have a few ideas. How about I put my number in your phone, and you can text me when you are free?"

"Perfect." She rummages in her bag, finding her phone and handing it to me. I notice she throws the brothers a self-satisfied smile but raises her eyebrows at them questioningly, as if in invitation. Smirking at them as they shake their heads, seemingly daunted by such open forwardness, I hand Geneva's phone back to her. She says her goodbyes before she sashays with swinging hips to the pastry bar and brazenly takes a few deliciously sweet treats to go, knowing that all three sets of eyes are on her, as well as a few from other guests in the restaurant.

The brothers utter "Whoa," and "Smooth," looking like they have just learned a priceless tip to add to their seduction repertoire.

"Amateurs," I scoff, then I notice a message from Xander letting me know they are at the airport, which is my cue that the apartment is free for me to drop the presents in, so I finish my breakfast quickly before I say farewell Ryan and Zack.

After running around checking Xander and Georgie out of the hotel, dropping the presents into Xander's apartment, and returning the hire car, I am finally back home where I quickly shower and change before walking the short distance to Geneva's hotel to meet up with her. She had messaged around midday and we had arranged to meet at 2pm. Knocking on her door, she opens it dressed in a sheer black, button up shirt, revealing a sexy red bra and G-string underneath. She throws me a voracious look, grabs my hand, and drags me inside, running her fingers down my firm chest as the door shuts behind me, watching my wicked eyes urge her further. Not that she needs much encouragement, nor do I, as the anticipation of her offerings has been building all morning, to the point where I am semi hard and needy for release.

Grabbing her hips, I press my body against hers, becoming entwined as her arms and one leg wrap around me, and our lips mash together. I become lost in the feverish fervor of lust and the sex is hard and fast, leaving me breathless and physically sated. Emotionally and mentally though, I feel like I have been going through the motions, almost detached in some way by wondering thoughts, like I was last night with her. I have no desire to get to know Geneva on a personal level, my interest in her body and my sexual gratification being the driving force for being here, like all my women. As I go down on her, licking and rubbing her clit, I realize how different this sexual interaction is from the one with Emily, as have all the other women now that

I think about it. Sex with Emily was an amazing stand out because I connected with her on a deeper level, and the contentment I felt afterward was terrifying in its newness, and disappointingly lacking since.

Geneva's shrieking orgasm brings me back to the matter at hand, and I'm aware of the hollowness inside of me. It's not long before I find myself running away again, desperate now for more than physical intimacy and I rebuke myself for not only letting Emily go again, but for letting thoughts of her interfere with what has up to now been a very pleasurable pastime. I also scoff at how unusual it is for me to be such a deep thinker. *Harden up, princess,* I berate myself.

***

Back in my apartment later in the day, Emily still plays on my mind. Reruns of our interactions throughout the wedding play on a loop in my head, and the heavy-hearted ache in my chest has become a constant companion.

Remorse sits like a bitter, foul taste in my mouth for not only hurting her *again*, but also dashing any chance I might have had of getting her back. *When did I decide I want her back?* Obviously, my subconscious knows something I haven't wanted to admit to and has been giving me clues along the way that I have been too arrogant and proud to acknowledge. Like the sucker punch of jealousy when Emily laughed with Georgie's brothers. And 'the woman I care about' thought when she ran away after finding me with Geneva. And the constant emptiness inside me that I vaguely recognize as disgust with myself for willfully hurting another person.

On deeper introspection, I realize my melancholy started around the time Xander and Georgie got engaged. I was thrilled for them but remember thinking for the first time that I would like to have such a special connection with someone; have someone look at me with love and adoration the way Georgie looks my brother. Someone who sees me for me, not for my wealth or charm or bedroom skills. And that I wanted more out of life than the shallow, quick lays I have been filling my time with. Emily was the only one I could see who provided all that.

However, between their engagement and wedding, I buried those thoughts, but the emotional symptoms remained. *Dickhead. You had that person but you've driven her way,* my narky inner voice informs me.

With a despondent sigh, dragging my lethargic body off the sofa, I resign myself to a shallow existence till I can find another Emily. For the second time today, my inner cynic berates me, *Harden up, princess.*

Chapter Eighteen

EMILY

London, six months later

It has been another busy night at the restaurant and my feet and legs hurt from all the tables I have served. I glance at my watch; only half hour before I finish, and I know I will be flopping on the bed as soon as I get home.

"Hey Em, can you take table twelve's order, please? I am busting to go to the restroom," Marguerite asks as she hurries past me in the direction of the toilets. In the latter stages of pregnancy, she has been struggling to hold her bladder.

"Sure. No problem." The wait staff have designated areas and tables but can often assist in other areas when the need arises, like now. A quick look around my area assures me that my patrons are all okay for now but some are close to needing plates removed.

Grabbing my ordering device, I turn toward table twelve and notice an attractive, well-dressed redhead seated there, sitting opposite a man with his back toward me. Strolling over to them, I admire the breadth of the man's shoulders and how his expertly tailored suit jacket hugs his lean physique. His dark brown hair is neatly trimmed around his neck, and he wears an air of affluence. The vague thought that he reminds me of Ethan flits through my head, and I scoff at myself because a lot of men who come in here resemble Ethan in their stylish good looks. Another beautiful couple enjoying the high life. Sighing, I hope that I will be brought here on a date one day. But as I have no romantic interest in my life, I will have to stick with sampling the food in the kitchen.

As I come alongside their table, they can't take their eyes off each other. I smile, guessing where their night will end as they both seem hungry but not for food.

"Can I take your order?" I glance smilingly from the lady to the man. Ethan. *Oh God, not him, not here.*

"Emily? Hi, how are you?" My smile slips momentarily, and my stomach drops as Ethan recognizes me. He looks just as good as the last time I saw him at Georgie's wedding. Feeling the awkwardness of this situation for both of us, I quickly put on my waitress smile again.

"I'm well thanks, Ethan. What would you like to order?" I ask smilingly as I turn back to the stunning redhead, who seems annoyed at being interrupted, although Ethan seems pleased to see me, going by the way his eyes light up.

I take my time tapping in the order, asking the woman questions on accompaniments for her meal, trying to compose myself before I need speak to Ethan again.

"Ethan, what would you like?" I ask, feigning a detachment I don't feel.

I notice a glint in his eyes and a twitch in his lips as he holds eye contact with me. His cheekiness and fun sense of humor were some of the things I liked about him and that doesn't seem to have changed. However, flirting with me while on a date with another woman is not something I can condone. I tighten my smile and raise an eyebrow as I wait silently for his order.

"I'll have oysters to start please." He grins and winks at his date. "And the eye fillet steak with mushroom sauce please, Emily." I tap in his request, then glance up at them both. "Will that be all?" They both nod so I throw out a fake smile at them and gather up the menus.

"Thank you. Your meals shouldn't be long. Enjoy your evening." Hastily I walk to the central counter to process their order.

Marguerite arrives back from the restroom just as I am finishing, and I give her a rundown on their selection.

"Oh, and if he asks anything about me, just tell him you don't know me very well," I add.

"What do you mean?" she probes, her beautiful features shaped in a quizzical expression. We have become good friends since I started working here three months ago.

"We dated a few times, just over a year ago. I thought we were really getting along well, then he stopped contacting me without any explanation. It became awkward because his brother married one of my best friends." After a pause, I chuckle. "I doubt he will but if he asks about me, just put on your beautiful French accent and pretend you don't understand."

"Okay," she giggles as an impish gleam lights her dark brown eyes. "I like your thinking."

As much as I try not to, my thoughts return to table twelve far too many times for my liking. Ethan. He has everything I ever wanted in a man. Compassion, good looks, intelligence, a great sense of humor, loyalty and generosity, and a caring heart. Remembering that he would frequently return to the London office, I wonder if he is back here for good, or still residing in Australia.

My gaze frequently returns to their table and the way tonight's date seems to be going, dinner is part of their foreplay. There has been lots of hand-touching, laughter, foot knocking, and flirting so it would be no surprise if bed is where they ended up tonight. *The pattern seems familiar to his gameplan with me,* the annoying thought flits through my head. *Funny that his date has similar coloring to me. I wonder if redheads are his type.* That might explain his initial interest in me, but I obviously didn't beguile him with flirtatious and smart repartee, like his date tonight. I realized a long time ago that I don't need a self-assured, opinionated, and impatient prick like him in my life.

While Marguerite serves table twelve's meals, I continue to painstakingly wipe down the tables and busy myself in the kitchen, all the while reminding myself that I am a much stronger, more confident woman now than I was then. After backpacking solo through France and Spain for six weeks and currently working in London, I am more comfortable in my own skin, and am not afraid to assert myself when needed. Finally, I am enjoying life.

Loitering in the kitchen, I wait for another table's meals and, when they are ready, I then realize I have to walk past Ethan again. Groaning, but straightening my back, I sail straight past him as if he is just another customer.

When the crowd in the restaurant thins, I spend more time wiping down tables as far away from Ethan as I can. I don't hate him, but I don't like him very much either. Georgie doesn't talk about him much because she knows how hurt I was at his rejection. I was still rediscovering myself back then, but in a way he did me a favor, because, had we been involved, I wouldn't have been able to provide the single-minded devotion to caring for Mom, nor explore and experience the world as a backpacker after she passed away, each bolstering my self-esteem along this journey of self-discovery.

Knowing my reluctance to go near Ethan's table, Marguerite clears their plates, then tallies up the bill when they decline dessert. *No doubt eager to feast on each other's sweet treats in private,* I muse cynically.

After they leave, Marguerite pulls me aside in the kitchen, just as eager to tell me what has transpired at Ethan's table, as I am to hear it.

"Emily, he is delicious. He said he thought you would come back with the food, then asked me to tell you that Gina and Xander say hi and they miss you." She chuckles. "He still seems interested in what you are up to."

"What makes you think that?" My forehead scrunches in confusion. I am sure she is teasing me, and certain she is trying to make me feel better about stumbling across someone who hurt me.

"Oh, just the way he turned to look for you, but then remembered the other girl across the table from him. He played it cool as if he knew you were working here all along."

Chuckling, I shake my head. "Oh, come on Marguerite. That doesn't mean he is interested in me. Just that he is intrigued by how I could pop up on the other side of the world. You are such a romantic and your pregnancy hormones amplify it." Grinning, I hug her, and as my shift has ended, I say goodnight. Donning my coat and scarf, I call out goodnight to the chef, Johan, Marguerite's husband, before making my way out the back door.

As it is 10pm, and quite cold, I am pleased I have my thick coat with me. Pulling my hood up over my head, I tuck my hands into my pockets to make the brisk walk to my apartment. Despite it being late, I am surprised as I turn the corner by the number of people still out and about. I haven't got used to how freezing or how busy London is yet. Although I miss the warmer climate of Sydney, I am very glad that I decided to take a twelve-month working holiday in the Northern Hemisphere. A change of scenery is just what I needed.

I have only taken a few steps onto the main street when I need to step aside for a group of six or seven people rowdily walking past. When they have moved on, I spot Ethan at the curb with the redhead. They are facing each other, oblivious to their surroundings as he pulls her coat collar upright to shield her from the cold, then leans in for a kiss.

Heaving out a sigh, I wrap my scarf over my nose and mouth and pull my hood further forward, then walk briskly past. I hope he doesn't recognize me, but then I reason that, huddled in my overcoat like so many others, my anonymity is safe. Then I chide myself that Ethan is too preoccupied to be aware of anything.

On the short walk home, I reflect on how fortunate I was to find this job with Marguerite and Johan on my arrival three months ago. My hospitality experience years ago while at Uni came in handy for this position, and it has allowed me to save some funds to travel, although so far I have only been taking short trips in the outlying regions of the city.

Some of the other restaurant staff are also backpackers, so I have had travel companions when exploring. I have it a bit easier than most backpackers, because I am staying at a central apartment owned by my friend Simone, who only uses the apartment when she's here on her international layovers.

Seeing Ethan tonight makes me revisit how tumultuous the last year and a bit has been, and how much I have evolved as a result. My heart has been battered, bruised, and shattered, and feels like it is encased in ice most days. But I have learned to survive through it all and am now a more resilient, self-sufficient person. The loss of my mother hit hardest though, and my already broken heart has struggled to recover since then.

It feels like a lifetime ago, but it was a week after Georgie's wedding when Mom passed away. I held her hand with mixed feelings as she slipped away, relieved that she was now at peace, overcome with the feeling of loneliness and the void that seemed to lie ahead now that I would have to pick up the pieces of my life.

Her funeral was a small, quiet celebration of her life, with all my friends—except Georgie and Xander who were still on their honeymoon, although they offered to come back.

While she had been in palliative care, I had started cleaning out the house, sorting and selling items that I would no longer need, arranging a storage unit for the stuff I wanted to keep, and listing the house for sale. It was during this process that I uncovered some old documents and photos, which I had never seen, that Mom had stashed away in a small wooden box at the back of her wardrobe.

When I opened the box, my world was rocked by a black and white photo of Mom holding a toddler, who I recognized as me, and a tall stockily built man who had his arm around Mom. On the back, she had written, 'Bruce, Emily and I' and it was dated thirty years ago, meaning it had been taken a year after I was born. Mom had always told me my father died not long after I was born. Was this him? She never spoke of him, so I had always assumed his death had been difficult to deal with, which I believed was why she never remarried.

As I dug further into the box, there was a marriage certificate and divorce papers. *What? My father hadn't died, only divorced Mom. Why had she hidden that all these years?* I had no answers and no one to ask, so I decided to do some digging.

Eventually, I tracked him down, living in London, which was the main reason for my trip overseas, to see if I could connect with him while exploring a part of the world I had always wanted to see. Realizing I had dual citizenship also made the destination choice so much easier. Funds from the sale of the house were invested as a backstop if I needed, but also to use as a nest egg when I return and decide what I wanted to do with my life. And what I wanted to do was find someone to love, and for them to love me wholeheartedly.

Letting myself into the apartment, I shake off my maudlin thoughts like I shake off the cold air. I have already eaten at the restaurant, and Simone is away, so I crank up the heating and hop into a hot shower.

Afterward, I sit on the lounge with a cup of tea and the TV playing quietly in the background. I check my phone, and notice I have a message about some nanny work in two days. Quickly, I accept the job and then send a message to Georgie.

Emily

You'll never guess who came into the restaurant tonight. Ethan! I didn't realize he was there until I served him and his very sexy date, so we were both surprised to see each other. How long has he been back in London?

Georgie

Wow. That must have been awkward. What did you do/say? He's been back in London full time for about four or five months now. Xander is going over next week, so I've asked him to check in with you.

I didn't expect an answer so fast, but remembered it was early morning in Sydney and Georgie always started early.

Emily

Oh, great. I'd love to catch up with Xander. Ethan didn't say much. Couldn't really, because his date seemed peeved that he

recognized me. Other than take his order, I didn't have much to do with him, because I hid in the kitchen. *smiley face emoji*.

Georgie

That's understandable. Gotta go, lovely. I'll be in touch with details of Xander's itinerary. Take care of you. Xx

Emily
Will do, gorgeous. xxx

Yawning, I hop up and pack a few things into a backpack in preparation for a day trip tomorrow with Rashida and Lorenzo to Windsor Castle, which we have been excitedly planning for the last week. A few hours at the castle is not enough to do it justice, but we try to see as many sights as possible on our days off, with the intention of going back to explore further if we find a place we particularly like.

My excitement for tomorrow's adventure is dampened though by buried emotions and memories that resurface, which I know I need to deal with before I will be able to sleep. The hurt and bitterness of Ethan's rejection still sting. I had considered him a friend, and really admired him, so his abandonment with no explanation after a night of fantastic sex had temporarily eroded my growing self-esteem. At the time, I felt like I hadn't been a good enough lover for him to pursue me further, but soon realized I was better off without him. My newfound self-respect (and some good solid advice from my friends) chided that, if he couldn't respect me by telling me he didn't want to see me anymore, then he didn't deserve me. Treating it as another life lesson, I had got on with the ups and downs of life.

I remembered Marguerite's comment tonight about Ethan seemingly still interested in me that I had laughingly brushed aside. Finding it hard to believe, I rationalize that it was just his curiosity that had been piqued, and, as it often is when you see an old school friend whom you haven't seen in years, a five-minute conversation is all it takes to slake the curiosity for another decade.

How do I feel about Ethan after seeing him? The words of "Gotye's" song spring to mind... *"Someone that I used to know."* Yes, that felt right, and I assume that Ethan would not give me another thought, and if he did, it would only be a passing comment to Georgie or Xander that he had seen me.

Feeling settled now, I amble off to bed, mentally checking off things I need to do in the morning before departing on our trip. Sleep eludes me for a while as I toss and turn, and my tired legs become restless, as they often do after a busy night.

Chapter Nineteen

EMILY

Damn. My alarm didn't go off and now I have half an hour before I need to meet up with Rashida and Lorenzo. Frantically, I throw on some tights under my jeans for warmth and several layers of tops. Then I put some bread in the toaster while I rush around and add my scarf and coat, hat, sunscreen, and water bottle into my backpack, as well as the power bank for my phone.

Grabbing the toast, I munch on it as I run out, slamming the door behind me. I could probably catch a cab to our pick up spot, but decide to power walk instead, figuring it will most likely be faster. Messaging Rashida on the way, knowing she will buy a coffee before the journey, I ask her to get me one as well. I very much need a heart start today after my restless night.

I make it to the departure point just as the bus pulls up and welcome the coffee Rashida hands me. She is always early, like I usually am too, and raises a dark eyebrow at me.

"What time do you call this? You only just made it in time." Her voice and expression are irritated, but I know she won't stay that way for long because her good natured, happy personality and zest for life usually return quickly.

"Yes, I know," I puff trying to catch my breath. "My alarm didn't go off. Thanks for the coffee. I'll buy you the next one." Her long black ponytail sways as she nods her head then looks around for Lorenzo.

There are quite a few people waiting, but it doesn't take long before we pay and board the bus, each sitting in a double seat, so we can reserve one for Lorenzo, who comes bounding on behind us and flops next to Rashida in front of me.

"What time do you call this? You only just made it in time, Lorenzo," I mimic Rashida, nudging her and we both laugh.

"You weren't at the hostel this morning, so I didn't think you would make it," Rashida added.

"Okay. Stop nagging me, both of you." His brow creases into a frown as he continues awkwardly, his Italian accent lilting, "I hooked up with someone, okay, and they were on the other side of town."

"Why does that not surprise me?" I shake my head, chuckling. Lorenzo is a good-looking man, fit, beautiful dark eyes, long lashes, and dark, curly hair that whorls over his forehead and ears. He has this boy next door appearance when dressed casually like he is today, but when dressed in his black trousers and white shirt as a barman or waiter, with his hair slicked back off his face, he is stunning. His personality is just as beautiful as his appearance: loyal, kind, assertive, easygoing, and charming. Just the sort of man I'm hoping to find one day. But, as he's gay, he'll remain a dear friend. Still, I acknowledge Lorenzo's traits are similar to Ethan's and have become the benchmark of what I'm looking for in a man.

Soon after, the bus takes off, and the driver introduces himself as the guide. He begins pointing out sights as we make our way out of the city, our heads swiveling to take in as much as we can, absorbed in the history and beauty.

Despite all the photos we have seen, the breathtaking splendor of the majestic stone castle, sitting on the highest point in its vicinity, is indescribable. The driver pulls over momentarily and all we can hear on the bus are exclamations of excitement as everyone jockeys for position to photograph the stunning view and lush green tree-lined avenue.

Continuing further up the road and stopping at the drop off point, I am in awe and speechless as I alight from the bus. The weight of history surrounds and engulfs me as I twirl on the spot, not knowing where to look first, and I notice Lorenzo and Rashida slightly ahead of me, looking just as amazed.

This is what I came to the United Kingdom for. To experience the wonders of the past centuries, painstakingly preserved for future generations. I wanted this to be the trip of a lifetime, and so far, I have not been disappointed. I hadn't realized what a fascination I have with historic architecture until I came to this part of the world steeped in antiquity and tradition.

I run up to my wonderful friends and give them a hug. Standing between them, resting my hands on my hips, and in an exaggerated posh English accent, ask, "Would m'lord and m'lady care to accompany me on a stroll to the Round Tower?" Lorenzo plays along and gives me a mock bow before hooking his arm through mine, while Rashida dips in a mock curtsy and hooks her arm through mine too. Laughingly we stroll up the slight incline to begin our exploration, along with a bevy of other tourists.

As we follow a guided tour around the interior of the castle, we take turns posing for photos in various rooms and taking selfies of the three of us. We stand in a huge vestibule, mouths gaping as we look up at the massive ornate vaulted ceiling. No matter how we try, we can't manage to get a photo of the three of us with the huge ceiling in the shot as well. Rashida and I are looking at my phone and laughing at some of the botched attempts that need to be deleted when Lorenzo strolls over and stands behind us.

"I think you two beauties have some admirers," he whispers.

Then a tall, good-looking man with dark hair and a close shaven beard, probably in his late twenties, approaches. "Hi. Would you like me to take a photo of all of you?" he offers in his American accent. We had noticed he and another fellow with sandy blond hair and a stubble shadow along his jaw, who seemed of similar age, tagging along with the guided tour as well, and at one point Rashida and I had glanced at each other, raised our eyebrows and gave a slight nod of our heads in admiration of the men, and their toned physiques.

"Thank you so much," I gush and hand my phone over to him. He takes the photo with Lorenzo between Rashida and me, then after a moment, he hands my phone back to me. Sneakily he has put his name and phone number into my phone as well. I look up at him and cock an eyebrow.

"That was a bit forward of you, Tom." He looks a bit sheepish but throws me a lopsided smile while Rashida looks over my shoulder to see what I am talking about.

"I couldn't pass up the opportunity to give my number to such a beautiful woman."

"Smooth. Very smooth," I reply, my lips tight but curling up in the corners as I try to hold back a grin. I can feel my face heating with a blush and curse my pale, freckled skin. Rashida giggles next to me and Lorenzo tuts as if in disgust at my reaction.

"This is my friend, Aaron." He points over his shoulder with his thumb and the man nods in acknowledgment.

"Hi. You guys don't sound English. Where are you from?" Aaron enquires as he looks to each of us in turn.

"I'm Emily, and I'm Australian. This is Rashida and she is from Egypt, while Lorenzo here is from Italy."

"What about you two? You both American?" I smile, looking from one to the other.

Tom laughs, and Aaron groans. "God, no." Although he sounds like he has an American accent. At my look of confusion, he clarifies, "Thankfully, I'm Canadian."

"Ahh, I've heard about your cross-border rivalry," I chuckle.

"Are you guys here on holiday or for work?" Lorenzo joins the conversation, and I am surprised that Rashida has remained quiet. I watch her as I listen to Tom, Aaron, and Lorenzo converse about their holiday plans and note that her eyes haven't left Aaron, but she lowers them shyly when he looks directly at her and smiles. *Wow, the confident, outgoing woman I know seems star-struck and speechless.* I nudge her gently on the arm and tilt my chin toward the tour group who are disappearing out a distant archway.

"We're going to catch up with the tour group, if you want to join us," I offer, but suspect they would have come along regardless.

Tom and Aaron join us for the rest of the day, and Rashida opens up more as she gradually becomes more comfortable. We learn that they are also backpacking around but have only just started their holiday, so we are able to provide them with tips on places to visit, transportation and pitfalls. They are checking into a different hostel to Lorenzo and Rashida, but not far away from them. We explain that we have all picked up jobs to help fund our stay and travels, so don't have a lot of free time. When Tom and Aaron's tour bus leaves earlier than ours, we say goodbye and the men exchange phone numbers so we can catch up at another time.

So many sights. I am suffering from visual overload as we clamber back on the bus several hours later and flop into our seats. My phone battery died halfway through the day from all the photos I have taken, so I am pleased that I had the foresight to bring along my power bank to recharge it, as well as Lorenzo's phone. The ever pragmatic and organized Rashida purchased several books with superb photos from the souvenir shop, saying she was more likely to look through those than thousands of photos on her phone. We have walked the entire day, rarely sitting down the entire time. No wonder my feet, legs, and back ache.

It is a much quieter trip back to the city as all the passengers have exhausted themselves exploring, with some, including me, nodding off.

When the bus pulls back into the depot, I groan as I stand and follow my friends out. Spotting a nearby café that we often frequent, we call in for some dinner. As backpackers, we tend to be careful with our money, so each of us orders different pasta options, the cheapest selection on the menu, and we share a bottle of wine.

"This pasta is not great. Much better at home," Lorenzo complains, but still wolfs down his meal, while Rashida and I roll our eyes. We hear this same complaint every time we have pasta, which is practically every other night.

"You are such a pasta snob, Lorenzo," Rashida laughs.

"You will have to come to my home to experience authentic Italian pasta for yourselves. Then you will appreciate why I grumble about pasta over here." Lorenzo casts an impish glance at us as he forks another mouthful of the offending bolognese into his mouth, then looks around the room before dropping his gaze again to his plate.

"When we are in Italy, we will expect you to show us this authentic pasta and all the wonderful sights you tell us about, Lorenzo. How much longer before we can go?" I enquire enthusiastically, calculating that it will be at least another month before I can afford the train fares and spending money.

After a few mouthfuls, Rashida pipes up, "Oh, don't forget about the cocktail party at the art gallery tomorrow night."

Lorenzo and I look at each other. "Yes, we know. It is very important that we don't let your boss down," we repeat Rashida's words that we have heard many times.

"The agency has it all sorted, so it will be fine," I comment, hoping to appease her anxiousness. "Do we have to treat you like one of your swanky VIP guests?" My comment is tongue-in-cheek and has the desired effect of making her smile.

"Of course. I'll be the most important person there," she mocks, her nose tilted in the air and waving her hand around like royalty.

Since meeting Rashida four months ago, there has always been an air of affluence about her, so the fact that she often works in the art gallery doesn't surprise me. It seems to fit with her well-educated personality. She will be the hostess at tomorrow night's function and not waitressing as would normally be the case, and I get the feeling she will enjoy hobnobbing with the gallery's wealthy clientele.

"Well, I have an early start in the morning for a nanny job for a couple of hours, and I am bushed after all today's walking. Otherwise, I would ask you back to my place," I explain as I stand. "Do you want to share an Uber?"

They both nod and stand as well. Knowing that my place is on the way to their hostel, Lorenzo hands over some cash and pulls out his phone to arrange the rideshare while Rashida and I pay for our meals, then we wait out front for the driver.

***

Yawning as I walk into my apartment, I reflect how different my holiday would be, if I hadn't met Rashida and Lorenzo in a Paris backpackers lodge when I first started my trip. I probably would have gone back home by now if it wasn't for them. We soon became firm friends, seeing some of the highlights of Paris together, and when I mentioned my next stop was London they decided to join me. Not long after arriving, we joined a temporary employment agency, picking up odd jobs to earn some travel money, which is also how I met Marguerite and Johan.

Simone is due in tomorrow, so I rush around tidying up before turning in for the night. My phone beeps as I am about to turn out the light, so I quickly pick up and read the message.

Lorenzo
Guess what, bella? Tom and Aaron are staying at our hostel now. The other one was booked out. Looks like you girls will get to see more of your cute American and Canadian. *smiley face emoji*

As I drift off to sleep, I feel blessed to have met my wonderful friends, who are like siblings I never had, and wonder if things will lead anywhere with Tom.

Chapter Twenty

Upon arrival at the art gallery the next night, I check in with Rashida and the caterer, who we have worked with previously, then help plate up the hors d'oeuvres in a back storage room. I am early, but always find it useful to get in and get organized before the event starts, particularly at cocktail parties, because invariably guests will arrive early and expect food immediately.

I am dressed in the customary black skirt and tights and a white shirt, with flat black, enclosed shoes. I would have preferred trousers, but Rashida mentioned that apparently, the gallery owner prefers the female wait staff in skirts. When I commented that the owner was sexist, she chuckled and commented satirically that he didn't believe he was but considers that skirts sell more paintings. Yep, definitely sexist, but who am I to argue when I am getting paid well for a few hours' work.

Rashida is dressed in a lovely fitted, dark gray shirt-style dress, stockings, and low heels that make her look very elegant.

A deep familiar chuckle causes me to look up from placing petit fours onto silver platters and see Lorenzo walk into the back room to start prepping the alcohol, and am surprised to see Tom and Aaron following not far behind. All are dressed for service, looking delicious.

"Oh, hi. I didn't expect to see you both here." Smiling a greeting to Tom and Aaron, I throw Lorenzo a subtle, querying glance.

Tom pipes up, "Yeah, after talking with Lorenzo yesterday, he convinced us to sign up with the same agency as you guys. Then, when the caterer asked if he knew a couple of barmen, he suggested us."

"Cool. Do you have a specialty?" I ask, making polite conversation as I look back at my task of filling platters.

"Yeah. A Screaming Orgasm."

I snort with laughter, as does everyone else, then look back at Tom with raised eyebrows and a smirk. He winks a sparkling blue eye at me as I ignore his blatant suggestiveness.

"Guess I walked straight into that one, didn't I?" I deflect, trying not to show how flustered his comment has made me. No way am I continuing this conversation here. Maybe not ever as I certainly am not the sort of person anymore to jump into bed with someone after such a short acquaintance. I don't mind flirting, but while I'm at work, I try to maintain a professional decorum, so tactfully put my head down and continue with what I am doing.

Fortunately, Graham, the caterer, calls us back to order by requesting a team chat to advise us of our roles and duties for the evening. Lorenzo will provide drink service while I serve food. Tom and Aaron are to start behind the makeshift bar, filling champagne flutes with Aaron assisting with either food or drink service where needed. With ten minutes left before doors are opened, we need to get cracking, so everyone heads off to their respective work areas.

As the gallery owner and Rashida open the front doors, they welcome the guests, directing them towards Lorenzo and me, standing nearby with filled trays, on their way to inspect the artworks.

The night progresses in much the same way with Lorenzo, Aaron and I circling between the patrons who are milling around, ensuring they have ample food and drink. From the snippets of conversation I've overheard, it appears to be a networking opportunity for the art aficionados of London's upper class, with at least one hundred guests present.

Rashida instructs us after about an hour that the auction will soon begin and we are to stand nearby, but only offer food or drink between each sale lot.

I venture back to the bar with Lorenzo while he tops up his tray with more glasses of champagne and orange juice. I'm relieved to put my tray down for a while as my arms are getting sore. We chat idly about the crowd with Tom and Aaron before I head to the back room to refill my platter, hoping that the night does not drag on too long. I am starting to feel very weary after an early morning start and a lot of running around after a two and a three-year-old for several hours.

As I return, Tom is carrying the drinks tray, while Aaron and Lorenzo start packing away the surplus alcohol.

"I thought I would get out from behind the bar for a bit and have a look around," Tom comments with a friendly smile as we walk side by side into the far gallery where the latest auction is taking place.

"Fair enough. Are you into art?" I ask.

"Hmm, not really. But I know what I like." His eyes glint and his smile softens as he gazes at me.

Unsure if he is coming on to me, or just being sociable, I nod in reply. We reach the far gallery and I stand at the outer edge of the clumps of bidders while Tom wanders through the groupings. At this point in the evening, the guests are more interested in the drinks on offer rather than the food, presumably to drown their sorrows over how much they have paid out, or for being outbid on a piece they particularly wanted.

I am watching with interest when I notice a plump, balding man with ruddy cheeks who I guess to be in his mid fifties approaching me from the side. I turn to face him, smiling, offering him a view of my tray of morsels.

He slurs, "No, I don't want food. Get me a drink."

"The drinks tray is circling around, sir. I'll try to grab Tom's attention for you." My smile is fixed in place as I remember I am here to do a job, and from several years' experience in the hospitality industry, I know that often involves dealing with rude and inebriated patrons.

"No, I don't want champagne or beer. I want a scotch." He spits out the words demandingly, glaring at me.

"I'm sorry, sir. We don't have scotch here tonight. Only beer, champagne, juice or bottled water." My tone is slightly apologetic and placating, and my features remain calm and composed. "I can get you a water or juice or perhaps you would like something to eat?"

"Listen here, you stupid bitch. I said I want a scotch. Get me one now." His voice is raised, and he tries to intimidate me by standing over me while he pokes me in the shoulder with his finger. His breath reeks of alcohol, so I assume he was well primed before arriving tonight.

Stepping back out of his reach, my heart is racing as it usually does in confrontational situations. My ex was an abusive asshole, so this type of situation is not unfamiliar to me, although I am more capable nowadays of standing firm.

Patiently and politely, I take a deep breath and, with my eyes fixed directly on his bloodshot glassy eyes, I explain again, "Sir, we don't have any scotch here on the premises, so I can't give you what I don't have. All I can offer you is champagne or beer, water or juice, and some food."

Grabbing my ponytail as he steps in close to me, and tilting my head back to look at him, he yells into my face. "Stupid fucking bitch. Don't you know who I am? Get me a beer then, fucking slut."

By now his tirade has drawn the attention of some of the patrons and I twist my head to release his hold on my hair. Struggling to maintain the balance of my tray, and twisting to place it on a nearby table, I step away again. He follows me and continues with his rant, quieter though, so only I can hear him. "I'll teach you a lesson. I'll fuck you up the ass right here, like the fucking slut you are." As I turn back to face the drunken man, I stand firm under his barrage of abuse. I have heard these types of threats before from my ex, so they fall off me like leaves off a tree. My back is strong and straight as I pull myself up to appear taller, hopefully, than my diminutive five feet four inches and glare coldly at the man. My responsible service of alcohol training kicks in and, sternly, as if addressing a disobedient child, I clip out my words.

"Sir. You are intoxicated and I can't serve you any more alcohol. Your abusive behavior is not tolerated here. So, if you wish to remain on the premises, I suggest you pull your head in and behave in a respectful manner. If you can't do that, you will need to leave immediately."

Watching me stand resolute and unmoving, my eyes icy, challenging him instead of cowering to his demands, he steps back and scoffs, "Who's going to make me? None of these wimps would dare to challenge a man of my power and wealth." He turns and waves his arm with disdain at the onlookers, swaying with his sudden movement. As I glance at the crowd, I notice the gallery owner making his way over.

"Okay. That's enough. Time to leave. I'll call a cab for you, sir." I state in a manner that tolerates no argument. A quick glance past him shows me that Tom, Lorenzo, and a few other men are nearby, ready to assist me if needed, a fact that seems to have permeated his alcohol addled brain as well. Looking directly at Lorenzo, I give him a small shake of my head, hopefully indicating that I don't need their assistance yet.

"What? Don't talk to me like that, you surly fucking slut," he snarls when he realizes that I am not backing down.

"The door is this way, sir. I'll ask you to wait outside, please." Extending my arm in the direction I want him to go, waiting for him to turn and walk toward it. The gallery owner approaches the man, nodding at me as if he will take over now.

"Simon. It will be best for you to leave, I think." Placing his hand on Simon's shoulder, as a conciliatory gesture, he subtly steers him away from me. I see Rashida over in the background on the phone, so assume she is calling a cab.

"I can't leave yet, Jerome. I want to buy the large abstract and it hasn't come up yet. All I wanted was a drink, and that bitch wouldn't give me one." The drunk turns to point his finger at me.

"In the state you're in, Simon, I couldn't have let you bid for it anyway. Why don't you head home, and I'll call you in the morning to let you know if it's still available."

"Hmph. I suppose so. But I'll outmatch any bid for it, so don't let it sell." Simon boasts as they move towards the doors.

As they move away, my cheeks balloon as I release a large pent-up breath. Lorenzo rushes in to give me a hug and steps back, then Tom wraps his arm around my shoulders, squeezing me in close, then relaxing his hold without removing his arm as my knees buckle. Their support and comfort are like balm to my jumbled emotions, and I feel tears welling behind my eyelids.

"Whoa. Are you okay? What was that all about?" they chorus, as I sag under their admiring gazes.

"He wanted a scotch, and when I told him we didn't have any, he went ballistic." I shudder as I remember his threats and am pleased that I have my friends here. "He threatened me, so I told him it was time for him to leave." I can feel my hands shaking with relief in the aftermath of the confrontation and I take another deep breath.

"He what? What did he say to you, bella?" Lorenzo fires up, angry that I had been threatened. Knowing how protective he is about Rashida and me, and not wanting to create any more drama, I place my hand on his forearm.

"I'll tell you about it later. Now all I want to do is go somewhere quiet and regroup. I'll be in the back room if you need me."

They nod, and I can feel their eyes on me, watching closely as I pace across the gallery into the ladies' room, desperate for escape. Resting my hands on the edge of the sink, my shoulders drop forward and my head hangs. Inhaling deeply several times, I try to restore my breathing and equilibrium, as Simon's verbal abuse has triggered memories of my ex's vilification.

I am proud of how I stood my ground tonight and acknowledge that anybody, regardless of whether they have had a traumatic abusive relationship or not, would be rattled by tonight's encounter. I didn't lose my cool though, or say what I wanted to, which would have aggravated the situation. I also didn't cower beneath the tirade. My outward persona projected a calm, confident and capable person despite my internal response screaming at me to take flight. I also reluctantly admit to myself that having a room full of witnesses who could defuse the situation was a totally different situation than being alone with your abuser in the sanctity of your home.

Feeling much calmer, I splash some cold water on my face and steel myself for the many questions I know will follow. Exiting the bathroom on my way to the back room, intending to begin the pack up of all the catering equipment, a deep, concerned voice, warm and smoky, surprises me from behind, as it asks, "Are you okay, Emily?"

Jumping, I shoot startled eyes toward the voice. "Ethan?"

"Sorry. I didn't mean to scare you." He gives me an apologetic smile. Pondering why he is here and why I hadn't seen him when mingling earlier, I'm aware of a tingling in my scalp and fluttering in my tummy that I've only experienced when Ethan is nearby.

"I'm fine, but still a bit jumpy." I flash a quick non-committal smile, continuing when he follows as I walk toward the back storage room. "I hadn't realized you were here tonight."

"I try to attend these auctions as often as I can and, although I arrived late, I am especially pleased that I came tonight," Ethan admits, as he falls in step beside me.

"Oh, why is that?" I'm only half interested in his response as my mind wanders off, wondering if his date from the other night is with him. He stops, then gently takes hold of my elbow, his warm hand halting my progress. My eyebrows rise questioningly as I turn to face him, peering at him, waiting for his answer.

"Because I am full of admiration for the way you handled yourself tonight. That must have been a very difficult situation for you." His magnetic green eyes glint with warmth and compassion. My heart does a flip-flop in my chest.

"Yes, it was, and it brought back memories I would rather forget. But I am no longer that cowering person you once knew." Despite what I've just said, my voice trembles and my eyes well up, so I bite my tongue while I pull myself together. Ethan is the last person I want to fall apart in front of.

"I never saw you as cowering or weak, Emily. I have always seen your strength and resilience. Now I see your confidence and assertiveness as well, which makes you even more of a force to be reckoned with." His warm, deep voice croons hypnotically as he brushes some hair from my face; his gaze locked with mine.

I blink several times, unsure if he is just trying to make me feel better, or if he is looking for another hook up now that our paths have crossed again. The cynical side of me suggests he might be trying to take advantage of my rattled state, but I know Ethan as a man of integrity, so instantly dismiss the thought.

Chapter Twenty-One

"You okay, Emily?" Tom's irritated voice interrupts us as he approaches, his eyes narrowing as he searches my face—as if trying to determine whether Ethan is hassling me— then his glance throws daggers at Ethan.

"Yes thanks, Tom. Ethan is my best friend's brother-in-law, also checking if I am okay." The two men are glaring at each other as if each of them is expecting the other to leave.

Huffing, I turn and comment to them both, "I have to go and pack up. Thanks for checking on me." Then march off, not particularly caring what either of them thinks. *Men!* Tom, I barely know, so don't understand why he is glaring at Ethan, like he is warning him off. And Ethandf, who has made it very clear he doesn't want to have anything to do with me, confounds me with his praise and also his territorial glare at Tom. I just want to finish my shift and get home.

The rest of the night is busy with packing up and stowing the equipment in Graham's van, so we don't have much time for talking about anything other than the job at hand. As we are about to leave, I see Jerome chatting to Rashida near the front doors. Jerome thanks us all for our hard work as we walk past and exit, and wait outside for Rashida to join us, arranging our lifts home in the meantime.

"I'll see you home, Emily," Tom pipes up, which surprises me, as well as Aaron and Lorenzo, going by the look on their faces.

"No need, Tom, but thanks anyway." My tone is sharper than intended and my smile feels forced, annoyed that he seems to think I need molly-coddling. I am no longer the person I was 12 months ago. As Ethan acknowledged, I am more able to assert myself these days, both verbally and physically (thanks to some martial arts training). So, in a carefully controlled voice, I continue, "Besides, it doesn't make any sense for you to pay for an Uber to see me home, then another to take you back to the hostel, when you can just share with the others."

He looks determined to argue when Rashida joins us, looking annoyed. She tells us quietly that Jerome is very sorry for what happened, then stops, like there is more, but she doesn't want to say. I make a mental note to ask her about it tomorrow.

My ride turns up, and I say my goodbyes. Tom moves as if to get in the car with me, and I turn to him, insisting, "Seriously, Tom. I am exhausted. I'll be fine. You go with the others." Before he can argue his case again, I hop in the car and shut the door, telling the driver to go.

I sigh as I drag myself out of the elevator, surprised as I approach my door to hear voices coming from my apartment, then remember Simone is home. I let myself in and chuckle to myself when I find her sprawled on the lounge sound asleep, her head drooping forward, and the TV on some crazy talk show. Picking the remote up off the floor, I turn the TV off. Simone stirs, lifting her head, still half asleep.

"Hey, Sim. It's only me. Why don't you go to bed, love?" She mumbles something, then stands and staggers to her room. Turning out the lights, I do the same, grabbing some pajamas and heading to the bathroom for a shower. I need to wash off the smell of food, and the bitter stench of alcohol and bad breath. Scrubbing my skin to get rid of that vile man's touch, my tears finally flow under the warmth and comfort of the soothing water, my sobs camouflaged by its splattering sound.

Despite the strength of will I displayed under his verbal abuse, no one likes that sort of confrontation. It rattles even the most hardened people, and truthfully, his volatility scared me, triggering awful memories of Bradley's tirades.

The difference tonight was that I had friends present who could have jumped in if necessary, and my months of counseling certainly helped me stay calm. As the tears dry up, I sigh deeply and wash my face again before turning the water off and hopping out. Totally wrung out, I remember to message Rashida before I fall asleep, letting her know that I am home safe.

The next morning, I wake with a start, hearing noises in the apartment, then remember again that Simone is home, and obviously up and about. Rolling over, I check the time on my phone. *Damn, it's only 7.3am.* Dragging myself out of bed, I pull on some clothes, tug the covers up neatly, and saunter to the kitchen, greeting Simone with a yawn.

We chat for a while about her trips and the occasional odd or troublesome passenger. Then I fill her in on what I have been up to, how I have met Tom and Aaron, regaling her with the story from last night, while I eat my yogurt and fruit and sip at my coffee.

"Geez, Em. You sure do attract some weirdos," she laments in her straight-talking manner, swallowing her tea before continuing, "I'm just glad that nothing more came of it."

"Yeah, me too. Hey. Guess who else I've run into, and was also at the Gallery last night?" Pausing, Simone shrugs, splaying out her hands in an 'I don't know' look, before I divulge, "Ethan."

"Oh, no way. Where? How?" she quizzes.

"He was dining at the restaurant a couple of nights ago, and I had to serve him and his date. They only had eyes for each other, so I'm surprised he bothered to ask how I was. After the other bloke abused me at the Gallery, Ethan approached me to make sure I was okay, which surprised me, because I hadn't even realized he was there."

"What are you going to do about him?"

"Nothing really. I don't expect to see him again and I certainly won't be contacting him, so I suppose it's moot." She nods as I shrug, then our conversation switches to more general topics before Simone says she has shopping to do and leaves.

I busy myself with laundry when I hear my phone buzz. *Damn, I must have forgotten to turn it off vibrate mode last night.* Picking it up, I quickly change the setting, then read the message.

Tom

Just checking to see how you are feeling this morning, and if you would like to catch up for a coffee.

Emily

Thanks. I'm fine. I'd love a cuppa, though. How about Lorenzo's favorite eatery Gianni's Trattoria? I'll send you the address.

Tom

I'll meet you there in an hour?

Emily

Sounds great.

***

The café is packed with its lunchtime crowd, some standing at the bar for their espresso shot. I sit at an outside table while I wait for Tom under the shade of a large black umbrella, enjoying the cooling breeze on this very warm day. Sipping some cold water, I fan myself with a menu, trying to dry off the perspiration from walking to the café, while I glance around at the mixture of stylishly dressed office workers and casually attired tourists.

A blaring horn down the street startles me, and turning my head in its direction, I spot Tom darting between cars on his way to meet me. I watch as he approaches, once again taken by his athletic physique, and his easy jogging style weaving in and out of the pedestrians indicates he does a lot of running. He is barely breathless when he stops a few feet away from me and hasn't even broken into a sweat.

As he advances with a huge grin, I am surprised when he stoops to peck me on the cheek and murmurs, "Hello, beautiful," as he sits opposite me.

Raising a single eyebrow, I look directly at him, my lips pressed into a hint of a smile and tilting slightly in one corner. "Taking liberties again, Tom? We barely know each other." I am half joking because, even though I quite like Tom, I certainly don't want him to think I am an easy lay. I would like to get to know him far better before getting too involved with him. I have been there, done that, and have learned to take the time to assess a man before getting too involved.

He chuckles and winks at me. "I'm very keen to know every part of you, Emily."

"Huh. I bet you are," I parry cheerfully. "Do you get many women falling for that line, Tom?"

"A polite man doesn't kiss and tell Emily," he hedges, wiggling his eyebrows comically, then the waiter arrives to take our order.

"So, Em, what's your reason for traveling halfway around the world and ending up in London?" Tom questions as our coffees arrive, his light tone holding an underlying note of seriousness, his blue gaze fixed on mine.

My smile slips a bit, and I drop my eyes to stare into the coffee mug cupped in my hands as a wave of sadness hits me. "Well, I lost my mother a few months back and, while going through some of her papers, I discovered some information about my father, who I never knew. So, I thought I would take the opportunity to see what I could of the world and hopefully get to meet my father in the process."

"Wow, that's so sad. Sorry about your mom." His big warm hand stretches across the table to grasp mine, offering comfort.

"Thanks, Tom. Mom had been sick for a while, so, as hard as it was to lose her, she was finally free of the suffocating pain." Sighing, I continue in a small voice, my eyes evading his. "Lots of mixed emotions, mingled with surprise and hurt that she hadn't confided in me about my father." Hot tears well in my eyes as I look back up at him with a sad smile. I have deliberately pushed those painful emotions aside till I was strong enough to evaluate them, and the fact that I have opened up to Tom hints to me that now might be the time to do some deep introspection. Well, not right this minute, but soon.

"Have you contacted your father at all? Maybe you should?" he encourages supportively.

"Yes, I sent a letter to the address I found, and searched for him online through his social media. So far, I haven't heard anything, and I don't expect any sort of relationship to come of it. I just wanted him to know that Mom had passed away."

"I'm happy to help you in any way. Just let me know," Tom offers with an earnest expression, his thumb gently rubbing the back of my hand.

"Thank you. I appreciate that." My response is sincere as I peer into his eyes, my gaze softening as I throw him a warm smile.

Suddenly, I become aware of distant church bells chiming the time. "Oh, my God. Is it 2 o'clock? I've got to get to work." Frantically I pick up my few belongings, find some loose change to give to Tom to pay for my coffee, and thanking him for a lovely time, I stand and rush down the street.

Chapter Twenty-Two

ETHAN

Sitting at the end of the bar drinking my coffee, I lean back against the wall, my eyes aimlessly wandering around the bustling café, while my mind questions why I am feeling downhearted today. Everyone has days when they feel dejected or down, but I don't have too many fortunately, and I can usually brush it off when I do. But I don't understand why this low feeling has lasted over the last few days. It's not as if I'm down. It's almost a hollow feeling or a perplexing numbness. I can't quite define it and that's giving me the shits.

Exhaling a heavy sigh, I glance disinterestedly out the nearby window and my heart beats an upbeat tattoo against my ribs, thrilled at the beautiful sight of Emily alone under the shade of an umbrella. Instantly I stand, noting distractedly that the heavy feeling has miraculously disappeared, and smiling, I start making my way to the door to say hello. But I am halted in my tracks when she stands and is kissed on the cheek by that waiter from last night at the gallery.

Taking a vacant seat where I can observe them without being detected, I watch as they exchange a few words, then she chuckles at something he says as they take their seats. My fists clench, and my jaw tightens as my teeth grit together. *What does she see in that ass-hole? Can't she see he is playing her?* She laughs and my hard, scornful gaze lashes the man, my lips pressing together with displeasure. The drumming of my heart a few moments ago has turned into a burning sensation in my chest as memories of Emily laughing like that with me hit like lightning. I just want to storm out there and drag her away from that womanizer. *She is too good for him. He will just use her, then move on to the next conquest.* My thoughts turn inward and my internal voice screams, *Just like you did.*

Slumping in my chair, I acknowledge again how poorly I treated Emily and remember how alive she made me feel. She lit a warmth and depth of emotion in me that I haven't felt since. *Maybe that is why I have been despondent since seeing her again in the restaurant a few days ago. Is my subconscious hankering for her presence?*

As much as I have tried forgetting Emily, I have been unable to. She is always there in the shadows of my heart and mind, popping out at the most unexpected times, occasionally in my dreams, often when I am having sex. My orgasms have never been as explosive or as intense since I dumped Emily, either.

Louisa even commented the other day about my penchant for red-heads over the last year, instead of blonds, which used to be my type. Knowing that she was insinuating I have been trying to fill the void left by Emily by seeing women with similar attributes, I told her to mind her own bloody business. She is right though, and I had acknowledged that to myself a while back. Not that I would tell Louisa that.

Since Emily, I have always felt like a part of me was missing. Don't get me wrong. Life continued as normal after her, but the feeling of emptiness remains to this day. I just haven't had the same thrill of the chase, or the driving need for sex. And I have yet to find someone with the complexity of fragility and strength, resilience and tenderness that

Emily had. I regret dumping her, and with hindsight, know she was good for me. In fact, the best thing that has ever happened to me, and I ran like a scared rabbit. I thump my fist on the windowsill in frustration.

While I watch, a myriad of expressions flit across Emily's face and I find myself smiling with admiration at her natural beauty and eloquence. Then her expression drops, turning serious, and I scowl as the bastard pats her hand comfortingly.

A slight growl rumbles from my throat. *Take your hands off her, you prick.* I feel my forehead scrunch, wondering where the hell that came from. *What's wrong with me?* My emotions are topsy-turvy and my thoughts are in turmoil. As I scowl out the window again, I see Emily peering into what's-his-name's face, her expression softening and a smile playing on her lips. With a start, she jumps up, grabs her things, and runs off down the street. *Did that bastard say something to upset her? I'll punch his lights out if he did.*

Jumping to my feet, ready to do just that, his startled expression at her sudden exit penetrates the red fog clouding my better judgment. *God, I must be losing it*, I groan, chiding myself for being so ridiculous. Huffing out a rough breath, I relax my clenched jaw slightly and unfurl my fingers, running them through my hair. *What the fuck just happened?* My usual espresso shot, which I finished just before Emily arrived, has never caused such an adrenalin rollercoaster before, so it probably wasn't that, I rationalize as I plop back into the chair.

Emily has me unsettled to the point where I want to hurt a stranger because he is with her. *You're jealous.* My inner voice decides to mock me. *Surely not.* I've never been jealous of anything before. Well, maybe Xander when I was a kid, because whenever he came home from boarding school for the holidays, Mom seemed so devoted to him, as if I didn't exist. My mouth drops open, and my eyes narrow and crinkle between the brows as I think that through. I don't remember ever consciously acknowledging that situation before, and it explains why Mom said I was naughtier when Xander was home. No doubt trying to get her attention in whatever way a child can.

"Oh, this is fucking ridiculous." Scoffing to myself, frustrated at my introspection, I stand quickly and pace out the door, giving the American a scowling nod as I pass him. He is intent on his phone conversation, paying no attention to me, and a snippet of his flirtatious conversation with someone reaches my ears. I could be mistaken, but I get the feeling it isn't Emily he is talking to, so I pause nearby, pretending to check my own phone while eavesdropping.

"I'd like that, Silvina. I can't wait to hold you in my arms again," the scumbag murmurs. "Where? Great. See you then, babe," he croons. Chuckling to himself, he gets up, throws some money on the table, and struts off in the opposite direction.

"What a lowlife." Fuming, I pace in the direction of my nearby office, steam coming out of my ears because I am so angry. Stringing Emily along with his flirtatious charm and arranging a hook up with another woman within five minutes of her leaving. "Fucking bastard," I mumble to myself, wanting to warn Emily about him so she doesn't get conned and hurt. *But would she believe me?* Probably not, particularly after the way I abandoned her. There is a burning need within me to protect her though, and I don't understand why, or how to do that.

My anger-fueled pace has abated to determined strides by the time I reach my office, my mind running through scenarios and consequences of alerting Emily about her friend's deception. *Huh, that's rich, coming from you; a player warning a woman off another player* jibes a sarcastic inner voice. At least I have principles, I concede, because I never chase a woman unless I am single.

Even though work consumes me for the rest of the afternoon, I can't shake the niggling, unsettled feelings. I know Emily won't welcome my interference and wonder how I can broach the subject, but then a disarming thought strikes me. If she's with me, she won't be with him.

Checking the time on my watch, dinner at the restaurant where she works seems like a good place to start.

***

Peering through the window as I approach, I spot Emily behind the counter, processing an order. I smile at the way she has her bottom lip trapped between her teeth as she concentrates on entering the items into the ordering system.

Pushing open the door and stepping inside, Emily lifts her head and, when she sees me, her courteous greeting smile slips at the corners and becomes forced, as if she is groaning inwardly but must stay professional.

"Ethan. Hello," she states in a pleasant tone that I recognize as her waitress voice. "How can I help you?"

"Emily. How are you today?" Giving her a small nod, I raise an eyebrow in wry amusement, sensing she would rather avoid me like she did last time I was here. "Do you have a table available, please?" I ask, schooling my features into an unreadable expression. I watch her eyebrows raise as she gives me a glassy stare, before checking the table bookings.

"Certainly. This way, please." Delighted, I follow her, admiring the way her black trousers stretch across her cute, well-rounded bottom, and my hands tingle, remembering how soft and malleable her butt cheeks were. Her stride is purposeful, and I almost walk into her when she stops next to a table against a wall near the back of the room. "Here you are, Ethan. Someone will be with you shortly to take your order," she states as she places the menu on the table before marching off.

Taking the seat facing the rest of the dining room, I have a view of the counter and the front door, and recognize the waitress at the other end of the restaurant as the hostess from the gallery last night.

She chuckles at something Emily says as they pass each other, and Emily disappears behind some swinging doors that I assume lead to the kitchen. The other lady brings water to my table and takes my order, and the restaurant starts to get busy with the dinner rush. A waiter, also from last night, circles the tables dispensing drinks from the bar. Even though Emily hasn't come near my table again while I eat my meal, I can see that she is busy at the other end of the restaurant and notice that she frequently glances my way with a confused look on her face. Chuckling to myself, I suspect that she assumed I would have a date tonight, but is baffled that I am dining alone.

Emily is at the counter again, settling a patron's bill, and I am finishing the last of my steak when a loud voice cuts through the conversational noise of the restaurant.

"You!" he bellows, and I glance up, along with all the other diners, and notice Emily's look of astonishment, before her professional mask is fixed firmly in place. "You caused so much trouble for me last night," he continues to yell. The abusive drunk from last night has recognized her and the hairs on the back of my neck stand up, sensing that this man looks like he intends making trouble. While Emily talks to the man, presumably about his table booking, the hostess from last night comes over as moral support and takes the loud, obnoxious, middle-aged man and his younger male friend to their table, next to mine.

Once they are seated, the rotund older man starts bellyaching to his guest about how Emily had embarrassed him last night. The younger man wears a sardonic expression like he knows his older associate well enough to accredit his poor behavior as the cause of his problems.

Emily stays well clear of our area, obviously to avoid a repeat of the previous evening, but her Italian-looking waiter friend returns to the men's table with their drinks, and then to take their order. As he hasn't taken any other food orders while I've been here, I assume that the women didn't want to be exposed to the older man's wrath. As it is, he is still cranky and surly, barking out instructions on how many minutes he wants his steak cooked for, and going into a mini-rant when advised that his preferred brand of wine isn't in stock. *What a douchebag.* All the while the younger man sits silently, tight-lipped, and with a steely stare at his associate, as if he is not happy with the other man's attitude but is reluctant to say anything.

My meal is finished, but I decide to linger a bit, in the hope of catching Emily, but also to keep an eye on the buffoon next to me. The waiter returns with wines for the other table and when he turns to clear my table, I politely ask him for a peppermint tea. Smiling, he nods and walks away. While I wait, I pull my phone out of my jacket's internal pocket and catch up on some emails that I wasn't in the right mindset to respond to earlier. The pregnant French lady who served me here once before returns with my tea.

"Is there anything else I can get for you, sir?" she asks courteously.

"No, nothing at the moment, thank you. But can you give this to the young lady over there?" Nodding in Emily's direction, who is back behind the counter again, I hand over my business card. Her gaze flicks between me and the card, appearing reluctant to do as I ask, then she flips it over and reads my short, handwritten message on the back, saying, *"Call me if you need help with this fellow, or anything else."*

Nodding, she smiles and returns to Emily, handing her the card, and after a few words, Emily turns the card over, quickly reads it then looks at me and nods. Even though she is surrounded by her friends in the restaurant, my concern is for her safety, and she seems to appreciate that.

While I pour my tea from the little white teapot into my cup, I am aware of the waiter returning with the meals for the men next to me. The obnoxious man is waving his arms around, talking loudly, regaling the younger man with stories of his financial prowess, and the waiter hesitates until he stills his arms before placing his plate down.

"This isn't what I ordered," he bellows, pushing the plate to the middle of the table.

"Yes, sir. This premium steak is cooked precisely four minutes like you asked." The waiter, to his credit, holds firm, with a neutral expression on his face.

"Take it back and bring me the lobster I ordered," he yells.

"Sir, lobster is not on the menu, so you couldn't have ordered it. I can bring you some salmon, but the kitchen is very busy and there is about half an hour wait." His lips press together as if holding back the words he would really like to say to the customer.

Fortunately, before the situation escalates any further, the younger man pipes up, "Simon, why don't you eat the steak so we can discuss business?" he cajoles, then gives Simon a friendly smile. The man appears to weigh up the situation and drags the plate back toward him, huffing, then glaring at the waiter, he orders a scotch on the rocks. The waiter nods and quickly retreats.

While I casually sip my tea, I overhear them talking about the situation at the gallery last night while they eat. It appears the younger man is Simon's attorney.

"I can't see what I can do, Simon. No charges have been laid, and if we push it that far, there are many witnesses who will attest in court that they saw you verbally abuse the woman. She has made no effort to confront you tonight, so I think you would be better off dropping the matter." The waiter returns with Simon's drink, taking away the empty wine glasses as Simon continues his complaining.

"What about my reputational damage? Surely there is something we can do about that?" he blusters.

"Yes, I think you should publicly apologize to the woman. That way you show you are acting in good faith, admit you made an error of judgment, and the matter is closed. If she decides to sue you for psychological trauma, then either offer her a payout or do a deep dive into her background to discredit her. I don't believe it will come to that though." My hackles rise and my blood boils at the callous and jaded advice, even though I understand it is often common practice in big business when reputations or huge amounts of money are at stake.

Simon huffs and downs his scotch then asks, "What about a non-disclosure agreement?"

"That could be a possibility, but I will have to investigate it. In the meantime, I suggest you clean up your act and stay well clear of that woman." Good advice from the attorney, but Simon doesn't appear to be a reasonable person.

Not long after, the attorney leaves and Simon stays behind, with another scotch on the rocks, glaring at Emily as she moves around the restaurant. Thankfully, she doesn't appear to notice. Simon eventually pays the bill and leaves and a short while later I see Emily talk to the hostess, and then wave goodbye to her waiter friend, before she disappears through the kitchen doors.

As another pot of tea arrives, I settle my bill and sit and ponder what I can do to help Emily if she is approached to sign an NDA.

Simon's bullying tactics indicate that he gets drunk and abusive quite frequently, so I shoot off a couple of emails to the gallery owner and Ramon, my head of security asking for details on Simon, and stress to him to look into Simon's background and similar cases of verbal abuse, because I suspect this isn't going to end here for Emily. I also message Louisa for a catch up tomorrow, with the intention of creating a contingency plan in case Emily needs it.

Then I wonder why I am going to so much trouble for someone I have previously rejected.

Shaking my head, chiding myself for getting involved, I am about to return my phone to my jacket pocket when it vibrates in my hand. Glancing at it, I don't recognize the number.

"Hello."

"Ethan. It's Emily," she whispers, her voice trembling slightly. "That fellow from the restaurant is following me in his car."

"Where are you?" Immediately I am on high alert, and wishing I could somehow teleport myself to her to make sure Simon doesn't find her. I jump to my feet and race out the door.

"I'm in an alleyway behind the grocery store three blocks east of the restaurant. Oh God, he's just driven past the alley again," her voice quivers.

"Is the grocery store open, Emily?" I quiz her as I start running down the street. At her meek "Yes," I tell her to go inside, reassuring her that it will be well lit and public, and there will be security cameras, so if he tries anything it will be recorded. "I'll be there soon, Em."

Chapter Twenty-Three

ETHAN

My heart is pounding as I shove open the glass door and pace inside, my eyes frantically searching for Emily. I can't see her. *Oh God, he hasn't gotten to her, has he?*

"Emily," I call out. "It's Ethan."

I hear a whimper from the back corner of the shop and see her poke her head tentatively around the row of shelves she is hiding behind. My relief is so great to see her that I rush toward her, wrapping her in my arms, feeling her tremble as I tuck her against my body and rest my chin on her head.

"It's okay, Em. I've got you. It's okay." Cooing the words repeatedly, she gradually relaxes enough to pull out of my arms. She tilts her head up and looks into my face, her eyes moist from the tears she is blinking away, and gives me a tight, almost embarrassed, smile.

"I'm sorry to put you to so much trouble, Ethan," she murmurs. "But I panicked when I saw him following me."

My hands cup the base of her head, and my thumbs rub over her cheeks, brushing away the few tears that have spilled. "No trouble at all, Em. Tell me what happened," I utter, desperate to kiss away her troubles and make her feel safe. But I need her to trust me again first.

"I left the restaurant through the back and walked round the corner to the main street like I always do. When I walked past the restaurant, I noticed him on the other side of the road leaning against a bright yellow low sports car. He recognized me and shook his fist at me, then hopped in his car." Her words are hurried, and her voice is wispy. Her breath catches in her throat, so she inhales a long breath as if trying to calm herself before continuing. "I heard it start up with a growl and he drove off in a hurry, so I paid no further attention to it until I heard it behind me. I turned and saw him about three car lengths back, crawling along, as if following me. I thought I was imagining it, but I turned down a side street, just to be sure, and he followed me, still crawling along. I zig zagged a bit through various streets until I could get far enough away from him to hide in the alley. That's when I called you."

"You did the right thing, and I am very pleased you called me. Now, let's get you out of here." Taking her hand, I stride to the counter, with her almost running alongside me. Paying for a bottle of water, I thank the shopkeeper for allowing her to stay safe and out of sight. I hear her gasp, and when I turn to look at her, she is frozen to the spot. "What is it, Em?"

"I can hear his car, Ethan. He's outside," she stammers breathlessly.

The brightly lit shop is like a goldfish bowl, with easy visibility from the outside looking in, but not as easy to see out due to the reflections in the dark windows. Pretending to look for other items along the window, I assess the location of the car, then formulate a plan.

"Okay, Em. Here's what we are going to do. We are going to walk outside with our arms around each other, just like a loving couple who have popped out for a late-night snack." While speaking calmly, I grab some random items from the shelves and pay for them, asking that they be put in a bag. "I'm testing a theory here that he won't follow you if I am with you. But let's just throw him off the scent a bit, hey?" Emily stares at me wide-eyed and nods. Pulling a peak cap out of the bag, I pull it down on her head, so the brim shadows her fair skinned face, then readjust her coat hood so it sits high on her shoulders to hide her distinguishable red hair.

"Are you ready?" I coax as I place a beanie on my head and can see Emily's courage bolstering, then a determined glint appears in her eyes when she tilts her head back and her eyes roam over my face.

"Yes. Let's do this," she agrees decisively, lifting her chin, her voice carrying a strained tense edge, her wariness apparent.

Bestowing her with a genuinely warm smile, I admire her spunk and, placing an arm across her shoulders, I walk us out of the shop and it strikes me that holding her like this feels so normal, so right.

"Thank you so much for doing this for me, Ethan," Emily murmurs with soft appreciation.

"Not a problem at all," I assure her with a quick squeeze of her shoulder, pulling her tighter against me.

We get almost a block on the nearly deserted, sparsely lit street and Emily suddenly tenses. "That's him. The yellow car." The vehicle turns a corner and drives towards us at a slow, prowling pace.

"Play along with me here, Em." My heart is pounding, and my senses are on high alert.

"What?" she questions, staring but not seeing me.

"Follow my lead, Em." I steer her toward a nearby shadowed doorway alcove and turn her so her back is pressing against it. Facing her, I step in close and grasp her waist with one hand, my head lowered, so it looks to a passerby like I am kissing her, my large frame shielding her from direct sight while my arm closest to the road leans on the wall just above her head.

Her trembling hands rest on my chest. "Grab my phone out of my jacket pocket and take some pictures of the car and driver." As she hesitates, I stress again, "My phone, Em." She nods and I feel her hand reach under the flap of my jacket and remove it. "Good girl." I speak softly, encouragingly. "Now, take some photos." I can hear that the car is close, estimating it is right opposite us, but daren't look around. Emily positions the phone under my raised arm, and I hear her drawing in deep breaths as she focuses on taking snaps.

The sound of the car fades, and I wait an excruciating minute or two before turning my head to ensure it is out of sight, then cast my concerned glance back to Emily, who is staring at my phone. Placing my hands along her trembling jaw, I stroke my thumbs gently across her dampened cheeks, then tilt her chin up so I can peer into her shiny eyes. She draws a deep breath and bestows on me a brave tight smile. "It's okay, Baby Girl. It's okay."

"Thank you, Ethan." Her soft-spoken voice falters. "I don't know what I would have done if you hadn't been here." Wrapping my arms around her, I pull her against me in a soothing hug, inhaling her subtle lavender scent. I don't know who is deriving the most comfort; Emily or me. Holding her in my arms, safe and secure, is a relief and a lump of emotion develops in my throat as it dawns on me how terrified I was that she was in danger.

Nestling against me like this, a warm closeness overwhelms me; that she belongs in my arms. An involuntary sigh escapes me, and I briefly close my eyes in contentment before realizing we need to get out of here. Releasing my hold and placing my hands on her shoulders, I step back but remain in the shadowed alcove, blocking the exit.

"Em, we need to get you out of here." Slipping my phone out of her hand, I quickly press a number on speed dial, and the call is picked up on the third ring. "Hi, man, can you come pick me up at this location?"

"Sure thing, Ethan. What's going on?" Ramon questions in his usual brisk manner.

"I'll tell you about it when you get here. Can you bring the SUV, because I have a friend with me?" My eyes flit between watching the road and Emily.

"Yep. On it. Be there in about ten minutes."

Disconnecting the call, I check the photos Emily took and text them to Ramon, knowing he will get his security team to track the vehicle, then slide my phone into my pocket.

"How much further is your place, Em?"

"About a ten-minute walk. The apartment I share with Simone is on this road." Her voice is stronger, and she seems to be breathing normally again.

Lifting her chin with my forefinger, I peer into her upturned gaze, stating calmly, "I don't mean to scare you anymore than you are, Em, but I don't think it is safe for you to go home tonight."

Her forehead creases and her spine stiffens when she answers, "I should be fine, Ethan. He's gone now. But if you wouldn't mind walking home with me, I'd appreciate it."

"I'd be happy to, but I don't want him knowing where you live, laying in wait for you," I try reasoning with her.

"I think that's unlikely," she comments with disdain.

"Probably not normally, but an hour ago, you would have thought the same, and yet here we are. This guy seems like a lunatic, and if he has gone to so much trouble stalking you, I don't think you should underestimate him, Em," I point out matter-of-factly, and I can see my words sinking in, resonating with her. Just then I hear the growl of the sports car as it cruises past us on another lap and, going by the startled look on Emily's face, she has too.

Bending my head, my hands clasp her face, my lips claiming hers as I again try to hide her from the lowlife scumbag. Well, that is my honorable intention, but when our lips meet, the latent chemistry between us ignites a fire within me, and my tongue probes her mouth insistently, conjuring buried visions of her naked beneath me.

Losing all sense of time and place, I know that I am where I want to be; with Emily in my arms. Craning her neck, her tongue dances with mine, and her warm hands press against my chest, but she jumps, breaking the kiss when my phone vibrates. Sighing, I remove my hands from her face, sliding one under my jacket flap to extract it, glancing at the incoming text.

Ramon

GPS says I am at your location, but I can't see you. You ok?

Turning to look out at the street, I spot our big black SUV parked by the curb, lights off, but engine purring. Quickly I text him back.

Ethan

Any sign of a yellow sports car?

Ramon

No.

Ethan

Coming out now.

Grabbing Emily's hand, I step out of the shadows, holding her behind me as I look up and down the street. Ramon spots me and hops out of the car, striding in front of the vehicle to open the rear passenger door.

Dragging Emily out of the alcove, we rush across the footpath. Stopping at the rear door, I guide Emily into the back seat before I clamber in next to her. Ramon shuts the door then paces around to the driver's side and steps in, putting the car into gear while buckling his seatbelt before gunning the vehicle out of the area.

"Thanks, man. Really appreciate you coming to get us at such short notice." Stretching forward, I grip his shoulder, squeezing it because I can't slap him on the back. Ramon nods, acknowledging my thanks, and his steely eyes make contact with mine in the rearview mirror.

"Wanna tell me what this is all about?" he questions brusquely, his no-nonsense security guard manner in place, a side of him I fortunately don't often see.

"This is my fault," Emily's quiet voice chips in, and Ramon's piercing stare stabs at her, flaying her for putting me in supposed danger, before returning to the road. To her credit, she doesn't quake under his scrutiny, unlike many others I know, but continues in a firm, quiet voice, "I called Ethan for help because I was being followed."

Ramon nods and glances at me, so I answer his questioning look by filling him in on the sequence of events that started last night, and how I don't want her to go home tonight as a safety precaution.

"Wise choice," is all he says, but I know this man of few words will be discussing the situation at length with me later. We are as close as brothers, and straight talking, sometimes brutal conversation, is a necessity. He, Xander, and I have shared many scrapes, and trust each other implicitly.

It is only a short drive and as we pull into my apartment building's driveway, Ramon swipes us through the security gate, ever vigilant while we wait for it to open and close behind us, then proceeds to the designated underground parking spots for my apartment.

The elevator takes us directly to my penthouse level apartment and as we exit into the vestibule, Emily states again, "Ethan, I really don't see the need to stay here. If I just sit it out here for a little while, then maybe you or Ramon can drive me back home. The creepy guy won't know where I live then."

"He knows where you work Em, so it won't take much for him to follow you from work again, but not be so obvious about it next time," I counter, believing that to be very likely, as I walk us into the lounge area.

Ramon, who's followed close behind us, adds, "Yep, very probable." His phone buzzes and he steps away, moving up the hall toward the bedrooms to answer it, speaking quietly and in one-word answers.

"Look. Em, just make yourself comfortable for one night, and we can work out the rest in the morning. You've had quite a shock tonight and I'm sure the adrenaline will wear off soon," I tell her. "Do you have to let your flatmate know where you are?"

"Oh my God, I hadn't thought about Simone. Yes, you're right." Her voice sounds worried for her friend, rather than herself, but I suspect the full impact of tonight hasn't hit Emily yet. "Is there somewhere I can go to call her?"

"Sure, follow me." Leading the way to the cozy, cream and tan toned tub chairs in the far corner from the kitchen separated by a floor-to-ceiling wall unit containing books and artwork pieces, I leave Emily to make her call, running my hand through my hair as I turn back toward the kitchen. My adrenaline-charged emotions are only now settling into normality and I feel wrung out, so I can't imagine how Emily is feeling.

Grabbing two crystal glasses on the way past the nearby bar nook and splashing a generous helping of scotch in both, I amble back into the kitchen, dropping some ice cubes into them, and then perch on a high-backed stool at the kitchen bench. Ramon drags himself onto the stool next to me, sighing heavily, which means he has some not so great news.

"Okay, spit it out," I comment flatly, as I push the scotch filled glass over to him. We often sit here like this, mulling over things because he has an apartment a few floors down, so he can be at the ready whenever we need him. Lately though, he has sub-let his apartment to a military buddy he has recently employed and has been spending time in Xander's penthouse not far away, while Xander is in Australia.

"Well, the security check on Creepy Guy shows he is a loose cannon, particularly when he has had a few drinks. And he is known for abusing, manhandling, and hitting women, so it is a good thing Emily was quick witted enough to hide and call you."

"Geezus." Groaning, I rub my forehead wearily. "What do you suggest we do?"

"I think Emily shouldn't go to work for a few days till he finds another target to stalk. But she should probably have a security detail just in case." He takes a swig of his drink, then turns to me. "Speaking of quick-witted, that was a great idea hiding in the doorway. Even I had difficulty seeing you." Smirking, he continues, "Interesting photo angles, though, taken from under your arm. How did you manage that?"

"Oh, fuck off." Sighing heavily again, I utter, "Emily took the photos. I was shielding her from sight, okay?"

"Shielding her how? Like blocking the doorway with your big head?" Ramon mocks, but before I can answer, "Fuck off" again, Emily returns to the kitchen.

"No, Ethan did a wonderful job by pressing me against the wall, pretending to kiss me." She says it with such innocence, but it doesn't sound like I was 'protecting' her.

Ramon gives me a side eye glance and a stupid smirk, nodding and says, tongue-in-cheek, "Pretended, huh?" I throw him a baleful glare.

"Did you get onto Simone, Em?" Changing the subject, I ask about the arrangements for some of Emily's belongings to be dropped off. She asks for my address, which I give her willingly, so she can text Simone.

"Emily, Ramon says the man who followed you is not a nice character at all and suggests you don't go into work for the next couple of days."

Her head snaps up, a worried look on her face, and she blurts, "Oh, but I have to work. I need to pay my rent."

"I understand that, but it is not safe for you to go to the restaurant right now. Can you pick up some temp work elsewhere for a few days?"

Exhaling loudly, Emily weighs up my suggestion as a compromise. "I'll try. Ramon, how long will this go on for?"

"Hard to say, but guys like that usually lose interest in a subject fairly quickly, transferring their anger to someone else."

"I'm so sorry to have involved you both in this. All I did was refuse to serve the guy some alcohol we didn't even have in to serve and it has blown so out of proportion."

"This is not your fault, Emily. This guy targeted you tonight because you stood up to him, calling out his bad behavior. You were well within your right to refuse him service. The fact that he has stalked you as payback is on him. He has the issues, Emily, not you." The vehemence in Ramon's words must surprise Emily as much as they do me, because we wear similar wide-eyed looks.

"I've never heard you say so many words before." Ramon issues a guttural humph at my jibe and downs his scotch.

Emily snickers then says, holding back a smile, "I'll let Rashida and Lorenzo know, so they can be careful too," and scurries away to make another call.

"Want me to arrange someone to tail Emily? Make sure she is safe?" Ramon queries, certain that is my preferred option.

Nodding, I reply, "Yeah. Thanks, mate. But tell them to stay out of sight. I don't want her spooked by someone else following her." He gives me a sardonic side eye as if I should have realized that was a given.

As shrewd and direct as ever, Ramon stares into his glass as he swirls the half-melted ice around it and probes, "What's going on between you two?"

"Nothing. We just have some history, and I did the wrong thing by her." I can tell from the way he eyes me that his bullshit meter is ticking in the red zone. "I'm just trying to make it right," I add flatly.

"If you say so," is his only comment, dripping with cynicism.

Chapter Twenty-Four

EMILY

After I hang up from telling Rashida of tonight's events, I sit in the quiet nook in Ethan's apartment, my head in my hands, reviewing how bad things could have gone, and grateful that Ethan had given me his number in case I needed it. This apartment is huge, and I can vaguely hear the men's voices, but not what they are saying. Thankful that I could lean on them when I needed to, and that they could give me some practical advice, I rack my brain trying to work out how I can repay them. Despite being in similar verbally abusive situations with Bradley, he had only stalked me after we had broken up, and I knew his triggers so felt more capable of managing the situation and being able to de-escalate his anger.

Tonight, that man's behavior was totally unexpected, making it far scarier than anything I had encountered. My panicky thoughts scattered, leaving me adrift in a sea of turbulent emotions, past traumatic scars rearing their ugly heads to compound the current distressing scenario. Ethan's clear-headed actions had got us to safety, but his presence had added another layer of disturbed emotions. Not as scary, but equally as volatile.

When he hovered over me in the doorway, holding me close to him, his head lowered near mine, inhaling his delectable sandalwood scent, I wanted so badly to feel his lips against mine, to feel the incendiary passion that we once shared, the obliterating, mind-numbing lust that demanded satiation. Past haunting the present again. Then his lips meshed with mine. I know it was to distract me from the yellow sports car prowling past us, but my gasp was from the zap that shot like electricity from my mouth to my feet when our lips touched. His mouth is just as divine as I remember, entrancing and sinful, rich and flavorsome like chocolate, and just as decadent. And just like chocolate, you can't stop at just one taste.

My rollercoaster of emotions is taking its toll, and I am feeling very tired and wiped out, probably due to the adrenaline wearing off. Again, I shake my head in my hands, thoughts wildly circling, wondering how to extricate myself from this situation. I feel sure that if I stay here with Ethan, I will be lusting after him now that he has awoken those feelings I fought so hard to bury. And I don't want to be a 'pity fuck'.

"I'll take them to her myself. I need to see that she is okay." Hearing Simone's voice, loud and assertive as if she is speaking to a difficult passenger, I stand and lumber through the doorway to the kitchen, scrunching my forehead as I see her and Ramon in a stand-off. Ethan wanders in as well, his phone in hand, and seems just as confused as I am by her raised voice and Ramon's steely glare and intimidating stance.

Simone catches my movement over Ramon's shoulder and shrieks, "Oh sweety. Are you okay?" as she side-steps around him. She rushes across the room to draw me into a huge bear hug as I nod to her, dropping the canvas duffle bag of my clothes but doesn't give me a chance to reply before she pulls away slightly, waving her arm in

Ramon's direction. "This muscle-headed shit for brains wouldn't let me see you." I catch the pissed off eye roll he throws toward Ethan as he stomps away in the opposite direction and Ethan's returned shrug.

Trying to keep the peace all round, I respond wearily to her concern. "I'm okay now Sim, but was pretty frightened earlier. Ramon came to get us, so he was probably trying to protect me from any more emotional upheaval."

"Humph," she scoffs. "Wait, what do you mean by 'us'?"

"I told you on the phone." Sighing, I clarify, "Ethan came to help me when I called him, and Ramon came to pick us up. Ramon and Ethan feel it best for me to not return home or go to the restaurant for a couple of days, just in case."

"Ethan?" she questions with a disparaging tone, as if the penny has just dropped for her as to which Ethan I mean.

"Yes?" Ethan responds to his name. He has been leaning on the kitchen bench behind her, texting on his phone and pretending to not pay attention to our conversation. Even in my tired state, it is comical to see Simone spin around with surprise at the sound of his voice, her mouth agape, while he looks at her from across the room, expecting her to continue her question to him.

"Him?" she mouths when she turns back around. Pressing my lips together, trying not to smile, I nod. Her eyes widen, her anxious gaze locking onto mine as she probes, "Are you going to be okay here?" Again, I nod, rubbing her upper arm gently to ease her concern, knowing what she is really asking is if I will manage to be in Ethan's presence because of how much he hurt me.

Ethan has moved next to us and butts in. "Of course she will be." I can't miss the edge of haughtiness in his voice.

I yawn. "Yes, Sim. I'll be fine. Thanks so much for dropping these things over to me." Her glance flits between me and Ethan before scrutinizing me further, then she nods and hugs me again, whispering in my ear, "Call me if you need anything."

Simone turns and addresses Ethan. "Will this elevator take me back to the foyer?"

"Yes. Thanks for helping out tonight, Simone." He walks her to it, pressing the button and the doors slide open.

"Look after her, or you'll have me to answer to," she warns, stepping into the elevator and glaring at Ethan. He gives her a respectful nod and waits for the doors to close before walking back over to me.

"You have some wonderfully loyal friends, Emily," he comments with a warm smile.

"Yes, I do." My smile is tight and weary. "Would you mind showing me where I am sleeping, Ethan? I am wrung out and just want to go to bed."

"Of course." He takes me on a tour of the apartment, pointing out the study where Ramon has escaped to, and I take the opportunity to thank him again. Ethan continues by showing me his bedroom, which is just down the hall from the guest room where I will be staying. I am quite impressed with the styling and décor throughout, providing a casual air of luxury and elegance, with my room no exception. It is large and spacious, with its own ensuite, and the oak-colored furniture and varied russet tonal furnishings provide an inviting warmth and coziness.

"You should have everything you need here, Emily, but let me know if you want anything else." His words ring in my ears after I thank him, closing the door behind him as he leaves. Ethan is the perfect host, and I keep reminding myself to view him that way, and that our earlier kiss was just a result of the situation.

Showering, I scrub my skin trying to remove the residual crawling sensations of being stalked, then rummage through my bag for some clothes, dressing in some short satin pajamas that I rarely wear, and slide under the covers of the comfortable king-sized bed. Musing that the bed is not too hard, nor too soft, but just right, just like the nursery rhyme, I chuckle to myself and question why Simone packed these nightclothes, but their sleek softness, combined with the luxurious ambiance makes me feel safe and pampered, like I am in a five-star hotel with not a care in the world. Sighing contentedly, I quickly fall into a deep sleep.

***

Next morning, the smell of coffee wafts into my room, rousing me from a turbulent night of tossing and turning, resulting from dreams of being chased, and hot, torrid sex with Ethan.

Startled to realize I am not in my own room, I bolt upright. Yesterday's events break through my morning fog, and I groan knowing I have to face Ethan again. Not quite sure how I will look him in the eye after all the deliciously wonderful ways we enjoyed each other's bodies in my dreams, I draw in a deep breath, get up, wash my face, and change into some jeans and a t-shirt, tying my long hair into a messy bun, then navigate my way back to the kitchen.

Ethan is behind the bench, cooking up some breakfast, while Ramon is perched on a stool at the end of the opposite side, texting on his phone.

"Good morning." The sunshiny lilt in my voice has both their heads spinning around, their gazes boring into me, and I give them a beaming smile. *Why wouldn't I be smiling, having two gorgeously hot hunks to start my day with*, I ponder, salivating over their toned physiques displayed beautifully in their snug fitting gym workout gear.

Blushing at where my crazy mind is going, I deflect by asking Ethan, "What are you cooking? It smells amazing." Ramon gives me a nod but remains silent as I pad barefoot past him to sit on a stool at the bench as well.

"Scrambled eggs. Some protein after our workout. Would you like some too?" Ethan's intense gaze shifts to a platonic expression before he turns back to the stovetop and stirs the eggs some more.

"Yes please, but only if there is enough," I reply, my voice a touch breathless, as I feel my own eggs cooking from the heat my core is generating at the sight of Ethan.

His blue t-shirt stretches across his broad sculpted back, his arm band tattoos clearly evident, while loose-legged black running shorts with a tighter fitting underlining sit on his narrow hips, shaping his firm rounded buttocks. Ramon is similarly dressed, his large biceps bulging under the ribbing of the t-shirt sleeve, tattoos prominently displayed in a long pattern down both arms.

"Plenty to go round," Ethan comments as he lifts four pieces of toast out of the toaster and places them on some waiting plates, then scoops the eggs out of the pan onto the toast. He pushes the plates in front of Ramon and me, before turning to get more eggs from the refrigerator.

"Ethan, you eat these while they are hot. I can cook my own," I offer.

"It's fine, Emily. It won't take long." Deftly, he cracks and beats the additional eggs.

Not wanting to be waited on, I spot a coffee machine on the bench and saunter over to it. "Would either of you like another coffee, then?" I enquire, letting the scrambled eggs cool a bit, but am surprised by Ramon's smirk when he responds with a "yes please", and Ethan's aghast look.

"It's okay. I'll make it in a minute, Em," Ethan expresses in an airy manner, but as he looks up at me, his smile is tight and his set expression seems to hide his irritation before he turns to add the beaten eggs to the heated pan. My eyes ping-pong between his back and Ramon's watchful glance as he eats, trying to decipher the undercurrent I feel.

Ramon's mouth tilts up at one edge and his eyes glitter with mirth as he mocks in his deep gravelly voice, "Ethan is very precious about his coffee machine, Emily."

"Aah." I acknowledge, tilting my head to hide my smile when Ethan turns and glares at Ramon with a look that says, 'fuck off'. I am loving the banter and friendly rivalry between these two men.

"Do you mind if I make a coffee, Ethan? I am a trained barista and promise not to break it?" Ethan huffs at my request and grumbles something I can't hear over the noise of the overhead exhaust fan. When he says nothing further, I raise an eyebrow and giving Ramon a smug, tight lip smile, I ask them their coffee preference and expertly get two coffees underway, serving a long black to Ramon who has finished his breakfast, and a flat white to Ethan who is just sitting down to eat his.

Taking my plate to the coffee machine, I scoop a forkful of egg into my mouth while the coffee crema drizzles into my cup, then another forkful while I steam the milk, then pour the fluffy, silky liquid artfully into my cup.

I move to stand opposite both men while I finish my eggs. Ramon holds his cup in both hands and lifts it to his mouth, then groans. My head jerks to look at him, as does Ethan's, and I notice his blissful expression as I glance at him. "Oh, that is good," he says on a sigh. Peering at him, I try to decipher if he is having a dig at me, but he turns to Ethan and continues, "So much better than the shit you call coffee."

Ethan rewards him with another glare, picks up his cup, and sips at it, his eyes closing briefly in enjoyment.

"God, yeah. It is," Ethan acknowledges and takes another gulp, while I smile to myself. As I've finished my breakfast, I collect the dirty plates and cutlery, bending to stack them in the nearby dishwasher.

"No need for you to do that Emily," Ethan protests.

"I may be your guest Ethan, but I am not a freeloader. I'm happy to do whatever I can to thank you for coming to my rescue," I state, my chin high and my shoulders held back. My voice is strong and determined, my reasoning is clear as I stare at him, but I realize my choice of words could have been better when he peers at me, his green eyes flashing with sexy devilment as if I have just offered sexual favors as repayment.

I hear Ramon choke on his coffee, so lowering my gaze, straight-faced but feeling my cheeks warm, I clarify, "To help around the house." Hurriedly finishing my coffee, I also add my cup to the dishwasher.

"Okay." Ethan tries hard not to smile, although the roguish twinkle in his eyes as I glance back up at him when I close the dishwasher indicates his appreciation of my unintentional innuendo.

Fortunately, my phone rings and, excusing myself, I answer it with relief. "Hi Rashida." I move into the small nook I used yesterday. When I return to the kitchen a short time later it is empty, so I head to the guest room where I am staying, noticing Ethan and Ramon huddled over a laptop as I pass the study, both focusing intently on the screen. Ethan points and exclaims, "There," so I continue unnoticed down the corridor to collect my purse and backpack. Returning a few minutes later, I poke my head through the doorway into the study. "I'm heading out to meet Rashida and Lorenzo. Do I need a pass or something to use the elevator when I come back?"

Their heads snap up at my words, their expressions hard and fixed, almost ruthless, making me take a step backward. Ethan stands and walks over to me, his persona shifting to the congenial businessman that I am more comfortable with. "We've arranged with the doorman for you to have a keycard. Just see him on your way out so he can give it to you." His tone is cool and matter-of-fact, as if I am running an errand for him, and nodding in acknowledgment, I glimpse Ramon quietly talking to someone on his phone.

I turn to leave when Ethan's voice halts me. "Oh, and Emily..." I look back over my shoulder at him. His eyebrows draw together and, resting his large warm hand on my shoulder, his expression softens as he urges, "Call me if you need anything. I'll text you Ramon's number as well."

"Okay. Thanks," I mumble, baffled by the tingling in my shoulder at his touch and the apparent concern in his voice. I walk away, feeling Ethan's gaze boring into my back, but catch sight of him slipping back into the study as the elevator doors shut. Maybe I am imagining things because of my heightened emotions over the last twenty-four hours, but there is a prickly undercurrent of yearning when I am near him. Reminding myself to be extra careful being under the same roof as him, and not get carried away with his charm, I approach the doorman as instructed, then head out onto the street.

Chapter Twenty-Five

EMILY

Rashida and Lorenzo are waiting for me in the bustling plaza outside the recruitment offices because I need to explain to them and my staffing officer why I am unable to return to the restaurant for the moment.

Hugging me tightly, they ask several times if I am okay. After providing them with all the details, and why I am staying with Ethan, they agree that is the best thing to do for now, relief evident on their faces that Ethan was on hand.

"Rashida, are you still working at the restaurant tonight?" I query. When she confirms that she is, I ask that she explain my absence to Marguerite and Johan. "Please be careful if you see that man in or around there, and don't leave alone."

Lorenzo pipes up that he will meet her and escort her home for the next couple of nights, just to be on the safe side. We continue by discussing our upcoming trip to Scotland when they advise me that Tom and Aaron will be joining us. Then we finalize some of the arrangements before they take off for work, leaving me free to speak to the staffing officer. After a bit of shuffling around, she manages to secure some more shifts for me as a nanny as well as some barista work, starting straight away in a cafe where I have previously worked.

When I step back outside, the beautiful sunshiny but cool morning has morphed into a hot, airless midday on the city streets. Traffic is heavy, and vehicle fumes mix with wafts from garbage cans sitting on the curb ready for collection. My nose crinkles with distaste as I wander past, soon savoring the delicious bakery and coffee aromas as I walk the short distance to the café.

Yippee, just in time for the lunchtime rush, I moan inwardly, but knowing that I need to save more money for my trip away, I grit my teeth and plaster on a smile as I greet the café staff. I like working here because they have a good system, and all the staff are friendly and professional. The manager waves me toward the coffee machine, yelling above the noise to "just make coffees. Tahleeah will take the orders."

By the time the café shuts a grueling four hours later, my feet and back hurt, and I have a headache building from the noise, heat, and lack of food. The other barista and I pumped out hundreds of hot beverages and iced coffees to the diners and takeaway customers, with very little opportunity to look at anyone or anything other than the coffee machine. However, I have noticed a big, burly, serious-looking man on the few occasions I glanced outside. Once he was on the phone, another time he was reading a newspaper and, as I exit the café, I recollect vaguely thinking it odd that he seemed to linger so long but was nowhere to be seen now.

Oh, you are imagining things, Emily, because of last night's scare, I chide myself, trudging through the still busy streets. Realizing I haven't had a chance to check my phone all afternoon, I drag it out of my pocket, noticing two messages from Ethan from earlier this morning, wondering where I was, but nothing since. I shoot off a reply, letting him know I am on my way back to his apartment, sighing as I remember his place is much further away from this part of town. My poor tired feet throb at the thought of that additional walking, sidestepping slower fellow pedestrians, until I spot a rental e-scooter parked up ahead. With relief, I process the payment, don my helmet and scoot uptown.

After parking the scooter on the corner half a block away, I walk the short distance to Ethan's apartment building, pondering how nice soaking in a hot bath would be when a horn blares behind me. Although that is not unusual in this city, I turn my head to see what the commotion is about. A motorcycle zips in very close to the front of a car and speeds up the road past me. *Idiot,* I curse to myself, but then recognize that his clothing and size seem very similar to the fellow who had been lingering around the café. His helmet hides his features so I can't be too sure it is the same man but other than thinking what a freaky coincidence it is for him to be here I shrug it off as some random wearing commonly comparable clothing. Thinking nothing more of it, I greet the doorman and let myself into the elevator which whisks me to the 32nd floor.

Silence regales me as I step into the apartment. Wandering to the kitchen and then past the study to see if Ethan is home, I am relieved that the place seems empty. I have no idea what sort of business hours Ethan keeps but expect he won't be home for at least an hour or two, so decide to take a long hot bath.

Traipsing into my room, I drop my backpack onto the bed then move to the ensuite and run the bath. Too fatigued last night to take much notice, I spy bottles of high end bubble bath, body wash, shampoo, and conditioner, as well as rolled washcloths, sitting on a shelf at the end of the almost freestanding bath.

Wondering who Ethan entertains here on a regular basis to warrant supplying them, my jaw clenches and a burning sensation churns in my stomach. Returning to the bedroom I rummage through the bag Simone brought over, before up ending it onto the bed.

Taking stock of what I have here, I realize that I'm limited to a few days' worth of clothing at best, and hoping I won't need to be here more than that, I conclude that I will need to wash yesterday's and today's clothes in preparation for work over the next couple of days. I notice an envelope addressed to me sticking out from underneath the pile of clothes, so pull it out and turn it over, discovering that there is no return address. *Hmm, how odd,* I muse, but throw it back on the bed to read after my bath.

After I fumble through my backpack looking for my cordless earphones, I grab my phone then wander into the ensuite. I add some of the beautiful lavender-scented bubble bath, before turning off the water, undressing, tying up my hair, and stepping into the deep bath.

Earphones in, eyes closed and humming to my favorite playlist while I relax, it occurs to me that the water has cooled so I must have been soaking for a while.

Sighing and sitting up, I lean forward and pull the plug, then stand and look for a towel. I can't reach the ones hanging under the window without getting out of the bath and don't really want to drip all over the shiny tiled floor. Then I become aware of a noise behind me and flinch when I see Ethan leaning against the doorframe, holding one out for me, with desire curving his mouth and sparks lighting his sensuous green eyes.

Startled, I gasp, covering my breasts with one arm, while the other conceals my mons. "What are you doing here?" I yelp, not sure which hand to move so that I can take the towel from him.

"No need to cover up, Baby Girl. I remember your exquisite body vividly," Ethan drawls in his sexy husky voice, loud enough for me to hear over the music in my ears.

"Get out, Ethan," I snarl. "How dare you come in here unannounced." Gritting my teeth, my forehead creases into a scowl and I glare at him, doubly annoyed because I can't be intimidating in this hunched pose.

Totally ignoring my rant, his gaze devours my body, then he approaches with the towel stretched between his hands. He raises the fluffy white cloth as a visual barrier, as if to protect my modesty (a bit late for that), and allows me to grab at it so I can wrap it around myself. Once I am covered and have tucked the towel corner underneath the top edge, securing it in place, I rip the earphones out of my ears, gripping them in a clenched fist to stop myself from throwing them at him.

"I did call out to you, but you obviously didn't hear me over your humming," he justifies with a hint of mockery in his cool voice, holding out his hands to help me step out of the bath.

My eyes bore into him, and I press my lips together into a tight, straight line, trying to assess his sincerity. Giving him the benefit of the doubt, though, I place my hands on his upturned palms and gingerly step over the high edge of the bath. My gaze narrows when he continues to hold my hands, his thumbs rubbing over the back of them, leaving an electrified trail in their wake. His soft, tantalizing touch fires memories of our evening of torrid sex, the intense tingling sensation I remember gripping my body like a vise. *Damn the man for his impact on my traitorous body.*

As if realizing from my etched expression how pissed I am with him, he states, "I'll let you get dressed, then we'll chat."

"Thanks. Pity you didn't do that earlier," I bark at his retreating back, my cutting words unaffectedly fall off him and I hear him chuckle as he exits the room.

Drying myself with anger-fueled vigor, I stomp into the bedroom to dress, throwing my clean clothing back into the duffel bag. Bundling the dirty garments in my arms, I spot my letter and collect it too, marching down the hallway to find Ethan on his laptop at the kitchen bench.

"Where is your washing machine?" I hiss, surprised steam isn't coming out of my ears. Ethan lifts his head and, being the wise man he is, stands without saying a word—although he tries to hide a smirk—and walks into a wide butler's pantry that I had been unaware of. When I follow him, he points to the top-of-the-line front loader machine and dryer tucked around the corner. "Thanks," I spit as I stride past him. Dumping my armful of clothes on top of the machine, I open the door and throw the clothes in, but then become aware of eyes on me and turn my head. "What?" I snarl at Ethan, who is watching me with an inscrutable expression. Turning to face him, my hands on my hips confrontationally, I scowl and taunt, "Are you going to gawk at me washing my clothes too?" Ethan puts his hands up, as if in surrender, releases a pent-up breath, and then walks back out to the kitchen. Shutting the washing machine door harder than I intended, it slams, but is somehow cathartic. Twisting the control knob and loading the detergent, I set the washer in motion, and pace around the utility area till I can better control my fury, then remember the letter I was going to read. I retrieve it from where it has fallen on the floor and carefully open it.

Dear Emily

Thank you for getting in touch. Yes, you have the right
person. I was once married to your mother, Joanne, but
now have a grown up family here in England who have
no idea of my previous life in Australia. And I have no
desire to disrupt the status quo.

However, I am prepared to meet up with you on a
one-time only basis as you are on vacation in England.

Please email me to arrange a meeting date and time on
bruce.baxter234@gmail.com.

Sincerely,
Bruce Baxter

Dropping to sit cross legged on the floor, with my back against the washer, I re-read it several times, trying to define how I feel about the contents. I am pleased that Bruce took the time to respond when he could easily have ignored me altogether. But I am disappointed that he is rejecting me again, albeit after a brief meeting out of curiosity.

Sighing heavily, I drop the letter into my lap and rest my head against the machine, closing my eyes. I didn't expect to play 'happy families', but I had hoped to have a more encouraging, welcoming response.

Tears slowly trickle from the corner of my eyes as my inner child feels the sting of rejection, and I swipe them away with annoyance. The rational adult part of me recognizes that Bruce is at least prepared to meet with me, so I should be happy with that. It also reasons that my anger with Ethan made Bruce's letter seem, irrationally, like another slap in the face. Uncertain whether I will arrange a meeting with him if he is so reluctant to know me, I wish, not for the first time, that I could discuss it with Mom.

Just as I wipe another lot of tears away, Ethan's soft concerned voice asks, "Em, are you okay?" Sighing heavily, I open my eyes and blurrily see him crouching down in front of me, his brow crinkled.

"Yes, I'll be fine," I respond, my voice thick as I hold the letter while I awkwardly get to my feet. "What is it with you, sneaking up on me and watching me?" I grumble, my tone flat, watching as he also stands.

"You've been in here for a while. I just wanted to see if you were alright." Genuine concern rings in the timbre of his voice. "I'm sorry I made you cry, Em." Then he extends a hand and gently wipes the damp tear trail from my face with his thumb.

"*You* didn't," I retort with an edge of bitterness and an element of truth, knowing my anger with him wouldn't have resulted in tears. His eyes flash with hurt, or maybe injured pride, but before I can work out which it is, his head tilts slightly, his brow furrows and his expression shifts to one of puzzlement. I hold up the paper in my hand and add, "I got some news that didn't sit well."

"Do you want to talk about it?

"No. I'm still too annoyed with you Ethan to discuss the letter rationally." My words are clipped and terse, but honest.

"Fair enough. How about I get us a drink and we can talk about what happened earlier?" he offers in a conciliatory manner. Studying his open and friendly countenance with narrowed eyes, I nod in agreement but with an air of suspicion because Bradley used this ploy on me many times. He would lull me into a false sense of security only to lambast me, laying all the blame at my feet. Ethan turns and walks out, while I lag behind, doubting Ethan would use the same tactics, but I am on guard nevertheless.

"Would you like tea, coffee, wine, or something stronger?" Ethan, the ever-courteous host, asks as I return to the kitchen.

"Tea, please." As I sit at the bench next to where his laptop is positioned, I watch him moving around, opening cupboards, getting out the necessities, offering me a selection of teas, and I take note of where he keeps them so I can make my own next time.

After he places my cup in front of me, he wanders around the bench and sits next to me. "Em, I apologize for encroaching on your privacy earlier." Ethan pauses, and when I don't respond, he continues, "I had called out to you several times and when you didn't answer I went looking for you. When I saw your things dumped all over your bed and heard what I thought was moaning from your ensuite, I thought you were hurt." Pausing again, assessing my expression to gauge my reaction, he continues again when there is none. "Then, when I saw you were okay, I was mesmerized by the sight of you in the bath. I couldn't look or walk away, even though I knew I should. I didn't mean to embarrass you and understand you being angry with me. Please forgive me."

Turning my head and lifting my gaze to stare at him, I blow out a breath and give him a small nod. "You had no right to do that Ethan. You forfeited any right you may have had when you ditched me," I vent, still pissed with him. "Don't do it again."

"Not without your permission." His face wears a mischievous expression as he throws me a cheeky smile, and I struggle to stay angry.

Chapter Twenty-Six

EMILY

While we sip our tea, Ethan comments, "I thought we might have dinner in about an hour if that suits you." I nod in agreement. "In the meantime, tell me about your day. You caught up with Rashida and Lorenzo, didn't you?"

"Yes, and Lorenzo will be accompanying Rashida back to the hostel after her shifts, just in case the crazy man decides to stalk her too. I also spoke with my recruitment officer and they have offered me some different work, so I won't be at the restaurant for a while. I managed to pick up four hours' work this afternoon in a café.

As we continue to chat Ethan mentions that Xander flew in today and will probably want to check in with me to ensure that I am alright, even though Ethan filled him in on my current circumstances.

Now that my anger has subsided, Ethan's charm and relaxed conversation has me relaxed and laughing. I feel like we are back to the comfortable, easy friendship we used to have and am thrilled that he seems to feel the same way.

While I clear the tea mugs, Ethan takes the elevator downstairs to collect our dinner order from the concierge and, while eating, he enquires, "Do you feel up to talking about your letter, Em?" I consider his question, not sure if I want to discuss it just yet, but figure Ethan would be as good a sounding board as any. I fill him in on how I came to learn about my father, and how I had reached out to him after my mother died and I pass the letter over for him to read.

"How do you feel about this?" He sits looking at me, his face unreadable as he pushes the piece of paper back to me.

My shoulders hunch, my head lowers, and I ponder his question, evaluating whether my feelings have altered now that I am in a more rational frame of mind.

"Disappointed and hurt by his rejection, but totally understanding of his decision." My head lifts, I bite my lip and meet his gaze before speaking. "After no contact from him for thirty years, I didn't expect him to be champing at the bit to get to know me, but I thought there might be some semblance of excitement about me." A frustrated humph sound escapes my throat, and my lopsided smile is edged with bitterness.

"I can appreciate that. Are you inclined to meet up with him?" His expression and tone remain neutral. I can see why he is such a successful businessman. He gives nothing away but absorbs more than he lets on, asking astute questions and really listening.

"I don't know." My gaze drops again to my clasped hands resting on the table. "When I was a little girl, all I wanted was a daddy; someone who would sit me high on his shoulders, play games, and tickle me, like I saw other fathers doing. But as I got older, I recognized my mom's resilience, strength, and love and was satisfied with that. In my mind, he was dead. A nameless ghost, a procreator, no different from a sperm donor."

Tears well in my eyes and try to rapidly blink them away. It feels like a dam wall has been opened inside of me. Heaving a sigh from the depths of my soul, I continue, my voice husky and a bit wobbly. "But finding out his name made him real, you know?"

He reaches over and captures my hands in his, his expression impassive while his eyes follow his thumb as it rubs over mine, and he waits patiently for me to finish.

"I suppose deep down I contacted him because I yearned to be accepted and loved as his 'little girl' and wanted to put a face to the name. So, his one and only meeting request slashes my inner child's expectations to pieces, and that's what I must come to terms with." I watch Ethan as he nods in understanding and then I blurt out, "It hardly seems worth the effort to meet up if he doesn't want to acknowledge me, though."

"That decision is yours to make, Em. But think about how you will feel in the future if you don't take the opportunity. Will you regret not meeting him? Regardless of whether a relationship with him continues, you will at least know you met him, spoke to him, know what he looks like, and have memories of him." Pausing for his words to sink in, he adds, "You're not a quitter either, Emily. You have fought through some tougher situations than this, at the hands of someone who professed to love you. You may feel hurt at Bruce's apparent rejection, but you have picked yourself up and recovered after going through much worse." Again, he pauses, seeing acknowledgment of the truth of his words light in my eyes. "Think about it from Bruce's perspective too. Maybe there was a reason he hadn't contacted you?"

"What do you mean?"

"You're a very fair person, Em, who normally looks at both sides of a situation. There could be a possibility that Bruce and your mom came to some sort of agreement." At my puzzled expression, he elaborates, his voice softening. "Although he loved our mother, Xander always begrudged her for leaving him with his father, and his resulting boarding school existence. It was only when he married Georgie that he spoke to Mom about it and learned she and Xander's dad made an agreement to share him, with her only getting access to him in the school holidays. With an adult perspective, he was able to rationalize and forgive, knowing she only had his best interests at heart."

Comprehension must have shown on my face because he pats my hands, then releases them, leaning backward into his chair. "It's entirely up to you, Em."

"Thank you, Ethan." My heart swells with how much I value his opinion. I stand and step next to him, bending to kiss him on the cheek to show my heartfelt gratitude for our chat. He turns his head, so my kiss lands on his smooth lips.

Pulling back marginally, he purrs, "You're welcome, Emily." His warm breath fanning my mouth robs me of breath. My eyes widen and an involuntary whimper escapes. Standing upright, I take a step backward, watching his expression shift from dreamy to mischievous.

I need to get away from him, so I scoop up my letter, tucking it into my rear jeans pocket, then I gather up the dinner plates, carrying them to the kitchen and placing them in the dishwasher. "Thanks again for dinner and the chat." He nods, his eyes following me like a tiger stalking its prey as I move around the space. "I'll just put my washing in the dryer, then head to my room. I have an early start in the morning," I babble, and escape into the butler's pantry, hearing him snicker once I am out of sight.

As I switch the clothes over, I ponder on what is wrong with me as my desire for Ethan burns through me, consuming my thoughts. My emotions have been all over the place the last couple of days, which is unusual. Now I think about it I can trace it back to seeing Ethan again in the restaurant. I thought I had put all those feelings behind me, but my body seems to be craving him. *Him or sex in general?* my inner voice torments. *Hmm, good point.*

Pacing around the pantry, inhaling and puffing out deep breaths, my mind goes round in circles. I need to get laid by someone other than Ethan, to work out the cause of this emotional upheaval. Tom springs to mind, and our upcoming trip to Scotland might be the perfect opportunity. At least with him, I can justify it as emotionless, casual sex, but with Ethan, I already have emotional hang ups from our history.

Unfortunately, sex, as infrequent as it has been over the last 6 months, hasn't been as good with anyone else as it was with Ethan. I have too much baggage where Ethan is concerned to come out unscathed, so the sooner I can return to my apartment and my normal life, the better.

When I am more in control of myself, I poke my head out of the butler's pantry and look around to make sure Ethan isn't in sight. Then I scurry down the corridor, past his study, and into my room, relieved that he is on the phone and facing out the window when I go by. Busying myself in my room, I stow away my limited amount of clothing into a couple of drawers and place my toiletries in the ensuite.

Sitting cross legged on the bed, I drag out my phone and begin drafting a response to Bruce Baxter. I can't bring myself to think of him as 'father', even though I have used that term for him in discussions with others because it makes talking about him easier. I want to mull over my decision before I send off the email. I'm pleased I talked with Ethan about him and, even though he affirmed a lot of what I was thinking, it opened some emotions I hadn't even realized were bottled inside me.

Leaving my room to check on the drying clothes, I notice Ethan has his head in his laptop as I wander past.

"Would you like a drink or anything, Ethan?" I inquire politely, stopping outside his door.

"Huh? No thanks." He barely lifts his head, so engrossed in whatever is on his laptop.

When I return with an armful of freshly dried, sweet-smelling garments, I call out goodnight as I venture past without stopping, only vaguely hearing from the study a mumbled response. After I sort my clothes and get ready for bed, I climb under the covers, savoring the fresh smelling crisp white sheets, and the comfortable mattress before I drift off to sleep.

Running as fast as I can, I can't escape the yellow sports car that is chasing me. No matter how many twists and turns I make it is right on my tail the whole time, taunting me. Looking over my shoulder again, I flee into a dark alley, smashing into a brick wall. Petrified, I turn around, watching the yellow sports car slow a few feet from me, creeping closer and closer, knowing that I have nowhere to go.

"No. No. Please don't," I yell, expecting it to crush me against the wall, but it stops, its front fender barely touching my legs. It menaces me by revving its engine loudly, then backing off, again and again. Screaming, I thrash against the wall, managing to slink past so I am free of the car, but the driver's door opens. Panicking, my rasping breath leaving white clouds in the bitterly cold alley, I whimper as I stare at the darkly clothed figure unfolding from the car.

When he straightens, I sob uncontrollably, terror filling me. The man is huge; his black hoodie stretched taut across his broad chest and bulging biceps, his long legs like tree trunks. One massive hand reaches up and drags the hood off his head. Recognizing the man from the cafe, I screech, "No. No. Please don't." His huge, booted foot thuds on the pavement, echoing as he steps toward me.

He stretches out his arm to grab hold of me, but I press myself as hard as I can against the wall. It gives way, disappearing altogether, and I step backward, my eyes fixed on the giant, menacing man, who for some reason doesn't move. I take another step, falling down a manhole, and just manage to grab the sill, holding on for dear life as my feet swing in open space. Futilely screaming for help, I know I can't hold on much longer. My breathing becomes choppier as my arms strain to hold me.

A shadow falls over me and, expecting to see the frightening man looming above me ready to stomp on my hands, another smaller framed figure, ghostly in appearance, stands at the edge, looking down at me. "Help me. Help," I plead, but the figure rotates in slow motion away from me, his head turning back to watch me. "No. No. Bruce. Please don't go," I scream, but the figure drifts away without giving me a second glance. Just as my fingers are about to slip off, sending me plummeting into the darkness, I hear my name called from a distance.

"Emily. Emily." The voice is more insistent, getting closer and closer. "I've got you, Emily. I've got you." I gradually become aware of a strong wide band holding me, making me feel safe. "Wake up Emily. Wake up." A scent I recognize, a voice that calls to my heart; both permeate the black fog, slowly lifting me out into the light and warmth. "That's it. I've got you, Em. Wake up. I've got you."

Opening my eyes, my head flicks around as I frantically try to work out where I am. My stiff body is still in flight mode, and I try pushing away from the constraints around my upper arms. The room is mostly dark, apart from a pool of light from a bedside lamp surrounding the bed. The sheets are bunched at the end of the bed. A gentle deep voice coos in my ear, soothing away the last of the panic. "You're safe, Emily. I've got you. You're safe." My breathing and senses start to return to normal and I look up into worried green eyes. *Ethan.* I sigh with relief, realizing his strong arms are the bands that hold me. That I am safe, and it was all a dream. My head drops to his chest and my arms wrap around him in a tight grip, hanging on to my salvation with all I have. Then I ugly cry, my tears glistening on his lightly tanned, hairless chest. Ethan tucks my head under his chin, stroking my hair and back in comfort, shushing me until my tears dry up.

"I'm sorry," I utter in a small voice against his chest, wiping away the moisture on my face.

He gently pushes my shoulders away from him, frames my face with his hands, then looks deeply into my eyes with an expression on his face that I am too muddled to define. "Oh, Em, don't be sorry. You had a bad dream. There's nothing to apologize for." His hands sweep the hair off my face before he lowers his mouth to kiss me on the forehead. "Do you want to tell me about your dream?" He kisses my forehead again before tucking me under his chin, my cheek resting on his collarbone.

"It's so confusing, Ethan. I was being chased by a yellow sports car and it had me pinned against a wall. But the man that got out of it was a huge, muscly man, fierce-looking, intimidating, just like the man I saw a few times earlier. The wall disappeared, and I stepped away from him and fell down a manhole, dangling by my fingers. Then this thinner, shorter man, who was gray and ghostly, appeared, looking down at me. I begged for help, but he turned and walked away. Then I fell. But you caught me. How? You weren't in my dream?"

"I heard you yelling and came to check on you. You were screaming and thrashing in your sleep. I wrapped you in my arms, talking to you till you woke up." His voice is soft and gentle but has a distinct catch in it when he mentions my screaming. "Can I get you a drink of water or something?"

I give my head a small shake. "No, but thank you for coming in." Lifting my head, I look up at him. "Please don't leave me just yet."

"I won't, Baby Girl. How about we lie down, and I hold you until you fall asleep?"

"Yes, please." I yawn, and lie down, then Ethan follows, dragging the covers over us. I readjust to lie on my side, with my head nestled on his shoulder and my arm across his chest. Ethan wraps his arm around my shoulders, occasionally stroking my hair. His gentle touch reminds me of how Mom used to comfort me after a nightmare when I was little, assuring me I was safe and loved. That same sense of safeness and well-being washes over me as I lay in his arms.

Chapter Twenty-Seven

ETHAN

Emily's soft snuffling noises tell me she has finally fallen asleep after her nightmare. And I am in heaven. She snoozed against me like this on our one night of sex, but I don't recall feeling so in sync with her, nor so much pleasure in having her so close, both physically and emotionally. A warmth fills me, and for the first time, I feel truly content. Inhaling the light floral fragrance of her hair, I smile and close my eyes, thoughts of protecting and pleasuring Emily lulling me into sleep.

My morning hard-on is throbbing as I grind it against Emily's delectable bottom, my arm reaching over her front, slipping under her satin pajama top so my hands can fondle her breasts. I'm obsessed with them; their soft whitish pink color, their weight, their squishiness. They fit so perfectly in my hands that I never want to let them go. The thought flits through my semi-conscious mind that this dream seems more intense and realistic than yesterday morning's dream about her. Moaning as she pushes back against me, I bend my arm, which rests under her head, crossing it across her chest so my hand rests on her opposite shoulder, holding her even closer.

She arches her neck, rubbing her head against my jaw, making incoherent sounds as her hand reaches behind me to grip my butt cheek. Strangely, I can feel the warmth of her hand, but not the skin on skin sensation like I have when my hands rest on her breasts. *Damn pajama pants*, I grumble to myself. *Wait, why am I wearing pajama pants?*

Coherency seeps into my foggy brain, recognizing that I usually sleep naked, and it dawns on me that the beautiful, warm figment of my imagination nestled against me is, in fact, real. *What? Why is Emily in my bed?* Flinging my eyes open, I blink a few times until they adjust to the sunlight streaming through the edges of the closed blind, then look around the room, realizing it is my guest room. The one Emily is currently sleeping in. With me.

She stirs against me, my movements having woken her. Regretfully, I slide my hand from her breasts, letting it rest on her stomach while my other arm drops to the bed. I know the moment she is fully awake because she pushes away from me with a start and sits up. Her sleep-fuzzy eyes stare at me with confusion.

Propping my head on my hand, I smile at her as if waking up next to her is as natural as breathing. "Good morning, Em."

"Ethan. What are you doing in my bed?" Her voice is husky from sleep and there is a wariness in her eyes.

"You had a nightmare. Do you remember? I came in to console you?" As if clarity returns to her sleep-addled brain, she looks around the room, then back at me, and nods.

"You asked me to stay with you until you fell asleep, and I must have drifted off as well," I elaborate.

"Thank you for staying." Her smile is shy but grateful. "I'm sorry I disturbed you."

"Don't be. I've had the best night's sleep in a long time." Rolling to my back, I make sure the bedclothes are covering my rigid erection, then, with my hands behind my head, I peer into her eyes. "Do you remember your dream?"

"Yes, it's coming back to me. Very strange. And terrifying. And it's even stranger waking up with you, holding me tight against you." Her focus seems to turn inwards. Recognizing the awkwardness of the situation, I roll away from her and clamber out of the bed, ensuring my back is to her so I don't embarrass her with my raging cock protruding from my pajama pants.

"What are you up to today?" I enquire, looking over my shoulder at her, catching sight of her hungry eyes checking out my back and pajama-clad buttocks. "Like what you see?"

Her eyes widen and fly to mine. "What? Oh. Um. I'm working today."

The pink hue of her blush is so endearing that I fight hard against grabbing her and kissing her senseless. Instead, I walk to the door and casually say, "Okay, well, I'll probably see you later then."

Pacing into my ensuite, I hit the shower. I needed to get out of her room before I took advantage of her sleep-numbed state. Horniness courses through my body from being so close to her, yearning to be inside her. Her scent still lingers on my skin and as much as it galls me, I need to wash it off if I expect to walk around without a hard on all day.

While I stand under the cool water, I try to occupy my mind with today's meetings. This tactic has been a surefire way of deflating my engorged cock in the past, but not today, as memories of Emily's round, soft breasts, and shapely buttocks assail me, keeping my cock ramrod stiff and pulsing with need.

Turning my back to the water and gripping my shaft in my right hand just below the head, I run my thumb over the slit, smearing pre-cum around the head, inhaling deeply as pleasure takes over.

My cock swells painfully, and my hips twitch as I stroke from tip to base, my thumb and forefinger sliding over my glans, dragging and stretching the skin. With every stroke faster than the previous one, I feel my balls tightening, intensifying the pressure, electrifying me with a driving need to cum. My breathing is heavy, my eyes closed and lost in the sensation, when, like a pressure cooker, the internal pressure explodes, spurting out a stream of creamy fluid as my throaty groan echoes off the tiles. My hand squeezes out the last droplets before I lean against the wall of the shower, replete and inhaling deeply.

Fuuck!

Emily always makes me cum hard, with the force and volatility of a volcanic eruption, temporarily frying my brain in the process. Panting, I let the water wash over me, cooling my heated body while I wait for my head to clear. The post-orgasmic feeling of lethargy and sleepiness kicks in and I know I will need a good, strong coffee before heading off to work.

By the time I am dressed and heading out the door with coffees in hand, there is no sign of Emily. I poked my head into her room earlier to make sure she hadn't fallen asleep, but the bed was made and the room tidy, so I assumed she had gone to work.

Ramon is leaning against the passenger side of the car as I come out of the building, opening my door and taking his coffee from me so I can clamber into the back. While he drives, I ask, "You found out any more information on the driver of the yellow sports car?"

"No, nothing that we don't already know, but I should be getting further reports in today. The car hasn't been spotted near Emily's apartment though."

"Good. Hope it stays that way."

Ramon nods and sips his coffee while navigating the traffic with one hand on the wheel, then winces and groans. "You made this coffee, didn't you?" he criticizes, looking at me in the rear-view mirror. "Where is Emily?"

Taking a sip of mine, I grumble, "Fuck off, the coffee's fine," while trying not to turn my lip up at its bitter, burned flavor. "Emily's gone to work this morning."

"Geez, E. You didn't think to let me know?" Ramon chides with frustration.

"What's your problem? You can track her, can't you?" My mocking tone borders on indifference because I know Ramon, who is exceptional at his job, whines when he doesn't have control over every situation.

"Yeah, but that's not the point. Surveillance requires keeping a close eye on someone, which I can't do if I don't know where she is." Shaking his head and huffing out a breath, he mumbles to himself, probably calling me all the names under the sun, while he makes a call.

Ignoring him, I gaze sightlessly out the window, mindlessly sipping my coffee as I watch the streetscape slip by, remembering the feeling of Emily curled against me. It isn't just the physical enjoyment, which is outstanding, but the contentment I feel with her goes much deeper. It's like I finally feel complete, which is strange because I have never felt like I was lacking in emotional fulfillment. However, she fills a void in me I wasn't aware of.

Smiling, I ponder on the thought of waking up next to her every day, then scoff at myself for being so fanciful. As the car comes to a halt, I unwillingly drag my mind back to the day ahead and tell Ramon I will check in with him later as I step out onto the curb.

The morning passes like any other, and in between meetings, I text Emily because she has been at the back of my mind all day.

Ethan

Sorry I missed you this morning. How is your day going? Where are you working today? I'm not sure what time I will be home.

Emily responds mid-afternoon, letting me know she has been working in the café today, and that she is just heading to a nannying job on the other side of the river. I like the idea that I will see her tonight. I've never had a woman living in my apartment, and even though Emily has been with me for only a couple of days, I am really enjoying her company. Just as I am about to put my phone away, another text beeps. "Damn," I curse as I glance at it.

Lainey

Are we still on for tonight, Tiger?

Ethan

Sorry. Change of plans. I'll call you in a few days.

I'd forgotten all about Lainey. I messaged her last week, vaguely arranging a potential hook-up for this week. The anticipation of Lainey's exquisite assets normally has my loins stirring by now, yet here we are, and all I can think about is Emily. I need to do something about this insatiable desire I have for her, I muse as the Finance Manager waves me into the boardroom for our meeting.

I am back in my office poring over more contracts, thankful that the finance meeting didn't string on for too long when there is a tap at the door and my brother's distinctive deep voice remarks, "No rest for the wicked, hey bro?" Standing, I slap him on the back as I pull him in for a hug.

"Zee. So good to see you, man." Stepping back, I return to my desk, and Xander sits opposite me. "I thought you were arriving this morning?"

"Yeah, damn delays at the stopover with backlog from bad weather. Good to see you too, brother." Rubbing his jaw wearily, he continues, "Tell me what's been happening."

I fill him in, most of which he already knew from our emails. However, as I was able to explain about certain aspects and contractors that are best not put on paper, my phone buzzes with a message from Ramon telling me he is downstairs waiting to drive me back home

"That was Ramon. He's downstairs. Wanna catch a lift with me and have dinner at my place?" I suggest to Xander, who is showing the effects of a long flight.

"Yeah, that will be great. Thanks, E. I'll just grab my things and meet you down there." Xander heads back to the spare office and I shuffle paperwork and my laptop into my bag, slinging it over my shoulder and riding the elevator down to the ground floor with my personal assistant. Pamela is efficient, quiet, and friendly enough, but not quite the loyal friend and confidante Carly in the Sydney office was.

As I step into the waiting town car after bidding Pamela good night, Xander is chatting with Ramon, who tilts his chin to me in greeting as he turns in his seat and drives away, continuing to chat with Xander about Georgie and security requirements for an upcoming garden show. Conversation between us turns to fitness and training as well as Xander's plans while he is in London for the week.

In what seems like no time, Ramon is parking in the underground car park of my building. Getting out of the car, we casually stroll to the elevator and head up to my apartment. As we step out, we halt as the delicious aroma of food cooking teases our nostrils and stomachs. Xander shoots a questioning glance between Ramon and me, each of us wearing a similar puzzled expression. It's almost comical watching Xander's double take when our expressions flick to beaming acknowledgment when we simultaneously announce, "Emily," and eagerly pace into the kitchen, Xander following close behind. And there, standing at the cooktop with her back to us stirring a large steaming pot, is Emily, a vision of loveliness in her sweatpants and t-shirt and damp hair loosely draping down her back.

"That smells fantastic, Em." She jumps and spins around as I speak. Her look of relief when her eyes land on the three of us quickly turns to a bright, beaming, all-encompassing smile.

"Hi. Sorry. I didn't hear you come in with this fan going," she explains. "Xander. So good to see you."

"You too, Emily. Although I didn't expect to see you here." His smile is polite, and he turns to me with a chiding glare for not filling him in.

Emily snickers and glances at me, as if not too sure how much to say. "Yeah, it was a bit sudden but it's temporary."

I fill Xander in while Emily rummages under the bench for another pot which she fills with water before placing it on the hob.

"Are you all eating here or heading out tonight?" Emily asks. When I confirm we are staying in, she continues, "I hope you're all hungry then because the spaghetti bolognese is nearly ready." Even if we had plans to go out, I know I would have changed mine to try the mouth-watering meal. If it tastes as good as it smells, I will be in heaven.

Busying myself with placing cutlery and condiments on the table, I notice Xander and Ramon grabbing glasses and red wine, apparently just as eager as I am to eat.

A large pot of rich, meaty sauce and perfectly cooked spaghetti is devoured while we chat. After telling her Georgie misses her, Xander asks Emily how much longer she intends backpacking.

"I think I will stay about six more months, which gives me heaps more time for traveling." Then, addressing Ramon and me, she continues, "Which reminds me. I am heading to Scotland on Friday and then I'll head back to my apartment when I come back the following week."

A jolt of alarm shocks me and I notice Ramon's head snap up as well. "Are you traveling alone, Emily?"

"No. I'm going with Rashida, Lorenzo, Tom, and Aaron," Emily responds as she scrapes the last pieces of spaghetti from her plate.

Her response is innocuous enough, but suddenly panic rises in my chest. *Tom? She's going away with Tom?* Instinctively, my lips tighten, and my eyes narrow.

"Be careful of Tom," I warn. "He strikes me as a player and not very trustworthy." I can't stop the sour words spilling from my lips, a hard, disapproving tone edging my voice.

Emily's smile vanishes, her jaw clenches and her face is cold. "I suppose it takes one to know one, Ethan." Ramon scoffs and chokes on his mouthful of wine, his shrewd eyes watching the interplay between us with merriment. As is Xander, who glances at me with raised eyebrows, his lips pressed together, holding back a smirk. It's as if he's saying, *'she's got you there,'* and is eager to see my response, the bastard.

"I don't want to see you get hurt, Emily." I hope she can see the sincerity in my eyes.

"I've been hurt before, Ethan." She sparks my guilt, then continues with a lifted chin. "I'm a big girl and will deal with it."

Standing, Emily begins to clear the dishes and, as she moves to the kitchen, announces in a tight voice, "Oh, by the way, I meant to mention to you both. There has been a big, burly, tattooed fellow hanging around the café where I have been working the last two days." I cast a furtive glance in Ramon's direction while she bends to load the dishwasher. "I have also seen him drive past here. Maybe I am being overly suspicious and it's probably just a coincidence, but you asked me to let you know if there was anything unusual."

Chapter Twenty-Eight

ETHAN

"Geez," both Xander and I exclaim with anxiousness.

"Hmm. That's worrying. What does he look like?" Ramon, unfazed, queries with a straight face while Emily fiddles with her phone.

"I've just sent you a photo of him," Emily replies, quite calm considering it appears yet another man is following her. Picking up the empty pots from the stovetop, she carries them into the butler's pantry, obviously with the intention of scrubbing them in there.

"Fuck," Ramon hisses, turning the phone around for Xander and me to see the photo. Big and burly is an accurate description of the man. "Fuck, fuck, fuck," Ramon curses in a quiet voice, his fist thumping the table.

"What's up? Do you know him?" I'm thinking the worst, like he is some dangerous criminal, and trying to work out why he would be following Emily.

"Yep," he fumes.

"Your man's been made?" The ever-astute Xander accurately reads the situation as we huddle over the phone, and when Ramon nods, he continues, "What will you do?"

"Wait. What? Is he the bloke you had tailing Emily?" I finally catch on. "Yep, he's definitely been made."

"Why did you have a man tailing me?" Her clipped words are thick with condemnation, causing our heads to shoot up to see Emily standing beside the bench. Her eyes are narrow and hard, her lips tightly shut and nostrils flared, her body rigid.

Taking a deep breath, I explain, "Em, we were trying to protect you by making sure that stalker from the other night doesn't come anywhere near you." My words fall flat. She scowls and her glowering eyes bore into me.

Incredulous, she explodes. "You protect me from a stalker with a stalker?" Then she snarls, "How does that even make sense?" She huffs and shakes her head, her hands clenching and unclenching like she is restraining herself from hitting us.

With a tightness in my chest, I tentatively stand, rub my neck, and sidle over to her, reaching for her hands, but she quickly steps out of my reach. "When you put it like that, it doesn't make sense," I offer in a soft conciliatory tone, acknowledging her valid point of view.

"Don't patronize me, Ethan. Neither of you considered discussing this with me. Nor took into account how unnerving it was when I realized another person was following me. What am I? Some sort of charity case to make yourselves feel better?" she spits like a hell cat.

I grit my teeth, not liking being the target of her fury, and despite wanting to bite back, I recognize that now is not the right time and that there is an element of truth in her words. I want to console her but surprisingly, a strange vibrancy courses through me seeing her in this little spitfire mode. Wrestling with the need to comfort her lovingly in my arms as well as the competing urge to pick her up caveman-like and march us into the bedroom, I fight hard to maintain a calm demeanor.

Glancing to the others for back up, which is not forthcoming, my hand splays innocently across my upper chest. "Emily—" I start to reason with her, but she cuts me off.

"Don't." Holding her hand up, she pauses before spinning on her heels and marching off toward her bedroom. As if remembering her manners, her voice is terse as she throws over her shoulder, "Nice to see you, Xander."

Huffing, I flop back into my seat, blowing air from my puffed out cheeks through my pursed lips. "Whoa!"

"You handled that well." Xander's words drip with sarcasm as he smirks at both of us, as if pleased he was nothing more than a by-stander. No doubt chuckling to himself about regaling Georgie with the details later.

"Thanks for your input, *mate*." Turning, I mock Ramon and he gives me a smug, sideways smile.

"Hey, I've seen enough battle action to know when not to engage. Particularly with an angry female," he scoffs. "Although I am impressed with Emily's ability to spot a tail."

"Oh, fuck off, the pair of you." Frustrated with this outcome when my intentions had been well meant, I stand and sink my hands deep into my trouser pockets. With my back to the others, I stare at the sparkling pinpoints of light in the inky blackness outside the window, too deflated to appreciate their beauty.

While Ramon and Xander discuss the security guard's level of training, and how impressive it is that Emily detected him, I ponder how I can make it up to her. She is right, I acknowledge again. I should have discussed it with her, and I need to apologize for not considering the impact it could have had on her.

Like Ramon, I am also very impressed that she spotted the security detail. Covert surveillance is a specialty and usually very few trained operatives get spotted. "Fuck," I growl, frustrated with how this innocent enough idea blew out of proportion.

An audible yawn breaks my reverie, and I hear Xander ask Ramon to drive him home. Turning and after saying farewell to them, they depart. My mind is racing, thoughts circling, both justifying my actions but also understanding Emily's stance. Irritated with myself for my gaffe, I hope Emily can forgive me because we seemed to be making some progress in getting to know each other better, and I would like to get back to that position.

Deciding to go for a run because it usually clears my head, I trudge into my room to get changed. When I come out again, I wander up to Emily's door and poke my head inside. She is lying on the bed, texting. Her eyes look red and blotchy, and I feel lousy that I made her cry. She glances up and sees me, then returns her attention to the screen.

Digging my hands into my short's pockets, my shoulder leans against the door frame. "Em, I'm sorry I hurt you. That was never my intention." Compassion laces my voice and, lifting her head again, she regards me with an unblinking, focused expression.

Pulling in a huge breath before loudly releasing it, her voice is quiet but has an acerbic edge when she admits, "I understand why you felt I needed a security detail, Ethan, but I'm angry because you didn't think it necessary to tell me." Pausing, she watches me nod then adds, with a cutting intonation, "Most men I've known always try to control my life in one way or another, and I'm sick of it. I will no longer be a doormat for others to walk over. Regardless of whether it is good or bad, if it involves me, I demand to know about it.".

"I'll bear that in mind." Respectfully conceding, I dip my head slightly and give her a tight smile. . "Okay. I'm going for a run."

As I turn to walk away, I hear Emily murmur, "Thank you for apologizing, Ethan." Her rant seems to have expelled the last of her earlier fiery anger, and she puffs out a breath. I bend my head very slightly in an appreciative mock bow, and my heart swells in my chest. *Maybe there is hope for us yet.* Smiling, I slip away to pound the pavement, feeling less concerned now we have established some mutual understanding.

While running, I reflect on why Emily's angry reaction hit me like a punch in the stomach. Of course, my ego was knocked down a peg or three because my decision to have her followed created fear in her, hurting her. I deluded myself that by not saying anything she would be none the wiser by the time she went back to her apartment, so it would be a moot point.

Up until now, I hadn't considered physical surveillance as stalking but, after overhearing Ramon discussing it with Xander, to all intents and purposes it is. Even if the intent is to protect someone from external threats, the surveillant, if spotted, could instill fear in the person they are following, as is the case with Emily. Then the surveillant becomes the stalker in the eyes of the law.

All this introspection has me questioning who I was really protecting. Myself or Emily? Hiding behind my arrogance of supposed good intentions, my need to protect her also allowed me to know more about her and her friends, and is something I couldn't admit to myself. I've come to realize that I desperately want to be part of her life. Having her tailed afforded me that voyeurism, thinking (erroneously) that I could be prepared for any obstacles that arose in my relationship with her. However, the few reports I've received have been nondescript. *So, who is the real stalker here?* my conscience berates me. A brainwave hits me: *I'll charm her with honesty and openness, showing and telling her of my growing infatuation with her.*

Sweaty but buoyed by my newfound revelation, I bounce out of the elevator when I return home with the plan of finding Emily but she's not in her room. Hearing the sound from the television, I traipse in its direction to the other end of the apartment and find her asleep on the lounge in the pajamas that I love on her. Warmth fills me as I peer at her captivating beauty, her face clear and peaceful in slumber, like an angel. Picking up the remote, I switch off the television and slip an arm under her neck and the other under her legs, lifting her and pulling her against my chest, inhaling the floral scent in her hair. Emily stirs when I press my lips in a soft caress to the top of her head as I walk.

"Ethan," she mumbles, lifting her head to look at me, her eyelids blinking as she battles to keep them open. "What are you doing?"

"Taking you to bed, Baby Girl." I move towards the bedroom.

"Mmm, okay." She breathes a soft sigh, closing her eyes and settling back into my arms as if that is exactly where she wants to be. I know that's exactly where I want her to be. Then her body tenses and her eyes fly open, fully alert. "Wait. What?"

"Stop squirming, Em, before I drop you," I grumble, my grip tightening when she tries to wriggle from my hold. "I'm taking you to your room."

"Oh." I can't tell whether she is deflated or pleased with that information, but I reluctantly relinquish the delicious sensation of holding her by depositing her gently into a sitting position on the edge of her bed. As I bend down, her mesmerizing eyes hold mine and I can feel her soft, warm breath whisper across my cheek. With my arms still around her back, she surprises me by lifting her arms and clasping them around my neck. Her gaze focuses on my mouth when she purrs, "Thank you, Ethan."

Time seems to slip into slow motion. My lips descend on her slightly open mouth in a tiny, fluttering kiss, then another, and another. Emily sighs, her eyes closed, and I inhale her breath as my mouth hovers over hers. I want so much more of her, but battle my warring need and chivalry. Wanting Emily to come to me willingly and not feel that I have taken advantage of her sleepy state, I pull back, but Emily has a different idea. She holds me in place and pulls my head down to her soft pink lips, meshing them with mine in a gentle, ardent kiss. Leaning backward, she drags me with her, and I topple on the bed next to her, twisting so that I land on my side, facing her.

"Are you sure this is what you want, Em?" I'm holding myself tightly in check, making sure that she is very clear on her decision before I let go.

"Yes," she coos in a sexy drawl. "Don't you?"

"Of course, I do. I want every bit of you, Baby Girl. Desperately. But I need you to want me, this, desperately too, not because you feel obligated to have make up sex." My hand brushes the hair off her face, peering directly into her sparkling eyes, noting them shift from sultry to serious, questioning and narrowing slightly.

"You think that's what I'm doing?" she queries with a testy edge to her voice.

"I don't know. I hope not." Exhaling loudly, I point out, "I'm trying to make sure you are involved in this decision, Em. I heard you earlier and am giving you the opportunity to discuss it before we go sailing into something we might regret in the morning." Blinking, she absorbs my words and I watch her expression soften again, a slow, grateful smile tilting the corners of her lips.

"I really appreciate your consideration, Ethan. Thank you." Her warm hand cups and caresses my face, her thumb gliding over my cheekbone. Huskily, she utters, "I've been yearning for you for days now, so there is no 'obligatory make up sex' involved." Shy sincerity shines in her face. "Kiss me, Ethan."

Chapter Twenty-Nine

EMILY

Ethan's hungry lips claim mine, impassioned and insistent. Our breath mingles and his warm hand cups the side of my head, his thumb stroking my temple. He throws his thick, heavy leg over me, laying it between mine. His stiff cock feels like a steel rod against my thigh and my lower abdomen responds with a dull ache and a hot dampness between my legs. His tongue probes my mouth and I reciprocate. This man is a sensational kisser, driving my lust to heights I have not experienced with other men. My fingers run through his hair, gliding over his back, tracing the sculpted muscle definition.

His hand draws a line down my throat to my breast, cupping it, squeezing it, and his moan vibrates against my lips. He grips my hip with his free hand, pressing me harder against his rigid dick.

"Too many clothes," Ethan rasps, his jaw tight as he shifts his weight to roll me onto my back. Pushing upright, he moves to stand between my legs and peers down at my splayed body with a dark, devilish look.

Taking my hands, he drags me into a sitting position, then lifts my pajama top over my head, flinging it somewhere behind me. "Ooh, exquisite." His dark gaze is glued to my ample breasts. Reaching out, his hands caress them with reverence, my nipples hardening under his touch. I am melting inside and want all of him.

Desperate to touch his skin, I slip my hands under his t-shirt, stroking his tight abs and protruding pecs, feeling them twitch under my touch. He moans as my fingertips trail over his nipples. He flings his head back, a deep rumbling growl escaping his open mouth.

Lowering his head, his dark eyes blaze, gleaming with the obvious intensity of his arousal.

He grips the hem of his shirt, ripping it over his head before pushing me backward so I fall onto the bed. Holding my hands above my head, he bends, hovering his torso over mine. With a small sideways swaying motion of his chest, his nipples brush over mine in an erotic, titillating dance. His cock rubs against the apex of my legs, driving me insane with need, and I squirm against him.

Ethan gives me a roguish smile, then glides his hands down my arms, over my breasts, tweaking my nipples before continuing agonizingly slowly over my stomach, stopping when he comes to the waistband of my pajama bottoms.

He traces his fingers along the edge, before tucking the tips under the band and dragging them down my legs and over my feet.

"Fuck, you're beautiful." Lifting my head at his exalting tone, I take in his mesmerized expression which banishes any concerns I may have held about his sincerity, or the tokenism of his earlier statements. His eyes look at me like a thirsty man lost in a desert looking at a glass of water.

Dropping to his knees, his hands widen my legs and he kisses the insides of my thighs, deliberately skipping where I want him the most. I groan out his name, eliciting a chuckle from him. My head flops back onto the bed, and he teases me again in the same way.

He licks the delicate skin at the top of my thigh. "I know…" His mouth skips to the other thigh, licking it identically. "Baby Girl." His thumbs separate my folds and his hot expert tongue swipes through the wetness. I twitch against his mouth, then the velvet warmth of his tongue flicks at my nub, making me buck forward.

An ecstatic sigh escapes me, and I give in to the pleasure bubbling in me like a boiling kettle. He torments me with his tongue over and over, occasionally blowing on my wet, pulsing button, making my hips thrust against his face.

He stops abruptly, just as I am about to reach my crescendo. Whimpering, I open my eyes and see him stand, take an appraising look at me, then leave the room. It takes a moment or two to sink in. Bereft and baffled, I lift myself onto my elbows, looking around, staring at the doorway, my thoughts racing.

Just as I am about to call his name angrily, he walks back into the room.

"Why did you leave?" I grumble.

"Condoms." He waves a strip of foil packets in the air. "Did you miss me?"

Sitting up, I stare at him and arch a sardonic, impish eyebrow at him. "No, I was just about to finish what you started."

"Really?"

Prominently displayed through his jocks, the outline of his cock is right in front of me, teasingly demanding attention. Gazing at it and deciding it was time for payback, I wrap my arm around Ethan's hips, placing my hand on his well-shaped bum cheek, squeezing it. With the other hand, I cup his balls, smiling at his sharp inhalation, then slide my hand slowly up his rigid shaft.

My eyes shift to his handsome face, seeing his darkened gaze fixed on me, flashing with need, and trying to predict my next move. My tongue peeks between my lips, slowly and suggestively licking them. His breath flows out in a low, steady, rapturous sigh, his eyes momentarily closing as my fingers trace the tip of his penis.

Out of the corner of my eye, I catch sight of the condom packets dropping to the floor. Sliding my hand down his shaft, I repeat the upward motion, but continue to his waistband, dragging it down with both hands to expose the head of his cock. As it proudly juts out, I flick it with my tongue, lapping at the droplets of pre-cum leaking from his slit. His hips twitch and he growls, then grabs both sides of my head, pulling me away.

"Enough," he grunts, inhaling deeply. "Not yet." His tone is crisp and complex; moderated and defensive, tightly controlled, pained, displaying his urgent need.

I pull his pants down and his dick bounces out as if announcing its presence, smugly erect and ramrod stiff, almost poking me in the eye.

Ethan shuffles out of the pants pooling at his feet. His face is serious with the fierce intensity of his restraint. He grips my shoulders hard, bruising them, making me wince. My heart starts pounding wildly and there is a tightness in my chest like I can't breathe. I watch him closely, warily, concern creeping in and dissipating my lust as shadows from my past infiltrate the fog of desire.

I scramble further up the bed, breaking free of his grip on me. I try to make sense of my panic, and the thought flashes through my brain that Ethan is not the sort of person to physically hurt a woman. But my scarred emotions react regardless of common sense.

A flash of concern sparks in his eyes as he detects my sudden apprehension.

"What is it, Em?" His baffled look turns to horror as he notices the faint blue shadow of his thumb beginning to appear under my collarbone that I can see out of the corner of my eye. "Oh my God,

I'm so sorry, Em." He reaches out to touch me, then pulls back, rooted to the spot, his voice cracking. "I hurt you. I'm so sorry." He holds his head in his hands. His posture crumples. "I swear I didn't mean to hurt you." With my continued silence, he sighs heavily, his eyes downcast. "I'm so sorry, Em. I'll leave." He stoops to collect the clothes, then walks to the door.

"Ethan, wait." My softly spoken words halt him, and he turns his forlorn face round to me, a glimmer of hope flitting across his gaze. Calming myself by taking some deep breaths, I begin to think rationally again. His honest and heartfelt remorse rings true in my gut, and I can grapple with the scarred emotions, shadows, and doubt and lock them away.

When I pat the bed, Ethan comes to sit next to me, the clothes held in his hand covering his groin. "Will you hold me, Ethan?"

His eyebrows rise as he questions, "Are you sure?"

"Positive." He scoots closer and wraps his arm around me while I drop my head to his shoulder.

"What just happened?" Ethan murmurs in a thick tentative voice, which I feel rumble through my body.

Feeling stupidly embarrassed about my reaction, I huff out a breath and lift my head. "Sometimes different situations bring buried trauma to the surface." Hesitating, I gently take hold of his hand that sits over his crumpled shorts in his lap. When I continue, my voice is small and deflated while I gaze at our clasped hands. "Your grip on my shoulder caused a flashback of when my ex held me the same way lots of times after sex, while he would berate me, telling me how worthless and useless I was." I feel Ethan's hand clench, squashing my captive fingers, so I wriggle my hand to make him aware of it. "After demeaning me, he would use similar words to apologize or beg for forgiveness." I feel Ethan wince.

"But they were cold, aloof, with a detached quality that made them unbelievable. It was like he thought that was what I wanted to hear. I soon realized that it was just another power play so that I could never use a lack of apology against him." My voice trails off. Ethan doesn't need to know all the details of what Bradley did to me, and I prefer not to relive those awful memories. Ethan pulls me closer to him, hugging me with gentle strength. He is such a caring, considerate man, respectful of others, and that is one of the many things I love about him.

Lifting my head, I turn to look him in the eye. "You, on the other hand, were genuinely mortified that you had hurt me. You can't fake that. Your honesty and integrity are so much of who you are, Ethan. I'm sorry my past ruined a special moment."

"Thank you, Baby Girl, for sharing that with me and for believing in my sincerity." He places a feather-soft kiss against my forehead. "Again, I'm truly sorry I hurt you. Now, and in the past."

Nodding in acknowledgment of his apology, a question haunts me that I need to ask.

"Why did you ghost me in Sydney?"

He sighs heavily, his expression grim. "I'm ashamed to admit that you scared me." My confusion must show on my face because he clarifies, "I felt something for you that I had never felt before, so I ran, scared. I'm not proud of that and have regretted it since. Then at the wedding, you looked so beautiful, and I was knocked for six by my feelings for you and embarrassed at how I had hurt you. I just wanted to flee again, but stupidly decided to lose myself in alcohol and an opportunistic female, hurting you again by doing so."

Not sure what to say to his admission, I just nod, then utter, "Thank you for apologizing."

We sit in silence for a while, both lost in our thoughts, while Ethan holds me. My eyes are getting heavy, and as much as I try to hold it in, a yawn slips out.

"Are you working tomorrow?" Ethan asks and I nod. "What time are you starting?"

"Eight o'clock at the cafe. Why?"

"I'm still concerned about the stalker, Em, and your safety. Can we talk about having a security guard keeping watch over you?"

"I don't really think it's necessary, Ethan," I comment, rolling my eyes at him, and continue as he opens his mouth to speak. "But I'll meet you halfway. I don't like the idea of being tailed, but I do see the sense in it for a bit longer. How about Ramon's man follows me tomorrow? I will be heading off tomorrow evening, catching the train with the others, so I'll be out of harm's way and won't be alone much anyway."

He ponders that for a moment, then nods. "Yeah, that should work. I'll let Ramon know."

"On one condition." Ethan throws me a wary glance. "I'd prefer the big burly man. He shouldn't be taken off the job because of me. And I'll feel a lot more comfortable with a recognizable face."

This time Ethan bows his head in agreement, but not before he gives me a cheeky grin, uttering, "Agreed." I'm sure he thinks me a novice playing in the bargaining game, but I've come to realize that I need to manage others' expectations and align them with my own, so we are all working toward the same goal. "I'll get my phone and let Ramon know. He'll be pleased." Ethan slides off the bed and stands, and I take great pleasure in ogling his perfect, toned bottom as he pads to the door.

While he is gone, I put my pajamas on and climb under the covers, surmising he will go to his room when he finds his phone. Curling up on my side and snuggling into the cozy warmth, I reflect on my emotional rollercoaster ride tonight. Uneasiness to anger, acceptance to exhilarating passion, fright to confidence from feeling respected. *Geez. No wonder I am so tired.* Drifting into a half-sleep, I stir when Ethan cuddles in behind me, spooning me. Making a soft humming sound, I delight in his heat and strength and the feel of his still hard cock pressing against the cleft of my bottom, then give in to sleep.

Chapter Thirty

What's buzzing? The thought penetrates my mental fog as I groan at the infernal noise that wakes me. Lifting my head, I squint one eyed through the darkness at the brightly lit display of my phone on the bedside table. *Oh, fuck. It's four-thirty in the morning,* I groan again, and my head drops to the pillow.

With my eyes closed, I reach in the direction of the annoying phone, swatting at it to shut it up, but it just keeps buzzing. "Uggh." Rolling onto my back, I twist my head in the direction of the noise and narrow my eyes, peering at a dim glow coming from the other bedside table. "Huh?" I try to make sense of the shadowy silhouette on its side in my bed, outlined by the faint light. Then I remember where I am.

"Ethan?" My croaky voice is barely audible, and I try again, husking, "Ethan." I roll onto my side and give him a slight shake.

"Huh? What?" he mumbles, rolling onto his back, his eyes cracking open. Suddenly aware of his phone buzzing, he half turns, reaching for it and finally silences it. Returning to his back, he flings his arm above his head and groans.

"Why is your alarm going off so early in the morning?" I grumble. My eyes are more accustomed to the dimness, and I notice his head snap toward me at the sound of my voice, as if unaware of my presence.

"So I can go for a run. Morning, gorgeous," he greets me, suddenly sounding fully awake. I can hear the dreamy smile in his voice as he turns over to face me. "Are you always grumpy when you wake up?"

"Only when someone's alarm wakes me at some ungodly hour," I protest. "Why are you so happy?"

"Well, I was having this wonderful dream about a beautiful woman and a vibrator, and when I wake up, she is in my bed." He reaches out and turns on the bedside lamp, which casts a soft light over the bed.

How can he be so damn sexy first thing in the morning? Even his voice is smooth and seductive, like chocolate, and hits right at my core, thawing my grouchiness. Of course, his huge sexy, cheeky grin helps as well.

"Really?"

He chuckles at my droll sarcasm and scrunches closer, wrapping his arm around my waist. His rock hard erection is flattened between my lower belly and his taut abdomen, and I feel the heat from his balls pressing against me, lighting the latent fire within me.

Pressed against him like this is like an incendiary bomb has dropped in my vagina, its thrumming intensifying into an urgent need. Ethan plants a trail of small, soft kisses along my shoulder, up my neck to my mouth, plundering it with a searing open mouthed liplock.

"Mmm." His moan brushes against my mouth while his serpentine tongue probes its depths, coiling and weaving with mine in an erotic dance. Undoing the buttons of my pajama top, he pushes one side off my shoulder, exposing my breast. "Better," he murmurs as he lifts his head, watching his hand circle and engulf it. Shifting position, he bends, his tongue lapping at my nipple while he squeezes my flesh.

My neck arches as a pulsating thrum swamps my pussy and I let out a heavenly sigh.

Ethan moves his hand to free my arm from the gaping top and nudges me onto my back. Flinging back the covers and propping himself on an elbow, his hips and cock press against the side of my hip with his lower leg draped over my shin.

Ethan's hand reclaims my breast, his talented tongue alternating between them, flicking and scraping my nipples. My back arches, my plump breasts and pink tipped peaks clamoring for more as waves of desire cascade through my body.

My other hand reaches to stroke his bum cheeks, tracing his defined thigh muscles as his head moves from side to side. I trail my nails up his thigh and circle his firm butt cheek and he growls in pleasure. Moaning, the heavy ache in the pit of my stomach surges wet heat between my legs. Releasing my breasts, Ethan's playful fingers blaze a tingling trail over my abdomen when they drift to the waistband of my pajama bottoms, tugging them down while I lift my hips.

As soon as my bottom lands on the bed again, I free myself of my pajama pants from where they are tangled under my knees. His hand returns to glide over my lower belly, his eyes lightening to a golden green and blazing with hunger as they wash over my nakedness, heightening the tingling and pleasurable ache flooding my body. He places his large hot hand on the sensitive skin of my inner thigh, and I eagerly spread my legs wide.

"Ohh, you are so gorgeous, Baby Girl. So frigging fuckable," he drawls in a soft voice, thick with emotion. Stretching to grab a condom from the strip on the bedside table, he rips it open with his mouth and expertly rolls it on, while his hungry eyes sweep my body again, as if he is undecided where to focus his attention.

He cups my pussy, groaning at its heat, then he slips a finger between the folds so his palm rests against my pussy. My hips twitch, begging for more of his exquisite touch. His finger delves deeper into my slick cleft, stroking upwards, then halting on my clit.

A long, slow, breathy sound of exhilaration flows from my open mouth, my neck arching and my eyes closing. His cock twitches against my thigh.

"You are so wet, gorgeous." Then drops his head to suck my nipple into his mouth, flicking it with his tongue tip, while his finger continues stroking and halting, pressing the sensitive button. My fingers grip his head, my eyes fling open, my other hand glides over his hip, my thumb stroking the side of his cock, feeling it pulse at my touch. He moans and I sigh heavily. Lifting his head to peer into my lust dazed eyes, he purrs, "So frigging beautiful."

"Ethan, I need you," I plead, my voice breathy and urgent.

"Mmm, I know, Baby Girl," he whispers, delighting in sliding his finger through my slit again, this time circling the nub. He casts a devilish grin at me when I whimper, my hips jerking against his hand, and pushes himself up to a kneel, repositioning himself between my legs.

Gripping my hips, he raises them off the bed, pulling me toward him, and I wrap my legs around his waist, overlapping my ankles to lock him in close to me. Moving his hips, his dick slides through my folds, edging my dripping entrance. Slowly, he pushes inside me and I love the familiar burn of him spreading me as he feeds me his length until he is most of the way in. I had forgotten how amazing he feels, so all encompassing, overtaking not just my body but my senses and mind as well. Then he retracts, pulling out of me. My eyes fly open, feeling his loss instantly.

"Don't worry, Baby Girl. I'm nowhere near done with you yet." He grabs my legs behind the knees, unlocking my ankles from his waist and lifting them over his shoulders. Gripping my hips, he lines his cock up with my entrance again, then plunges into me. Deep. As I let out a mewling cry, he stills and growls a protracted groan. "Oh, fuuuck." Ethan withdraws, then buries his thick shaft into me, his eyes dark and glazed as he drives piston-like into me, as if his urgent need is chasing oblivion. My fingers curl, bunching the sheets in my hand. My eyes roll upwards and my breath pants with every thrust.

The fire in my belly explodes, spreading through me causing my body to clench vice-like on Ethan's penis, forcing him to stop moving. Crying out, I shatter into a million pieces around him.

When my contractions relax enough, he pounds into me again, furiously charging to his own orgasm. A guttural grunt rumbles from him as he cums, his cock pulsing vigorously inside me. He drops to the bed, his upper body falling between my legs onto my flushed chest. His hot, heavy breath pants against my neck, my own chest rising and falling rapidly from my labored breathing. As our orgasm-dulled senses return to a semblance of normality, Ethan withdraws and rolls onto his back.

"Fucking amazing," he marvels, drawing out the words as he stares at the ceiling.

I turn to him, vaguely noticing the pink hue staining his chest and neck. It's his beaming expression and wide, sated grin, though, that mesmerizes me, and I instinctively reciprocate with my own elated smile as I utter, "Incredible."

We lay in silence for a while, basking in the glow and lost in our thoughts. My heart swells as I gaze at him, drinking in his handsome features and attractive physique. And what a great lover he is; considerate, patient, and skilled. His cheeky adventurous nature shines through in either a glint in his eye or the corner of his mouth lifting, like it did earlier when he said he wasn't finished with me yet.

True to his word, he sure did finish me off. Silently, I chuckle at my lame joke. I love his thoughtfulness, like last night, wanting to take himself away from me because of my traumatic flashback. I love his integrity and strength of character and his cheeky banter with Ramon and Xander. I love everything about him, except his occasional bossiness, but even then, I can usually see that it stems from a place of caring.

Oh, my God. I am in love with Ethan.

Probably not surprising, now that I think about it, because no man can hold a candle to him. Even after he ghosted me, he was still the benchmark I rated others against. *Maybe it's post-coital euphoria,* my cynical side questions. *All those blissful, happy endorphins running through me.*

No, I don't believe that, because faint seeds of my love for him have been buried within me for a while now, occasionally peeking out, before being pushed back down. I realize how much a part of my life he has become in such a short while, and how much I am going to miss him when I head off on my trip later tonight.

Rolling onto my side, I place my hand on Ethan's chest. His heart is beating steadily, his eyes are closed, and he appears to be asleep. Then he lifts my hand, drawing it to his mouth, and kisses my palm, sending shooting tingles to my heart.

My amorous gaze eats up the sight of him as he clambers off the bed to dispose of the condom. By the time he returns, I have relocated further up the bed with my head again on my pillow, so I can still ogle Ethan as he returns. I can never get enough of him.

"You look well fucked, my angel." Ethan smiles as he climbs back onto the bed with a contented sigh.

"Mmm, the god of fucking did me over reaaal good," I gush drowsily.

"The god of fucking, hey?" he quips. His chin lifts slightly and his chest puffs proudly. A satisfied smile sits on his face, obviously liking my praise, and I inwardly smile at how like a little boy he is sometimes.

After a moment, he asks, "Is it tonight you are catching the train?" When I nod, he continues, "How are you getting there?" Filling him in on all the details, we arrange for Ramon to drive me to the station to meet my friends there. "Will you message me to let me know you are okay, Em?"

"Of course, but I'll be fine, Ethan," I remark, admonishing gently. He crooks a finger under my chin, tilting my head back to peer into his eyes.

"Every day, Em. I want to hear from you every day."

"Really?" I counter, nearly scoffing, surprised by his insistence.

"Yes. I need to know you are okay when you're so far away." His voice is determined, assertive, leaving no room for argument. Then he softens it to almost a whisper, and he bashfully adds, "I don't think you realize how much you affect me."

My mouth opens and closes, wordlessly and my heart flips wildly at his words; thrilled that I mean more than just a friend to him.

My wide eyes scrutinize him, while I wonder if I am reading too much into his statement. *Maybe he just means the physical, sexual effect because our chemistry is fiery.* If it was just about the sexual chemistry though, I chide, then the brazen Ethan I know would link his concern back to our next fuck session. *But his coy demeanor suggests that his meaning is something deeper, something he grapples with defining,* the niggling thought prods at my emotions. *Or is it a jealousy thing, knowing that Tom will be away with us?*

With my mind whirling, I croak, "Okay. Every day." Then an unsettling thought questions whether I have been emotionally manipulated. *Oh, please don't let him be one of those...*

Ethan nods, and we fall into an awkward silence. Shifting, I check the time on my phone, realizing I need to be at work in an hour and a half, so I set an alarm in case I fall asleep again. Ethan moves behind me, wrapping himself around me. "What are you doing?"

"Setting an alarm, so I'm not late for work." Replacing my phone on the bedside table, I settle against Ethan's warm body and feel his flaccid cock pressing against me.

"Mm, good idea," he murmurs close to my ear. "What time do you have to start?"

"Seven," I yawn.

"Want me to drive you?"

"Thank you, but no. Traffic is usually crazy, so it will be faster if I walk. Besides, you have my security man tailing me," I remembered. "What's his name?"

"Ramon calls him Mav, short for Maverick."

"Hmm. Okay." Spent from our lovemaking, the cozy warmth soon puts me to sleep.

Chapter Thirty-One

EMILY

The day has been crazy busy. Despite setting the alarm, Ethan and I snuggled for a while longer, fondling and kissing in a glorious way to greet the morning. Ethan made some toast for us while I had a quick shower and dressed, hurriedly running out the door and making it to work right on the dot of start time. Since then, it has been flat out, with barely any time to stop.

Throughout the day, I frequently found myself reflecting on Ethan and our torrid lovemaking. With the sanity of distance, I revisit my assumption that I love him, turning it over and over, concluding that my love for him is real. The fledgling feelings I had for him when we first met have only grown into a passionate, respectful, wholesome devotion. His demand for daily communication hints that he feels the same way, but is yet to admit it to himself.

Occasionally alternating with another barista or wait staff to do table service to get my body moving, I notice Mav sitting in a secluded corner of the courtyard, and on one instance took him a free coffee, making out that he was another customer, and thanking him so much for all he was doing for me.

Now I am back at Ethan's apartment, packing the last of my belongings. My phone buzzes with a message from Ramon, who is taking me to the station via my apartment so I can collect a few more clothes and switch over some items from my bag.

Racing downstairs after glancing around the room to make sure I have everything, I am taken aback to see Ramon standing next to the open rear door when I expected him to be sitting inside the car. Smiling warmly at him, I do a mock curtsy. "Why, thank you, kind sir."

Ramon's lips turn up at the corners, his tone dry and droll when he responds. "Just get in the car." I salute him, chuckling, as I clamber into the back seat and watch him shake his head as he paces to the driver's door and slides into his seat. After a few moments of silence, and still feeling awkward being chauffeured around, I blurt out, "Mav seems like a nice bloke."

Ramon's eyes flick to look at me in the rearview mirror, his eyebrows raised, as he responds, scoffing, "Nice? Hardly. The man is a cold, savage beast." After a pause, he continues, "Although he really appreciated the coffee you gave him."

A little while later, Ramon parks the car outside my apartment and, as I am about to step out, I turn to him. "Would you like to come up? I shouldn't be long." He hesitates as if pondering. "Yeah, okay."

Ramon is in full security mode as we enter the building, his head swiveling, surveying the lobby. When we get to my door, he holds back while I unlock it, again perusing the quiet hallway. Offering him an instant coffee, I turn on the kettle and get out cups and coffee jar, then drop my bag in my room and rummage through the drawers while the kettle boils. Suddenly, I hear a familiar voice filled with vitriol. "What the hell are *you* doing here?"

Rushing into the kitchen, I see Simone wrapped in a towel and Ramon with hands on hips, both standing silently glaring at each other.

"Sim? I didn't expect you to be home."

"I got sick and came home early. Why is *he* here?"

"Ramon is driving me to the train station, but I needed a few more clothes for my week away. I thought he might like to wait here rather than in the car." When she grumbles, I gently admonish, "Be nice, Sim."

Ramon pipes up, "I'll wait in the car." Obviously trying to defuse the situation by removing himself.

"Stay and have your coffee," I address Ramon then turn to Simone. "I won't be long, and we'll be out of here and leave you in peace." Simone gives Ramon one last glare then huffs off to her room. Ramon's gaze follows her seeming to appreciate her shapely body and long legs which is interestingly at odds with his tightly pressed lips and hard jaw line.

I return to my packing and when I'm finished, I pop my head into Simone's room and find her sitting propped up on her bed, earphones on, and scrolling on her tablet. Grabbing her attention, I wait till she removes her headphones. "I hope you feel better soon, Sim. Sorry for the intrusion, but we're leaving now."

"Alright. Be careful. Let me know when you are back," she croaks. Blowing her a kiss, I grab my bag and throw it over my shoulder before returning to the living room. "I'm ready," I comment to Ramon, and we make our way back down to the car. Fortunately, I remember the card for Ethan's apartment and hand it over before we get out of the elevator.

On the drive to the station, I text Rashida and Lorenzo to let them know I won't be long. I also text Ethan to let him know my progress. Then, when Ramon parks the car, he accompanies me to the designated meeting spot under the large clock in the central hall. When Rashida and Lorenzo see me, they both run to hug me but halt wide eyed and mouths gaping when Ramon steps forward to shield me.

"Thanks, Ramon," I move next to him and gently touch his arm. "These are my friends" Nodding he steps aside, and they hug me, keeping a watchful eye on him.

"Be careful, Emily, and call me if you need anything." He studies me with his level gaze then flicks a glance at Rashida and Lorenzo. As if interpreting some silent message about keeping me safe, Lorenzo gives him a short sharp nod.

Before he turns to pace away, I wrap my arms around Ramon's waist, hugging him. "Thank you for everything you have done for me. You don't know how much I appreciate it, Ramon."

Stepping out of my arms, he peers down at me with a slight surprise in his eyes. "I'm going to miss your morning coffees," he reveals with a slightly awkward bashfulness. I haven't known Ramon long, but I know he is not a sentimental man, so this is as close as I am likely to get to him saying he is fond of me. "Call me if you need anything, Emily," he says again and then he disappears out of sight.

Rashida and Lorenzo, who are standing either side of me, hook their arms through mine, both excitedly asking questions about Ramon as we saunter toward our platform.

Chapter Thirty-Two

It's Xander's last day in the office before he goes back to Australia, and we are sitting in the dullest, slowest meeting ever. I look at my watch for the umpteenth time and can't believe only five minutes have passed because it feels like an hour since I last checked it.

My mind drifts again to the amazing, wonderful night cuddling and fucking Emily. I have never felt so content, or so horny. Everything about her turns me on, from the way she brushes her hair back off her face, to her cheeky grin, and her rarely seen temper. Sex with her is mind blowing but last night, I felt another level of intimacy. Almost like she was a part of me. I felt something similar when we went out together a while ago, and it made me run, thinking I was no good for her. But our early morning love making felt far more intense; familiar, comforting, immensely pleasurable. Emily's frightened flashback meant I had to adapt to a gentler approach with her, and that brought out a softer side of myself, one I didn't know I had within me. With hindsight, I realize Emily is the only woman I truly feel comfortable and relaxed with.

"Ethan." Xander's bark snaps me out of my delightful daydream and my startled gaze shoots toward him. His expression is a mixture of irritation and wry amusement which makes me aware of the goofy grin I am wearing.

"Sorry," I utter and feel my face flush with embarrassment, because I rarely lose my game face in a meeting, even if my focus is sometimes lacking. "What was your question?"

"We wanted to know if you had any input on the proposed plans," Xander taunts, his face serious but with a gleeful twinkle in his eyes. *Damn, he is enjoying catching me out. I will be hearing about this for a while.* Fortunately, I had prepped for my meeting and referred to my notes for my questions.

A while later, Xander and I are leaving the conference room when he quips, "I bet I know who put that stupid grin on your face."

"You can talk. I know exactly when you are thinking of Georgie. You get this stupid sappy look on you." My retort is met with a glare, and I grin, knowing my barb hit home.

He changes the subject while we walk to our offices. "Are you still going to the Building Awards next weekend?"

"Yes. I'm driving up Tuesday morning, because I want to check out some potential acquisitions between Birmingham and Manchester," I tell him.

"Okay. Keep me posted." He turns in the direction of his office, halting to add, "Be careful and stay safe, brother."

"You too," I answer.

When I sit at my desk, I check my phone. No messages from Emily, but I know she is working so probably hasn't had the opportunity to do so. I quickly type a message to her before I get involved with work.

Ethan

Hope you are having a good day, Angel. Travel safe and please let me know when you arrive.

The rest of the day passes in a blur of activity and just as I am wrapping up, a text from Emily comes in, letting me know that she is on the way to the station. Ramon offered to drive her because he is still concerned and I am relieved that he did. Not only because I wasn't sure what time I could get away today to take Emily myself, but I think I would have lost it if I had seen that Tom bloke coming on to her. I'm not happy that they will be traveling together, but Emily has to work out for herself what sort of two-timing cad he is.

I hang on to the reassuring thought that Emily wouldn't have slept with me if she had feelings for Tom. She just isn't that sort of person. That is probably the only thing that will get me through this next week without her. And the hope she will message me every day like I asked.

Walking into my apartment seems unnaturally quiet without Emily. Yet the crazy thing is that up till a few days ago, I loved the solitude and peacefulness of the place, where I could do what I wanted, when I wanted. But since Emily has been here, I find myself seeking her out, not necessarily to chat but just to watch her or know what she is doing. I know that sounds creepy and stalkerish in itself, but she has a soothing presence that draws me to her. I always feel more fuller in the heart when near her.

Wandering into her bedroom and seeing it clinically organized and devoid of her belongings, just the way it was presented to her, rips at my heart. *This is going to be a damn long week.*

Damn. What is wrong with me? I throw the television remote to the other end of the long sofa a short while later, frustrated that I can't settle into anything. The dinner I normally cook for myself and devour with enjoyment tasted like cardboard and I only ate half of it. Despite having a cleaning lady, I throw a pile of laundry in the washing machine, memories of Emily crying in here springing to mind, making me even more morose. Then I thought the distraction of channel surfing the television might help, but no, everything irritates me.

Stomping into the bedroom, I change into my running gear and plonk on the end of the bed to put on my shoes. Quickly I text Ramon.

Ethan

Just heading for a run. Usual route if you want to join me.

His response is immediate and disappointing, but I admit I would not be good company tonight.

Ramon

Nah, man, I'm good. Thanks though.

Pounding the pavement, lathered in sweat, my hot breath fogs in the cool night air. I am pushing myself harder tonight, doing the circuit twice, trying to rid myself of my dismal mood. I am exhausted as I stagger into the lobby and see Ramon, who jumps to his feet when he spots me faltering through the door.

"You okay, man? What happened?" The uneasiness in Ramon's voice tells me he is worried about me. Nodding to him, I stoop over with my hands on my knees as I try to catch my breath and reflect that, going by my dripping, disheveled appearance, he has good reason to be. I stand upright and wipe an arm across my sweaty brow, then place both hands on my hips as I draw in a deep breath.

"Yeah... Did the circuit... twice... Best time ever," I boast falteringly between breaths.

"Dickhead," he growls and glares at me, then stomps toward the elevator. Following him, I get there just as the doors open. When we step inside, he snaps, "Fucking idiot. I thought you had been mugged or something when I hadn't heard from you." Shaking his head, he continues, irritated, "I got to the point of tracking your whereabouts, you shithead."

"Ohh, so nice that you care so much," I mock, remorseful that I have caused him to worry. I know he would never track Xander, Louisa, or myself unless he was concerned for our safety. "Seriously. Sorry mate. After one round, I hadn't chased the doldrums away, so kept going."

"Yeah, I know the feeling," he grumbles. I throw him a quizzical glance as we step into my apartment. Moving to the fridge I grab two bottles of water and throw one to Ramon. He seems on edge tonight, which is unusual for the normally cool controlled man I know.

"You worried about Emily too?" I enquire, slowly unscrewing the bottle cap. While I gulp my water, I feel the icy coolness travel down my parched throat as I watch Ramon scrunch his face, then sip from his bottle before taking his time recapping it.

"Yeah, my gut senses some trouble around her, and it's bugging me that I can't work out what it could be." Ramon was renowned for his gut feelings, which mostly proved accurate, so this news unsettles me more.

"Do you think it is about the crazy bloke?"

"No. Nothing more eventuated from our leads, but he's been dealt with." Ramon's brooding expression matches his tone.

"Dealt with how?"

"Just a quiet word to a friend of mine. All above board," he responds. As if sensing my scrutiny his reserved mask slips back into place and he retorts, "I'll head off then, now that I know you're not lying in a gutter somewhere."

"Yeah, okay. Thanks for your concern, buddy. Oh, by the way. Have you been using my cologne?"

Ramon's mouth gives a sardonic twist and an eyebrow raises as he scoffs, "Hell no. Why?"

"It seems to be evaporating. I'm down to half a bottle and I only bought it last week." I respond, slightly baffled by this occurrence.

"You're probably over-using it, pretty boy. You know you don't need to use it head to toe, don't you," is his droll, straight faced, smartass reply.

"Oh, fuck off. Get out of here, jarhead," I tease with an affectionate smirk, and he paces to the elevator, chuckling.

After showering I sit in my study for a while doing some work, till I feel tired enough to go to sleep. My king size bed seems far too large and empty tonight, and I toss and turn for a while. Even though she hasn't slept in my bed I am missing snuggling into the warmth and coziness of Emily's body.

The next morning, I am sick of my own company so text Ramon and Sanjit, a good friend from university who I haven't caught up with for a while, to see if they want to meet me for breakfast. Both soon reply yes, so I get changed and eagerly head out to meet them, looking forward to the distraction.

It is a beautiful, sunny spring Saturday morning as we sit in a popular café with views of the river, marred only by the occasional mild waft of sewage when the breeze blows in our direction.

The three of us catch up and we idle away the time.

With bellies full of delicious food and coffee, we part ways, and I walk back to my apartment, filling the afternoon in with dreary but necessary work. I am just wrapping up when I hear my phone buzz with a message. Guessing it will be Emily—or more accurately, hoping it will be her—I realize that she hasn't been at the forefront of my mind today like she was yesterday. In some ways this thought is comforting, knowing that I can carry on my normal existence without feeling like I am obsessing over her. But I have missed her companionship... and the warmth of her body.

Walking to the kitchen bench to pick up my phone, a combination of disappointment and delight washes over me that the message is from Mario, from our Los Angeles office.

Mario

Just checked in to my hotel. You feel like clubbing tonight?

So, I quickly respond.

Ethan

Hey, man. I assumed you would be arriving tomorrow. Yeah, clubbing would be good. When and where?

Mario

Took an earlier flight so I can have a rest day *wink emoji* tomorrow before seeing your ugly mug in the office on Monday.

He continues with the time and location of our catch up, and I quickly check my watch, mentally checking off what I need to do beforehand.

Packing away my paperwork, I wonder why Emily hasn't texted yet, but expect she will be out and about sightseeing with her friends, so decide to send her a quick message.

Ethan

Hi, Baby Girl. Thinking of you, and wishing you were here. Hope you are having fun. Can't wait to hear about your day.

Chapter Thirty-Three

ETHAN

While Ramon drives me to the office Monday morning, I reflect on how quickly the weekend has passed. Normally, a lingering buzz from the weekend's excitement fizzes through me, but I don't feel that today.

The nightclub with Mario was thrilling, enlivening the senses with its loud pumping beats that permeated my soul, enticing me into the writhing throng like a surfer is drawn into the ocean keen to ride the next wave. Lots of beautiful women displaying their assets, and in his usual form, Mario was on his game and had several women keen to take advantage of his attention.

For me, I danced the night away, and despite several blatant invitations and opportunities for a quickie in the restrooms, none of the women aroused me enough to accept. And for some bizarre reason, my stomach knotted, making me feel like I was betraying Emily. We haven't made any commitments to each other and can't even say we are dating. But I keep coming back to how Emily, with just a simple smile, sends me into a spin, my heart racing and blood pulsing on its rush through me. When I acknowledged those feelings, there was no point in staying at the club, so I left Mario to his game playing and caught a cab home. Once there, I noticed a text from Emily telling me about her sightseeing, which brought a smile to my face and an ache in my heart.

I arranged to meet up with my sister, Louisa, yesterday and it was a nice casual lunch at her townhouse. Hers is the last in a row of whitewashed terraced houses and next door to an upmarket menswear store, so I took advantage of the visit to do a bit of shopping as well.

Louisa and I chatted over the beautifully cooked salmon and kale, avocado salad, which was paired with a crisp chardonnay. She had returned from Australia about a week ago after one of the many international long-haul trips we all do, so was a bit quieter than her usual bubbly self. Her body may have been suffering from jetlag, but her shrewd mind wasn't and she spent time grilling me about Emily in her subtle sledgehammer way.

"Xander mentioned to me that a mutual friend of yours and Georgie's had been stalked earlier in the week and she had been staying with you. Is that the same Emily I met in Sydney when you were going on a date with her?"

I pause before I answer. "Yes, it is."

"Oh, that must have been an awful experience," she commented, then sipped at her wine, looking at me over her glass. "I didn't realize you were still dating?"

"We're not. I only ran into her again in London a week or two ago." I roll my eyes at her. "I'm sure Xander has already told you all the details, sis, so quit the interrogation," I reprimand.

She adopted a mock hurt expression before asserting, "Can't I ask about your love life?"

"No," I barked coldly, returning my attention to the last of my meal. My expression and tone might have been enough to make someone else change the subject, but not my bloodhound sister. She just can't leave well enough alone.

"Why did you stop dating?" she probed with mock innocence. My God, she was infuriating. *No wonder she has so many successes in the courtroom.*

Huffing out a sigh, I glared at her. "Geez, Louisa. Why does it matter?" Her raised eyebrows and insistent stare tolerated no refusal to answer. This was her attorney face, and I had always empathized with victims of that stern, authoritative expression. I immediately understood why they usually caved quickly. Just like I did. "I ghosted her after a couple of dates, okay?" My grumbled, embarrassed admission made her look at me momentarily with derision before she slipped back into her attorney mask.

"You're an idiot," she scoffed. "So why did she call you for help then?" I could see her mind ticking away, trying to put the pieces together.

"Didn't Xander tell you?" I crossed my arms, trying to gauge how much she knew, and how much she was fishing for answers.

"I want to hear it from you." A mischievous glint flashed in her eyes, belying her otherwise expressionless face.

Knowing she wouldn't let up until she got her answer, I tsked and huffed, speaking in a deadpan voice. "I bumped into her when I went to a restaurant where Emily happened to be working. Then again, at an event where she was part of the catering staff, I witnessed her getting abused by the guy who later stalked her. I wanted to make sure she was okay so dined at the restaurant again, and the stalker dude was there and recognized her. So, I slipped her my card with a message to call me if she needed help. And it turned out she did." I paused and gave Louisa a tight lipped side-eye glance. "Satisfied?" My question dripped with sarcasm.

Louisa's face softened, and she smiled warmly, like a sister instead of an attorney. "That was very noble and kind of you, Ethan. I'm very proud of you for helping her out." I blushed and lowered my head. But of course, that wasn't enough for her. "But how did she come to stay at your place, and where is she now?"

"You ask too many damn questions, Lou. I'll answer, but no more. Okay?" When she nodded, I clarified, dropping my gaze to where my fingers twirled the wine glass. "The guy kept driving up and down the street trying to find her. I was walking her home, and he cruised past again. So, I hid her in a doorway until Ramon could come and collect us. He was worried about the guy following her to her apartment, so we thought it best for Emily to stay at mine for a few nights." Louisa opened her mouth to speak, but I jumped in before she could get a word in.

"Emily is currently in Scotland with some backpacker friends."

"Hmm. Interesting."

I glanced up to see her watching me closely, an inscrutable look on her face. "What does that mean?" I groaned, demandingly.

"Do you miss her?" she probed.

"Oh, fuck off. I thought you agreed no more questions," I barked. "You are my sister, not my counselor."

"True," she noted in her most conciliatory tone. "And as your sister, I'll tell you my thoughts for free."

"Do you have to?" I interjected, groaning. She responded with a beaming grin, and I could tell that she thought she had it all worked out, and I was instantly wary.

"I think you are missing Emily terribly." I quirked an eyebrow at her with no effect as she continued. "In fact, I think you are falling in love with her," she stated with smug satisfaction.

And if she thought I would confirm or deny that rash statement, she had misjudged me. "You've lost your mind, sis," I scoffed. "Projecting your own wishes onto me, are you?" I watched her smug expression shift into sadness, stabbing me in the heart. "I'm sorry, Lou. I didn't mean to be cruel. But I don't want to discuss how I feel about Emily. Okay?"

We chatted a bit more about Georgie and Xander, regaining our jovial ribbing and teasing, and I gave Louisa a huge, warm hug before I left. Her words haunted me though. I spent the rest of the evening analyzing my feelings for Emily and whether I was falling in love with her. There is a lot to love about Emily; her warmth, caring, thoughtfulness, and sincerity, her soft heart and genuine down to earth nature, her sharp wit and sense of humor, loyalty to her friends and her resilience in overcoming some difficult situations.

My heart swells and I catch myself wearing a goofy grin when thinking of her. She touches me deeply and I am struck by how deflated I feel with her not around. *Is this how she felt when I dumped her?* That agonizing thought fills me with sorrow that I hurt her in such a way. Yet I am grateful that she still wants to have anything to do with me. *I wonder how she feels about me. I know she likes me, but is she falling in love with me too? What if she doesn't feel that way about me? What will I do? Is this love?* I don't know for sure, but I feel like it is the beginning of it. For me, anyway. I feel safe with Emily, I trust her, we communicate easily, and both are prepared to compromise. She has so many incredible qualities all wrapped into one beautifully stimulating and challenging package. Love is such a scary word, though, and I'm not sure I want to label my feelings yet. All I know is that I want to spend a lot more time with Emily and can't wait for her return.

"Ethan, you okay?" Ramon's voice breaks through my reverie, and I realize we are stopped outside my building, while I sit staring out the opposite window, apparently entranced by the passing traffic.

I throw him a quick, tight-lipped grin as I respond, "Yeah. Thanks, mate. Just thinking a few things through." He nods, but his watchful gaze feels like he knows what I have been thinking about. I trudge into the office building, greeting colleagues with a smile I don't feel as we wait for the elevator. *And so my Monday begins*, I muse, deflated and dreading the day.

No matter what I do, I can't seem to shake the funk I am in. I am moody and snappy and have little patience for anyone. My back-to-back meetings only irritate me more. My jaw is aching from clenching it so tight, holding back what I want to say. And I am feeling the weight of my workload piling up, knowing I will be away from tomorrow and not able to clear it for a few days.

Before I head into my next meeting, I notice a text from Emily that came in earlier, lifting my spirits immensely.

Emily
I've just realized I've left my hairdryer at your place. Can I call in and collect it, please?

Thinking it an odd message because she's in Scotland and can't collect it till she returns, I don't have much time to think about it as I pace to my meeting, so shoot back a response.

Ethan
Sure. I'm out of town for the rest of the week, but message Ramon when you're home to let you into the apartment. I'm looking forward to seeing you when I get back.

Emily
Ok. Thanks. Me too. So much to tell you.

By the time the last meeting of the day is finished, I am bushed, so when Ramon picks me up, I fall into the back seat and breathe a sigh of relief. Ramon lifts his sunglasses to peer at me with hard, steely eyes through the rearview mirror.

"Busy day?" His question is innocuous but there is a sharp edge to his voice, like there is a double meaning to it.

I feel my eyebrows furrow as I return his gaze, trying to decipher his meaning and why he seems angry. "Yeah, crazy busy," I respond. He drops his sunglasses over his eyes and starts the car.

"Just a reminder, I'm driving up north tomorrow for the week, and should be home late Sunday," I prompt.

"Yep. I remember," is his short, sharp answer.

Chapter Thirty-Four

EMILY

Well, so much for my wonderful trip to Scotland, I fume.

Here I am, Monday morning, sitting on the train for a four-and-a-half-hour trip back to London, after only two full days of sightseeing. Why? Because Tom propositioned me. Then became quite insistent, refusing to take no for an answer, no matter how many times I rejected him. He kept harping on about how good we would be together, telling me what I should be doing, where I should be going, and kept putting his arm around me.

He creeped me out so much I couldn't sleep, and as we were in the same dorm room, I had no way of protecting myself from him. The best option was for me to leave. Maybe I was running like a frightened bunny, but I wasn't taking any chances with him. The more I saw of him whilst we were away, the more I saw red flags of his emotional manipulation. *Been there, done that, not doing that again.*

Rashida and Lorenzo fully understood my situation and agreed I should go home, and told Tom and Aaron to find other accommodation and travel separately. Despite the altered arrangements, they knew our itinerary and I suspected Tom would continue to hound me at every location. Aaron wasn't very impressed with Tom either and apparently had a quiet word with him, convincing him it would be in his best interest to split the group. Yes, I'm disappointed that I didn't get to see as much of Scotland as I would have liked, but I was able to tick a couple of items off my bucket list at least.

To fill in my time on the train, I have messaged my employment agency to advise them of my availability. I discovered yesterday that I hadn't packed my hairdryer and couldn't recall stashing it with my belongings when I left Ethan's place. So, I messaged him, asking if I could come collect it, deliberately omitting the fact that I am coming home early. I didn't want to tell him about Tom via message because he will get all protective and want to 'rescue' me, and I need him to see that I can manage most difficult situations by myself. Also, I am slightly embarrassed that I shot Ethan down when he expressed his concern about Tom a few days ago, and want to apologize to him directly.

When Ethan tells me he will be out of town for the remainder of the week, I am disappointed because I won't have the opportunity to explain face to face.

So, when the train is about an hour from its destination, I message Ramon.

Emily

Hi, Ramon. I stupidly left my hairdryer at Ethan's place, and Ethan asked me to contact you when I am home so you can let me in to collect it. I am on my way home, about an hour out of London, and wonder if I can arrange a time for you to let me into the apartment, please?

Before I had a chance to put my phone away, it rings, and I am surprised to see it's Ramon.

"What's going on, Em?" he asks abruptly, all business and ready to act.

"I'm on my way back to London—"

"And?" He talks over me before I can finish.

"And I am safe and sound, so you can stand down now, soldier." My voice is calm but firm as I recognize his concern for my safety. I hear him breathe a sigh of relief. "I'll tell you about it when I see you."

"Okay. I'll meet you at the station. What time is the train due in?" That's what I like about Ramon. His direct manner means you know where you stand with him, and he doesn't mince his words. I tell him my estimated arrival time and he agrees to be there before he hangs up.

Relieved that he will be collecting me from the station, I watch the beautiful countryside speed by while I sit with a book in one hand and a cup of tea in the other. I laugh at myself because watching the ever-changing scenery means I haven't read much of my new book. Pity, because I really love this author, and have been anticipating reading the story of a billionaire and his love interest meeting on a flight, and an unexpected stopover bringing them together. Never mind, now I am back in Simone's apartment, I should have ample time to read.

As the train pulls into the station, Ramon messages me to let me know he will meet me under the huge skylight in the concourse. I reply, then stand, throwing my duffle bag over my back, and shuffle off the train with the other passengers.

Like every city's major train station, the concourse is bustling, but Ramon is not hard to find, his large muscular frame easy to spot, swathed in dark clothing and his usual dark aviator sunglasses, particularly as no-one is standing within eight feet of him. It's like his bulky height and vigilant military stance emanates a menacing barrier around him.

"Why is it you scare people away?" I ask with intrigue, waving my arm around as I approach him, indicating the clear area.

"Just lucky, I guess," he smirks and shrugs his shoulders. Nodding his head toward the exit, he comments with a tinge of embarrassment as he paces in that direction. "I don't like crowds, and prefer to have room to move." I am practically running to keep up with him, and he must realize I am lagging because he turns to look for me, then shortens his stride so I can keep up. We make it to the street quicker than I would have alone and as he opens the rear door for me, I peer up at him and smile.

"Thank you for doing this, Ramon." He nods his head to the side telling me to get in the car, so I drag my bag off my back and throw it into the back seat, then clamber in after it. He paces around to the driver's side, throws open the door, and slides in. Twisting in his seat, he looks at me, his gaze brooking no argument. If I didn't think of him as a friend, I would be quite intimidated by his interrogatory look.

"Spill," he orders, his face unreadable, and eyes unblinking. When I explain to him about Tom continuing to come onto me after I repeatedly refused him, Ramon's expression hardens, his lovely gray eyes turning dark and stony, glittering with anger, his mouth tight-lipped.

Ramon just nods, his words clipped as he utters, "You did the right and safest thing." Apparently appeased, he turns in his seat, slips his sunglasses over his eyes, starts the car, and drives off.

As we approach Ethan's apartment block, Ramon explains, "I'll park, and come in with you to activate the elevator, but I will be in a No Parking zone, so will have to return to the car. I'll keep circling the block till you come out."

"Okay. Sounds good. I won't be long." We climb out of the car and Ramon waves to the doorman as we pass, then presses the button for the elevator. When it arrives and the doors open, he reaches in, swiping his card and pressing the correct floor button, then steps back and the doors close.

When the doors open at Ethan's apartment, I rush down the hallway to the guest bedroom, my loafers silent on the tiled flooring. Even though I have permission to be here, I still feel guilty being in the apartment without Ethan present, and without being a 'guest'. So, I scurry into the guest bathroom and see my hairdryer, right where I left it on the vanity. Grabbing it and winding the cord around the handle as I hurry out, the sound of a chuckling male voice flows out as I pass Ethan's bedroom, stopping me in my tracks. *Is that Ethan?*

I turn toward his bedroom doorway, confused when an elegant dark haired, slender woman sashays out in a tight fitting skimpy black dress that barely covers anything. My eyes widen and my mouth drops open as I watch her stop and stare at me, just as surprised as I am. She quickly recovers and her bright red lips twist into a smirk, and she haughtily invites in an alluring husky voice, "You're welcome to join us if you like."

Drawing together what little composure I have left, I shake my head, and babble, "forgot my hairdryer" as I wave it in the air and scurry toward the elevator, thankful that the doors open as soon as I press the button. When they close again, I slump against the side wall, my legs buckling underneath me, my emotions warring with each other for supremacy. Deceit, humiliation, betrayal, anguish, hurt, and some I can't identify. My heart feels like it is being wrenched from my chest, and tears well in my eyes. My head is spinning and my stomach clenches, settling like a heavy kettlebell in my gut. My throat tightens painfully, and my lungs feel like they are in a steel vice. *How could Ethan do this to me?*

Chapter Thirty-Five

Unfortunately, the elevator arrives at the ground floor faster than I would like. All I want to do is hide in here but I know that Ramon will be waiting for me. Reluctantly I stagger teary-eyed through the foyer, but it is not till I am outside on the pavement that the tears flow. My head is lowered and, using my empty hand to shield my face, I just stand on the footpath weeping, unaware of passersby or traffic. Suddenly, a big strong hand bites into my upper arm, and I raise my head in fright.

"Fucking hell, Emily. Get in the car," Ramon orders, his strong grip escorting me to the hastily parked vehicle. Ramon gives me a quick glance over his shoulder, and without saying a word, he pulls out from the curb and speeds off

When my weeping abates, I rummage in my bag for a tissue and swipe at my tears, then become aware of Ramon pulling the large SUV over. We are at my apartment already.

When I reach for the door handle, I hear a loud click, and my head swings to Ramon who has turned in the front seat to watch me. *Has he locked me in?* Shaking his head, he lifts his sunglasses to rest on his head. His piercing gaze pins me in my seat and his stern clipped voice commands, "Tell me what happened."

I inhale deeply, steadying my voice before speaking. "There was a woman in the apartment... coming out of Ethan's room and I heard him in there, laughing. She was dressed... well, she wasn't wearing much." My voice wobbles and I draw in a steadying breath. "She said I was welcome to join them." I hiccup out the last words along with a loud sob.

"What?" he barked. "Are you sure? Who was she?"

"I don't know," I snap. "Why did you take me there if you knew he was home with someone else?" I spit, on the defensive now that he doesn't seem to believe me.

"Whoa. Whoa. Hold up." His hands fly up and his voice is conciliatory. "I didn't know he was home, Em. I wouldn't have taken you there if I did." He pauses, making sure I recognize his sincerity. At my nod, he continues, "I'm not Ethan's keeper, so am not aware of all his movements, but I dropped him at work this morning and thought he had a hectic day." Ramon's brows furrow with the ambiguity of his words. As if another thought crosses his mind, his face hardens, "She didn't hurt you, did she?"

Mollified, I lower my gaze and shake my head, mumbling, "Not physically." Realizing that whatever Ethan and I had is apparently over, I feel deflated. "I knew I shouldn't have fallen in love with him."

"It'll work out, Em," he offers, his voice thoughtful, then he reaches under his seat and states, "But something's not right here. Tell me what the woman looks like." I can see his mind ticking away as I describe her again and watch him place the laptop he's brought out on the center console.

"Ramon, I just want to go upstairs. It's been an emotional couple of days. Why don't you bring the laptop up and I can answer your questions over a cup of tea."

"Sounds good," he answers and shifts in his seat as if to get out, then his mouth twists with distaste as he says, "Wait. Is Simone home?"

I shake my head and Ramon unlocks the SUV and slips out, holding my door for me while I step down and drag my bag through the opening. He takes it from me as we walk into my building, his laptop in his other hand.

Inside I make us both a cup of tea while Ramon sets himself up on the kitchen bench and mumbles to himself as he intently watches the screen. "What are you doing?" I ask when I put his cup in front of him.

"Scanning the camera footage from the lobby," he answers distractedly.

"How are you able to do that?"

He gives me a cheeky grin and a conspiratorial wink. "It's ironic how easy it is to get into the system." I watch over his shoulder as he fast-forwards through the footage and glimpse myself on the screen walking to the elevators. Ramon stops and rewinds, slower this time, staring at the screen.

"That's her," I exclaim, pointing at the screen. Ramon replays the footage till he gets a good clear image of the tall, dark haired woman. "But she was in skimpy, sexy clothes when I saw her." I stare at the woman on the screen dressed in nondescript jeans and t-shirt with a large bag over her shoulders.

"You're sure that's her?" Ramon peers at me, his eyes searching mine.

"Yes. But I don't understand the change of clothes."

"Maybe she didn't want to be obvious about the reason for her visit," he suggests diplomatically.

"True," I answer. "So, what happens now?"

"I'll do some digging and see what I can find out about her." Checking his watch, he closes the laptop, gulps his tea, and puts his big hand on my shoulder. "Time for me to run. Are you sure you're okay here alone?"

I roll my eyes at him and sigh heavily. "I'm hurt and disappointed that Ethan is playing around with another woman while I've been away. I thought we had something special. Obviously, he doesn't feel the same way. I'll get over it. I did last time he dumped me, and I will again."

Picking up his laptop, he moves toward the door but pauses when I add in a flat tone, "Ironic isn't it that I rejected Tom to be faithful to Ethan."

"Yep," is all he says before he leaves. Shutting the door behind him, I contemplate that Ramon probably can't say much because Ethan is his employer and friend, and he knows where his loyalty lies. Well, lesson learned. Ethan fucking Wiggins is persona non grata as far as I am concerned.

Later, as I busy myself unpacking my bag, I analyze for the millionth time my relationship, or lack thereof, with Ethan, looking for indicators of his cheating behavior. I must be a gullible fool because he seemed so sincere, and caring. Yet after only two days away from me, he is in bed with another woman, like I never existed. Uggh! Bastard. *I deserve better than that fucking prick,* my inner voice roars in my head, while I throw clothes across the room, calling him all the names under the sun. "Well, you can get well and truly fucked. I hope your dick drops off with some sexually transmitted disease," I fume, voicing my thoughts aloud. "Then you'll be a gutless, prickless asshole."

Flopping on the bed, my anger exhausted, I feel hollow, numb and trembly. And I sob. Noisy ugly crying until I have no tears left. I just lay there, in a state of emptiness for I don't know how long, until my stomach growls, reminding me I haven't eaten since breakfast.

Heaving myself off the bed, I trudge to the kitchen, open the fridge and stare inside, not interested in food, but knowing I need to eat something. Lethargically, I make some toast and a cup of tea, then mope around the lounge room, staring mindlessly at the television.

My phone pings with a message from Rashida checking I arrived home safely. I send a quick response, avoiding my turmoil, feeling embarrassed that I've been easily taken in by most of the men in my life. Besides I don't want to ruin her trip, because she is such a good friend that she will want to come back if she knows. It can wait a few more days, and by then I might have more control of my emotions. For the same reason, I am pleased that Simone is also away because I couldn't bear her telling me what a fool I am for getting involved with Ethan again. I can't even tell Georgie what has happened because she will tell Xander, who will hound Ethan. And I don't want him to feel forced into being with me.

My phone rings, making me jump because I was dozing on the lounge, apparently for a while when I notice the time as I pick up the phone. My voice sounds sleepy, and my throat is dry and croaky—probably from sleeping with my mouth open—as I answer.

"Hello, Emily. This is Victoria, from the employment agency," a very pleasant well-articulated female voice states. "You emailed earlier today that you're available for work again. Is that still the case?"

"Yes, it is," I respond in a much clearer voice. She informs me of more work at the café again, which I eagerly accept. After ending the call, I breathe a sigh of relief that I won't be sitting around mulling over Ethan.

I suddenly realize that I need to wash and iron my work clothes, so with a heavy heart I drag myself through my chores. However, my thoughts keep torturing me with the few memorable loving moments that Ethan and I shared, but I am out of tears for him.

Before I go to bed a while later, I check my phone and am surprised by an email from Bruce Baxter. While we were on the train to Scotland, I told Rashida and Lorenzo about my quandary over whether to meet with him and decided to email him then and there, before I lost my nerve again. So, his unexpected suggestion to meet this coming Saturday afternoon makes me nervous. Great, another flaky male who doesn't want to get to know me. Just what I need. *Not.*

Chapter Thirty-Six

EMILY

Working in the café has been a godsend today. As I suspected, I have been too busy to think of anything other than the next coffee order or clearing and wiping tables. I still feel hollow and know that my normally sunny disposition is hiding behind the dark gray cloud hanging over me. But I keep reminding myself that I have had it worse, and there are many thousands in the world far worse off than me.

I didn't have a great night's sleep, understandably, but being out in the big, wide, vibrant world, instead of the narrow dark, dingy place inside my head, has lifted my spirits somewhat. It has given me a brighter perspective about meeting Bruce too. Even though he has no intention of keeping me in his life, I know I will regret not meeting him. It has been a heartfelt desire since I found out about him and my bruised and battered heart needs an uplift. So, I rationalize that, if I go into the meeting without expectations, then I can't be disappointed.

In my break, I email him and arrange to meet him here at the café, where I am on familiar ground. I really wish Rashida was here though, because I could use some moral support. Ethan had offered to go, but that won't be happening now, because he is out of town. And for obvious reasons, I wouldn't have asked him even if he lived next door. I'll let Ramon know where I am going, more from a security perspective than needing him for moral support, and I sense he will be far happier that he knows my whereabouts when meeting someone I know nothing about.

It's nearly lunchtime rush hour and, in between the milk frother hissing steam and the noise of the espresso machine, I hear a familiar deep male voice and look up to see Mav wearing his standard apparel sunglasses. His broad chest and thick biceps are imposing and his ever-present 'don't mess with me' air is like a force field, other patrons keeping their distance. He nods at me, while placing his order with my colleague, and I throw him a beaming smile, pleased to see a familiar face. He is like an anchor to a boat drifting in choppy seas, diminishing my feelings of abandonment and loneliness just by being here. When his double shot short black coffee is ready, I take my break and deliver it to him. Typically, he is sitting in a corner of the fenced off area, scrutinizing the passersby.

"Hi, Mav. How are you doing?" I put his cup down.

"Good." Dragging his glasses down his nose, he looks over them to answer me, then dips his head and eyes toward the paper cup, "Thank you," before sliding the glasses back in place.

Tilting my head slightly, my eyes narrow in puzzlement as I ask, "Are you still tailing me?"

"Nope. Just here for the coffee." Lounging back in his chair, his expressionless face gives me no indication of whether he is serious or mocking me. While he removes the plastic lid, I inwardly chuckle at how much he is like Ramon. *What is it with these big, macho men not conversing like normal people? Maybe they're worried about giving away too much information.*

"Okay. Well, enjoy." I have only taken a step or two away when a thought stops me in my tracks. Turning back to him, I blurt out, "Mav, this is going to sound weird, but hear me out." Again, his shrewd green eyes peer over his glasses at me, hardening suspiciously.

"Long story short, I've arranged to meet my biological father here on Saturday afternoon. A man I know very little about, have never met before, and who doesn't want my existence to upset his status quo." Mav removes his glasses while I am speaking, holding them in his hand, while he brings the lidless coffee cup to his lips with his other hand and sips it. His eyebrows raise, his deep-set eyes are fixed directly on me as if questioning not only why I would meet up with someone in such circumstances but also why I am telling him this information.

"My friends may not be back from Scotland in time to be my moral support. Ethan is out of town, and I've imposed on Ramon enough, although I will let him know. Just wondering, if you're not doing anything, would you be able to loiter in the background like you've been doing? I'd feel far more comfortable having a familiar face nearby." My question hangs in the air for an agonizing few moments while he sips his coffee again. Heat suffuses my cheeks, and I am about to walk away when he answers.

"Yep. Okay. What time?" He slides the sunglasses back on and shifts his head slightly as if he is looking past me.

"One thirty." A short sharp nod is the only confirmation he gives me. Okay. Got it. End of conversation I acknowledge internally and, with my short break over, walk back to my post behind the coffee machine, grumbling about the damn uncommunicative macho men in my life.

Chapter Thirty-Seven

EMILY

I check my watch again and huff out a breath because only five minutes have passed since I last looked at it. My stomach is in knots from the thought of meeting Bruce Baxter shortly.

The week has disappeared in a blur and here I am, working on Saturday morning, mainly to fill in time so I am not sitting moping in my apartment. If I keep myself busy, I don't have time to think about Ethan, or so I delude myself. Thoughts of him, his cheeky grin, and the way his eyes light up when he looks at me creep through my defenses, stabbing at my heart and making me wonder who he has in his bed today.

His persistent text messages earlier in the week have now stopped because of my lack of response. He also made a couple of frantic phone calls to check that I was okay, which I appreciated, but let go to voicemail. My simple cold response of "All good. Busy," to the third call, however, must have sent the desired message that I want nothing to do with him because all communication has stopped.

While I reflect on why Ethan even bothered to text and call me when he is involved with someone else, questioning again how little

I really knew him, I spot Mav entering the courtyard, no doubt early, to assess the area.

The morning crowd has tapered off and only a few people are taking advantage of the post lunch calm and balmy weather, sitting at the bench tables leisurely catching up with friends. I make Mav a coffee, then finish up my work, grab my bag, and yell to the manager that I am out of here.

Mav is positioned in the far corner of the courtyard, facing toward the crowd, in his typical surveillance mode black t-shirt, which hangs from his thick broad shoulders, draping over his rock-solid torso, and finishes over the waistband of his camouflage style trousers. Sunglasses hide his eyes, and I can feel him watching me as I stroll toward him and place the coffee cup in front of him.

"What's this?"

"It's my way of saying thank you for helping me out today." He nods and says thanks while I saunter to an empty table not far away, wondering if Bruce will recognize me.

While I wait, my fingers fidget nervously with the table condiments and signage and my gaze peruses any newcomers, hoping that Bruce won't leave me hanging by not turning up. My stomach is churning, and I check my watch again. One-thirty. I pull an old photo of Mom, Bruce and me when I was a baby that I found in Mom's things out of my bag, hoping it will help me recognize him. Thirty years have passed since the photo was taken, and I try to imagine what he will look like now in his late fifties.

When I look up again, a middle-aged man of average height and stocky build saunters into the courtyard area, his silvery gray head turned toward the café. My heart thumps in my chest, certain that this is him. He turns his head, casting his gaze around the seating area and his eyes lock onto mine. His head jerks back slightly and a flash of surprised recognition crosses his face. As he hesitates, I recognize him as an older version of the man in the photo and give him a tentative smile, wondering if he will hightail it out of here now that he has seen me. Thankfully, Bruce wanders over with a stiff gait.

"Emily?" he queries in an easygoing tone. He seems self-assured and confident, his refined voice quiet and unemotional. His high forehead is framed by a thick straight hairline, neatly trimmed and brushed back off his face. His straight nose, hooded brown eyes, cheeks puffy with age, and thinnish lips are set against a backdrop of clear smooth, pinkish-beige skin, making him still a good-looking man.

"Yes. Bruce?" Extending my hand in the direction of the seat opposite me, I continue with a friendly smile, although my voice quavers. "Thank you for coming." Tugging at his trouser legs as he sits, he scrutinizes me closely and rests his lightly tanned forearms, with cuffs rolled up, on the table, his hands clasped in front of him. A fluttery feeling circles my stomach as nervousness assails me like I have been unexpectedly called into the principal's office. My mind scurries trying to find something else to say.

"You look just like your mother," Bruce utters in his strong English accent. "Sorry to hear of her passing."

"Thank you. A lot of people have said that. I've always put it down to the red hair." My eyes drop to my clenched hands and remember the photo of us I am still holding. Passing it across the table, I show it to him. "I thought you might like to see this. I found it when I was cleaning out Mom's stuff." My eyes get watery, and my voice is a bit shaky with remembered emotions and better times with Mom.

"This was taken just before I left," he volunteers, an edge of sadness in his voice. "You were about one, if I remember correctly. Yes, we had just celebrated your first birthday."

"What happened? Why did you leave?" The words blurt out and I soften them by adding, "Mom always made out that you died."

"Yeah, that was probably for the best. My visa expired and I had to return here. Joanne wanted to stay in Australia. I tried reapplying but the process took several years. In the meantime, communication between your mom and I stalled as we got on with our lives. When I filed for a divorce because I met and fell in love with my current wife, it became non-existent." Bruce pauses, as if reflecting on those times, and adds softly, "I always remember your birthday. Even though I never send you anything, I always buy a cupcake to celebrate it and honor you." His voice is wobbly, and I feel tears well in my eyes, surprised and touched by his admission. He seems to be just as surprised by his revelation.

Clearing my throat and blinking away the tears, my voice cracks when I answer, "From your letter, I didn't expect you to say something like that. But thank you for telling me."

Bruce simply nods his head, then asks as he hands the photo back, "Did your mom ever remarry?"

"No, never. If she had any romantic interests, I wasn't aware of them. Whenever she spoke of you though, which wasn't often, she always seemed wistful." I don't want him thinking Mom had been pining for him all these years so add, with a bright fondness, "We had a very close relationship. She worked hard to provide for us and was more like a best friend once I reached adulthood. I miss her terribly." To lift the somberness of my words, I ask, "Tell me about your family."

"Well, I have four kids, two daughters and two sons. The eldest son is twenty-eight, the youngest son is twenty-six, and my twin daughters are twenty-four. They are all working in good jobs and my wife, Liz, works part-time as a schoolteacher." There is pride in his voice, which is to be expected, but it stings that he doesn't feel that way about me.

"Nice. I'm also a schoolteacher, although I've been doing a lot of temp work while I'm here. What sort of work do you do Bruce?" I ask thinking that this is no different from the conversations I have with customers in the café and while I understand I'm a stranger to him, it makes me sad that our relationship is not likely to change.

He tells me that he is an accountant for a large organization and is hoping to retire in the next few years, and I discover he enjoys reading and outdoor activities like hiking. He smiles warmly when I tell him I am the same and we laugh about how much Mom hated those things. He shares a memory of trying to get Mom to go bushwalking before I was born. I ask him about his childhood, which he brushes off lightly as ordinary, and that he was an only child, with his parents both deceased.

"What about you, Emily? Are you married?" he enquires, seemingly curious.

"No, not married. I was engaged, but that broke up about eighteen months ago. No one serious since then. So, I am exploring the world before I get tied down," I answer, making light of the topic that still hurts.

There is a slight pause and I ask the question I have been eager to know the answer to. "Why don't you want your family to know about me?" His lips draw together and his forehead creases in a frown and he sits silently, his gaze scanning the courtyard. Patiently, I wait for his response, and when I think I won't get one, he returns gruffly, "Because I'm ashamed of how I didn't stick by you or Joanne. The obstacles seemed far too hard at the time." His words are clipped, and he sighs heavily before continuing, "Liz, my wife, doesn't know I was married before, and I don't think she will handle it very well. Particularly as you and Joanne have the same coloring and look very much like her." I immediately surmised the implications for him if his wife realized she looked like a copy of his first wife. Not a good situation to be in. But it also alludes to how much he loved my mom by falling in love with someone who looked like her.

"I understand your dilemma. Difficult for your kids to accept as well, I guess," I acknowledge, compassion coloring my tone. "Why did you say yes to meeting me at all?"

"Curiosity, mainly. To see what sort of woman the little girl I remembered had turned into. To reassure myself that my leaving worked out for the best for you both." We sit in silence for a moment or two, neither too sure of what to say next, when Bruce's phone dings, startling us both. While he reads the message, I check the time on my phone, surprised that an hour has passed already.

He puts his phone back into his shirt pocket and smiles warmly at me, the corner of his eyes crinkling. "I have to head off. It's been an absolute pleasure meeting you, Emily. I'm so pleased you contacted me." He sounds sincere as he stands, and I am confused and hurting that I am losing him again while my inner child screams at me, *You're not good enough for him to want to get to know more about you.*

"Oh, okay. It is a pleasure meeting you too, Bruce." I mutter, extending my hand to shake his, but he surprises me by pulling me in for a hug.

He releases me and asks, "How long are you in London for? I'd like to stay in touch and maybe meet again if that is okay with you."

My head is nodding as vigorously as one of those toy dogs you put on the car dashboard and my mouth feels like it is stretching from ear to ear. Beaming at him, I am as ecstatic as a little girl whose daddy had promised her a special treat. "I'm not sure how long I will stay here, but I'd like that very much. Bye, for now, Bruce."

"Bye, Emily." His voice trembles and again he smiles, then turns and walks away. My eyes follow him, and he turns and waves before disappearing behind the shrubbery.

Standing rooted to the spot, dazed and still looking in the direction of where Bruce walked out of sight, two arms suddenly wrap around me as a warm body collides with mine, making me stagger sideways. Rashida gushes, "Ohh, Emily, was that him? Tell me, tell me. It looks like it went well." Looking around, I spot Lorenzo moving in for a hug as well, but he stops and stands nearby, which I find a bit odd until I hear Mav's strong, crisp voice behind me.

"Are you okay, Emily?" He looks like he is ready to drag Rashida off me. Gathering myself, I step out of Rashida's embrace as I answer.

"Yes, thanks, Mav. These are my friends, Rashida and Lorenzo." Rashida's jaw drops when she turns around and sees Mav's imposing figure behind her. He simply nods, eyeing them both, obviously satisfied I am in safe hands.

"Your friends are here now, so I'll head off."

"Thank you so much. I really appreciate your help," I babble, leaning in and wrapping my arms around his waist. His body is like hugging a tree trunk, hard and immovable. Catching him unaware, his arms splay out in front of him, like a barrier around me, as if he is unsure whether to return the hug or tough it out. Knowing how uneasy he is, I quickly release him and step away, making light of the situation by adding playfully, "I owe you about a dozen coffees." With a decisive nod, he strides away.

Plonking myself on the bench seat, Rashida and Lorenzo assail me with a barrage of questions about Bruce and Mav, which I answer before returning the questioning to them about their trip. Feeling bewildered and muddled, I know I need some quiet time to digest all the afternoon's happenings, so listen with detached interest as they fill me in on their many adventures.

Chapter Thirty-Eight

ETHAN

Finally, I am back home after a week traveling the northern countryside. Breathing a sigh of relief as I park my car in the basement car park, I step out and stretch my aching body.

The return trip was a five-hour drive, so I am tired and deflated. Some of the potential developments appear fruitful, others will need a lot more investigation. I think in future I will send one of my managers to do the research because a lot of the meetings were a waste of time. Either that or I will condense the trip into two days, fly into Manchester, and hire a car. It was necessary to make this trip because of the awards ceremony and it seemed to make sense at the time to combine into one longer trip my attendance at the ceremony with the research activities. I won't do that again.

Grabbing my laptop and luggage from the trunk, I amble to the elevator, leaning against the wall while it travels to my apartment. When I step into my apartment, it looks just as I left it, and I am struck with a sense of longing as I remember coming home to beautiful-smelling dinners cooked by Emily, or the sound of music permeating the sterile space, both making it feel homely and welcoming. Instead, the only sound is my footsteps echoing on the marble and timber floors. And the smell? I sniff the air. Well, there is nothing distinctive or discernible other than a hint of cleaning products.

Trudging down the hallway to my study, I put my laptop bag on the desk then move to my bedroom, dropping the luggage in my walk-in closet, with the intention of unpacking later. As I walk to the bed, I notice how scrupulously clean and tidy everything seems to be. *Wow, this new cleaner sure is doing an amazing job. The place is cleaner than most hotels I've stayed in.* Pushing the thought aside, I flop on the bed and stare at the ceiling with my hands behind my head. I should probably get some food, but it's Sunday night and I couldn't be bothered going back out to a restaurant. I'm not really feeling hungry either, so ordering in would be a bit of a waste. There should still be some bread in the freezer and some cheese in the refrigerator, so I decide to have a toasted cheese sandwich in a little while.

Looking back on the awards ceremony, it was typically a glitzy, glamorous occasion, and a long night of boring speeches. Although, it was also a good opportunity to network and catch up with some friends and associates. And, like previous years, lots of people had too much to drink, so there were many opportunities for hook ups. Unlike previous years, I wasn't interested in anyone. I just felt lethargic and indifferent, and still do. I put some of that down to homesickness, being out of the normal routine, but then it dawned on me that I was feeling like this for a couple of days after Emily left.

Emily. I am bewildered and hurt by her lack of contact and there is a constant ache behind my breastbone that I frequently find myself subconsciously massaging. I've only had two messages from her this last week. One was friendly, like Emily is, asking about getting her hairdryer from her room here. The other was later in the week and an obvious brush off after I had sent several texts and a couple of frantic voicemail messages to ensure she was okay, all unanswered. Three words are all I received back after the last voicemail, where I urged her to let me know she was okay. Three cold little words: "All good. Busy." I took the hint and left her alone, realizing I was being an obsessive jerk, just like her ex. And she doesn't need another one of those in her life.

I remember that, while I was away, about mid-week, a flippant comment I made to a barman about having girlfriend issues spawned an introspection of my feelings for Emily, posing the question of when I had started thinking about her as a 'girlfriend'. At the time, I finally admitted to myself that she is well and truly embedded in my heart and that I am miserable without her, so would be honored to have her as my girlfriend. I suspected she was more guarded with her feelings than me due to our previous track record. She is warm and giving, and I feel I know her well enough to know she would have vetoed sex between us if she didn't have strong feelings for me.

But now, I don't understand what changed for her. *Did she end up hooking up with Tom while she was away? Was she playing me all along as some sort of payback for ditching her so rudely in Australia? Did my heavy handling of her frighten her more than she let on? But if that was the case, why did she sleep with me later? Does she have some sort of hangover from her ex-boyfriend where she needs to give a man what he wants for the sake of getting out unscathed?* I keep going round in circles, asking the same questions without any feasible answers. All I know is that I have a thick lump in my throat that won't go away and a perpetual hollow feeling in my chest. Now I understand why Xander was such a prick after he ditched Georgie in the early stages of their relationship.

Sick of myself and my internal contemplation, I plod to the kitchen and rummage around making two toasted cheese sandwiches. I also message Ramon to let him know I am home and frown at his single word reply. "Good." I know he is a man of few words, but normally he would respond with something more.

Knowing I should finish writing up my notes from the trip, I can't be bothered, so decide to zone out in front of the television. Much later, my phone dings, waking me from my slouched position on the lounge. Grimacing as I straighten the kinks out of my neck and shoulders, I read the message from Ramon.

Ramon

Normal time tomorrow?

Ethan

Yep, sounds good. Thx

Noticing the time is after midnight, I take myself off to shower and bed. But I can't help diverting into Emily's room just to relive those memories cherishing the way I felt close to her. I quickly check the bathroom for her hairdryer, but it's not there. *She must have picked it up already.* The thought drives home how much she didn't want to see me. *I wonder why Ramon didn't say anything though.* Shrugging my shoulders, I am too tired to give it much thought and traipse back to my room.

The next morning, I meet Ramon in the underground parking garage. He is leaning against the vehicle, waiting for me, and I fist pump him in greeting. "How's it going, bro?"

"Good. Glad you're back." Short and sharp response from Ramon as per usual, but I sense something is off, and watch him pace around the car to get in the driver's seat.

"Everything okay?" He makes eye contact with me through the rear-view mirror while he reaches for his sunglasses in the upper compartment.

"Yeah. Just got a tricky situation I'm investigating."

His cryptic response prompts me to question, suddenly alert, "Anything I should know about?"

"Yeah, but I'll tell you about it when I have a few more pieces in the puzzle." I trust Ramon and know he usually puts out fires before I even become aware of them.

As we drive out of the parking lot, I remember to ask him, "Did Emily contact you while I was away about getting her hair dryer?"

Ramon's head snaps to the rear-view mirror again, his manner coy as he states, "Yes. Why?"

"I noticed last night that it wasn't there and assumed she had already collected it. Just disappointed to have not seen her." Ramon nods and turns his gaze back to the traffic and after a moment I voice a question as casually as I can that has been plaguing me. "Do you hear much from her? She seems to be incommunicado with me for some reason."

"A bit here and there, but she is flat out with work." His answer seems evasive, which intrigues and angers me, spiking a burning jealous sensation in my stomach. *Are he and Emily getting it on? Is that why he is evasive? Is that why she is not communicating with me anymore?* Fuming, I rip my laptop out of its bag, open it with more force than needed, then pound on the keys as I type for the rest of the journey.

The rest of the week continued in the same vein as Monday and I brood after another solitary dinner on Friday. The hollow feeling inside me and a grumpy irritability are my new status quo. I am sure I am making life hell for those around me, but I can't seem to shake the blues, no matter how much running or working out I do.

I am resigned to the fact that Emily wants nothing to do with me and assume she has moved on. The nagging question that remains is why. Did I do something to scare her away? Racking my brain, I can't think of anything other than her flashback where I bruised her shoulder, but I thought we resolved that. So why did she dump me? Aside from the fact that my ego is battered because I've always been the dumper, not the dumpee, I can only assume it was payback for ghosting her. Anger and disappointment battle it out over her apparent pettiness, shouting louder than my heart's conviction that Emily is not that sort of person. I can't count how many times I have picked up the phone to text or call her, only to push it away again, reminding myself to respect her wish to avoid me.

The part that surprises me most though is my loss of sex drive. It's almost like Emily took it with her because, for the first time since my pre-teen years, I don't even feel inclined to jerk off. Two weeks without any form of sex or masturbation is a record for me, and not one that I wish to crow about. Nor do I want it to continue for much longer because I am frustrated and living the life of a hermit. What's that old saying? *All work and no play makes Ethan a dull boy*, certainly is a true account of my life right now.

Ramon has driven me to work every day, as usual, but I totally avoid the subject of Emily. If he is with her, then good luck to him, but it will be awkward seeing them together. And if she isn't with Ramon, it's probably a good thing, but then there is no point in discussing the situation with him because I have lost her to someone else.

With a total lack of interest, I tidy up the kitchen and load the dishwasher, trying to decide what *fun* activity will keep me occupied until bedtime. I've watched re-run after re-run of my favorite TV shows and sports games. Looks like I need to go for a run to get myself out of the apartment and exhaust my body.

Yes, I need to get out of here, but my body needs a break from the grueling punishment I've inflicted on it over the last couple of weeks. Then I remember an invitation to an art exhibition tonight at Simon's gallery. *I wonder if Emily will be working it?* A thrill of excitement runs through me, and my decision is made.

I change clothes quickly and head to the elevator and then the parked car, impatient with the necessary travel time because I just want to be there to see Emily. Even if she won't talk to me, I am convinced that seeing her will eradicate these doldrums and I will be able to move on.

Butterflies stir in my stomach as I stand outside, looking through the large glass doors. Taking a deep breath, I steady my nerves, and repeat the words, 'Play it cool' like a mantra in my head.

Donning my savoir-faire cloak, I push open the doors and stride inside, nodding confidently to a few familiar faces. I notice that Rashida, who is again the hostess, does a double take when she sees me, and her smile almost slips before she plasters it in place as she approaches.

"Ethan, hello. You know the routine. Have a look around, and the bidding will start in fifteen minutes." Her voice is elegant and professional, but not as warm as I remember it.

"Thank you, Rashida. How was the trip to Scotland?"

"Mostly enjoyable, and certainly worthwhile seeing." She seems surprised by my question but also wary to not give anything away about Emily.

"Mostly enjoyable?" I subtly press her.

"Yes, you know how it is. Constant traveling can be exhausting," she quips evasively, her face inscrutable, correctly surmising I am fishing for information.

"So true," I respond as she extends her arm in a cordial invitation to enter.

Wandering around, I give cursory regard to the artworks, none of which pique my interest, purely because my attention is focused on scanning the room for Emily. I can't see her, and after an hour standing at the back of the bidding crowd, there is still no sign of her on the catering crew.

Disappointed, I leave, bidding Rashida a goodnight. I nearly blurt out, "Tell Emily I said hi," but figure she is not likely to pass on the message anyway. Then my pride's inner voice berates me. *If Emily wants to play games, let her. I'm not buying into it.*

Storming back to my car, I sit in the driver's seat, wondering what I should do now. Going back to my apartment to sit around aimlessly biding time does not appeal. *Maybe I should go to a bar, but which one?* Remembering there is one near the restaurant where Emily works, I make my way there but divert to the restaurant instead.

You are such a loser, I chide myself after sitting in the parked car for an hour. It is well past Emily's usual finish time, and there is still no sign of her. When I got here, I stood out front peering in for a while, making out I was reading the menu on the window. Nope, she didn't appear to be working. Instead, I sit in the car, deluding myself that the sight of her getting on with her life would be enough to get me out of this funk. *You are no better than the stalker who followed her,* an inner voice hounds me. Disgusted with myself, I fire up the engine and charge off.

Chapter Thirty-Nine

ETHAN

Saturday morning, I sigh, screwing my nose up at the foul coffee I have just made after an intense workout at the downstairs gym. My phone dings with a message as I pour the coffee down the sink.

Ramon
You home, E?

Ethan
Sure am.

Ramon
Great. See you in five.

Obviously concerned about my disconnected mood of late, Ramon has been dropping in and just hanging out a bit more frequently.

I crank up the coffee machine again, taking more care not to overfill the filter basket or scald the milk, so by the time Ramon comes out of the elevator, the coffee is ready for him. He accepts it dubiously, and fist pumps me in greeting.

"What's going on, man?" I ask as he props himself on a bar stool at the kitchen bench.

"Been researching that tricky situation I was telling you about and I finally have it sorted." Before I can respond, he continues, shrewdly watching me, "And it involves you."

"Me? How?" My eyes scan his face, trying to gauge whether he is serious.

"Well, you know how Emily messaged asking to collect her hairdryer?"

"Yeah."

"I dropped her off here on the Monday before you went north..." Ramon begins to elaborate.

"Wait. On the Monday? She came home from Scotland early? Why? What happened? And why am I only finding out about this now?" My incredulity turns to glowering annoyance at being kept in the dark about this, trying to fathom what could have scared Emily away.

Rolling his eyes at me, he continues, "I'll get to that in a minute. When Emily came back downstairs, she was in tears. She said that she heard you laughing in your room and this sexily clad woman came out and spotted her, inviting her to join in. Understandably, Emily was heartbroken and ran."

"What? I don't understand." I can feel my forehead furrowing so deeply, I am sure my eyebrows are touching. I perch on one of the barstools.

"E, shut up and let me finish. Then it will make sense." Ramon pauses, watching my mouth open as I am about to say something, then close it again to let him finish. "We went through the video footage from the foyer, and Emily identified the woman, although she was in jeans when she entered the building. So, I've been scouring footage for previous weeks to see if this has happened before, and how the woman got access to your apartment. It turns out she's your new cleaner. And here's the kicker. She's been running a call girl service from your apartment."

"What? Fucking what?" I roar. "How?"

"Well, as your cleaner, she has access to the apartment. She has been arranging for her patrons to arrive with a take-away food bag as if they are deliverymen. As you know, the concierge doesn't let anyone ride these elevators unless they have a card. When the concierge call up, she is already changed into her sexy gear and takes the elevator down to meet them. Then she brings them in and 'does the business'."

Ramon waits, letting that sink in, and watching my mouth opening and closing like a goldfish. "That's why Emily heard a male voice when she walked past your bedroom. Unfortunately, but understandably, she assumed it was you." His voice softens on this last bit, eagle eyeing me, knowing that it would hurt me. Yep. It's like a sucker punch in the solar plexus. My mind is reeling. How could Emily think I would do that to her? Apparently, I'd spoken those words aloud, because Ramon answered with the sensitivity of a sledgehammer.

"Well, your history as a 'love 'em and leave 'em' guy hasn't done you any favors there. Neither has the fact that you ghosted her in Sydney. Why wouldn't she think that you'd taken up with someone else when she heard a male voice in *your* apartment? She was no longer staying here and was going away so, in her mind, you had free reign again to do what you liked."

Putting aside Emily's assumptions for the moment, and blinking rapidly while processing this shocking information, my voice is grim as

I work through the pieces of the puzzle. "How did the cleaner manage it? And why not use a hotel? Surely that would be easier."

"I know it's a lot to take in, E, but think about it. She was your cleaner. She could do the deed, make the bed, and take away any rubbish afterwards. Sheets could be left in the drier and no one would think anything of it. As a cleaner, she could be here for a couple of hours without anyone questioning it." Pausing, he shrugs then adds, "I suppose a hotel carries its own risks. It could get quite costly too, particularly if booked for a week or more, and that would eat into her takings. Using your apartment, there are no expenses, and she is being paid double income—from you and her clients."

Another piece falls into place when I remember a question that I asked Ramon several weeks ago. "And that would explain the vanishing cologne," I conclude flatly, shifting to outrage as I continue, "Her fucking clients were using my fucking five hundred dollar a bottle cologne!" I thump my fist on the counter, the noise bouncing off the hard stone surfaces.

Astounded that this had been going on under my nose, my words are clipped when I stand and seethe, "Fucking bitch." Pacing while Ramon drinks his coffee, I inhale deeply, trying to find a sense of calm so I can think logically and clearly. Tersely, I ask, "How did you put it all together?"

"It's taken a while to get the evidence together. A bit of a sting operation, and a few covert cameras around the apartment." My narrowed eyes snap to his, and he simultaneously anticipates my thoughts. "Yes, including your bedroom. Don't worry, they will be removed. Others opposite the lift downstairs to see how frequently she has been escorting clients up here. And a trip sensor near the elevator entrance here. We were able to tap into her calls, and one of my operatives posed as a client, so we could see how the whole racket worked."

"Fuuuck. What can we do about this mess? I want her gone. I'll ring the agency Monday," I snarl.

"We could have her charged, but most likely, it won't stick. She will get off due to illegal entrapment and surveillance."

"Fuck. There must be something else," I snap with frustration.

"Yeah, I've been thinking about that." His look is sly, devilish and challenging, pausing to ensure he has my attention. "We could catch her in the act, plant a supposed client, and have you walk in on them. That way you get the satisfaction of kicking her out and having her escorted from the building."

"I like your thinking. Arrange it as soon as possible." Ramon nods in agreement, a menacing grin crossing his face.

My mind is now in damage control mode, imagining potential ramifications, when I request, "Can you do a sweep of the place to make sure she hasn't got the place bugged or hidden any cameras of her own? I don't want to end up being blackmailed for living in my own apartment."

Ramon stands and takes a few steps to the sink, placing his cup in before turning to walk past me. I grip him on the shoulder, extending my free hand to him in a handshake, grateful he is such a good friend, a brother from another mother. "Thanks, bro. I don't know how to repay you."

He swings a thick bulging bicep around my neck in a mock headlock and pulls me in for a man hug, then steps back, releasing me. "Just doing my job. And you can thank Emily for stumbling across the woman." His eyes widen like he didn't mean to mention Emily.

"Yeah, you were going to tell me about her," I prompt, solemnly.

He watches me closely and appears to be mulling over the right words to use but, like ripping off a Bandaid, he spills the details. "Tom made a move on her, which she rejected, but he kept persisting. The group were sleeping in a dorm and she didn't trust him to leave her alone during the night, so she came home."

"Good girl," I utter to myself, then bark, "I knew that creep was no good."

"Thanks for looking out for her, man." His astute gaze pierces my soul, acknowledging my longing for her, and I drop my gaze.

"You need to let her know it wasn't you in the bedroom," he puts forth softly, almost beseechingly. Sighing, I give him a tight-lipped smile and nod. He waves two fingers near his forehead in a cross between a salute and a hat tip gesture, then walks to the elevator and disappears inside.

Fueled by antagonism toward the cleaning woman, I pace around the apartment to see if anything is missing. There doesn't appear to be anything missing, but I am experiencing a sense of violation because my private space, my sanctuary, has been invaded. People I don't know or trust have been handling my personal possessions, making me feel sick, unclean, and very angry. I can't fathom how someone would go to such lengths, not only the arrangements in getting into the building, but the laundering and re-sprucing the apartment, when surely a hotel would have been more of a walk-in, walk-out practical solution. As a result of her activities, I now have to live, for a short time at least, with covert cameras recording my every move. *So much for sleeping tonight,* I muse.

Like they have all day, my thoughts turn to Emily as I get ready for bed, a habit that has developed lately. Instead of daydreaming and reminiscing about her like I have every day, I ponder whether I should take Ramon's advice and let her know it wasn't me that she heard in my bedroom. *If I were her, would I believe me?* Probably not. It sounds like a convenient excuse. Knowing that she doubts my faithfulness to her lances me like a spear to the heart. But as Ramon said, my track record as a womanizer doesn't provide much credibility to my claim of faithfulness. I am at a loss as to how I can make her believe me. *That is, if she will even speak with me*, I reason with skepticism. But I know I need to try to make her understand how I feel about her.

Ticking off my options, I consider texting or phoning her. *She has probably blocked me. No, that won't work.* Maybe I can write her a letter. *She will probably throw it in the bin. So, no guarantee that she will read it.* Maybe Ramon will tell her. *That makes me look like a shy, gutless teenager. No, suck it up, Princess. Be a man and approach her.* Yes, that feels right. *She can see my sincerity that way.* But how do I get her to meet me? Remembering the old adage, I decide to 'take Mohamed to the mountain'.

Chapter Forty

The beginning of a new week and the first stage of Operation Win Emily Back is in play. Yesterday, I contemplated at length Ramon's comment that Emily was crying when she left my apartment, concluding that, surely, it must mean she has strong feelings for me. So, drawing on my project planning experience, I've devised a strategy which is my new goal.

Now that I understand the reason for her silence, I am enthusiastic about proving to Emily she can trust me with her heart and that I will stand by her no matter what. Stage one in progress—a dozen long-stemmed red roses delivered to her apartment today, with a card simply reading, ***It wasn't me in the bedroom. Ramon will verify. I miss you. Please come back.***

Surprisingly, everyone in the office today seems much happier. Pamela even commented this morning that I seem to be in a good mood, and when I affirmed that I am, she uttered a very dry, witty, "Thank god for that." I held back a smile because her clever sarcasm often cracks me up, but also makes me realize, and regret, how difficult I have been.

I feel energized now that I have a plan regarding Emily and am confident that I can allay her fears regarding my fidelity. I am a skilled negotiator after all and have worn down even the most hardheaded, obstinate power brokers over time. And I have all the time in the world where Emily is concerned because I don't intend letting her go.

By mid-afternoon, the notification about the flowers arrives. I expect Emily will still be at work, so probably isn't even aware of them yet. However, I am antsy about her reaction and hope she will message me later. Despite being in meetings all afternoon, I am upbeat in anticipation, so the time goes quickly.

When I get home, there is still no message from Emily, which I am disappointed about, but rationalize that she could be working at the restaurant and hasn't had time to go home. Or she might be wondering what to say in reply. Maybe she doesn't want to seem too eager with her response. Who knows, but I am patient and can wait.

Ramon drops in later that evening to hang out and mentions Emily, so I press him for further details.

"I called in to tell her about what the cleaner was using your apartment for and showed her some of the footage," Ramon explains. "Like all of us, Emily was shocked at the audacity of the woman." He looks at me expectantly, like a kid with a secret who is bursting to tell you what it is.

"Did she say anything else?" I prompt impatiently and watch cheekiness twinkle in his eyes, and a playful smile plays along his lips. He quickly masks his features into a deadpan expression, though.

"She's a smart girl and put two and two together herself. Even commented that she understood it wasn't you in the bedroom. She even sounded regretful that she jumped to that conclusion." I nod and grin, then he adds, "I reassured her that it was a logical conclusion and that you wouldn't hold it against her."

"Yes," I exclaim and high five him. "Thank you, bro."

I sound him out on my plans to win Emily back, which he approves of, but cautions that she is embarrassed by her groundless assumption and thinks I hate her because of it.

Heeding and reflecting on his advice after he leaves, I understand how she feels, but it adds to my determination to tell her I love her. *Funny how admitting that I love her doesn't scare me anymore,* I muse. *It has become so much a part of me that it is like the air that I breathe. I can't live without it. And I can't live without her. I have experienced not having her in my life and know I don't want to go there again. The sooner I can tell her, the better our chance of a future together.*

For the first time in a couple of weeks, I go to bed with a smile on my face.

The next morning, I pay Emily a visit at the café. Thankfully, Ramon let it 'slip' last night when she was working, so I drop by just before the lunchtime rush. Using their app as I approach the cafe, I pre-order my coffee, knowing that Emily will call out my name and hand it to me. I'm hoping to speak with her, let her know there are no hard feelings and, if this next step in the strategy doesn't pan out, then I will hang around until I can talk with her.

As I stand hovering near the counter behind a couple of other people also waiting for their orders, I catch an occasional glimpse of Emily as she moves around behind the coffee machine. Her beautiful red hair is tied back in a ponytail, which sways and shimmers as she moves. I can't help but smile when I see her, my heart hammering in my chest, and a sense of wholeness filling me. *Oh, I have missed her gorgeous, smiling face,* I reflect as I draw in a long deep savoring breath. Apparently, my cock has missed her too, because I feel a sudden throb and flush of warmth spreading from my groin as my cock stiffens. *Yes,*

I'm back, I crow internally, acknowledging that Emily is the only one who can get me from flaccid to rock hard at just the sight of her.

Watching and admiring everything about her, she calls out the names of other patrons, moving out from behind the machine to place their cup on the counter for them to collect, before disappearing behind the machine again without any form of contact with them.

"Ethan," she yells, but this time she holds the cup and looks around for the owner. When I step forward and walk toward her with a beaming smile, her unblinking gaze holds mine and a small smile upturns her mouth while her face flushes a soft pink.

"Hi, Em," I murmur, my eyes raking over her beautiful, freckled face, deliberately touching her hand when I reach for the cup and feeling an electrical jolt shoot through my hand and arm.

"Hi," she whispers breathlessly, blinking as her hand, engulfed in mine, continues to hold the cup.

"Can we talk?" I offer a touch huskily, still beaming at her, as I feel emotion rise in my throat.

Nodding, she responds softly, "Can you give me five minutes?"

"Anything for you, Em," I gush with sincerity. "I'll wait at one of the tables for you."

Giving me a closed-mouth smile and nodding, I remove the cup from her hand as she moves back behind the coffee machine.

I turn and amble towards the tables but glance back over my shoulder and spot Em peeking from behind the machine, watching me, which puts a spring in my step. Taking a seat at a nearby small round table against a potted plant, I sit watching the patrons shift and change, then see Emily come out the side door and make her way towards me.

As she approaches, I stand, wanting to pull her into my arms and kiss her. At the very least, hug her. But I also don't want to come on too strong, so I bend and kiss her on the cheek like good friends often do.

"Hi. Thank you for the roses," she says with a grin, seeming more her confident self, hopefully because she can see my feelings for her haven't changed. "I can't stay long, because it's getting busy," she adds apologetically as we both sit, and I suspect her last comment is probably a safeguard measure in case our discussion goes awry.

"No problem. I just wanted to see you. I've missed you, Em," I murmur, stretching my arms out and placing my hands on either side of where hers rest on the table.

"Ethan, I'm so sorry I jumped to the wrong conclusion," she apologizes. "I shouldn't have doubted you." Her gaze drops as she lets her embarrassment show.

"Em, it's fine. It was a logical assumption. In the same circumstances, I would have thought the same." My thumbs reassuringly stroke the soft flesh of her inner wrists. "Only difference is, I would have barged in and belted the living daylights out of whoever was with you." Her lips move into a faint smile, her eyes widening with the vehemence of my last statement.

She blushes, and I notice her chin quiver slightly. "Will you forgive me, Ethan?" she pleads, her voice catching in her throat.

"I already have, gorgeous girl." Her worried eyes fly to mine as if to gauge my sincerity, and I give her a smile that could melt steel. Sliding my fingers between her palms, I hold her soft, pale hands, enveloping them in mine. "And I want to spend as much time with you as I can. I know you have limited time today, but will you come out to dinner with me tomorrow night? I want to take you on a proper date."

Her beautiful smile beams at me, as she answers softly, "Really? I'd love to go on a date with you Ethan."

"I thought we could go to a place where you feel comfortable, so maybe Marguerite's restaurant? But if you would rather be somewhere else, I'll happily go wherever you want to go."

Emily ponders my suggestion for a moment, then replies in her sweet, sensuous voice, "I'd like that very much, Ethan. Thank you." Pulling her phone out of her shirt pocket, she glances at the time, then sighs. "Sorry, but I have to get back to work."

"Okay." I smile, my eyes warm with admiration as I watch her stand, then follow suit, leaning in to peck her on the cheek. "I'll text you the details." She nods and takes a few steps before I call out, "Don't forget to unblock me." Emily turns and smilingly gives me a thumbs up, then pivots and walks back to her coffee machine. My lustful eyes rake appraisingly over her curvaceous figure, longing to hold her close.

Lingering in the courtyard for a while longer to finish my coffee and just be within Emily's vicinity, I am pleased that this meeting went as well as I had hoped. With the initial awkwardness out of the way, my aim for dinner tomorrow night is to get back to the undeniable and indefinable connection we have together.

After I begin walking back to the office, I decide to hail a cab. As I slide into the rear seat, I revel in the exquisite sensation of arousal that Emily has brought to life again and eagerly anticipate tomorrow night's dinner.

Chapter Forty-One

EMILY

After Ramon told me about the scenario in Ethan's apartment, I was mortified at misjudging Ethan, assuming he would want nothing to do with me, or that he suspected my lack of contact was because I didn't want to have anything to do with him. If the truth be known, my residual low self-esteem issues made it very easy to believe he would seek solace elsewhere, particularly with his playboy background. I was also hurting so bad, that I couldn't bear to talk to him or have any messages from him, so I blocked him.

The more time that passed, the more I believed he had moved on, justifying to myself that he knew where I lived so could come talk to me if he really wanted to. The fact that he didn't come to see me proved my case, I felt.

Ramon's news upset me more than I let on. How could I be so judgmental, so reactive, when I profess to be all about conciliation and talking out issues? After spending the rest of the evening in introspection, I didn't feel worthy enough to contact Ethan straight away and assumed he had wiped his hands of me for misjudging him.

Until the roses arrived. Just when the constant ache, and my nightly tossing and turning going over every little thing that he had said and done, had started to ease and vestiges of my pre-Ethan-self showed glimmers of returning.

When I came home to see the flowers on my doorstep, my heart pounded, and I was as excited as a giddy schoolgirl, hoping they were from Ethan. But I also felt a twinge of guilt that I should have sent something to him to apologize.

I re-read the card so many times, and wanted to send a message of thanks, but what could I say? 'Thanks for the roses' sounded so indifferent, like we hadn't had a special connection. 'I'm sorry,' didn't seem enough. I was still mulling over the best choice of words when I saw his name pop up on my order screen at work, anxiously waiting to see if it was him. And I am so pleased it was.

He doesn't seem to hold a grudge against me, thankfully, and seems keen to pick up where we left off, I reflect while sitting at home on the sofa, yearning to spend time with him at dinner tomorrow night. *Dinner What will I wear?*

Jumping up, I race to my room and rummage through my wardrobe, which is minimalist at best, searching for something perfect. I know Marguerite's restaurant isn't high class dining, but my pride dictates getting dressed up for a date.

One garment after another is flung on the bed with dissatisfaction and I exhale a long breath, deflated. Most of my clothing is geared around traveling or working, so no smart-casual dresses magically appear in there. *I won't have time tomorrow to shop for something so I will just have to make do with what I have,* I sigh in frustration. Then Simone and Georgie's words pop into my head about mixing and matching functional everyday clothing into smart outfits, so I stand, biting my bottom lip, my brow furrowed, staring at the pile of clothes, trying to find inspiration.

Hmm, wide legged black woolen blend trousers that I bought on a whim during a sale. *They might work*, I consider and put them to the side. *What top to wear with them, though?* My eyes fall on a thin ribbed, black, long sleeved turtleneck top. *Yes, that will work, and the long sleeves will be good for the cooler night air.*

But it needs more.

Then I spot, hidden at the back of the wardrobe, a gray with black spots hip length suede jacket that I brought with me from Australia, but had underestimated how cold a London winter is, and realize that it is better suited for a coolish summer night here in London.

Decision made, I finish tidying up my mess and return to the sofa, unable to settle with watching television or reading, so I make a cup of calming chamomile tea. Startling me, my phone dings and I feel a grin crease my face when I note the message from Ethan.

Ethan

Gorgeous girl, I'm so pleased we talked today. I've been thinking of you all afternoon and can't wait till tomorrow night. I'll pick you up at 6.30pm. Table is booked for 7pm.

Emily

Sounds wonderful. I haven't stopped smiling. I'll be ready and waiting.

xx

Ethan

Good night, Em. Sweet dreams. *heart emoji*

Emily

*Night, Ethan. You too. *blowing kiss emoji**

Whooping, I happy dance around the kitchen. So excited am I that I need to talk to someone, so I ring Rashida, babbling my news down the phone. She is happy for me, but I sense from the reservation in her tone that she doubts Ethan's staying power in a relationship and is worried I will get hurt again. She is echoing sentiments we've discussed previously, but she hasn't seen the soft, warm adoration in his eyes when he looks at me. Hanging up the phone, I make a mental note to discuss my concerns about this to Ethan.

I have had a day from hell at the café, mainly due to my mental fuzziness, distraction and daydreaming about Ethan. My pride in my work took a blow because I messed up so many orders and had to remake them, something I rarely do. The manager was getting so annoyed with me that he switched me to waiting tables instead, so my feet are killing me. The only bright spot was a sweet message from Ethan about midday that made me feel all warm and fuzzy inside.

Ethan

Six and a half hours to go before I see you again. This has been the longest day ever. Every minute is torture.

Emily

Mine too. It has been the worst day. Can't wait to see you.

Fortunately, my shift finished at four-thirty, so I had plenty of time to get home to shower and change, which meant I have been sitting around ready and nervously watching the clock for the last half hour.

I've checked my appearance about ten times, wondered if I am too dressy, or not dressy enough, rummaged through my wardrobe again, and come up with nothing better than what I am wearing.

My hands are clammy, and my nervousness builds as the time gets closer to Ethan picking me up. My heart is racing, and I have a swarm of butterflies in my stomach, and I suddenly realize I don't know whether he is coming to my door, or if I am to meet him in the lobby. Frantically I search for my phone, then feel frazzled when there is a knock on my door. Taking a deep breath, I walk over to it, trying to look calm and unaffected, but the warmth from my flushed cheeks is a dead giveaway.

When I open the door, my knees feel like they will buckle beneath me and my heart hammers against my ribcage. My God, Ethan is gorgeous. He takes my breath away and I can't help but stare at him.

His stylishly tailored light gray suit, teamed with a black shirt, unbuttoned at the collar and tieless, just a peek of hairless chest showing, hugs his fine masculine body. His eyes are mesmerizing, captivating me as I watch what appears to be desire, admiration and joy flash in his gaze while a beaming smile lights his face.

"Hi," I breathe the word as a sigh, my eyes locked on his.

He frames my face with his hands, then presses his warm, hungry lips against mine in a light, yet seductive, kiss full of promise. My heart lurches into my throat and a sense of wholeness fills me. My hands hang on to his muscular upper arms, not wanting the kiss to end. Oh, I've missed him so much.

Ethan lifts his head, his face hovering over mine as his eyes brush over me. His lips move into a smile, and I feel his warm breath as he murmurs, "Hi, beautiful." He gazes at me a moment longer, then drops his hands and continues in a soft husky voice, "Are you ready to go?"

Blinking, trying to collect my thoughts because his kiss fried my brain, I squeak, "Oh, ah. Yes." I turn and reach for my purse from the stand near the door, then Ethan steps backward as I walk out the door, locking it behind me. He places his large, warm hand in the small of my back as we amble the short distance to the elevator. Once inside, he wraps his arm around me, his hand resting on my waist, pulling me against him.

"I've missed you," he utters, turning his head and planting a short, soft kiss on top of my head."

"Me too. Again, I'm sorry I thought wrongly about you."

"No need to apologize, Em. It's done with, so let's forget about it." He smiles down at me as the doors open and we walk out, his arm still wrapped around my waist.

As we exit the lobby onto the street, I look around for the black SUV without any success. "Where's your car?" I question, not expecting that we would walk to the restaurant, thinking that my already sore feet would be killing me after that amount of walking in my high heeled boots.

Ethan chuckles and leads me to a low-slung sports car that, even stationary, looks fast. Turning to him and smirking, remembering his muscle car in Sydney, I mock, "You really love your sports cars, don't you?"

With a grin that spreads from ear to ear, he confirms, "Sure do, particularly when I can get this baby out onto the motorway."

Opening the large passenger door, I slide into the sumptuous black and tan leather seats, admiring the craftsmanship and attention to detail. "Wow. Classy," I gush as he clambers into the cockpit.

"Just like the classy lady sitting next to me." He complements his suave charm with a wiggle of his eyebrows and a flash of heat sparks in his eyes. The engine growls when he fires it up and, shifting into gear,

Ethan merges into traffic with skilled restraint of the overwhelming power. The speed, comfort, and handling are superb, and we are at the restaurant in no time.

Marguerite greets us as we walk in the door, her eyes widening with obvious surprise when she sees Ethan and I together. She steps forward to hug me, and I introduce her (properly this time) to Ethan. She gives him a tight-lipped smile as if pleased we are together and apparently more than friendly. When Ethan points out that we have a booking, she turns and checks the table list.

"Okay. I'll just relocate you to a quieter location. Table 35. Follow me." Ethan has his hand in the small of my back again as we follow, and my lips twitch up at the corners as I realize she is taking us to a secluded corner.

After we are seated, Ethan leans toward me and queries in a hushed, conspiratorial tone, "Her French accent is far less obvious tonight, or am I imagining it?"

I nearly spurt out my mouthful of water as I laugh and confess, "Marguerite's accent is normally very faint. When you first saw me here, I asked her to put on a thick accent as if she didn't understand English very well, so you wouldn't badger her for information about me."

"Minx," he responds, chuckling. "What would you recommend from the menu?" Looking very at ease, Ethan leans back in his chair, stretching his legs underneath the table as he contemplates the menu. As his foot brushes against my crossed ankles, tingles shoot up my leg and my eyes flick to his face, catching the barest hint of a cheeky smirk, as if flirting with me. Instead of moving my feet, I keep them right where they are but twist my top foot, gently rubbing it over his lower shin. My lips lift at the corners from his sharp inhalation. With a raised eyebrow, my gaze devilishly holds his as I watch a fervent, lustful flame dart across his eyes at my touch, but he quickly dampens it to a warm regard.

We chat about the menu while teasing each other with frequent touches of our feet, and then, surprisingly, Lorenzo comes to take our order. Bending, he gives me a hug, and greets me in his usual manner, "Ciao, bella." Out of the corner of my eye, I notice Ethan's body tense and his expression harden.

Smiling, and pleased to see Lorenzo, I answer with my normal response, "Ciao mio caro amico." I continue in English because my Italian is rudimentary at best. Lorenzo has tried his best to teach me, but gets impatient when I don't understand the gender differences in the language. "Ethan, this is Lorenzo. Lorenzo, this is Ethan," I introduce them both and observe a relaxing in Ethan's posture and facial features as he recognizes the name.

Shaking Lorenzo's hand, Ethan prattles off Italian like it is his native language, then translates for me. "I just thanked Lorenzo for being such a great friend and looking out for you." Nodding, I turn my gaze to Lorenzo, smiling at him. "Yes, you are a true friend."

"My pleasure," Lorenzo responds with a beaming smile for me. "Now what would you like to order?".

After he leaves, Ethan remarks with a hardened gaze that I can't quite interpret, "I believe you had to cut your trip to Scotland short." From his words, I assume his hardened look is disgust with Tom because his expression shifts from taut to meaningful, and his eyes soften as he continues, "I'm so relieved you were traveling with true friends like Rashida and Lorenzo who stood by you. Would you like to talk about the trip?"

Smiling at him in reassurance that I am okay with what happened, I elaborate, "We'd seen some great sights before Tom hit on me. Unfortunately, no matter how many times I said no, he didn't listen.

Ramon probably told you we were staying in dorm accommodation, so I didn't want to take any chances and came home. But there's still more I'd like to see in Scotland."

"Best that you're rid of him. I hope you've blocked him too," Ethan responds, his outspoken manner a further indication of his dislike of Tom.

"Yes. Most definitely," I agree wholeheartedly.

Lorenzo brings our meals, then returns with our drinks. "Buon appetito." He grins and strides away, seemingly pleased that we both look happy. While we eat, Ethan asks about the sights I managed to see while away and I babble excitedly about my highlights.

"One day soon, I'll take you to see a few more castles," he adds as we finish eating.

I feel myself beaming at him and gush, "Oh, that would be wonderful, Ethan." Filled with enthusiasm at his keen interest in the happenings of the last couple of weeks, I regale him with updates on meeting Bruce and the positive outcome.

"That's fantastic, Em. I'm thrilled you followed through, despite your doubts. I'm sure you would have looked back and regretted not taking the opportunity while you could." He sips his wine with a thoughtful expression. "Do you think you will see him again?"

"I'd like to, but don't really expect a lot of contact," I reply before I explain the situation with Bruce's wife and family.

Chapter Forty-Two

ETHAN

After lingering over dessert and another wine, I drive Emily home and, holding hands, walk her up to her apartment. Once the door is unlocked, she pulls me inside with her.

The apartment is quite warm, and Emily removes her suede jacket while I remove my suit coat. Standing facing me in her black sweater and trousers, her svelte, elegant and very sexy figure brings a hardness to my loins that is both welcome and insistent. My aching cock desperately demands release from the strangling confines of my jocks.

Emily raises her hand to my cheek, cupping it and then skimming the palm toward my chin. "Thank you so much for a wonderful evening, Ethan," she husks, her pupils dark and dilated. I love that sexy look on her because it usually means she's aroused.

Framing her face with my hands, I look deeply into her eyes, murmuring, "It's not over yet," and my mouth descends on her upturned lips. The kiss is hot, slow, and tender, igniting into a searing, passionate rediscovery of each other's mouth. Tongues twisting and tasting, lips soft but ardent. I drag my hands over her shoulders and down her back, landing in the dip near the top of her buttocks, pulling her against me.

She moans into my mouth at the feel of my hard bulge against her belly, rocking her body against it. My cock throbs at the movements and I groan.

Lifting my lips from her mouth, I draw in a lungful of air, our faces so close we can feel the other's breath. Our eyes lock in a shared understanding. We want each other. Frantically. Her hands glide over my chest, and she circles a finger of each hand around my nipples, their jutting pebbles outlined through my shirt. My hands squeeze her ass, holding her against me, loving the feel of her body heat against my sensitive shaft. Leaning back slightly, she undoes some buttons on my shirt, her eyes drinking in the sight of my defined pecs, one finger tracing the cleft till it gets to the top of my abdomen where the shirt buttons are still done up.

Emily raises her eyes, looking at me through her fair lashes, and gives me a teasingly seductive closed-mouth smile, with just the tip of her tongue peeking out to lick her lips while she undoes the rest of the buttons.

Bending my head, I lay a trail of tiny kisses up her neck and along her jaw, then back to her neck. My hands move up her sides to her delightfully full breasts, cupping and squeezing them through her sweater and padded bra, my thumbs rubbing across the front where I estimate her nipples to be. Her hands tug my open shirt from my waistband, then slip underneath, feathering over the ridges and valleys of my torso, leaving a tingling trail in their wake.

Her head dips and her luscious tongue flicks over my nipples, shooting an electrical jolt straight to my balls. I exhale deeply, my eyes closing, savoring the delicious sensation of her warm, wet tongue laving and flicking my small, hardened tips. Then her lips encompass one, gently sucking hard.

Groaning, I feel my dick throb and twitch, straining to be released. When her hot hand cups me through my trousers, I buck against it, nearly shooting my load then and there. Needing to slow things down, I take her hand and bring it to my mouth, kissing the palm.

In a throaty voice, thick with desire, I share, "I desperately want you, Em, but there's something I need to tell you."

Her expression shifts from sultry to searching, and I vaguely note her body tense as she questions, "Oh?" like she is preparing herself for bad news.

I scrabble around in my head, trying to find the words to tell her how I feel. I have so many thoughts and feelings that I can't define and haven't acknowledged before, let alone verbalize them. I want to express myself honestly and articulately, however, my cock's insistence on release is fogging my mental sharpness. As if to prove my point, I reveal in a dreamy tone, "You own my cock, Baby Girl. It won't stir for anyone but you." *Crap, that's not what I wanted to say.* I meant to say how much she means to me. Hearing my words, although they're true, I run a hand through my hair and fret over my artless wording, particularly when I glimpse Emily's crestfallen features before they change to a guarded derision.

"Oh? You've been testing that theory, have you?" Her sarcastic, sneering tone and raised eyebrow confirm her dashed hope for different loving words. I can see the angry redhead tugging on her chains of restraint and know I need to defuse the situation before I lose Em altogether.

"No. Definitely not," I try to backtrack and clarify. "In the past, I would often feel horny before I went to a nightclub or bar, anticipating a pickup." Her look of derision tightens, but I soften my voice to almost a whisper. "But since you, I only feel horny with you, or when I'm thinking about you, which is every minute of every day." Taking hold of her hands, I instill as much honesty and love into my gaze and voice as I am feeling when I painfully admit, "I haven't even wanted sex with anyone else since seeing you in the restaurant a few weeks back. That's what I mean by 'you own my dick', Em."

She scrutinizes my face, and I can see the flame of anger dissipating in her eyes and the set of her mouth, but a tinge of hurt remains in her softened features.

"Okay. So, us, this..." She pauses and moves a hand between us. "It's all about sex?"

I shake my head and sigh heavily, taking her hands in mine again. "No, what you and I have isn't just about sex," I protest firmly. Frustrated by my ineptness, my voice catches with frustration as I admit, "I'm not expressing myself well because I've never had to think about, let alone put my feelings into words."

Taking a deep breath, I elaborate. "Us. We have a special connection that I can't put into words, but something just clicks with us. I'm infatuated with you, Emily, and hovering on the edge of love. I don't know what to call it. Pre-love maybe because this feels amazing. All I know is I am falling in love with you." Smiling lovingly and feeling like a weight has been lifted off my chest, I notice her eyes welling with tears, even though her face is beaming.

Reaching up, she places one hand behind my head and grins. "And I am falling in love with you too, Ethan." She then pulls me in for a soft, sensuous, loving kiss.

When we come up for air, I press my forehead against hers, and ask, "Can we consider us officially dating now?"

"I thought you would never ask," she responds with a sly grin, leading me into the bedroom.

Emily quickly undresses while I watch mesmerized, then unbuckles my belt, unzips my fly, and pushes my trousers and underwear to the floor. My rigid dick bounces out, gleefully enjoying its freedom by standing proudly erect. Emily stares at it, hungrily licking her lips.

"Nothing more appealing than a woman who goes after what she wants," I tease, with my hands on my hips.

With a cocky expression, Emily pushes me, and I fall on my back onto the bed. Stunned, but horny as hell, I watch her with smoldering, hungry intensity as she kneels on the bed, then hovers on all fours over me. "You said I own your cock. I'm just claiming what's mine," she mutters with sultry pride, then slides onto my rigid pole.

I groan in ecstasy at the feeling of skin on skin each time she rises, sliding further down with every descent. I grip the sheets and clench my jaw, trying to stop myself from cumming when she takes all of me inside her. Sitting upright, impaled on me, she has a look of euphoria that I will never forget. When she rides me, increasing her tempo to a frenzied pace, I can't hold on any longer. As I feel her tightening around me, the pressure in my balls boils like a bubbling pot on a cooktop. She cries out, her body tensing as her muscles clench in orgasm, and I hold back with the last vestige of sanity. With a fierce grip of her hips I heave her off me, exploding over my stomach as she collapses onto the bed beside me.

When my vision returns and my brain fog clears, I turn my head to see Emily sprawled on the bed, wearing a blissful expression. "Are you okay, Baby Girl?"

"Sure am, your hugeness." Her voice is soft and dreamy, and she sighs, satiated. "But why did you lift me off you?" she questions.

"No condom," I answer, stretching behind me for a box of tissues to mop up my mess.

"Ooh," she breathes with realization. "Whoops. Guess I got carried away."

Rolling off the bed to dispose of the matted, soggy mass of tissues in the bathroom wastebasket, I use Emily's washcloth and some hand-wash to wash away the stickiness.

When I return, Emily is curled up on her side between the sheets. I snuggle in behind her, resting one arm over her waist, bending it to hold her breast. I kiss a trail from behind her ear, down her neck and along her shoulder, then return to her ear, whispering, "As much as I love the naked feel inside you, gorgeous, let's not risk a pregnancy just yet."

"I'm on the pill, Ethan, so your hugeness can go naked as often as he likes," she chuckles.

Growling with delight, I tweak her nipple and grin as Emily makes a low rumbling noise that sounds like a purr, then pushes her bum against my groin.

My love for this woman just keeps building, and I know we will face whatever challenges arise together.

Chapter Forty-Three

EMILY – Epilogue

Six Months Later...

True to his word, Ethan brought me to Scotland for a week before the craziness of the next few months begins. We flew into Edinburgh last night and are staying just outside of the city in a luxury floating hotel permanently berthed on the waterfront. I never knew places such as this existed until I met Ethan, and he continually opens my eyes to the other world of the rich and famous.

Everything about this hotel is sumptuous, with a glorious old-world charm, a stunning dining room, and exquisite food. Dinner last night was an amazing three courses, and we were so full we needed to take a walk afterward in the brisk, bracing air to help it digest before we went to bed.

Bed. We sure made use of the king sized bed and, as usual, my McSteamy ensured I was well pampered with three or four orgasms. I was delirious in the pleasure zone and lost count. Not that it matters. My man is built for pleasure. Whether giving or receiving it in any form, he excels. Every day, I grow more in love with him, and never truly understood how huge my capacity for love was until he made me whole.

Standing on the deck outside our cabin, admiring the harbor views while Ethan sleeps in, I reflect on the months since we officially started dating. Ethan has proven to be not only a consummate lover but a wise and patient financial adviser, pragmatist, and my grounding force. He has welcomed my friends as his, just as I have welcomed his friends. There have been many social activities, and I now count Louisa, Ethan's sister, as close a friend as Georgie, Simone, and Rashida. Georgie, of course, was thrilled to learn that Ethan and I are dating, and we have even made a trip back to Sydney to catch up with her and Xander. While there, we arranged for all my remaining personal effects to be shipped to England because that will be my permanent home now.

I've met up with Bruce a couple of times and introduced him to Ethan, and I believe Bruce has talked to his wife about his previous marriage. He is still working through some of that friction; so contact has been spasmodic.

Rashida and Lorenzo have finished touring around and, as their visas have expired, they have both returned home. We still stay in touch and have met up a few times in Italy.

Apparently, Ethan and Ramon set up a sting operation to catch the cleaner in the act, with Ethan kicking her out. Ramon tipped off one of his buddies on the Vice Squad and, after an official investigation, they were able to catch and arrest her in another luxury apartment.

I moved into Ethan's apartment two months ago and am loving being in a relationship with him. Simone was sad to see me leave her apartment, but is happy that things are working out for us. My work in the café and restaurant has continued, but I am not doing nights in the restaurant any longer, so I can spend my evenings with Ethan.

Despite applying for several teaching positions now that I am a British citizen, I have been unsuccessful. If truth be known, I don't really want to be bringing home the amount of work that a teacher has to do out of hours. If I have learned anything from my trip to the United Kingdom, it is that life is too short to be bound to textbooks, lesson plans, and curriculum changes.

Even though the café work is physically tiring, I enjoy chatting to my regular customers and the set hours where I can pack up and come home, although I do miss the mental stimulation and challenges of teaching. I enjoy the flexibility and independence of having my own money as well, despite Ethan's wealth. He usually pays for our trips away or dinners, so I have been able to save a fair amount.

Ramon takes care to call before he drops into the apartment nowadays, just so he doesn't walk in on us in a compromising situation. He will often drive me to work and wait till I make him a coffee if we haven't had time for me to make him one in the apartment.

Lately, he and Mav, as well as some of their ex-military compatriots, have been coming to the café every couple of days. From what Ramon has said, I have been able to deduce it is like a support group, where they can talk or not, and just be with like-minded people who know all about the internal scars from military life. It also appears to be a bit of a team meeting because when I take their coffees to them, they seem to be discussing some operation or another.

Ramon will often point out the ones who are living rough, so I arrange with the café manager for them to collect food that can't be resold the next day. Apparently, Mav does a patrol around their hangouts every couple of days to make sure they are ok as well.

For such big tough, menacing looking men, they sure look out and care for each other. I suppose it comes down to the adage 'you can't judge a book by its cover' because Ramon and Mav are big softies under that hard macho exterior. Ramon also mentioned to me recently that the stalker fellow had found several other targets over the last few months, but surprisingly is now in rehab due to a court order which also states he needs to atone for his abuse to his victims.

Despite being thankful the awful man left me alone and saw the error of his ways I am perplexed how it got to that outcome, and recall wondering if Ramon or Ethan had anything to do with that.

I still chuckle at the ongoing sniping between Ramon and Simone on the few occasions they see each other. Simone even messaged me the other day to say she had the 'unfortunate experience' of Ramon being seated in first class on one of her flights, and that she had to attend to him. I would have paid good money to be on that flight and watch their baleful stares and listen to their sarcastic comments to each other.

On our nightly runs around the streets of the relatively new sub-divisions where Ethan lives, we have passed several new high-rise de-velopments and some vacant shop spaces on ground level. We had commented previously on the lack of coffee shops in the vicinity of his apartment, so when the shopfronts became available for purchase or lease, I began pondering the possibilities of a start up café business. Working closer to home would be an advantage, but I didn't have enough savings to get anything off the ground. Ethan, as he has done with other start ups that he believed had the potential to succeed, as-sisted with some seed funding, and regulatory and contractual advice. So, when we return from this week away, I will be throwing myself into managing fit out contractors and arranging equipment deliveries. Recruitment has begun for staff, and I hope to utilize some of the backpacking hospitality staff during busy periods. I'm also hoping to use it as a base for training courses in the hospitality field once I get up and running. We have also discussed the possibility of establishing a creche for the children of Ethan's staff, where I can utilize my teaching skills without the need to fit into a tight curriculum.

On a personal front, my confidence and self-worth has increased tenfold thanks to Ethan's collaborative and caring approach and understanding. Don't get me wrong, we still have disagreements, but we know when to disengage, and after the heat of the argument has died down, we manage to find a way to resolve the conflict. We have both learned compromise in the process.

I hear Ethan call out my name so step back inside, smiling at his sleepy morning face. His hair is tousled, he is sitting up with the sheet pulled over his manhood and squinting around the room trying to find me. Blinking a few times, he scrunches up his face and scratches his scalp, then smiles as I pad over to the bed. "Where have you been, gorgeous? I missed you in our bed."

Sitting, I peck him on the lips and chuckle. "I thought you needed a sleep in after your athletic endurance last night, so I've been out on the deck watching the harbor come to life."

"Mmm, that was some workout." Putting his arms around my waist he pulls me down to him. The bathrobe I'm wearing falls open and his hand slips inside, circling a tender nipple. "Where's my proper good morning kiss, woman?" His mouth descends on my lips, his tongue parting them, and he ravages me in a thorough, scorchingly passionate, breathtaking kiss, just like he does every morning.

When he pulls away, I can't do anything for a few seconds. My eyes remain closed, my mouth agape as my mind tries to process what happened. You'd think by now I'd be used to this overwhelming lust that his kiss spikes in me and lasts all day. As a result, every day I am a hot mess of randy wantonness, just about ready to rip his clothes off when he comes home. And of course, I do my best to drive him into the same perpetual state of lustful excitement as well.

Just when I am coming back to earth, Ethan's hand slips between my legs, a finger sliding through my cleft. "Just the way I like you, Baby Girl. Deliciously wet for me."

My hand reaches his semi erect dick, stroking it while he slides inside me and finger fucks me slowly and we start our morning by making each other cum

Several hours later, we are in a hire car driving on a castle trail. Having already seen some ruins, we are on our way to a magnificent looking Abbey to wander around. The countryside is an amazing patchwork of greens and browns, and it's not long before we find the Abbey, which leaves us both speechless. We spend a couple of hours wandering around, viewing the famous stained-glass window and the Nave, as well as the tombs.

It's been an absolutely wonderful day and, as we exit through the large wooden doors, Ethan stops on the bottom stone step. When I step down, he takes my hand and turns me toward him. Then he stands there, looking at our joined hands. I am about to ask if he is okay when his soft loving gaze meets and holds mine.

"Emily, since we've been together, you have brought me joy I never knew existed. You make me whole and when I'm with you it feels like home. My heart calls out for you, and when I see those feelings in my heart in your eyes too, I feel like we are one. You turn me inside out and you will forever be a part of me. I can't live without you, Em. I cherish and adore you. You are my addiction, my life and I'm hopelessly in love with you. Will you marry me?"

Pulling my hands out of his, I raise them to cup his face, standing on tip toe to kiss him tenderly. My eyes blink away the welling tears so I can gaze into his beautiful face. He looks worried, as if he doubts that I will say yes. *Silly man.* Putting him out of his misery, I gush, "Yes, Ethan. I would be honored to marry you. Yes. A thousand times yes. I am so in love with you. You are my home, and the love of my life, my everything." This time I kiss him with all the love I have.

THE END

About the Author

Kerrie Maxon has been a lover of romance novels for since she was a teenager. She has thought about writing a book for many years, jotting down ideas in several notebooks and phone apps without really doing anything about it because life got in the way. However, after breaking an ankle while on holiday in 2022, she decided to make the most of her idle time by finally getting her ideas into some sort of cohesive outline. One chapter led to many and finally became a completed novel.

Now, Kerrie is a contemporary romance author living in the beautiful south coast of New South Wales with her husband and cat. Her family consists of two daughters and three step-kids, their spouses and seven grandchildren, all of whom keep her busy. Kerrie has worked in office administration all her working life, often proofreading others' works and reports, so words are her passion.

Thank you for reading **Built For Pleasure**. I hope you enjoyed **Ethan and Emily's** story.

Keep an eye out for follow ups in the **Drake Enterprises** interconnected standalone series. Other titles in this series include:

Built For Sin

Built for Pleasure

Stay up to date on upcoming books, visit Kerrie at:

www.kerriemaxonauthor.com

admin@kerriemaxonauthor.com

facebook.com/KerrieMaxon

instagram.com/kerriemaxonauthor

tiktok.com/kerrikcd9ui